SCREEN SHOT

SCREEN SH⊕T

A NOVEL

JOHN DARRIN

KÜNATI

CLEARWATER | FL | USA

For information, contact Kunati Inc., Book Publishers in Canada.
USA: 13575 58th Street North, Suite 200, Clearwater, FL 33760-3721 USA
Canada: 75 First Street, Suite 128, Orangeville, ON L9W 5B6 CANADA.
E-mail: info@kunati.com.

FIRST EDITION

Designed by Kam Wai Yu
Persona Corp. | www.personaco.com

ISBN 978-1-60164-168-7   EAN 9781601641687
Fiction

Published by Kunati Inc. (USA) and Kunati Inc. (Canada).
Provocative. Bold. Controversial.™

http://www.kunati.com

TM—Kunati and Kunati Trailer are trademarks owned by Kunati Inc.
Persona is a trademark owned by Persona Corp.
All other trademarks are the property of their respective owners.

Library of Congress Cataloging-in-Publication Data

Darrin, John.
  Screenshot : a novel / John Darrin. -- 1st ed.
     p. cm.
  Summary: "A techno-thriller that poses provocative questions about
justice, revenge and the influence of Internet culture on modern ethics and
morality"--Provided by publisher.
  ISBN 978-1-60164-168-7 (alk. paper)
  1. Internet--Moral and ethical aspects--Fiction. 2. Executions and
executioners--Fiction. I. Title.
  PS3604.A765S37 2009
  813'.6--dc22
                                    2008056140

DEDICATION

For Anne, of course.

ACKNOWLEDGMENTS

My son, Josh Darrin, for his plot ideas and technical expertise.

My agent, Jacques de Spoelberch,
for recognizing the possibilities and guiding the creation.

The Deadly Prose Critique group for their contribution to my literary education,
and especially Biman Nath and BJ Ryan for their detailed and helpful critiques.

My publisher, Derek Armstrong and editor, James McKinnon,
for their support of my work and their effots to improve it.

Chapter One

The First E-mail

To: members@hackdoor.com

From: screenshot@heroscents.com

Subject: Extravagant retribution

Message:

At approximately 7 PM GMT today, Screenshot will present the first-ever, live Web execution. Click on the link below to view.

Pay attention. The broadcast time is approximate. The image will appear just moments before the event.

We're having some fun now.

http://kills.torchsense.com/imageclick/
CID=00000b7c79a99a5070cfg0

Seth Mathias

The gunshot startled him. He hadn't been expecting that. But an appropriate start to a live execution, he realized.

The sound came from his computer speakers while he stared at the blank screen, expecting a visual alert before the show began. The noise was round and deep and over so fast he thought he might have imagined it. With almost no knowledge of guns, Seth guessed it was something big. It sounded like an impressive bullet.

His screen brightened from the center out, like one of those graphic conceptions of how the big bang must have looked if anyone could have been watching. A neutral image formed, a wide-frame shot of a streetscape, clearly urban, clearly impoverished. A few people moved in and out of view, passing in front of the typical city row house centered in the picture. The house was indistinguishable from its neighbors—rundown, dirty, some unintelligible graffiti on the foundation, three concrete steps leading up to the front door. Sunshine and jacketless pedestrians, all African-American, said the location could be almost any urban setting with a significant black population where the sun was shining on the mid-June day. Pretty much any city.

Seth watched, along with 7,382 others, according to the web site visitor statistics automatically recorded by the domain host, and displayed on the counter in the lower right corner of his screen. The camera seemed to be in a car across the street from the house, probably an SUV from the shape and size of the window that it pointed through. A truck and two cars, older American models, passed by the camera so quickly that Seth couldn't identify them.

The image flickered and telescoped to the front door, narrowing the field of view, sweeping left and right across the house before returning to the door. A red laser sighting dot came on, centered on the door, and held still, like a stain on the fading paint. A whirring noise accompanied the camera movement as it panned left and right, in and out. A sturdy, solid sound, the kind that Seth associated with something made in Germany, over-designed and built to last.

The front door to the row house opened and a young black man came out, dressed in oversized Los Angeles Lakers gear, purple and gold, the satiny pants cinched at crotch level, the baseball hat reversed over a black skullcap. He stood there for a few moments and surveyed the scene, looking for something or someone. Or maybe nothing and no one, like a lookout.

After several seconds, he turned his head and said something to someone out of sight inside the house then started down the three steps. Another young black man followed him out the door. He stopped and raised his arms out like a dictator presenting himself to his subjects.

Without warning, everything exploded.

The speakers exploded with a staccato banging, like rapid hammering on a metal roof, each bang distinct.

The SUV window exploded in a mist of glass particles, momentarily fogging the view before falling out of sight.

His screen exploded with strobing flashes, one for each bang, irradiating the view and blinding the image.

The door to the house exploded; wood splinters and brick shards spun and whirled through the air in every direction.

And the man exploded, disintegrating into a bright mass of meat that fragmented and bounced and splashed in every direction.

"Shit," Seth yelled to no one, almost toppling his desk chair as he convulsed away from his laptop, the carpeting holding the legs in place like Velcro.

He pulled himself back in, leaning toward the screen like that would help him see through the smoke from what he would soon learn was twenty .50 caliber bullets. He could still hear the reverberations of the automatic weapon; sounds not real, but not an echo either. More of a memory as his eardrums stopped vibrating. He stared at the scene as the image cleared. The same scene, but now with a front door and some remains that looked like the results of a successful suicide bomber.

Seth picked up his cell phone, pressed the voice dial button and said, "Wes school." Keypad tones beeped through the earpiece, and after several rings, Seth's son answered. He was in his senior year as a computer science major at Cornell.

"What was that all about?" Seth asked him.

"What?"

"That killing on the Internet you told me to watch. You're not watching it?"

"Dad, I just finished class and I'm on my way to the café to meet some friends. I haven't been watching anything."

"Then why did you want me to watch it?"

There was a momentary silence and then Wes answered, "Watch what? I didn't tell you to watch anything that I can remember."

"I got an e-mail from you this morning forwarding some other e-mail notification about a first-ever live execution on the web. You said I should watch. You don't remember?"

"I remember fine. I didn't send anything. I never heard of this execution. You sure it was from me? Check the header and tell me what it says."

"The original was sent to a mail list by someone calling himself Screenshot. It says it was forwarded to me by wes.mathias@cornell.edu. That's your e-mail, right?"

"Damn. I gotta go. Somebody's zombied my computer and they're using it to spam."

After hanging up, Seth continued to watch the scene unfold on his monitor and thought about that. This wasn't spam. And it wasn't sent to just anybody. It was sent from his son to him, giving it absolute credibility, assuring that he would watch.

Who would want him to witness a murder? And why?

❖　　❖　　❖

Philip Hurst

From his leather chair, Philip released the joystick and closed the weapon's control link, erasing any electronic trail between the gun and his trigger. The camera automatically zoomed out to its default original shot, and he sat back to enjoy the rest of the show in the quiet comfort of his luxurious home office. Alone in the exclusive condo where he lived, he could give it his full attention. Attention it deserved.

At first, he saw only the clearing smoke as it rose out of view, on its way to join the rest of LA's pervasive summer smog. He could only imagine the thick smell, trapped in the confines of the SUV, made by almost 900 grams of detonated WC860 propellant, 45 grams for each of the twenty bullets.

Someone screamed, and then someone else joined in, until it sounded like a rock concert filled with crazed teenage girls. A man entered the picture from the left and tiptoed toward the corpse, looking around in rapid, jerky motions, ready to dive for cover. Philip tapped the Print Screen key on his keyboard and took a different kind of shot, a screenshot, a single still frame of his computer monitor image, saving the file as Act1Pic1.jpg. By the end of the day, he would be at number eighty-seven.

As the witness got closer, he stopped. Stopped his tiptoeing, stopped his nervous glances, and possibly stopped breathing as he stared at the carcass that was, moments earlier, Redoucelle Washington, regional drug kingpin for a four-block territory in Los Angeles' south-central district, and the recent beneficiary of legal technicalities that allowed him to escape his third murder rap. The first two dismissals resulted from the disappearance of certain witnesses, and sudden neurological disorders with others, causing their memories to fail. Redo, as everyone knew him, was a celebrity in his neighborhood.

Several others, all men, all black, edged into the picture. One of them bent over the body of Redo's lookout and probed out of the camera's sight, then he popped up, hollering for someone to call 9-1-1. Collateral damage, Philip thought, not concerned that one of the minions had gotten in the way of Redo's requital.

The screams subsided and some women started to clear the edge of the frame and come into view, aghast with maternal horror at the murder of someone else's son. Sirens provided new background noise as they grew closer, and soon police, fire and emergency medical personnel swarmed over the area.

As the police organized the scene, the SUV became an object of interest, and they cautiously approached it. Guns drawn, the cops shouted commands to drop any weapons and put any hands where they could be seen. Philip chuckled and thought, not gonna happen, but raised his hands in mock surrender anyway. When the police could see inside and verify the SUV was unoccupied, they holstered their sidearms and peered through the still intact windows, avoiding the gun barrel and careful not to disturb anything.

Philip's straight-ahead view from the gun's perspective limited his sight, and he couldn't see what they were doing around the other sides of the SUV. He wished he could have seen their faces when they found the label stenciled on the crate that concealed the weapon everywhere except the gun slit. The name had been an ironic thought that flitted through his mind as he made his plans many months earlier. The thought brought a chuckle, and most things that got a chuckle from Phillip got acted upon. So his trademark, his brand, was born. Or rather, plagiarized.

ACME DRUG REHABINATOR. Patent Pending, the stencil read, in bright red block letters.

Philip watched the investigation of the crime scene for another twenty minutes while the police strung yellow tape everywhere and examined the interior of the SUV. A uniformed policeman approached the plainclothes detective who seemed to be in charge, and told him something, pointing at the weapon. The detective didn't seem to understand, and more discussion ensued before they both walked directly toward the barrel-mounted camera and bent down to stare, faces slightly scrunched as they studied the device.

The detective keyed his shoulder mike and asked the listener to describe what they were seeing. Philip couldn't make out the reply, but he knew what it was. Philip was seeing the same thing. Along with 23,019 others, according to the web site traffic counter, with viewership increasing as the word spread through the Internet community. The detective climbed into the front seat, moving out of sight. The image shook momentarily, confirming that the authorities were onto the Internet broadcast, and they were stopping it.

Almost twenty-five minutes, Philip thought. Let's see what's on the other channels.

He tapped some keys and the screen went blank momentarily, then opened a new image of the same scene from a different perspective. This one looked down from an elevated location and showed a broader view of emergency vehicles and personnel, curious crowds and news teams.

The new view gave more panorama, and showed two men standing near the SUV, one of them using a shoulder mike. He raised his arm and pointed up, aimed to the right of Philip's vantage point, and swung his arm slowly toward the camera. When he passed it, he stopped and, still talking into the mike, reversed his arc until Philip was looking directly at the tip of his right index finger. He figured that they knew about the new view.

When the new image wobbled and went off, Philip checked his computer clock again. Thirty-six minutes had elapsed, and by then the counter showed 461,594 current viewers. This is viral, he thought, spreading like Ebola through the Net community. He estimated that if viewership continued to grow this fast, the servers would become overloaded and a denial-of-service interruption couldn't be far off.

Philip hummed while he did some more tapping. Almost immediately another view opened, aimed from a point across the street, on the crime-scene side. It showed, among other things, two policemen on a row house roof, probably securing and investigating the camera that had just gone blank. This is perfect, he thought, and wondered which would run out first, the six cameras he had pre-positioned or the server capacity. After one more camera change, it turned out to be server capacity. When viewership passed the 900,000 mark, the image shut down, and he got the "page cannot be displayed" error message signaling server collapse after just forty-nine minutes. Philip started surfing.

He watched his work dissected through the afternoon as the 24/7 cable news channels covered the story with a diligence so pervasive and trivial that it threatened to exhaust public interest before bedtime. Every network and each station said the same things, interviewed the same people, and the individual reporter became the only way to differentiate. By dinnertime, Redo Washington had no secrets left. Of course, he didn't need any.

When all the chaff was separated, the wheat was pretty

sparse. Everyone agreed that Redo was an extreme sociopath, that he certainly deserved to at least be incarcerated forever, and execution was an acceptable alternative for many. Someone had posted an accurate description of the weapon that Philip had built himself from a World War II vintage Browning Automatic Rifle, or BAR to the GIs who lugged them all over Europe and the Pacific by its folding handle, like some lethal luggage. The communications and Internet technology used were state-of-the-art. Beyond that, it appeared the police knew virtually nothing. That was good. They would know what he wanted them to know, when he wanted them to know it. His spokesman would see to that, Philip knew, confident that his unwitting spokesman had received his e-mail and watched the event.

The many eyewitnesses could only describe the event, not the perpetrator. Forensic evidence from the car would likely be useless. It had been stolen four days earlier from its registered owner—Redo's mother.

The intercom office buzzed, interrupting his amusement and alerting him that the caterer had arrived, and his guests would follow soon. He logged off each site with care, leaving no trace of his physical location, and minimal traces of his virtual one, his computer security configured for privacy. On his approval, the doorman let the caterer in, and their staff and supplies arrived at his suite by the time he locked the door to his office and set the intrusion alarm. No one except Philip entered that room. Not friends, not family, not guests, not cleaners, not girlfriends.

His three-bedroom home spanned two stories at the top of the secure Pacific Heights co-op building, looking out over the city and San Francisco Bay. He'd converted one of the bedrooms into the office, and there was also a den, living room, kitchen, dining room, loft, and two and a half bathrooms.

While the caterer set up, Philip got himself ready. Casual elegance was the dress code for dinner, and he chose a blue silk Brooks Brothers blazer with a faint rose windowpane, medium grey linen slacks, and John Varvatos Venetian slip-ons. Informal enough to relax his guests, but exclusive enough to remind them of his taste and his resources.

There would be five guests, and the topic would be politics. The participants included the chairman of the state Democratic committee and his wife, there to keep Philip buying into the political process; Philip's business manager, with his wife, there to do the talking—the process held no interest for Philip, only the results; and Philip's current girlfriend, Laura Fascio, an ambitious young lawyer from a firm that did occasional work for him, and who would like to do more, invited for dinner, and providing the dessert.

"The Meet Your Representative rally is set for Tuesday the eighteenth at the St. Francis. We should—"

"I can't make it," Philip interrupted the chairman.

"Oh?" he replied. "This is a very important event. There will be a lot of high-level contributors there, and your presence sets a strong example for them."

Elliot, the business manager, checked his PDA and said, "There's nothing on the calendar, Philip. Are you sure you have the right date?"

"Elliot, not everything I do is on your calendar."

Philip held up his hand, stopping Elliot before he could protest. "And, no, it is not something that I can re-schedule. You'll just have to get along without me this time. You can arrange a video message from me if you like. That's the best I can do."

After wrapping up the business, Philip poured a round of cognac, his signal for everyone to relax for a little while and then leave.

"Has the committee prepared a statement regarding the Screenshot events," Elliot asked the chairman. "Are you going to take some official position?"

Philip suppressed his excitement at someone finally raising the subject, keeping his reaction neutral.

"The killing? I haven't actually seen it," the chairman replied. "I'll have to view it tomorrow and poll the other members. I expect we will take a strong law and order stand, possibly even renew our calls for Internet regulation. What's your opinion, Philip?"

"I oppose any attempts to regulate the Internet. It is futile to even try. Look at the Chinese. Even they have only succeeded in driving it underground, and they have to relent more each day. Google is there, for Christ's sake. There's no stopping it, Ben. If you want to take a symbolic stand, that's fine, but you can't win this one."

It was Philip's longest speech of the evening, by three sentences.

Laura lingered long after the other guests left, and well past her normal exit time. That time was always right after some unremarkable sex, usually consummated before the eleven o'clock news.

"Oh, wow," she thought. "What did you take?" Unaware that she asked this out loud, she started when he answered.

"Take? Nothing. Can you stay?"

"You keep that up and I'll move in." She apparently didn't

intend the double entendre, but Philip caught it.

He smiled without answering and thought about the beneficial side effects of his Screenshot high.

"We'll have to do this more often," he agreed. *A lot more often*, he thought.

Chapter Two

Seth

After the call to Wes, Seth watched the show until the screen went blank and then typed a new command, entered his user ID and password, and surfed some of the Internet forums he used for various research. At one forum, several members had captured the streaming video and posted it on their web sites where they kept it in constant rotation for everyone to see. Now he watched the replay, concentrating, sticking his tongue out slightly so that he looked like he had three lips, ready now to study the events calmly.

The review shocked him more than the original. He saw the entire event in detail, with his brain fully engaged instead of half shut down. The shots were not like the automatic weapons that he saw on the news, AKs and ARs and MACs chattering like over-revved mopeds. This was more like a big Harley at idle, each explosion slow and deep and distinct, each resonation overlapping the next.

He watched the rerun once—it was enough—then got up and paced. The confines of his RV, his current home, couldn't contain the energy of his reaction, and he needed more space, space to go round and round instead of back and forth.

Outside, the day was sunny and clear, no surprise in San Diego. He walked the circle around the camping area at Lake Jennings. Seth had seen people die before. First-hand. In one terrifying episode a year earlier, the episode that led to his current lifestyle and his efforts to distance himself from the memories, he had killed several people in self-defense, surprising himself with latent abilities he'd never known in his forty-four years. And more importantly to him, the year before that he had watched helplessly while disease killed his wife, and had held her as death won the lingering war of attrition. Senseless death held no shock value for him.

This presentation, however, did. Real-time murder, in the vivid splatter mode of slasher movies, available for anyone with a computer and modem. Not even his first-hand experience with violent death blunted the impact of the fifty-caliber butchery he had just witnessed.

Even though the walk was in a circle, it put some emotional distance between him and his initial repugnance at the broadcast, and he returned to his surfing to learn more about it. The prevalent attitude on the Internet forums supported the killer. Many people thought him some sort of vigilante hero, standing up against sociopaths and the ineffectual and corrupt justice system that let them go free. Others argued that the logical conclusion to that was anarchy. Several others cheered for that conclusion. Most of the forums, however, made no mention of justice or anarchy, they just thought it was a cool show, and speculated on the possibility of another episode.

Seth disconnected, deciding in an instant that he wanted to know more about the murder that someone had made sure he watched. He picked up his cell phone and dialed Sid Beecher, the publisher of the *San Jose Mercury News*, Seth's current, and temporary, employer.

"Did you see it," Seth asked.

"You mean Screenshot? Yeah, I saw it. I've got people on their way."

"Listen, I'm in San Diego doing the interviews with the nuclear fuel people for the terrorist piece. I want to take a break from it and head up to LA and look into this Screenshot thing."

"No, I'd rather you finished the nuke piece. I've got others in LA. That story will be deader than a road kill Frisbee by the time you get there."

"Sid, someone hacked into my son's computer and sent me a phony e-mail to make sure I watched it. That takes some knowledge and resources. Who would go to that trouble? And why?"

"Screenshot?"

"I doubt it. I'm nobody. I can't imagine this Screenshot would pick me for something. It's probably a prank, but it can't hurt to look."

"Okay. Drop the nuke piece for the moment. Get me a fresh perspective on this Screenshot. Something for the Sunday edition."

Getting to LA for Seth involved relocating, only without the packing and the movers. The thirty-six-foot trailer was like a very big, very luxurious hotel room connected to his big Dodge Ram pick-up truck, using a tractor-trailer style hitch mounted in the truck bed. It had all the amenities of home, and with the dish raised and the GPS locked on, he was fully connected to the Internet and television. But the biggest attraction of this lifestyle was the view—he could change it at will.

He decided to start for LA right away and went back on-line to search campgrounds. Malibu Creek State Park sounded good, in LA County, on the northern edge of the city, but isolated, set in the hills and woods. He entered the address and MapQuest told him it was 169 miles up I-5. If he broke camp right away, he could be there for dinner. That simply involved putting loose items away, raising the self-levelers, lowering the satellite dishes, unplugging electric, water and sewage, and paying his bill. It took forty minutes.

Seth liked driving the Interstate, especially pulling the trailer. No excitement, although the scenery on I-5 was a lot better than most. The drive was uninterrupted time to think, to consider what he had seen, and how he would approach it. He had seen a murder, certainly, but a very extravagant one. His limited knowledge of the motives for murder included passion and greed and religion and revenge and insanity and self-defense. But not entertainment. That was the stuff of fiction. This was a production, an expensive production, carefully planned and staged, not so much for results as for visibility. This was not intended to kill a specific person, but to exalt the act itself.

Whatever anyone thought about Redo and his qualifications for victimhood, this seemed like overkill. According to the stories on the Internet forums, one of those fifty-caliber bullets would have exploded Redo. Why the nineteen extra?

And why a remote-controlled weapon? It seemed like a curious way to flee the scene of the crime, so to speak. And why camera after camera, planning for the plug to be pulled on each one and having a back-up in place?

Unable to answer any of his own questions, Seth narrowed his focus and called Wes to see if he had learned anything in the meantime.

When he answered, Seth asked, "Did you find out anything about the e-mail? Any clues about the source?"

"Nothing. There's not even a record of it in my Sent folder or on the school mail server. I talked to one of my professors, and we're going to use it in computer lab tomorrow and see if we can find anything."

"Has anyone said anything about how much that whole thing would have cost? Cameras, Internet, remote control."

"Yeah. A lot."

"How much is a lot? A vacation? A car? College tuition? Retirement?"

"Ball park? College tuition. Couple hundred grand. I'm really guessing on the remote-control gun stuff, but according to what I'm seeing on the web, that's a good guess. And then there's all the setup. Yeah, college tuition."

"What are they saying on-line?"

"Everyone's wondering who this Screenshot guy is. Or guys. Seems like a big project for one person. Lots of technology involved, lots of different disciplines."

"Really? What disciplines?"

"Half a dozen types of engineering, crazy technology, even sociology. Who does all that?"

"What do they think?"

"Dad, it's the Internet. They think everything. From a superhero to a government conspiracy. Terrorists. The Klan. Big business. Methodists. You name it, and someone has posted an argument supporting it."

"Any realistic candidates?"

"The most popular seems to be government conspiracy. They have the resources and the technology and the stealth. The only thing I can't figure is the motive."

After saying goodbye, Seth considered that, and why someone wanted him to see it live. Maybe that was the coming attractions, he thought.

Chapter Three

Dr. Morgan Sicals

In 1985, the committee in Stockholm awarded the Nobel Prize in physics for the discovery of the Quantum Hall Effect, and, among its much more esoteric applications, QHE became the international standard for measuring electrical resistance, helping physicists better understand the movement of electrons through semiconductors. Dr. Morgan Sicals of the Lawrence Livermore National Lab near San Francisco discovered QHE in 1978. Unfortunately for Dr. Sicals, he was the only person in the theoretical physics world who believed that, and Dr. Klaus von Klitzing of the High Magnetic Field Laboratory in Grenoble, France was credited with the discovery in 1979 and awarded the prize. Dr. Sicals had since spent a great deal of time and energy trying to rectify that.

The effort cost him much more than the dollar value of the prize, but that was of little consequence to him. He wanted—required—that his work be properly recognized, that his superior intellect be acknowledged. Along his Quixotic journey, he accumulated some interesting artifacts, including mountains of correspondence that somewhere contained the phrase, "I'm sorry, but …" And he had documentation: his medical release from his tenure at the University of California, legal bills for his failed wrongful termination lawsuit, and the final discharge papers of his bankruptcy.

Sicals paid no heed to the Screenshot frenzy, his curiosity

failing to register anything not QHE-related. The dirt and grime and scratches and stains on the outside of the street-level Plexiglas window provided a little light and a lot of seclusion. The basement was his office, his computer laboratory, and a storage area for the furniture typically found in an apartment, all arranged for living a normal human life. Something he didn't seem to do very much. There was also a small kitchen, a bedroom and a bathroom, all used only when their functions were no longer avoidable.

The Screenshot-related Internet traffic finally reached a volume sufficient to get his attention, and he followed the threads and reviewed the video several times, making increasingly hasty notes with each new observation. He wondered if others in the various forums saw what he did, and started monitoring real-time chats. Impatient with what he considered the drivel being posted on the Internet sites by others, Sicals made one of his infrequent entries. His only concession to the abbreviated and hieroglyphic chat-room format was his screen name: QHEDoc.

"(QHEDoc). Screenshot may be a covert agent for the FBI's Tactical Enforcement Command."

"(n3tsl1ng3r). ??????"

"(sParKle210). whats that?"

"(QHEDoc). It is a clandestine branch of the FBI that conducts domestic abduction, interrogation, and execution of significant malcontents, working outside the regulation of the justice system."

"(bzs@wgUY). webster time. malcontent?"

"(QHEDoc). A troublemaker. TEC addresses those malcontents who threaten governmental prerogatives or secrets, but can't be publicly prosecuted because they have information that could threaten the government."

"(n3tsl1ng3r). u bin using, doc?"

"(QHEDoc). No, you buffoon. I don't use anything except my brain. Forget who Screenshot is or what he is doing or why, and consider *how* he is doing it. How much do you suppose that weapon cost? Several hundred thousand dollars at the least. And the time and trouble and risk to install it? And the cost of the communications gear? Why not just shoot this Redoucelle Washington with a sniper rifle? It has to be government sponsored."

"(bzs@wgUY). what 4?"

"(QHEDoc). That is what I'm going to investigate."

"(n3tsl1ng3r). g, thanks doc. don't u have something else 2 do? like, now?"

"(QHEDoc). Yes, I do. I'm going to find this Screenshot and prove that your precious Internet privacy is just another government myth. You will see soon enough."

The Second E-mail

To: members@hackdoor.com
From: screenshot@shocenters.com
Subject: Tuesday's special event
Mr. Washington died because I decided that he needed to.
Others will as well.
Stay tuned.
We're having some fun now.

Karen Larsen

The seventeen-inch LCD monitor at her workstation displayed

Screenshot's second e-mail, in twenty-point font, selected so she could read it over and over from across the junior-executive office where she stood, holding her chin with one hand and her elbow with the other.

The running joke within the Agency asked if her team should be issued guns or wireless PDAs. Special Agent Karen Larsen's own Personal Digital Assistant got a lot more use than her gun, but she resented the implication anyway. Her gun had never been used, or even unholstered, for any target not made of paper or metal. She knew that was true of most agents, but at least they had the possibility. She was never going to draw down on her computer.

Both her gun and her PDA were state-of-the-technology, upgraded with each new generation. In her imagination, she worked on a design to synthesize the two and create the ultimate law enforcement device: a password protected weapon that could pull up her e-mail. She just couldn't figure where to put the LCD screen so she wasn't aiming at someone while she was reading.

Karen Larsen's name brought to mind Nordic images—tall, blonde, athletic. That was a reasonable description of her father, Nils, before age bent the tall, grayed the blonde, and substituted a cane for the hockey stick. Karen stood five foot three, weighed a consistent 119 pounds, and had the distinct Korean features of her mother, Kyung-ja Park. Except for the blonde part. Kyung-ja had a recessive gene lurking there, and Nils had found it, unintentionally turning a pretty Asian girl into something of a sideshow freak.

The irony gnawed at Karen. On other educated, presentable and determined women, blonde hair was an asset, so much so that many of them faked it. On Karen, it was the other running joke in her department. More than the intelligence, more than the hard work, more than the eloquence, her hair defined her, as it always had. She became a fantasy to some, a mutant to others, and even worse to a few. None of these definitions included a serious professional, none included career advancement in the FBI.

That didn't matter to her at the moment. As soon as Screenshot had hit the Send key on the latest e-mail, threatening more mayhem, he had become the Bureau's responsibility. Karen wanted it to be her responsibility, but the Pittsburgh office of the National Cyber-Forensics and Training Alliance wasn't exactly the hub of FBI crime solving. Getting further down the decision-making organization would be possible, but difficult for anyone with English as a first language.

Her title made matters even worse: Special Agent-in-Charge, Digital Phish-Net. She only handed out business cards when required.

Despite its name and location, Digital Phish-Net employed some of the most powerful technology in the Bureau, and allied with private companies who could buy the FBI—Microsoft, Oracle, AOL—and all the other recognizable names of the Internet world. The mission of the Phish Tank, as they called it, was to jump on Internet fraud fast and hard, working in virtual time where crime syndicates came and went before lunch.

Screenshot went far beyond phishing and hacking, but he used the same tools. Catching him would require technological resource and know-how, and vast amounts of luck. Turning from her monitor, Karen looked out of her office door at some of that technological know-how, incorporated in the computers and software and people of the Phish Tank, all focused on the ephemeral world of Internet crime. Someone in Washington needed to understand these resources and their unique pertinence to this crime. Karen would have to make them aware, and she set about the task.

Her business-school training and her pre-FBI experience in the high-tech business world had taught her how to approach the problem. What was the mission? Where would resources come from? How would they be applied? And most important to her, who would lead the charge? She would make sure that her white paper to her boss would answer all of those questions.

Karen wanted to lead the charge, offered to lead the charge, justified leading the charge, but she knew that wouldn't happen, blonde hair or no. The message was always the same: agents solve crimes, geeks solve equations.

Chapter Four

Philip

Philip drove the big Lexus south on the 101 through the relatively light Saturday morning traffic. It was a ten-mile drive from downtown San Francisco, but the detour to the airport long-term parking doubled the mileage. Philip didn't care. Today's destination was his own private world, and the extra time to protect it was well worth the effort.

He reflected on how quickly things had cooled down, even with his second e-mail, since the Redo killing four days before. He looked forward to tomorrow's notice. That would shake them up a bit.

He drove to the selected spot in the long-term parking garage and got out, locking the car with a push of the button on the key. That key went into his pocket and he brought out a set of keys that he kept hidden in the Lexus and only used on the occasions of these particular trips. He walked to a 1998 white Ford cargo van and unlocked it. He rolled down the manual windows before getting in to let the truck exchange the air that had decayed for three weeks in the moldering interior.

Leaving the lot, Philip drove back almost six miles, retracing half his journey, to a mostly abandoned industrial area south of the city. Driving past the cracked loading docks and rusting trailers and empty cargo shells, he approached the one-story, warehouse-type building with a faded sign that read, AMTCo. It was attached to an identical building, sharing one full side wall, with its own doors and a similar old sign that read Nu-Way Chemical Treatment. The condition of the building and the name on the sign made it an unattractive destination.

AMTCo, like Nu-Way, was apparently closed for good, large locks securing the building. The oversized roll-up door for moving equipment in and out appeared to be sealed with steel bars welded to the metal door and the frame. The single incongruity was the security cameras, concealed in old, rusted spotlight fixtures, and not noticeable unless you looked very hard.

As he approached the building, Philip pressed the remote control on the van's visor and arrived just as the big door completed its spiral up into the housing above the opening, taking the fake iron bars with it. Inside, the building was an abandoned warehouse, big enough and empty enough to play a football game, as long as no one tried to punt under the twenty-four-foot roof. The other three walls were of concrete block, barren of any feature to interrupt the monotony of the peeling paint. The only break in the rectangle was the office area, a small cube at the front corner of the building, to the right of the roll-up door where Philip had driven in.

The roll-up door closed, and Philip got out and walked to the office. His footsteps echoed as the hard leather heels shuddered with each contact with the greasy concrete floor. The two interior office walls had old-fashioned wood paneling to waist height, and glass above, so the occupants had a clear view of the entire warehouse. The space was empty except for an old metal desk and broken chair, abandoned by the last tenant.

Unlocking the door, he entered a password into the keypad mounted behind a phony thermostat, turning off the security system. Getting the green light, he went across the office to a metal security door that looked like a small closet on the shared concrete wall. It was marked Do Not Enter, and seemed to be an unused connecting door to the attached building.

He unlocked it using a different key, and the door opened into a spacious, clean and well-equipped machine shop, the real Acme Machine Tool Company, officially registered in California with an ownership designed to be untraceable further than two parent companies up the corporate ladder.

The interior was the same size as its neighbor, but the similarities ended there. Fluorescent light fixtures tiled the high ceiling, bathing the room in a soft, uniform light that bounced off the white block walls and grey corrugated floor. Two rows of machines filled the floor space, and around the perimeter steel shelves and bins stored various metal and plastic materials, hand tools, machine parts, lubricants, fuels, cleaning supplies and other consumables. On the walls, engineering drawings and posters of Roadrunner and Wile E. Coyote cartoons were mounted, complete with an array of the ACME products that always backfired. Philip kept them to remind himself that things can always go wrong.

The machines were Philip's toys, his Ferrari and his Hummer. An ABL-1 Pillar Drilling Machine, the Omax 2626XP Waterjet Cutting Machine, a Bardons & Oliver 36TBC Turning Center, and the Sandvik Coromill 245 3-axis milling machine, among many others, for cutting and forming and extruding and shaping and finishing. Given time and design, he had the equipment and materials to build the Hummer from scratch.

Philip found retirement boring, even with the $73 million cash-out to manage, the venture capital investments to select, the boards to sit on. All of those involved someone else's challenges, someone else's dreams. He didn't regret the successful exit from his challenge; he regretted not having another one. He still wanted to be The Wizard.

It was a nickname well known in a small circle of engineers, programmers and venture capitalists. Philip liked the significance of the title, even though he didn't necessarily agree with it. What he did, what he had accomplished, wasn't particularly surprising to him, and he marveled at the esteem of others. What he did seemed to come easy, he didn't suffer any trials to achieve it, he didn't struggle through deprivations to succeed, there was no memory of years of rejection. After dropping out of Cal Tech, he simply drew some designs, machined some pieces, wrote some code, and the result made a lot of people rich, including himself and the engineers and programmers and venture capitalists who gave him the nickname. It *was* like wizardry, because it came that easily to him.

The zeal of talent unapplied, the hubris of too much money too easily accumulated, and the conscience that he didn't even notice wasn't there, all combined to create Screenshot. And Acme was its exclusive supplier.

Philip plugged in a video while he worked on the final preparations for his next device. On the screen, the calf seemed to develop elasticity, and to bounce at the end of the orange ribbon that crackled and flexed like a whip made of lightning. Animal rights had an altogether different meaning in Russia, and apparently being electrocuted wasn't covered. The narrative was in Russian, but the *show* was enough, and no *tell* was required. When the flame flickered out, the calf lay crumpled on the ground, smoke rising off it. Philip guessed that the operators were probably hungry from the smell of broiled beef.

The plasma Taser test had occurred and been taped two years

earlier. The concept was simple: a Taser without wires, one that could fire its lethal electrical charge and be stopped and started again and again. A conductive aerosol stream replaced the regular wires, and the heat of the electricity created the plasma wire that could lock on the target and move with it, just like real wires, as long as the spray was kept on and your aim reasonably good.

A simple concept maybe, but a design and fabrication challenge. Philip had several scorched and melted prototypes to prove that. The key, he found through trial and error, was the fluid and the pressure. Change either, and you could get quite an impressive explosion. The design originated in Germany, but was soon stolen by the Russians, which meant it was immediately for sale over the Internet, even though it was not yet perfected. Philip perfected it enough for his purposes.

The finished device looked enough like a robotic TIG welding machine to pass an examination by anyone except experienced welders, and even they might think it was a newer, better model. The electrical generator, several gas bottles, and a hydraulic arm, all mounted in an angle iron frame, looked harmless enough. And it fit nicely in the back of the Ford F-150 pickup that Philip bought on eBay, paying with a money order.

With the last ratcheting tie-down in place, Philip broke for lunch. He would come back later to pick up the pickup, and start the two-day drive to deliver it to the FBI. With one little stop in between.

Chapter Five

Seth

"Hello?" Seth didn't recognize the number on the Caller ID, and he couldn't place the 510 area code. That didn't surprise him, though. He'd been placing calls all over the country all week as his Screenshot research had proved more and more frustrating, trying to find a story buried in the event, not another one about it. In the end, he opted for more cleverness than insight, but Sid had liked the "Murder for Dummies" angle.

"Is this Mr. Seth Allen Mathias?"

"Yes. Who's this?"

"The Seth Allen Mathias who authored the piece of tripe in today's edition of the jingoistic tabloid down there in that theme park you call a city?"

Seth smiled. *Not a fan.*

"The very same. Did you enjoy it?"

"My enjoyment, or lack thereof, is immaterial. I demand that you provide proper attribution when you cite my work."

Even alone in the trailer with no one to read his expression, Seth's face scrunched.

"What work? I didn't cite anyone's work in the article. That was an opinion piece."

"Disingenuous. Of course you cited my work. Quote, 'There's even a theory that the Internet is bugged by the government, that anonymity is just a façade, set in place to encourage a level of candor that allows government a level of knowledge and control that is otherwise impossible.' End quote. You didn't read it somewhere. You read it in my own *opinion piece.*"

"*Your* opinion piece? Ohhh, yeah. You must be the nut who writes that blog about conspiracies. That was in the last one, wasn't it? Where you decided that Screenshot was an agent of the government, but couldn't figure out why?"

"There is no such word as blog, no matter how many times people use it. Check *any* dictionary. I write white papers. And I can assure you, I am no *nut,* as you call it. That is a theory which I have posited based on the facts available, and your neglect of scientific etiquette only demonstrates your ignorance. You clearly don't want your foolish readers to see my column as it would contradict your silly conclusion, so you plagiarize my content for your own benefit and ignore the source material. Typical in today's world, I am sad to say."

"Listen, Mr.—"

"*Doctor* Morgan Sicals, Ph.D., if you please."

"Okay. *Dr.* Sicals. I didn't plagiarize anything. I mentioned an opposing viewpoint. And who's to say I got it from you? You're not the only one positing *that* tripe."

"I challenge you to show me any other published document that uses my *agent provocateur* analogy that you so blithely stole."

Seth glanced at his watch and smiled again. What the hell, he thought, I've got nothing better to do.

"Can't do it, wouldn't try, don't care. Sue me. I challenge *you* to show me any legal precedent that defines my statements as plagiarism."

"I would not waste my time. Legal precedents be damned, there is professional courtesy to consider. There are rules for crediting others for the foundations of your work."

Seth stopped smiling. He felt some forlorn overtone, like the guy was genuinely hurt, and the fun went out of it.

"All right. I'm sorry. I'll be sure to mention you and your work in my next article."

"Don't patronize me. My work is sound, going back to the Nobel Prize." Seth sat up a little straighter and focused his attention a little more seriously as Sicals continued. "You think yourself a journalist. Well, do your research and check it yourself. You will find very few bodies of work to compare to mine.

"And while you're at it, maybe you could remind your readers of Archimedes. Do you even know who he was? 'Give me a lever long enough and a fulcrum on which to place it, and I shall move the world.' Give *me* a cluster of servers powerful enough and the storage space to hold their output, and *I* could take you by the hand and introduce you to this Screenshot personally.

"And, yes, I would appreciate a proper citation. I look forward to reading it." Click.

Seth took a moment to stare at the phone before reacting to the disconnect and clicking *end* on his cell phone. Nobel Prize? This guy won a Nobel Prize? Do they give that for lunacy?

His temporary *Mercury News* credentials got Seth into places he wouldn't normally be allowed, and one of them was the subscription-only Lexis-Nexis search engine. If anything was published about this guy, it would be there. He typed his query and references quickly filled the screen. He scrolled as more and more appeared. Three pages into it, Seth decided he had enough and clicked stop.

Starting with the oldest, he found articles with headlines like "Famed Physicist in Nobel Controversy" and "Committee

Investigation of Physicist's Claims." He scanned these just enough to understand the gist of the matter and learned that Sicals was indeed a very smart and respected scientist, at one time, anyhow.

As the dates got more recent, the tone deteriorated to name calling and accusations of scientific dishonesty and conspiracy. The stories got further and further apart as interest faded, until there was nothing at all for the last few years. Looking at the record like this, compressed into one extended story, it was just sad.

The Third E-mail

To: members@hackdoor.com
From: screenshot@crosstheen.com
Subject: Another execution
As promised, another live execution is planned. An announcement will be sent soon.
But wait! There's more!
YOU ARE INVITED TO PULL THE TRIGGER.
There are some requirements.
There is a $1,000 entry fee.
If selected, you must be ready to pay $10,000 for the privilege.
There will be no refunds.
You get one chance only.
You'd better be able to keep a secret.
To qualify, find and join the CROSSTHEEN forum under an anonymous user name and password. If you follow the directions that you find there, exactly, you will never be

identified. If you don't believe that, ask yourself why I did the first one myself.

If you are selected, you will be contacted with further instructions.

We're having some fun now.

Seth

Seth's computer chimed, alerting him that he had new e-mail. He clicked his Gmail tab and saw the sender was Rachel, his adopted daughter, and that brought on a visual of her with his new granddaughter, and that brought on a smile. Then he scanned across to the Subject field and saw, FW: Another Execution. That froze him, the smile developing a distinct rictal quality, and he knew the sender wasn't her.

He'd already read the original e-mail the day before, and it had led to his commission from the *Mercury News* to stay on the story. Slapping his belt looking for the case and not finding it, he swiveled his head around and spotted his cell phone charging in its rack. He was saying "Call Rachel home" before looking to see if it was even on and registering. She answered on the third ring, about an hour after the first one by Seth's anxiety-distorted reckoning of time. He tried to keep that out of his voice.

"Hi, Rach. How're you doing? And Brian? And Tessa?" His son-in-law and new granddaughter.

"Hi, Dad. I was going to call you later. We're all fine. How about you? Any progress with the nuke terrorists?"

"No, that's on hold. I've been working on another story all week. It was in yesterday's paper. I'll e-mail you a link to it. Listen, I had an e-mail crash today and lost about two days' worth. Did you send me anything recently?"

"A virus or something? No, I haven't sent anything since those pictures of Tessa in the park, what, two weeks ago. Is your computer all right?"

Rachel had always been maternal, but since her mother's death, she had taken on the responsibility of worrying about Seth, and he didn't want to give her any new cause for concern, like weird e-mails.

"No, just a glitch while I was cleaning out some old files. I'm checking around to see if anyone is expecting a reply or something."

"Geez. You must get a lot more e-mails than I do if you can't remember if the mother of your granddaughter sent you one."

Without even thinking about it, Seth could picture the teasing smile on her face, and that image neutralized his immediate anxiety. After the small talk and baby reports, Seth immediately called Wes.

He'd started to open the e-mail, but caught himself. Wes and his computer science lab instructor had been unable to find any trace of the first one on Wes's computer, no record that it had ever been there, and they were speculating that the hijacking of the e-mail account had taken place at the Internet Service Provider level, and the traces wiped off that server, or buried in the avalanche of other e-mail activity. Would they have better luck with an unopened e-mail?

Wes's cell phone answered with, "Sorry. I'm busy. Leave a message." Beep.

"Wes, I got another one of those e-mails. From Rach this time. I didn't open it. What do you want me to do with it?" Click.

Now he had to wait, and the anxiety percolated back to the

surface. The same questions. Who? Why? It was pacing time again, and Seth put the cell phone in his belt holster and set off around the campground.

He could think of only two possibilities: a prank or Screenshot. There was no doubt someone had targeted him for the e-mails, coming from the accounts of both his children. As far-fetched as the notion of Screenshot contacting him was, the possibility of a prankster was even more so. There was nothing Seth could think of that would put him on Screenshot's radar, unless he was somehow connected to one of the stories Seth had written over the years.

Before his wife's death, Seth wrote what he acknowledged as fluff— minor celebrity interviews, generic travel reports, personal-interest stuff, and even some pop-psychology—articles for air-line magazines, small-city periodicals and Sunday supplements. He couldn't imagine that any of those stories were linked to Screenshot.

After she died, he wrote nothing for almost a year. He'd tried many times, but could never stay with any one story through completion. Then came what he thought of as his West Virginia Adventure. Not in the roller coaster sense, unless it was an amusement park designed by Stephen King. Two days of running through the woods, chased by killers, trying to save an innocent woman, and failing.

When he got out of the hospital, he sold his home, bought the truck and trailer, and hit the road. Writing was not a problem after that, and he had plenty of work. He chased unusual news stories and dug into them, not for reporting, but for understanding. There were only a few of them, and he couldn't see how they might be connected to the e-mails and the executions.

The phone rang, and he saw that it was Wes on the caller ID. Even before he answered, he'd aimed himself back toward the trailer and picked up the pace.

Seth told him about the new e-mail and his talk with Rachel, asking him not to say anything to her unless they needed to look at her computer.

"After looking at my computer, I don't think we'll need to see hers. If it's the same sender, we'll get the same results. I would like to see yours, though, before you open the e-mail."

"I can't do that. Not without coming there. It's got all my stuff on it."

"Okay, then here's what you need to do. Get to a computer store and buy an external drive the same size as yours. Then get software that will replicate your drive contents on the new one. Not backup or copy. Replicate. It creates a mirror copy of your drive, bit by bit. Send that to me by overnight and we'll analyze it. Oh, and once you make the replica, go ahead and call me and open the e-mail so you can tell me everything that happens in real time."

That seemed workable, and Seth told Wes he'd send it right away. Then he was alone again, with nothing to do but consider the possibilities. One thing was clear: someone wanted something from him. Someone who knew his family. He wondered what it could be, and if he could deliver.

Chapter Six

The Second Victim

William Allen Sutter moved to Denver on a cold and snowy day in October, escaping his life-long hometown of Mankato, Minnesota. In accordance with Colorado law, he registered with the state on establishing residency, and twice again since. He only had seventy-seven more to go.

Glazer, as he liked to be called, was a Class 1 sexual offender. He nicknamed himself, a reference to the coating on his ample moustache after oral sex. Colorado wanted to know his location every three months for twenty years, and anyone who cared to could find out all about him on Colorado's SOR, Sexual Offender Registry, web site. Philip cared. Almost no one else did.

The manager of the athletic shoe outlet store didn't. He hired Sutter based on his appearance (clean and neat), personality (outgoing and friendly), job application information (mostly false), and the constant need for mature, and hopefully reliable, retail help. So far, he was pleased with his decision. William, as the manager called him, showed up on time each day, worked his shift, sold a lot of shoes and didn't complain. The customers liked him, and he seemed to like them.

Philip had found the almost celebratory story of his departure in the *Mankato Free Press*. He found no corresponding story in the *Denver Post* announcing Sutter's arrival. It went unnoticed. Philip found other press coverage of Sutter in abundance. After conviction for the abduction and repeated sexual assaults of twin eleven-year-old girls, Sutter had spent the next two years in the Minnesota State Prison in Stillwater until it was discovered that in another, unrelated case, the senior police investigator had lied under oath, calling into question his testimony in other trials.

The subsequent appeal frenzy threatened to overwhelm the resources of the state prosecutors, and they expedited solutions. Wherever they could get a reasonable plea bargain, they took it. Ten years and one day after his conviction, and looking forward to celebrating his thirty-third birthday there, Sutter boarded the bus to Denver.

All of this information, and a lot more on many kindred individuals, was stored in the external computer hard drive which in turn was stored in a small floor safe alongside an electro-magnet, wired to power up if anyone tampered with the safe, wiping the drive clean. Philip didn't worry about the possible loss of information—it was all readily available from public sources. He did worry about its evidentiary value.

He had installed the safe himself in the motor home that was one of the first toys he bought after cashing out. The $800,000 price bought a level of luxury and technology that eclipsed most homes, making up for what it lacked in size. Equipped with the high-speed satellite connections, wireless computer network, plasma screens, and state-of-the-art computers, it depreciated nicely on his tax returns as a business expense. As did the huge amounts of diesel fuel necessary to drive between his various business interests around the country.

Philip enjoyed the leisurely pace that driving a big bus required, and the dominant viewing station it afforded, high above all the other vehicles. As a board member for seven companies, and an investor in a dozen more, he always had somewhere to go, and an authentic reason for being there. LA, for instance, where he'd been three times before the Redo assassination.

The current trip to Denver, the last one for this project, came after three previous trips. Reconnoitering trips to establish the environment and patterns. Trips to research the life and crimes of William Sutter. Trips to plan his recompense. And this trip, its installation and use.

The Second Assassin

He read the simple instructions and subconsciously translated them into a language he understood: put your money where your mouth is, anonymously.

Geoffrey Keating's computer wallpaper, the image that provided the backdrop for all of his open programs, displayed himself with a dead snow leopard slung over his shoulders like some endangered species shawl, and the Eastern Sayan Mountains of Russia in the background. That leopard cost him over $42,000 to track, shoot, and smuggle to the taxidermist, so he figured a dead person was worth $10,000. More, with a picture.

He tried to poke holes in the instructions, looking for a weakness that would allow the authorities, or this Screenshot character, to identify him. His crude analysis found none. The $1,000 price tag qualified him as a player, someone serious about this opportunity and willing to gamble on being selected. And someone invested enough to pay the $9,000 balance if he won.

He'd never heard of Digital Gold Currency, but the research linked by the Crosstheen site made it look foolproof. He could open an anonymous account without any identification or background check, fund it with cash, a blind wire transfer or generic bank check, and conduct financial activities in complete anonymity. Transfers to other DGC accounts were instantaneous, no holds or validation.

"Jeh-fee," came the call from the other room, disturbing his seventeenth review of the Redo execution, imagining how it would feel to aim the gun, that incredibly cool gun, pull the trigger and watch Redo undo. The way she whined his name sounded like the cheap spelling, the Jeffrey spelling, in keeping with her image. He wondered if she even knew there was a proper spelling, a royal spelling, and if she would pronounce it gee-off-fur-ee if she did.

"Jeh-fee," Brynda called again. "Are you getting rea-dy?"

She wanted him to get dressed for dinner and the premiere of the road show of *The Lion King*. She dragged him to every event where there might be people with money or cameras. He was tired of these, and tired of her, and her expiration date was coming up soon. He wondered what it would cost him financially, and mentally prepared for the inevitable tantrum. Too bad he couldn't target *her* over the Internet. That would be a hunt he'd pay for.

The upside was that tonight he would premiere the new white Hummer H1 Alpha that had cost him $146,000. The bright white color, bush guards, light racks, and chrome step rails made it look like he was preparing for some designer war. He thought that the Rehabinator would look real nice mounted in the open cargo area.

Before shutting down, he funded a new DGC account with two $8,000 blind transfers from different banks, both to have a cushion in this new money market, and to stay below the $10,000 single-transaction radar. Picking West Coast branches that were still open, he made the transfers using the ID *b1gg@m3m@n*, big game man. By the time he dressed, the money was there, and he transferred his $1,000 gamble to the account number provided by Screenshot before leaving his dead leopard picture for the fake lions on the stage.

❖   ❖   ❖

Her snoring woke Geoffrey. Her appearance got him out of the bed, leaving her undisturbed, and still fully dressed. Falling into bed after the post-show parties, she looked like she tried to remove her extensive makeup using the white silk pillowcase. The nausea he felt could have been the hangover, or the grotesque vision of her face smeared in equal parts on her skin and on the pillow.

The 900 milligrams of aspirin washed down from the bottle of Belvedere Vodka he kept chilled in the fridge would take care of the hangover. She would be a bigger problem.

In his boxer shorts, Geoffrey checked his e-mail and found one from Screenshot. He opened it, and his day got better.

"You have been selected …" it began, and the headache disappeared, this news a far better analgesic than aspirin. The image of Brynda's abstract face faded, replaced by his expectation of aiming and firing the Rehabinator, and watching his target shatter under the fifty-caliber barrage. It would be far better than one clean shot at a wild animal, a big cat or a rhino that always fell dead immediately, the laser sighting taking any chance of a miss out of the equation. His abdomen fluttered, the same way it did just before having sex for the first time with a particularly beautiful woman, a woman who wouldn't give him a second look without his bank accounts and the trappings they bought.

The instructions provided a link to the Internet site where

he would control and fire the weapon, and the schedule to do it. He would need to be at his computer, ready to go, an hour beforehand. It also recommended complete privacy for at least two hours as the schedule varied with the target.

At the linked site, he found the return on his investment.

> The target is a white male, 33, brown hair cut short, 5' 8" tall, medium build. He drives a bright yellow Mustang. He is a convicted pedophile, having served 5 years of a 30-year sentence for a series of brutal rapes before being released on a legal technicality. This has been carefully researched, and there can be no mistake.
>
> At approximately 1:00 AM GMT, you will have a live video feed of the car parked in a shopping mall parking lot. At that time, control of the aiming will be enabled, and you will be able to move the weapon within a limited range—up, down, left, and right—using the arrow keys or a joystick. You will be allowed three minutes to practice before control will be disconnected. At that point you will transfer the remaining $9,000 to the same DGC account. Once the transfer is received and the target is within range, control will be returned to you.
>
> The weapon works like a high-pressure hose, but it throws electricity instead of water. Wait until the target is at the car door and stationary.

It wasn't the Rehabinator, Geoffrey realized. No projectiles, no explosions, no body parts.

> Sight on the target using the laser pointer that will

appear when the target is in the recommended kill zone. Press and hold the F10 key or the joystick button. You will see a stream of liquid spray toward the target, followed almost immediately by a bright orange glow along the path. The range of the weapon is approximately 40 feet, and it is positioned 11 feet from the Mustang's driver's side door. The sound and motion of the weapon may attract the target's attention, so be ready for any sudden movements.

As long as the stream is directed on the target and the F10 key/joystick button depressed, he will receive a 7 mA, 300 kV electric charge. The therapeutic effects of this vary with the duration. One second will get the target's complete attention. Three seconds will put the target on the ground, with disorientation and muscle spasms for as long as fifteen minutes. Each additional second will increase the likelihood of death until twelve seconds, at which time you will simply be cooking the corpse.

You may stop and start the spray at will using the F10 key or Joystick button. You have 20 seconds of fuel. Enjoy it.

DO NOT ENGAGE ANY OTHER TARGETS. AIMING AT ANYONE OR ANYTHING OTHER THAN THE IDENTIFIED TARGET WILL RESULT IN IMMEDIATE SHUTDOWN OF THE WEAPON.

We're having some fun now.

Geoffrey stared at the screen, dumbfounded, like the word of God had just emanated from his speakers. Was he dreaming? This was simply too good to be true. It would be like reaching out and touching the bastard, and he could picture it in his mind as if it were already a memory. The clock on the computer displayed

9:17, and he calculated that he had less than nine hours to get ready.

Getting rid of Brynda and establishing absolute privacy in his condo took first priority, and he felt a pressing urgency to get it done. He wished for more time, and yet he was impatient for six o'clock to arrive.

Having some fun now? No shit!

Geoffrey watched someone approach in the distance and nudged the new, top-of-the-line joystick he bought earlier in the day, trying to aim the weapon. Nothing happened, and he frantically checked the cable connection and then tried the arrow keys. Still nothing. He panicked and froze, something he'd never done with a rifle in his hands. He'd followed the instructions to the letter, the money transfer verified by a returned receipt. It had worked fine in practice, and now he was being robbed. And there was nothing he could do about it.

"Shit," he yelled, and got an unexpected answer.

"Jeh-fee? What's wrong, Snooks?"

What the hell is she doing here? I sent her shopping.

She walked into his den and whined an answer to his silent question. "Nothing fit. I'm retaining water. I can't try clothes on when I'm all," she waved her hands like she was trying to shake the water out, "… bloaty."

"Get the hell out of here. *Get out!* Don't come back."

He yanked her by the arm and she yelled, "Ow," and tried to pull away. Gripping tighter, he dragged her through the spacious living room to the front door, took the keys from her hand, and pushed her out, slamming the door in her shocked face. He ignored the clamor as she hammered on the door and screamed at him, asking why and begging to be let back in.

On the monitor, the target was almost to the car door, and a new message blinked at the bottom of the screen: Control Enabled. The weapon was his now. A nozzle had appeared in the frame, and a laser sighting dot shone on the yellow door like a red paint drip.

He grabbed the joystick as he sat, joggling the laser dot, causing it to trace squiggly lines across the Mustang. The target looked up at him, and Geoffrey had to remind himself that it was a camera, just the sound and movement catching the guy's attention. As he centered on him, the guy reached to unlock the car door and Geoffrey thought, now or never, and thumbed the button on the top of the joystick.

Chapter Seven

Seth

The car had so many wings and air dams and scoops that it looked like it was made from yellow Legos, and it would only blend in at a modern art exhibit.

As he waited for the next live Screenshot event, the image on Seth's screen showed a generic shopping mall parking lot on a clear and sunny day, centered on the yellow Mustang. With the preponderance of pickups and SUVs, and the Loews Marketplace Multiplex Theater in the background, just like with Redo, it could have been anywhere in North America. It had taken six tries to log on to the web site, and he only succeeded after typing "your password" in the box labeled Enter Your Password. Apparently Screenshot's instructions were literal.

After logging on, he'd waited almost twenty-five minutes before the screen came alive, right after the gunshot alert, which he was ready for this time. The camera seemed to be positioned on a pick-up truck, and Seth could see part of the sidewall and tailgate of the truck bed at the bottom of the screen. People moved back and forth on foot and in cars, but no one even glanced in the direction of the camera, so it must have been hidden. The background sounds were unobtrusive—traffic in the distance and occasional voices from outside the camera's field of vision.

Two rows away, a man walked toward the Mustang. He looked about thirty and carried a paper sack cradled in one arm, like the contents were precious and he didn't trust the paper to hold. There was no sign of a gun barrel, and Seth thought the range very close for the devastating effects of the Rehabinator. Then he noticed three computer graphic facsimiles of gauges had appeared in the bottom left of the screen, one labeled Amps, one Watts, and the other Seconds.

What the hell is that?

A hydraulic noise started, barely audible in the traffic din, and a red laser dot traced its way to the middle of the man and hung there. The movement attracted his attention, and he stared at the camera with some interest, looking like the curious dog in the old RCA logo, head tilted slightly to one side, eyes scrunched, unaware of the red dot on his chest. His right hand hesitated just short of inserting the key, and the left still clutched the bag.

A bolt of light flashed from the nozzle, accompanied by what sounded like an electronic yap, almost a cartoon noise, and arced to the man, knocking him down instantly. He lay there, stunned, for several seconds, looking at his body like he expected to see his organs exposed. The bag contained something liquid, and its container broke in the fall, spilling its contents in a pool around it. Two of the screen gauges simultaneously jumped with the bolt, but Seth hadn't noticed the reading, just the movement. The third gauge registered nineteen seconds, whatever that meant.

Finding no holes in himself, the man looked up again and tried to scramble backwards, crab-like, on his hands and feet. The laser dot locked on his left thigh and another bolt hit him, jerking him off the ground. It was over in an instant. The gauge readings again jumped unnoticed, and the seconds counted down to sixteen.

This time the man lay still, and Seth wondered if he was dead. After several seconds his head moved sluggishly, and he regained comprehension, looking with desperate fear at the camera.

The next bolt hit him in the side, waist high, and didn't stop immediately. The man's body seemed to levitate and do an airborne Irish toe dance, the torso stable and the arms and legs flailing. Many more seconds passed, seeming like they could be better measured as minutes, and Seth could see the gauges pegged at 7 mAmps and 380 kV, and 11, 10, 9 seconds counting down.

When the lightning stopped at nine, the man lay immobile, smoke rising off the scorch where the bolt had attached itself to his body. The contents of the bag, Seth guessed liquor, had caught fire and the man's left foot burned in the flame. Still, he didn't move, and Seth figured he was dead.

The laser dot moved around his body, like it was searching for something. It came to a stop on his face, and another short bolt of two seconds seemed to apply black makeup wherever it touched. The body convulsed, but with less conviction.

Then the camera rose and panned left and right. It finally came to rest on the winged medallion on the hood of the Chrysler P/T Cruiser parked next to the Mustang. Another bolt shot out and the ornament shattered before the flame suddenly stopped, the gauge at seven. Action on the screen froze, the flames became the only movement, but Seth just stared and stared.

After an interval that had no meaning for him, a passing of time unnoticed, a scrolling message appeared on the bottom of the monitor, like headline news.

ACME PEDIPHRYER, Patent Pending.

Chapter Eight

Karen

"Mr. Holcomb called while you were on the phone. He said there is an e-ticket for you on the 10:05 USAir flight to Reagan, and to be on it. Someone will meet you there. He wants to see you about Screenshot."

Karen's demeanor held its ground in the face of this surprise call from her boss in DC. It had been almost a week since she'd e-mailed him her treatise, her evaluations and recommendations on using Phish-Net in the Screenshot investigation. She hadn't really expected any response, let alone a summons to DC. Had her white paper proposing Phish-Net leadership in the investigation really gotten someone's attention?

"Thanks. I better wrap up and go. Did he say overnight or not?"

"He said don't bother to pack, you'll be there and back today."

The short flight gave her just enough time to scribble some notes and try to organize a presentation. There would be no time to prepare computer slides, no glossy handouts, just her thinking on her feet. She hadn't been so excited since ... well, since she graduated from the FBI academy and got an actual badge.

Someone she didn't know picked her up. Getting picked up indicated an urgency that rarely accompanied her visits to headquarters. The security guard greeted her and directed her to an executive conference room on the ninth floor. A high-level location told her it would be a high-level meeting, and she was pleased that her efforts commanded such attention. When she walked into the conference room, eleven section heads and field agents looked up at her and smiled. Several called out greetings, and some new faces gave her a thorough examination. Looking for dark roots in her hair, no doubt.

Dave Hendrickson, Special Agent-In-Charge of the Screenshot investigation, said a warm hello and told her to have a seat. He brought her up to speed on the twenty minutes that she'd missed. The FBI had a plan, he said. They needed her resources. About her paper, he said nothing. She'd prepared for the wrong meeting.

"Based on the limited analysis we are able to do of the Internet traffic to Screenshot's lottery, and the timing, we estimate that there will be no more than 5,000 lottery entrants this time. We're prepared to spend up to $5,000,000 on entrance fees. Taking into account other factors, such as timing, we project our probability of winning the lottery at 73 percent."

Karen understood what they were doing; she didn't understand why. "You're going to flood the lottery with entries and win? What then?"

"Then we'll use the contact with Screenshot to narrow the list of possibilities and delay the execution while we try to intervene. We might get lucky and get a clue to this guy."

"You can't stop it," she reminded them. "He controls the weapon. The best you can hope for is to give the victim another few minutes of life. Five mill to give someone like Redo Washington a few minutes? Can't we use our resources better than that?"

"The goal is not to give any Redos out there a better chance. The goal is to try to use the contact with Screenshot to get a better ID on him."

"How? Do you think he's going to tell us who he is?" She heard her own tone and realized she was letting her disappointment show through, and she softened her attitude. "Look, he's already demonstrated his ability to hide in the Internet. There are no clues there. When he signs off, he's gone."

"Karen, crimes are solved by legwork. You examine everything, you enter it into the record, you compare, you construct scenarios, you test them, you add new information. We gather enough information and we'll find the guy."

Karen swallowed her resentment at being lectured, at being patronized, and said, "Okay, what's the plan once we win? Who gets to pull the trigger?"

"You do. Not you specifically, but your office. We want to use your resources to create and send the entries, and to monitor and control the action. You will need to set it up as thousands of different e-mails."

"I can do that. What are we doing to intervene?"

"We'll have all our field offices on-line, live, during the video stream. As soon as it starts, we'll ID the victim and location. Urban Search and Rescue will be airborne in every city and cover their area. We'll use local law enforcement assets where we don't have coverage. We'll have all the cell phone providers available to get us the number of anyone we identify in the target area, and we'll try to disrupt the execution with a phone call to the victim while our guys get there. That should pretty much cover it."

Karen thought about offering her opinion that an attempt to disrupt would more likely lead to hastening the event, but a warning look from her boss, Stan Holcomb, told her to wait and talk to him. When the meeting ended, they went to his office.

"I don't want to hear about it," he started before the door even closed. "I read your proposal and passed it along. No response.

This is the plan now. We'll give it our best shot. If it works, everyone's happy. If it doesn't, we'll learn something."

"An expensive lesson."

"How much would you pay to know Screenshot's identity?"

"That's not the point. We're spending the money so that someone high enough in the food chain can point and say, 'See what we're doing?' There's not a sliver of a chance that we will find Screenshot with this. Is it worth it?"

"That's not our call. Our job is to come up with a plan that is doable and has a chance at success. It's going to be a long weekend. You better get back and get started."

Chapter Nine

Seth

The subject line on the e-mail was, FW: Execution Number Three. Seth knew immediately what that meant. The sender wasn't a relative this time: it was listed as Screenshot.

"Thought you might be interested," the text read before duplicating the original announcement. It was early, just two and a half days since the last execution.

> ---------- Forwarded message ----------
> To: members@hackdoor.com
> From: Screenshot@techssenor.com
> Subject: Execution v3.0
> V3.0 will take place Tuesday at approximately 7:00 PM
> GMT. Click on the link below and enter your new password.
> http://kills.techssenor.com/imageclick/
> CID=00000d4e57b88f5075csy066
> We're having some fun now.

After Wes's unsuccessful attempt to get anything useful from the previous two e-mails, they'd decided on a new course of action. He clicked the reply button, and in the space for his message he typed, "Who are you?" And then he waited. He waited twenty minutes and then brewed the morning coffee. Then he checked his e-mail. Then drank the coffee, and checked his e-mail. And finally concluded he was being foolish, and checked his e-mail again before going to shower and dress.

In the trailer shower, limited in both size and hot water capacity, Seth did the two things he always did—he scrubbed and thought.

His thoughts orbited around one nucleus: did Screenshot really send him the e-mail? The questions and the implications swirled in his head. Why? Was there really another execution scheduled? Why tell me about it? What should I do? Who do I tell? Holy shit!

Toweling his still dripping body, Seth checked his e-mail. Nothing but spam.

Dressed and brushing his teeth, Seth checked his e-mail. Not even any spam.

Realizing that he was obsessing on a reply, he grabbed his truck keys and wallet and drove to the nearby Denny's for some too-big breakfast, just to be away from the computer. But he couldn't escape his thoughts.

Still holding his keys after unlocking the trailer when he returned, Seth checked his computer and the little white envelope confirmed he had new mail. He found three spams and one message titled, Go here, from horse_cents@sensortech.com. Any other day, he would have deleted it as just more garbage. But not today.

Opening the document, he found a link, www.satchat. com/secret_nosh/, and clicked it without hesitation, not even considering the possibility of viruses or any other Internet hazard. Satchat turned out to be an Internet chat service, and secret_nosh, a private room. A listing of current users showed only one other ID: horse_cents. A dialog box asked Seth to create a user name and enter the password to access the room.

Seth typed his name for the user, and then wondered what

the password might be. Another game, like the second execution where he entered 'your password' to see the video. Seth typed in the same words and got nowhere. Looking at the message, Seth changed it to 'the password,' and then 'password.' Still nothing. He tried 'horse_cents' and 'screenshot' and every other related word he could think of, and finally slapped the keyboard in disgust and went to his kitchen.

Leaning against the refrigerator door, sipping the iced tea he had poured, Seth glared at the screen, still blinking *Enter password* and wondered why Screenshot would tell him to go there if he wasn't going to let him in. Seth straightened up and leapt the distance to the keyboard when the answer finally occurred to him.

He typed 'go there' and again got an empty dialog box asking him for a password. Shit! He re-opened his Inbox and read the instructions once more. 'Go here.' Typing that phrase into the password field got a rising-scale tone and the message, "Welcome to Secret Nosh." A new window opened, showing a list of room occupants in the small pane on the left, a large pane covering most of the screen for the chat record, and a third, smaller pane below it to enter his own text. All of them were empty.

Seth leaned back and sipped the tea, knowing that somewhere Screenshot, if it really was Screenshot, was manipulating him, and Seth was ready to let him.

He put the empty glass in the sink and involuntarily glanced over his shoulder at the still empty chat room. I should do some work, he thought, and sat back down to open his word processor to start the new Screenshot article the *Mercury News* had commissioned. He thought this new development might give him a whole new angle, and started making notes of the questions he had for Screenshot. The same rising chime tone sounded, startling him, and a pop-up said there was a new occupant in the chat room: Horse Cents.

Seth clicked the box and the Secret Nosh room showed a new entry in the chat record.

"Hello, Seth. May I call you Seth?"

Seth stared at the entry, wondering how to respond to such a civil question from such an anti-civil person.

"What do I call you?"

"Screenshot. Or maybe just Shot for short."

"How about Mr. Screenshot to keep it formal?"

"Formal, eh? Okay, Mr. Seth Allen Mathias. Formal it is."

Why do the weirdoes of the world insist on using my middle name, Seth wondered.

"What about Tuesday? Is there another murder scheduled?"

"Not a murder. Think more like capital punishment. Overdue retribution. You're the first to know about it. Everyone else will know Monday, as usual. Unless you want to tell them beforehand. I'm just giving you a heads-up."

"Why me?"

"I like you. I liked your article. Are you writing more? 'Murder for Dummies!' Very clever. And your conclusion was, well … interesting. So you think these events were coming attractions? Of what, do you suppose? Maybe you should think about the implications of that and make it your next article."

"That's not it. You contacted me before the article, before the first murder. You tricked me into watching. So again, why me?"

"Let's say I appreciate that other little episode in your life."

That brought a chill to Seth, tracing up his spine and tickling his brain, causing a shiver. His life contained few events that he would categorize as episodes. Only one, really.

"What episode?" he typed, thinking "disingenuous," as Dr. Sicals would say.

Instead of a reply, a new frame opened and a graphic popped up, a picture of an old news story. Seth had read it before.

"Wilderness Wilding" Survivor Released

Tuesday, March 6, 2007
By Pamela Gaye, Pittsburgh Post-Gazette

The man many call a hero, and some a vigilante, was released from the Davis Memorial Hospital today where he has been under treatment for injuries suffered in the two-day ordeal that came to be called "The Wilderness Wilding." Seth Mathias, 42, left the grounds alone, without responding to questions.

Deputy Sheriff Anne Ogilvie, the only other survivor, remains in guarded condition after surgery Sunday for a gunshot wound to her head. Doctors say she should recover completely.

The Wilding episode captured the attention of authorities when they found Mathias and Ogilivie, wounded and unconscious, at a remote lakeside campground in the Monongahela National Forest after Ogilvie went to the area following up on a suspicious traffic accident and didn't return. The event captured national attention when the subsequent search uncovered seven dead bodies, the result of a weekend of terror and tragedy.

Authorities believe that Mathias stumbled on the murder of Ken Slocumb and the attempted rape of his girlfriend, Angela Flynn, and intervened. No details have yet been released pending further investigation, but Sheriff Randy Mades confirmed that the dead included Slocumb and Flynn, and five unidentified males. Speculation is that the unidentified bodies are David and James Kaslich, Luther Praeger, Daniel Adderton, and Warren Sanders, Jr., all friends, and described by some of the local residents as a gang.

Interviews with family members of the identified and suspected victims seem to tell a story of a love triangle revenge killing, and the attempted rescue of Flynn. During their two-day rampage that followed, each of the unidentified male victims was violently killed, four of them by Mathias, apparently one at a time.

Sheriff Mades said that no further charges were pending, and that the results of their investigation would be released after review by District Attorney Marsha McLemore.

The other question on everyone's mind is *how*? How did Mathias, a middle-aged everyman, kill four reputed thugs? Mathias isn't telling. And neither are the victims.

"That episode," Horse Cents typed. "Is there more than one? Or are you treating the four of them as separate? You're still two ahead of me, you know. But I'm catching up."

Seth's near-death experience in the woods a year earlier was no secret. His evolution from Good Samaritan to vigilante had ultimately led to his current attempt to escape on the opposite coast.

"Big deal. You read the papers."

"Yes, I do. And the follow-up stories were rather graphic, wouldn't you say? Beating people with clubs, or choking them to death. Your point of view might be closer to mine than you think."

"It's not the same. They tried to kill me."

"Yes, with maybe a little revenge thrown in there at the end. And Redo and Glazer aren't trying to kill you? Aren't trying to kill our civilization?"

"Please, spare me the righteous justifications for murder and tell me how I know you are really Screenshot."

"I am hardly righteous. And proof? Tuesday's executioner will be a sign. We'll talk again after that. I think we'll be talking a lot."

"Wait," Seth typed, his list of questions unasked. But the chime tone descended this time, and the pop-up read, Horse Cents has left the room.

A sign of what?

Any sense has left the room, Seth thought.

Chapter Ten

Seth

"Special Agent Connelly. How can I help you?"

"Are you the person in charge of the Screenshot investigation," Seth asked the voice on the other end of the phone.

"No, sir. That is being run out of Washington. I am one of the local agents working the case. How can I help you?"

"I'm Seth Mathias, a reporter for the *San Jose Mercury News.* I ..."

"Excuse me, sir," Connelly interrupted, "all press calls are handled through our media center. I'll transfer you."

"Wait! Agent ... Connelly? I'm not calling about news. I mean not newspaper news. Screenshot contacted me this morning and gave me a message, and I wanted to pass that along to the FBI."

"A message? From Screenshot? What exactly was this message?"

"He said tomorrow's executioner would be a sign."

"A sign of what?"

"That's what I wanted to know. But he left the chat room before I could ask."

There was a pause. "Chat room? You mean Screenshot logged into an Internet chat room and announced that he was giving us a sign? And that's what you're reporting?"

"Yes. It was on some web site called Satchat and the room was the Secret Nosh room and his screen name was horse cents and he said we'll talk again."

"Yes sir. I've got all that. Please give me a phone number where you can be reached and I'll have an agent follow up right away."

❖   ❖   ❖

Breakfast didn't digest. No agent called. Lunch didn't get made. The phone didn't ring. Seth lost his patience.

"Special Agent Wilkinson. How can I help you?"

"May I speak to Agent Connelly, please."

"Agent Connelly isn't here. Is there something I can help you with?"

Irritation showing through, Seth said, "Yes, there is. You can tell me when someone will be calling to get the information I have about Screenshot."

"You have information about Screenshot? What information, exactly?"

"Exactly the same information I reported to Agent Connelly over four hours ago when he promised someone would get back to me."

"One moment, sir, while I check the phone log. You said around ten this morning?" Seth heard key clicks in the background. "What is your name, sir?"

Seth gave it to him and drummed his fingers on an imaginary keyboard listening to more clicks from Wilkinson's.

"I'm sorry, sir, but I don't find any record of your call or your information. Can you please repeat it for me?"

With less anxiety, but a lot more frustration, Seth told his story again.

"I'll pass this along to Agent Connelly and I'm sure he will get someone to handle it right away."

Seth understood patronizing, and that he was now the victim

of it twice. When he rolled it over in his head, he realized just how deranged he must sound. In a deranged situation, he wondered how he could sound otherwise.

It took eleven steps to pace from the entertainment center in the back of the trailer to the wardrobe in front, including the three steps up to the sleeping area. Eleven steps back. Was his information really that worthless? Could chat rooms be traced somehow, their occupants identified? Wes, his son, would know. His voicemail picked up when Seth tried to call, and he went back to his eleven steps. Who else?

Sicals. The guy was a kook, but he was a smart kook, and he seemed to know the Internet. Seth opened the incoming phone log on his cell phone to find the number and, as a precaution, saved it to his contact list. Then he pressed *dial,* and hoped this wasn't even kookier.

The phone rang twice and then connected with a flat, formal "This is Dr. Morgan Sicals." Seth waited for the voicemail instructions but got silence, then an impatient "Hello. Is someone there?"

"Oh, I'm sorry. This is Seth Mathias. We spoke earlier."

"I am perfectly aware of what I did earlier, Mr. Mathias. I don't need you to remind me. What do you want?"

Seth explained the e-mail and chat room discussion he'd had, leaving out that it was with Screenshot, and asked if it was possible to identify anyone.

"Are you researching another article in which you won't acknowledge my contributions? I don't have the time or the interest in assisting your pathetic essays. Please do not bother me with these inconsequential inquiries."

Seth stopped pacing in the kitchen and stood looking out the window above the small sink, wondering what to do. He could feel Sicals starting to hang up. What's the harm in telling him, he thought? Everyone already knows he's crazy.

"Wait, please. I really am sorry to bother you, Dr. Sicals, but I can assure you this inquiry is not inconsequential. You said you could track Screenshot. Here's your chance. He sent me two e-mails earlier today, and we talked in one of those Internet chat rooms. The FBI doesn't seem to believe me, and you're the one person I know who might be able to help."

The silence lasted so long that Seth began to believe Sicals had hung up on him.

"First of all, you don't know me," Sicals finally responded. "You apparently know my phone number. That we talked briefly does not constitute even the flimsiest of relationships. Second, you wasted your time with the FBI, as you apparently now understand. Who did you call there? Never mind. You called the local field office, didn't you? Unfortunate. You have made yourself known to them, and you are now part of their problem."

Seth started to speak, but Sicals talked right over him.

"Do you have the e-mails? Forward them to me now. q h e doctor at comcast dot net. Spell out doctor, no abbreviations, no spaces."

The line went silent and Seth figured now meant *now* to Sicals, so he set the phone down and went to his computer to do as instructed.

"Okay, they're on their way."

"Wait while I read them."

After several minutes, Sicals came back on the line. "I still haven't received them. Are you sure you did it right."

"Yeah, right here in front of me. q-h-e-d-o-c-t-o-r at c-o-m-c-a-s-t dot c-o-m."

"Comcast dot *net*. You're going to have to pay attention and follow instructions if you expect any assistance from me. Now resend them. And do it right this time."

After another extended silence, burning more of Seth's cell minutes, Sicals came back on line.

"All right. I've looked at them. There is nothing particularly useful. Tell me everything. Leave out nothing. Also, time stamp the events."

"Time stamp?"

"Tell me what time things happened, for God's sake."

Seth related the story for the third time, careful to do it in chronological order and to describe everything he could remember, including all of the passwords he had tried.

"Interesting. But another waste of time. There is no trail on the Internet, no record of these transactions. Identifying Screenshot requires live activity, something other than simple typed text. There's nothing I can do to help."

"Why live activity?"

"Because then you don't need a record of the transactions. You follow the transactions as they occur. Unfortunately, they occur in tiny fractions of a second, and they are mixed in with millions of others. It would be like tracking one set of cow tracks in a stampede. You need to work backwards, to find each one before it gets lost in the muddle."

Seth understood the metaphor. "You'd have to be in the middle of the stampede, and go backwards in time. How do you do that?"

"Packet analysis. But before you can do that, you have to identify the juncture of the packets to analyze. To do that you need ping triangulation. And then once you have done the packet analysis back to the local source, you need signal correlation to identify the single track that you are following. And to do any of these processes, you need massive computing power. Distributed computing power working from distant locations. In short, unless you are the NSA, it can only be done in theory."

Seth had no idea what Sicals had just said, and tried the only computer question that he could think of. "What about those supercomputers? Couldn't one of them do it?"

"I said *distributed* computing power, working simultaneously from at least three distant locations. Three supercomputers, yes. Or the massive parallel processing array of smaller computers, mainframes and even some high-end minis and network servers that I mentioned in our previous call. In other words, hundreds or even thousands of computers working simultaneously on the same problem. Sort of an intensive SETI initiative."

"What is that?"

"Mr. Mathias. You are hopelessly ignorant about all of this, and therefore wasting my time and yours."

"Doctor, it's Screenshot we're discussing, and I may be ignorant, but I am the only connection to him."

"How do you know that?"

The question sent a small tremor through Seth. "I guess I don't," he admitted, but then recovered. "But I am the only one that you have."

"Yes, that is so," Sicals answered. "Unfortunate. The SETI initiative is unimportant. It is simply the simultaneous application of tens of thousands of personal computers to do the work of several very large computers analyzing radio signal data from space in the misguided attempt to find other life in the universe.

You may read my critique of the project in my Internet publications. Volume Two, Number Seven, as I recall."

"And this ping triangulation?"

"Volume One, Number Eleven. Ping triangulation is simply a massive and simultaneous query sent to a particular URL—oh, I'm sorry, I forgot who I was talking to—sent to a particular *web site address* for the purpose of confirming its availability, and the round-trip time for the message to travel between the originating computer and the target web site. Two things happen when you do a massive ping campaign. First, you get times for each ping, and while any one or ten or even thousand such records is meaningless, once you start to record tens and hundreds of thousands, you can do data mining to determine certain probabilities, like the physical distance between the two computers.

"Second, the server will likely interpret the pings as a denial-of-service assault and take steps to protect itself, identifying and blocking certain transactions. This, too, done tens of thousands of times, leaves a record for probabilistic analysis.

"One source of records, that is, one computer somewhere launching the pings, will give you a circle of probable locations from the locus, the source. If you use three computers, the intersection of the three circles is the approximate location of your target server."

"What good does that do?"

"None, really. There could be hundreds of servers within the probable area. But once you have narrowed the search area, discovered which stampede you need to get into the middle of, in effect, you limit the amount of data to be analyzed to a manageable amount. Volume Two, Number Twelve: Packet Analysis."

Seth didn't ask the obvious question, knowing by then that

Sicals would continue.

"Packet analysis is simply the rudimentary examination of the content of any packet of information being transmitted. Since there are billions of such packets at any given moment, all jumbled together waiting to be assembled at their destination into a useful form, analyzing all of them is an impossible task. At some point in time, the theoretical computing power necessary adds so many of its own packets that it overwhelms itself. So you must narrow not only the source of the data, but also the type of data using some distinguishing feature. For example, video versus text or anything else. Sort of finding the three-legged cow in the stampede.

"Further analysis of these packets lets you make judgments, guesses really, of which ones are connected, which ones are going to be re-assembled at the target. Certain characteristics can be identified and applied to the packets coming behind, and you can slowly move back up the data stream to its source. If you could be in the middle of the stampede and find one set of three-legged cow prints, and if you could move back in time in very small increments, you could see the preceding set before they got trampled. And so on. This, obviously, cannot be done in real time. You must capture thousands of snapshots of the data flowing by and then work carefully backwards following the trail back in time as well as path."

"And this would lead you back to Screenshot?"

"No, but it gets you closer. Since he is using video streaming, it would be easier to do the packet analysis and backtrack to the host. But there is no guarantee that this host is in Screenshot's possession, or even his city or state or country. He could be in Boise using a server in Taipei. But once you have the server, then you have again narrowed the search universe. Now you can apply

Signal Correlation. Volume Two, Number Fourteen. Number Thirteen covered Asymmetrical Sequencing.

"Signal correlation again applies probability analysis to massive amounts of data. In this case, correlating certain packets with some other constant to link the connected packets into a single line back to the specific source. In Screenshot's case, correlating the commands from the target computer with the images on the screen. Simple. He orders the camera to pan right, the image changes, and we correlate the command and response signals. Eventually we get back to the specific computer."

Sicals stopped talking, and Seth couldn't start. He had no idea what to say, what to ask. It all sounded perfectly reasonable, but he didn't know if it was genius or delusion. Finally he spoke, more to break the silence than to address the information.

"And you invented all of this?"

"I didn't invent anything. I simply identified a mathematical process for accomplishing a complex task. Any competent mathematician could have done the same. No, let me correct that. There are probably two dozen mathematicians alive today who could develop the algorithms to do the analysis."

"I thought you were a physicist."

"Aahhh, so you did your research, Mr. Mathias. Very good. Then you know that I have been unjustly shut out of the world of theoretical physics. The resources to do my work are very expensive, and if you aren't supported by an institution, then you are irrelevant. It is another means for the few to control information and therefore our lives. But mathematics? If you have a pencil and a calculator, you can do mathematical research. And if you have time, you don't need the calculator. So that is where I have turned my talents."

"All right, Doctor. Where do we go to apply this theory to the reality of Screenshot?"

"*We* don't go anywhere, Mr. Mathias. I have no interest in this other than the theoretical applications of my theory. And as I said, it would take the NSA or an unlikely cooperation among many less well-equipped enterprises. So good luck, Mr. Mathias. Remember to watch behind you for the FBI."

"Wait. Dr. Sicals. Hello?"

The line stayed connected, but there was no response for several seconds.

"Maybe … No. They wouldn't. Never mind."

"Who wouldn't?" Seth asked. "Wouldn't what?"

"My mention of the FBI reminded me of something. But of course, they're not going to make their resources available for this investigation."

"What resources?"

"The FBI runs a rather sophisticated Internet crimes team. Mind you, their definition of crime covers some questionable ground, and I have watched them for years to gather information on some of the government's unpublicized activities. They have a cooperative relationship with many of the major commercial computer and Internet companies that would almost certainly be able to accumulate the necessary resources. The problem is that they have no interest in doing so. Just the opposite, in fact."

"What is this group? How do I find it?"

"It is called Digital Phish-Net, and good luck finding it. I must go now. Please keep me apprised of your efforts. It will provide some amusement."

This time the silence was a dead connection.

Chapter Eleven

Karen

Her boss had been right, it had been a long weekend. Creating and sending 4,884 distinct e-mail entries from 4,884 legitimate e-mail accounts had required a huge effort from her staff. And then it had been a long Monday before they learned that they had indeed won. Everyone took that as a sign that the plan was working, but Karen kept her opinion to herself. Now she would find out if she was right to be skeptical.

The monitors all over the building went live, and the bustle and activity of hundreds of people instantly stopped, like the announcer was describing the Blue Light Special at K-Mart, and all the shoppers wanted to know where to flock. But these people already knew where to go, some back to their workstations, others to conference rooms with big- screen monitors, still others to man the phones.

Karen sat at her workstation, set up in the large conference room, her senior staff surrounding her. Stan Holcomb and Dave Hendrickson and several others from the Hoover Building offices in DC watched from their own temporary workstations, directing their people, hoping for a break, any break.

The instructions in the return e-mail from their winning entry told her that they would only need the F10 button to fire the weapon, but that wouldn't happen. Their goal was to delay, to make Screenshot wait and hope they could intervene before he took control and pulled the trigger himself. She could use the arrow keys to pan and zoom the camera, trying to find clues about the intended victim before he or she became one.

One bank of three monitors remained dark. These would focus on the appropriate local FBI office and accept feed from any other law enforcement assets dispatched to the scene once it was identified. The agents and specialists monitoring these would provide information or recommendations to guide the response. All in all, it was a pretty impressive display of impotent technology, she thought.

The view now displayed on her monitor showed a dais with people milling around, most in civilian clothes, several in military uniforms, and even one that looked to be clergy. The distance was too great to identify either the uniforms or the people. The setting was outdoors, and the sun was shining off screen. It looked to be a beautiful July fourth, about to be spoiled.

A banner was partially visible in the background of the dais, and someone figured it was the bottom of the letters Americ and started matching the colors and font to any logos in the file.

"Someone's giving a speech," one of the agents called out.

"It's the fourth of July," came the response. "Everyone's giving a speech."

Karen heard the buzz of activity around her heighten as everyone scrambled, trying to contribute something. Behind her, Dave muttered, echoing all of their feelings: this could be happening anywhere the sun was shining. Into his microphone, she heard him say, "All right everyone, settle. Focus on the people. Find someone we know."

In the lower left corner, the message Camera Ready appeared, along with numbers that ticked slowly down from ten, not in steady increments, but randomly, as if the schedule was flexible.

Karen immediately zoomed in on the person at the far left, and moved slowly to the right, one person at a time, giving everyone a chance to recognize someone. No one did.

"Has anyone got anything?" Dave shouted when they got to seven. More buzzing. Then someone shouted, "Wait. Go back to the uniform." When she did, he said, "That's the Army of American Patriots uniform."

"Someone find out where they're meeting today," Hendrickson yelled. The answer came almost immediately. "Oh, shit. Oklahoma City. They're holding their Independence Day rally there."

That stopped everyone momentarily while they tried to process the symbolism, the Murrah Building and Timothy McVeigh still vivid in every FBI agent's mind.

"Get Helter's cell number. Get him on the phone. Figure out who is with him. Get through to someone there *now*."

General Anthony Helter, self-promoted in his own private army, had retired from the Marines as a Colonel when it became apparent that self-promotion was his only avenue above that rank, no matter how many years he put in. His fervent opinions, and his compulsion to announce them at any opportunity, limited his career possibilities. The Army of American Patriots shared his goals, and supported him whole-heartedly. That was an entry requirement.

The people on the dais organized themselves and took seats, some moving out of view, others replacing them.

"Dave, it's ringing. You'll have him on line one."

Karen picked up her own headset, held it to her ear without putting it on, and pushed the Line 1 button on her telephone to listen in.

"Major Wesley," was the answer to the ringing.

"Major, this is Special Agent Dave Hendrickson of the FBI. I must speak to General Helter immediately. It is a matter of life and death."

"Who is this? How did you get this number?"

"Major, please pay attention to me. I am with the FBI. There is no time for explanation. The general is in danger, imminent danger. I have agents on the way. Do not let him onto the dais."

"Look, I don't know who you are or what you think you're doing, but the general is well-protected. This is one of his most important speeches of the year, and I'm not going to interrupt him because some crackpot got my phone number. And if you really are the FBI, then I'm sure you would like nothing better than to disrupt his plans, to try to make him look foolish in front of his supporters. Now, please clear this line. We have a Republic to save."

The line went dead, and Hendrickson cursed. "Are the choppers airborne? How many and how soon?"

"Four. Sixteen men. ETA eight minutes."

"Eight minutes? Where the hell are they?"

"Eight minutes away," came the only answer the agent had.

The Third Victim

The light bulbs on the trailer-mounted electric sign, labeled as belonging to the Equipment & Tool Rental Service Center of Oklahoma City, blinked the word *Parking* in a visual echo, repeating it over and over again. Below the word, an arrow pointed to a field full of pickup trucks, campers, motor homes, SUVs, motorcycles, and the occasional passenger car. As well as local vehicles, there were vehicles displaying license plates from Arkansas, Missouri, Texas and all the other surrounding states, and from as far away as Pennsylvania and Montana. This temporary parking lot served the modest crowd filling the temporary bleachers not far from the rented sign.

The bleachers looked out over an empty field, big enough to accommodate a football game with plenty of room to spare. On other days, it did serve as a football or baseball or soccer field, or a picnic area for summer meals and Frisbee tossing, or a country and western band concert.

On this day, it served as a parade ground. The Army of American Patriots paid Oklahoma City a reasonable fee to hold their annual July fourth rally and fundraiser there, complete with a battalion of citizen-soldiers marching in full battle gear, and speeches justifying the need for this force to meet the threats to the American Way of Life. The parade would showcase their ability to fulfill that role, and bolster appeals for more contributions, for more sales of AAP t-shirts and coffee mugs and bumper stickers and official gun carrying-cases. Everything but a Ferris wheel and a bake sale.

The sign kept blinking while the crowd organized itself in and around the bleachers. It blinked while 300 soldiers marched to the blare of "The Battle Hymn of the Republic," played at distortion levels through the pole-mounted speakers. It blinked while they arranged themselves neatly in rows and columns, facing the stage, their weapons at ready, barrel-up, butt-end on the ground. Then it stopped blinking and went dark and quiet.

The Reverend Lucius MacFadden offered his invocation, blessing these good people as the last, best hope for America, and the sign hummed. A narrow, triangular metal box, mounted on top and not part of the original equipment, vibrated ever so slightly as motors inside spun into action, electronics came alive and radio signals messaged the network through the transceiver.

Councilman William Berry introduced the agenda and announced the pride of all of Oklahoma City to host such an important event.

In the box, pistons tickled levers into place, making minute adjustments, and lenses telescoped in and out, adjusting focal length for optimum viewing of wide-angles and close-ups, and every distance in between.

The pointy end of the wedge-shaped box, aimed toward the stage, wasn't really pointy. The last several inches had been chopped off, like someone had taken a bite of a piece of pie, leaving an opening about two inches wide. Plenty of space for the laser sighting device attached to the barrel of the Bushmaster M4 Carbine with the thirty-round clip and Izzy flash suppressor.

General Anthony Helter—Helter-Skelter as his troops called him—rose from his center seat on the dais, a seat mounted on a small platform to elevate it eight inches above everyone else on stage, with a single stair to dismount. His slow and deliberate trip forward took a lot longer than necessary.

Standing there, in his dress-blue uniform, a modernized copy of a Revolutionary War design, he allowed the applause to linger, his hands resting easily on the edges of the podium, his sincere smile reflecting his sincere gratitude for the adulation shown by the gathered crowd. His head swiveled left and right, taking in the scene without acknowledging it by gestures or nods.

"Thank you all for coming today," he finally started, quieting the crowd. "Thank you for your support for the Army of American Patriots, the rightful heirs to the legacy of George Washington and Paul Revere and Patrick Henry. Thank you, Reverend McFadden, for that sacred invocation, reminding us that it is the work of God that we do. And thank you Councilman Berry for your gracious words, and for the hospitality of this great American city."

Helter paused and let the crowd vent its energy in an opening round of applause. He noted its substantial volume, and judged that the later applause lines in his speech would set them into a frenzy.

"I see that some of you carry signs today, and I understand the sentiments, the outrage, that prompts them. That is what I came to talk about today, the threats to our society by a bloated government that allows, *encourages*, the erosion of the American way of life, the intrusion of foreign and evil elements. I see your signs are written in American English. There is no need for 'wetback spoken here' or gook scribble for *us* to understand your message. And I will be *speaking* to you in American English. You won't hear me say *oy vay* to make a point. I won't *axe* you any questions."

The first eleven rounds punched three holes in the security guard to Helter's left, one of those through his left ventricle, and he dropped to the floor without hesitation. Two more hit Helter in the arm and shoulder without damage to anything vital, and he looked down at the holes with curiosity. The other six perforated the stage, one of them passing through someone's foot before doing it.

The applause tapered off as the audience registered the stammer of the Bushmaster, and saw the fallen soldier. The other guard, positioned to the right of Helter and out of the line of fire, reacted first and tackled his leader, covering the general with his body. A courageous and futile effort. The last nineteen rounds, fired in three distinct bursts, put eight singed holes in his dress-blue uniform, with five of those making it through him and into various parts of the general. The most serious hit Helter in the crown of his head, and had just enough energy left to penetrate the skull and lodge in the frontal lobe of his brain.

At the same time, the sound of automatic weapons fire filled the air, recorded and played back over the speakers as if there were many more AR15s firing. The troops reacted like a school of fish, raising their empty weapons and swiveling as a single group this way and that toward the changing source of the noise. They saw the helicopters swooping toward them, and to a man, thought, *black helicopters, United Nations.*

The four helicopters raced toward the park, urged to incaution by their FBI dispatchers, themselves alarmed by what they were seeing on their monitors. In the lead chopper, Agent Timmy Olson leaned partway out the open doorway, his foot on the landing skid. He'd seen the war movies, the Marines dashing into some hot LZ, the first guy, the hero, holding his M16, ready to jump and cover. He loved those movies. He wished he'd been a Marine.

May Hutchins held her nine-year-old son lightly as he stood on the bench to see his father, Sgt. Ethan Hutchins, lead his squad in parade, providing the boy more balance than security. She smiled, proud of her family, proud of their friends, proud of what Ethan was doing for his country. The trip from Georgia in the rented motor home had been new and exciting, a chance to get away from work and carpools and housecleaning and cooking and play dates for Jason. Ethan looked good in his uniform, out there at the head of the other men, and she was happy all over again.

In Ethan's squad, Leland Lipscomb was prepared, alert to the responsibilities of a soldier, the guardians of everything good and sacred. Leland believed in preparation. He believed in their mission. He respected his leaders. He ignored bureaucrats. Like the one who sent the memo forbidding live ammunition at the ceremony. A soldier without a working weapon was a parody, and Leland was a serious man. Sixty-seven of his buddies felt the same way.

When the guard fell, and the loudspeakers echoed gunfire, the very large woman behind May, one of the first to panic, stood up and started sweeping people out of her escape path. Jason, knocked loose from May's grasp, bounced off the man in front of him, fell to the foot board, out of sight in the forest of churning legs.

May struggled to swim upstream against the crowd, breaking her arm and dislocating her shoulder in the attempt to reach him, her screams equal parts pain and despair. Jason, kicked repeatedly by stamping feet, was rolled off the open bleachers, and dropped twenty feet through the scaffolding that supported everything. On the way down, his head struck several of the metal supports, and he died before he hit the ground.

Leland saw the general and two of his fellow soldiers fall. He heard the gunfire all around him, punching little holes in the background noise of the incoming helicopters. He brought his weapon to ready, slamming the receiver back, and letting it spring forward, chambering one of his thirty real bullets.

Along with the sixty-seven other militiamen who chose to ignore the memo, Leland began spraying fire at the in-coming choppers, certain that they were under attack. 2,040 rounds arced into the sky, most destined to do no more then break windows, damage shingles and siding, scratch some cars, and aerate some lawns.

In the lead helicopter, Timmy Olson screamed, "They're firing at—" Before he could finish the observation, two rounds hit his body armor and stopped. A third, benefiting from the upward trajectory of being fired from the ground, snuck in under the edge of the Kevlar just above his hip, shredded a good deal of his intestine, bounced off his rib and came to rest in his right lung.

One hundred and thirty-three additional rounds hit the four helicopters before they realized they were under attack and able to break off their mission, flight controllers screaming into their headsets to *get out of there*. Six agents were wounded, two of them seriously. Tim Olson died before they landed, with his buddies still trying to stanch the bleeding.

Leland Lipscomb fired his last 5.56 mm round, certain he hit at least one of the damn one-world commies before his clip emptied. Most of the others were already running, and he smiled to himself as he turned to join them, noting that the helicopters were veering, breaking off their attack. He was proud of the performance of his buddies in this, their first real firefight. Those bastards will think twice before they try that again, he thought, wishing he had brought spare ammo.

In a moment of irony, as if one of his own bullets had followed a boomerang path, a single 5.56 mm round, fired without thought or authorization from the last helicopter as it banked away, struck him behind his right ear and exited through his lower jaw. Leland's eyes were still open when the paramedics got to him twenty-six minutes later, but they closed in the ambulance on the way to the hospital. Two of his fellow soldiers also died, and fourteen others were wounded, most by friendly fire and accidents during the retreat, but no one was ever able to attribute specific responsibility.

The panic worsened as the dead and injured accumulated within the sight of more and more of the crowd. People stumbled and fell down the wooden bleachers, and sprains were the dominant injury when the casualties were eventually totaled. Mothers tried to protect infants and children as others tried to trample them. The tramplers behind shoved the tramplers in front into the tramplers in front of them, and bodies piled up like a human dam, creating even more panic for those trapped behind. Some vaulted over the railings, and broken bones became the second most numerous injury.

The panic subsided somewhat when the loudspeakers came alive again, this time to the strains of the National Anthem. Some people, realizing the gunfire had stopped, themselves stopped and looked around, trying to comprehend the scene. These kernels of calm began to propagate and expand as those nearest to the originator stopped as well. The atmosphere settled and the quiet spread. Then the sign came alive again, its small gasoline-engined generator cranking up. Most eyes swung in the direction of this new and different sound in time to see the bulbs light up in an array of words.

ACME PATRIATTACKER. Patent Pending.

Karen

Karen stared at the scene on her monitor, unable to turn away, alternating between the shock of what she had witnessed, and disbelief that it could have really happened. She'd never thought the plan would work, that they would be able to intervene, but she'd never imagined it would lead to this, to an FBI firefight with apparently law-abiding citizens.

Silence settled on the room like nerve gas, freezing everyone in their place, staring at the monitors, their speakers quieter without the whooping of helicopter blades and the crack of gunshots. Even the screams still broadcast became more muted, background noise for the astonishment that everyone felt.

"Goddammit!" Hendrickson broke the mood, punctuating it with his hand slamming the desk louder than anything from the speakers. "Those people are fucking nuts. What's the damage?"

The agent monitoring the helicopter chatter had only a vague idea, and it wasn't good. "All four were hit by ground fire. We've got wounded, I don't know how many. One of the choppers is losing hydraulic pressure and may have to ditch."

"Where are the ground units?"

"Police, fire, and EMTs are all en route. The first should be arriving now. Our team is three minutes out if the roads stay open."

"Tell them first priority is the injured, but then I want every available resource collecting those weapons as evidence and detaining anyone in one of those ridiculous uniforms. By God, I'll ..." He didn't finish the thought, at least not out loud.

Karen watched several of the militiamen working frantically over Helter in the distance. She couldn't distinguish their activities, and the camera no longer responded to her joystick. Their urgency seemed to indicate that Helter survived, almost certainly wounded, probably gravely.

Emergency vehicles began to arrive, and within minutes someone draped something over the camera, cutting off her view. Seconds later another view opened, following the familiar script. This shot came from near the bleachers and clearly showed the sign and its message.

"Shit," someone said. "He used a sign."

Karen stared, her mind locked, but locked in a frenzy of thought, blocking out all of the action in the room and on the monitor. Hendrickson yelled for senior staff to meet *now* in her conference room, and everyone else was hustled out, some wondering if they were senior staff or not, and choosing *not* until notified otherwise.

After the meeting, where nothing was accomplished other than confirming the decisions already commanded and venting some of the anger and frustration, Karen tried to walk back to her office at a normal pace. She'd kept her mouth shut, knowing that "I told you so" was not an appropriate response to the events they'd just witnessed. Tasks had been assigned, and the investigation kicked off. Her own assignment was to wait, and she was glad for it.

Trying to appear calm and thoughtful, she controlled the impulse to break into a sprint, shouting all the way. FBI policy was to hold deleted voicemail messages in archive for thirty days. Thank God for the caution of the Bureau, she thought. Recovering the message from the day before took several levels of button pushing on her speakerphone, but then there it was, and she listened to it for the second time.

"Hello? Uh, this is Seth Mathias. It's about three o'clock here in California. I was referred to you about Screenshot. I spoke to the office here in LA, but they weren't able to help me. I received an e-mail message from Screenshot and then chatted with him in one of those Internet rooms. He said we would talk, well, communicate really, again after tomorrow's execution. He told me that the executioner would be a sign. He didn't say of what, but I guess you'll figure that out. Please call me back as soon as you get this."

It couldn't be a coincidence. It couldn't be just some wacko who said the right words without knowing their meaning. Could it? One way to find out, she thought, as she dialed the number he'd left.

Voicemail picked up, telling her the cell phone subscriber was unavailable and to leave a message. Instead, she disconnected, thinking he's probably already on the phone to the LA office raising hell. Shit. She dialed again and got the same result. Her third try got an answer.

"Mr. Mathias, this is Special Agent Larsen of the FBI. You left a message for me about Screenshot. Do you have some information for me about him?"

"Can you hold a moment, Agent Larsen? I have someone on

the other line." He disconnected without waiting for an answer.

Karen imagined he was having a conversation with some senior field agent in LA, getting instructions to get rid of her and come to their office instantly. He re-connected, and she held her breath.

"Not to be too rude about it, but what took you so long?" he asked. "No one at the FBI wants to talk to me until there really is a sign, and all of a sudden I'm important."

"I'm sorry I didn't get back to you sooner, Mr. Mathias, but as you can imagine, we've been very busy here this morning preparing for this latest event, and of course trying to find Screenshot. Have you spoken to the local field office again?"

"No. They took my information twice yesterday, but I don't think they believed me."

Good, she thought. "Did you tell them about the sign?"

"Yes, but I don't think they cared. I spoke to an Agent Connelly and then an Agent Wilkinson. They took the information and said someone would contact me. No one did, so I checked around and called this IC^3 thing and someone there directed me to you."

In her mind, Karen invented a bridge between the LA office reaction to Mathias' call and the referral to her from IC^3, the FBI's Internet Crime Complaint Center, and decided that she had been officially assigned to Mathias. And somewhere in LA and in Washington, there were call logs to substantiate it. At least enough to earn her only a reprimand when her boss discovered her decision to handle it herself.

She walked Mathias through his story again. The hint about the sign substantiated that it probably came from the genuine Screenshot, and the promise that he would contact him again gave her something to do about it. She wanted to be there when he made contact, and told Mathias she would be in LA that evening and they should meet.

"You'll never find me," he told her, sounding like he was on the run. "I'll have to meet you at LAX. Call or e-mail me your flight information."

"Fine. Please forward the Screenshot e-mail to me and I'll reply with my flight info."

She gave him her personal e-mail address, keeping it off the FBI e-mail server, and hung up. Smiling. She might get to lead the charge, after all.

Chapter Twelve

Seth

Seth's head pivoted back and forth, like he was watching a tennis match through his windshield instead of his left and right mirrors as he inched his way into the parking spot. The tiny gap between the extra-wide wheel wells and fenders of his Dodge and the Infiniti on one side, and the Taurus on the other, looked about the size of a golf ball. He biased his margin of error in favor of the much more expensive Infiniti, and watched the thin strip of light between his fender and the Taurus's shrink until it seemed paper-thin.

Goddamn miniature parking spots, he thought, knowing that the real problem was the size of the truck needed to haul his trailer. The only thing Seth hated more than driving the massive truck in LA traffic was parking it. The Taurus driver would be pissed that he couldn't open his door, and Seth hoped to be back and gone before then.

Carrying his computer-printed sign with Larsen's name, Seth stood outside the security checkpoint to wait for the deplaning travelers. The crowd around him undulated as it constantly transformed, people coming and going with each new wave of passengers washing down the pier, and he held the sign high above his head with each surge of the herd.

Unconsciously, he stopped scanning the crowd and watched one person, a clearly Asian woman with blonde hair, a striking combination.

While he stared at the woman, she looked at his sign and then at him and waved, more of a *hey taxi* gesture than *glad to see you*. For a moment he wanted to do one of those "Who? Me?" things, looking behind himself, but resisted. She didn't look the way he imagined her from hearing her on the phone, but then again, he'd imagined a female FBI agent, not a woman, and certainly not this woman.

Seth edged his way out of the crowd and they met near the escalator down to baggage claim. Larsen's smile looked sincere, maybe a little wary, like she was greeting a blind date. She dragged a carry-on bag on wheels with her left hand, which she let stand while she gave him an earnest handshake.

"Mr. Mathias, I'm so glad to meet you. I read your *Mercury News* articles on the flight out and I can see how you might have intrigued Screenshot."

Her unruffled appearance and animated good nature made Seth wonder what she was like before spending six hours on a plane.

Maybe the FBI springs for first class.

Despite his frustration with FBI agents and his residual annoyance with the parking experience, Seth smiled, somehow flattered that she'd read his writing.

"Thank you, I think. Please call me Seth. Can I help you with that?"

"No thanks, I'm fine with it, Seth. And please call me Karen."

"My truck is this way. Where are you staying? I'll take you there and we can talk on the way."

"I'm staying with you," she stated without hesitation. "Don't worry, I'll stay well out of your way and won't disturb anything." Seth stopped, and she spoke the last part to the empty space next to her while she continued ahead, never slowing. Seth jogged a few steps to catch up.

"I'm sorry, but you really can't stay with me. There's no room."

"Oh, that's okay," she replied as if he was apologizing instead of refusing. "I need to be there when Screenshot contacts you again, and the only way we can be sure of that is for me to be with you all the time until he does. Don't think of me as a guest. I'm your partner until we resolve this."

Seth was about to object again and she carefully interrupted.

"Look, Seth, I've lived in stuffy vans with cigarettes and coffee and donuts for days on stakeouts. I'm sure I will be fine on a couch or even in a chair. And I'll make us Eggs Benedict for breakfast."

He didn't have an answer for that, or any other valid objection except *I don't want you in my home*, and he wasn't going to say that. They arrived at the truck, and for some reason Seth wanted to apologize for it.

"Wait here. I'll pull out and then it will be easier for you to get in."

After she'd loaded her bag in the back seat and jumped in next to Seth she said, "Screenshot will probably contact you quickly to get your reaction to this fiasco. Helter is still alive, by the way. They did surgery to remove the bullet in his head and they expect him to recover, possibly with some brain damage."

Seth knew some of this from the news, but not the brain damage part.

"What's the plan if he does contact me?"

"Well, I'll be there and I'll have my team conferenced in to my cell and we can direct your responses and questions."

"That won't work."

"Oh, sure it will. We have instant communications with some of the best law enforcement minds—"

"No, that's not it. Screenshot knows me, he's researched me. He made that quite clear. If I start giving him phony answers or try to trick him into something, he'll figure it out and we'll lose him. Better I just go about it as I would naturally, and you see if you can get any information from that. Just tell me generally what you want, and I'll do it my way."

Larsen didn't answer right away and Seth let the silence drag on.

"Okay. You may be right. We'll do it your way."

Turning south on Las Virgenes Road, the exit sign should have read Another World instead of Malibu Creek State Park. The winding, two-lane road led through some spectacular mountain scenery for the four miles to the park campground. All that was invisible at night, and Seth watched for Larsen's reaction as he drove into the dark woods. He didn't get one.

When he pulled up to the trailer, he said, "Here we are. This is home, and the reason I drive this monster. Welcome to Malibu Creek State Park."

"I'm looking forward to it," Larsen said. "They tell me it's quite beautiful, a real contrast to LA County. I'm glad I brought the right clothes."

She knew, Seth thought, and she was letting him know it. They know where I live, and probably everything else about me. Everything.

Karen

"This is very nice," Karen said, looking around the efficient,

360 square-foot space. "Better than some apartments I've lived in."

"Let's see what you think after a night on the table."

She looked toward the dining area and back at Seth, and he said, "It folds down and becomes the second bed. The seat cushions and backrests are the mattress. I've never tried it."

Karen smiled and said, "Sounds like an adventure. But I thought the 37RLCS had the fold-out couch. Can I use that instead?"

"I see you know your RVs. Or is it just this RV?"

It hadn't occurred to Karen that her hurried research into his current lifestyle would cause resentment. It was routine for her. She forgot that her routine was his private life, and he might want to keep it that way. She decided to change the subject.

"Can we take a few moments and review the Screenshot information? I know it's late, but if he contacts you before we've talked, we might lose the opportunity."

"Sure. I'm not the one running on East Coast time."

While Seth took her drink order and got them each orange juice, she briefed him.

"I assume you watched today's events. Those people firing on us came as a complete surprise. No one realized Screenshot would be using a military weapon, or that he would broadcast the sounds of an attack over the loudspeakers. Our teams arrived by helicopter at precisely the wrong moment, and it was misconstrued as part of an attack. It was an incredible confluence of events, and Screenshot must be overjoyed at his luck. So you see, he might contact you at any moment. In fact, I was fully prepared to find out that he already had by the time I arrived."

"How did the FBI get there so fast?"

The information that the FBI had won Screenshot's lottery

had not yet been made public. In the meeting with Hendrickson, they had decided to try to hold that back, to see if they could get another chance. Karen felt that was a little self-serving for those who had made the decision to try to intervene, and she had little confidence the secret would hold long. Still, it was the decision, and Mathias could not know either.

"It's Oklahoma City. If there's any FBI office in the world that's ready to respond instantly, it's those guys. So, all we've got to go on is his first contact with you. Not very much. When he contacts you again, I need you to challenge him gently, push back a little on his directions, debate his opinions. All we can do is record everything and try to pick up any clues from that."

"Weren't you able to get any information from his broadcast? Track him through his internet connection?"

"No, that's not possible. We have no way of tracking him electronically."

"You couldn't do packet analysis while he was streaming the video," Seth asked.

"Packet analysis? Why?"

"To try to trace his messages back to his server."

Karen figured she was dealing with Internet ignorance. "Mr. Mathias, Seth, I don't have the slightest idea what you're talking about. Packet analysis is just a means to understand superficially what type of information is contained in a single, eight-bit piece of data. It can't tell us anything about where it came from."

"True. But when you include ping triangulation and signal correlation, you should be able to follow his electronic trail right back to his computer. Are you trying that?"

"Backtrack an Internet broadcast? How? To where? This isn't cowboys and Indians. This is electronic ones and zeroes. There is no trail to follow."

"Sure there is. You just have to capture the information and look. I know it's a lot of information, but that's why you guys have all that technology."

"What are you talking about?"

"Have you ever heard of Dr. Morgan Sicals?"

"I don't recall the name."

"Well, I spoke to him," Seth told her, "and he claims he can find Screenshot using those methods. Theories he's invented."

"Who is this guy? How do you know him?"

"He's a physicist who nearly won a Nobel Prize, and he has a blog with this stuff. I used his opinions in my article and he called me about it."

"How do you *nearly* win a Nobel prize? All that is supposed to be secret. And if he's that renowned, why is he writing a blog? Not quite peer-reviewed papers."

"Well, he's actually just a bit loony, I think. But aren't all of those guys? He's the one who told me about your Phish-Net. He said outside the NSA, you were the one group that could muster the computing resources to do it."

"Do what, exactly?"

Seth gave her his brief interpretation of Sicals' lecture, bolstered by his review of the entries on Sicals' blog. When he finished, Karen sipped her orange juice without speaking. After a moment, she got up and walked to the bank of switches and flipped them all down. The trailer went dark.

"Mr. Mathias," she asked, going back to his formal name for emphasis, "can you tell me where the light went? Can you show me any evidence that it was ever here? Can you backtrack it to its source with the switch off?"

She flipped them back on and continued, "That's the Internet. All we see is electro-magnetic energy. When it stops, everything disappears. The only way to save it is to store it on some medium, and even then, we have only whatever arrived at our end, not the paths all the little pieces took to get there, and certainly not the point where it started."

"That's not what Sicals says. Here. I printed out the entries for you," Seth said, handing her thirty-seven single-spaced pages. "The web site address is at the top. Hope you have better luck with that than I did. It put me to sleep."

"Well, I won't need it to put me to sleep. I'll e-mail the URL to my team and tell them to get me a report by morning. Then, if it's all right with you, I'd like to get some sleep."

"Sure," Seth said. "Bathroom's there. Go easy on the hot water. Ten-gallon capacity, and it takes a while to recover. But you already know all that, I guess."

"Thanks. Look, Seth. I'm sorry that we had to get some background on you, but in a case like this, we have to know who we're dealing with. A lot depends on who you are and what you know."

"You need to know where my trailer is parked and the floor plan? How does that help you catch Screenshot?"

"Until I got off that plane, you were a voice on a telephone. We have had thousands of calls, with everything from confessions to threats. For all I know, you're Screenshot." She smiled as she said it, making sure he understood that she was joking. "Knowing the floor plan could help me hide or get out, if I need to. Knowing where the trailer is parked let's me escape. So you see, just precautions."

Seth looked at her for a moment and then said, "Okay. Why

don't you take the bedroom, and I'll use the fold-out couch. You can lock the door as another precaution."

She guessed he wasn't convinced.

Chapter Thirteen

Philip

Philip arched his shoulders in a series of shrugs, front to back, back to front, and rotated his head from side to side while trying to keep his eyes on the rain-slick city street. He grimaced with each lift and flex, and gave up the exercise after several tries, forced to live with the stiff neck for just a little while longer.

The headlights of the on-coming cars suffused on the grimy haze the rental agency had left on the inside of the windshield, and it nearly blinded him with each encounter. He missed the GPS in the motor home, struggling to read the street names in the glaring dark of the early morning streetlights instead of listening to a soft, female voice telling him when to turn.

At least I'm awake, he thought. No chance of getting comfortable enough to doze off.

The marathon drive from Houston, his stopping-off point after positioning the Patriattacker, the drive straight through the night in the rental Buick to Oklahoma City, straight into the rainstorm that barreled in as the Army of American Patriots retreated home, left aches everywhere he had an active nerve. He'd left the motor home behind on this spur-of-the-moment trip, figuring it would be a faster and less conspicuous in-and-out if he drove. His motor home in Houston would provide cover if there were ever questions. Four AM, he thought, way too early. He decided to find a motel and sleep in the parking lot for an hour while the hospital came awake, and then let the bustle of morning shift-change conceal him.

Eleven hours earlier, he'd watched the plasma screen in the motor home while parked in a campsite outside of Houston. At first he smiled, almost giggled to himself, as a script he couldn't have written any better played itself out. Helicopters, firefights, frenzy. And news coverage. Non-stop news coverage.

As the day went along, the glee devolved to a growing anger as the real news of the Gunfight at the OK Park, as the press was calling the attack on Helter, sifted through the panicked early reports and finally started to get it right. Nine dead. And not one of them Helter.

The doctor at Deaconess Hospital verified this when he answered questions from the gathered media. He talked, seemingly more interested in showing off his skills than in protecting patient confidentiality, of the bullet lodged in the general's head, and the delicate surgery to remove it, and explained the need for the drug-induced coma to let the inflamed brain shrink back to normal size.

Philip didn't wait to hear the inane follow-up, mostly political and sociological questions that the doctor was neither competent nor willing to answer. Philip grabbed a few overnight travel necessities and the specialty toiletries kit he kept stashed in a bin in the back of a storage area, and shoved it all in his backpack. From the floor-mounted safe he took $7,000 in one-hundred-dollar bills and folded the fat wad into the pocket of his jeans. Then he hiked the three miles back toward Houston and the nearest car rental agency his Internet search found.

It took seven hours to get to the dark parking lot behind the Hospitality Inn, just a mile south of the hospital. Philip reclined the passenger seat, hands interlocked behind his head, and thought some more about the events of the previous day. When the selected assassin hadn't pulled the trigger, transparently delaying the execution, Philip had become curious about who was at the other end. And when the police communications activity on the Oklahoma City Metroplex emergency services radio feed, which he monitored on the Internet, directed emergency services to Helter's rally well before any overt action to cause it, he took control. He rightly guessed that the FBI had won his lottery, as he expected they eventually would, and law enforcement was trying to intervene. It was dumb luck that he'd pulled the trigger when he did and set off his attack just as the FBI choppers were arriving.

He awoke startled, and needed a second to realize the beeping was his wristwatch, and another to remember where he was and why. Time to go, he thought. At the Sinclair station on 50th St., he set the nozzle to fill automatically and scanned the area for any witnesses who might remember him when the police inevitably got around to canvassing the neighborhood and found a five AM fill-up paid in cash.

Seeing no one, he pulled the Denver Broncos cap lower on his head and went in to get the key to the men's room. Philip glanced around again before unlocking the bathroom door, and again saw no one else out that early. The room was reasonably clean, and the light and mirror sufficient for his needs. The door latch was spring-loaded to lock on closing, and he used a small piece of duct tape from his kit to disable it. After testing it to be certain he could regain access unnoticed, he returned the key and paid the uninterested kid in the office.

He parked on N. Portland Street and walked back to the station, approaching on the side away from the kid in the office.

Philip consciously forced the same, slow gait he'd used coming to get the key. The deliberate steps and hunched posture would make an accurate estimation of his height and age difficult, and his hands stuffed in his pockets, with the toiletries kit under his jacket, would distort any sense of weight. He went back into the men's room an older, slightly overweight five-foot-eight, and came out a young, six-foot-one thin man carrying a coat.

He carefully drove the last few blocks to the hospital, using the time to review the plan again and to settle his nerves. While the coming act didn't bother him, his lack of any similar experience made the conclusion uncertain, opening the possibility of exposure.

Behind the hospital, he parked, put on the clear plastic surgical gloves from his backpack, and got out of the car with a nonchalance that wouldn't attract attention. The gloves were a potential problem, being worn when he was clearly not involved in any sterile activity, but he was more concerned about fingerprints. He climbed the loading dock stairs into the shipping and receiving bay without encountering anyone. Orienting himself once inside, he walked down the hallway into the hospital proper, finding the remainder of his disguise, a freshly laundered doctor's smock, in a storage room.

The doorknob of the doctor's lounge wouldn't turn, and he had a moment of panic, almost rattling the handle in dismay, a move that he realized just in time would attract the attention of any possible witness, including anyone inside the lounge. Then he realized that the plain black pad mounted at chest height on the wall was an electronic security card reader, and he turned and walked away without hesitation. That wasn't in the plan.

He headed for a vinyl-padded bench a few feet from the door.

Taking off the smock and folding it into a bundle, he lay down and used it as a pillow to feign sleep, just another late shift worker or visitor grabbing a quick nap, while he watched the door and hoped. The next eleven minutes took a lot longer in his mind.

The door finally opened and a doctor, slipping his arm into the sleeve of his smock, emerged. Philip jumped like he'd been startled out of sleep and hurried to the closing door, catching it as the doctor walked away. Inside the break room were two round tables with four plastic chairs haphazardly arranged around each, a sink and counter-top with a coffee-maker, junk food and soda dispensing machines, and all the debris of snacking supplies and careless snackers, left behind despite the hand-lettered sign: Your mother doesn't work here. Clean up after yourself.

At the far end was a door marked, Rest Area – Keep Closed.

Inside, someone, probably an overworked resident, slept on the bottom bunk of one of the two sets of beds. His smock, complete with ID, hung from a hook on the opposite wall. Philip simply swapped smocks and, back in the lounge area, found the size was close enough. The embroidered name on the smock matched the ID, Dr. Evan Newsome. The stethoscope in the pocket got draped over his shoulders.

Following the signs to Intensive Care, Philip grabbed a clipboard from a wall-mounted rack outside a patient room and pretended to read it, head slightly down, as he walked and watched. Rounding a corner, he knew he'd found Helter by the presence of two uniformed men sitting outside the door. He walked by them without looking up and continued past the nurses' station, turning into the first corridor, out of their sight.

He took out the throwaway, prepaid cell phone, one of three he kept ready and discarded after a single use. He navigated the interactive hospital answering system, and got through to the nurses' station he'd just passed.

"ICU. Nurse Randall."

"Yes, hello," he said. "I'm sorry to bother you, but I'm Tony Helter's brother-in-law, and I'm trying to get through to my sister, his wife. She's in his room, but I can't get an answer, and that's got me a little concerned. Could you go and get her for me?"

"I'm sorry, but visiting hours haven't started, and there's no one in the room with Mr. Helter."

"Oh. That's odd. She called me a few minutes ago and I told her I would call right back. She said she was in Tony's room with him. Could you check for me? She was going to spend the night, and I'm concerned about her own health, and why she isn't answering if she's there."

"All right. I'll put you on hold."

Philip listened from around the corner and peeked to see her come out from behind the counter and head toward Helter's room. He stepped out quietly and followed just behind her. At the door, the police officer greeted her, and Philip followed her into the room with only the briefest glance up from his clipboard.

She looked around the room and turned to leave, nodding to Philip without any recognition or curiosity. As she did, one of the guards came in, an AAP militiaman complete with camo fatigues. Philip turned slightly toward him, looked him up and down and said, with arrogant authority, "Who are you?"

"I'm Sergeant Hastings, here to guard the general. No one comes in here without my permission."

"Well, you're here without my permission, and I need to examine the patient. Wait outside."

The man didn't answer or move, and Philip called to the

policeman in the hall. When he stuck his head in, Philip asked, "Is this man a relative of Mr. Helter?"

"Uh, no, I don't think so, Doctor."

"Then please remove him from the hospital immediately. This is private property, these are not public visiting hours, and he has no legitimate business here. If there is any complaint, he can take it up with the hospital administrator when he arrives at nine. Until then, please excuse me while I try to save this man's life."

While Philip talked, the policeman glanced at his ID. Philip noticed, and hoped that in the dimly lit room, he had at least a vague resemblance to Dr. Newsome. The cop looked up and said, "Sure, Doc. All right, Bert. You heard the doc. You gotta go. I told you to go easy on that soldier shit."

Bert's protests quieted when the door to Helter's room closed behind their departure. As he expected for someone with Helter's notoriety, it was a private room. Working quickly, Philip took the syringe and small medicine bottle from his pocket, flipped the hinged cover off the needle and drew seventy-five milligrams of succinylcholine into the cylinder. He injected this into the port on the IV dripping into the general's wrist, and put the syringe into his smock pocket with the plastic cover back over the needle. He had maybe ten minutes until the monitors over Helter's head, and at the nursing station, would raise the alarm.

When he stepped out of the room, the hall was empty, but as he turned the corner back the way he came, he nearly ran into the policeman returning to the room. Philip put one of his gloved hands in his pocket and used the clipboard to block the other one as much as possible.

"Excuse me, Doc," the policeman said. Philip nodded and started away.

"Hey," the cop called, freezing Philip. "Before you go, I wanted to ask how Helter is doing, if the news is right about brain damage."

Relieved, Philip half-turned toward him and said, "You know I can't talk about that, officer. You'll just have to wait for the public reports, like everyone else."

"Yeah, I suppose so," he said, adding almost to himself, "Although I don't know how they'll know. That brain was already damaged, as far as I can tell."

Philip smiled. He chuckled about the comment when he dumped his disguise in a laundry bin, and left the same way he came in. He almost made it.

"Wait, you phony," Bert yelled, striding hard across the parking lot toward Philip from a pickup truck. "I knew you was wrong. What did you do to The General?" He pronounced it with a capital *the*.

A quick glance around showed they were alone. Philip had just seconds to decide how to handle the situation. He had the skills, he knew, learned in lessons, but never practiced live. When the sergeant got close enough, Philip took one quick step at him with his right foot, and rammed the knuckles of his left hand, curled flat into a flesh-and-bone two-by-four, into his Adam's apple. Bert's hands jerked to his neck and he gurgled in surprise as Philip punched the butt of his right hand into Bert's nose. His knees buckled and blood spurted. Some landed on Philip and smeared on his shirt when he caught the man on the way down..

Bert surprised Philip by continuing to live, barely breathing in little snorts, while he dragged him behind the dumpster at the edge of the lot. He hadn't been taught how to finish the job, or rather, the blow was supposed to have finished the job, and he wondered what he'd done wrong. He rolled the unconscious Bert onto his chest and grabbed his chin and the back of his head and jerked it sideways, expecting to hear the satisfying crack, just like in the movies. Instead, he heard Bert exhale sharply, and then gasp a little inhale. He knew that very soon alarms would sound and soon after that, cordons would go up and cars would be checked. A man with blood on his shirt would attract attention.

Philip tried it again and still didn't succeed in snapping Bert's neck. He decided on brute force over technique and simply grabbed Bert's head and twisted it and then twisted it further. He didn't get the crack he expected. Instead, Bert went limp and stopped breathing.

He waited to get back into the car before removing the latex gloves that he'd worn the whole time, and which probably had been the subconscious tip-off to the dead guard that something wasn't right. These would get dumped with the shirt when he was back on the Interstate heading west.

Philip smiled. "That wasn't so bad," he said out loud as he turned south on North Portland Street. "I wonder if it was as easy for Mathias in old West-by-God Virginia?"

Chapter Fourteen

Seth

"What happened? ... How? ... When? ... Any leads?"

Listening to one-half of Larsen's cell phone call had all the excitement of calling attendance in school.

Seth noted that she woke as she went to sleep—fully arranged and good-natured, like she had been up for hours getting a head start on the day. She'd even tried to find the ingredients for the Eggs Benedict, with no luck. And, he found, waking with a pretty woman in his trailer, even one who slept with the door closed, added some cheer to his mood.

He finished making the omelets and toast as she disconnected and whispered, "Damn."

"What's wrong?" he asked.

"Change of plans. Screenshot probably won't contact you today. Someone got into Helter's hospital room this morning and murdered him. Three possibilities. Someone else doesn't like Helter. Screenshot has an accomplice. Or he did it himself. I'm betting on number three."

"So he was there?"

"That's what we're guessing. We have three eyewitnesses, but one of them has gone missing. The other two might as well have described you."

"I've got an alibi."

"Good thing," she said. Seth wasn't sure how to take that.

Feeling somehow infected for having communicated with a

hands-on murderer, and for possibly being suspected of being one, Seth served breakfast in silence, and they ate without talking or even looking at one another, each considering what to do next.

"What do we do now?" he finally asked the obvious question.

"That's what I'm trying to figure out. Staying here might easily be a waste of time. This is a new level. No Internet, no lottery. Just good old-fashioned murder. You may never hear from him again. Or he might wait to see what you write. Or there might be an e-mail in your computer right now asking what you think. I don't know. It's all a guess. I just hate to waste time waiting for something that might not happen."

They went back to eating their eggs in silence.

"Maybe I'll go back," Karen said, "and someone from the LA office can baby-sit you."

"Baby-sit?"

"Sorry. Bureau slang. You know what I mean."

The thought of Connelly or Wilkinson or someone similar shadowing him didn't appeal to Seth.

"Why don't you stay and not waste time? We could go check out Sicals and see if there's anything there."

"No. I looked over his papers. There's nothing there. It all sounds nice and logical, but logical in the human sense, not the virtual world sense. What he is talking about is like filming an avalanche and trying to trace one snowball from the end back to the start. Even if you could grab a single image, tracing it backwards simply isn't possible. There will be times, most of the time, actually, when it won't be visible, hidden by all the other snowballs. It won't matter how many frames you capture, most of them will tell you nothing about the snowball you want. And all those frames will suck memory like a silicon vampire. He's right about the NSA. They're the only ones who could even come close to the computing power and memory required."

"What about you and your commercial partners? He said you had some kind of cooperative agreement where the number of computers available would have sufficient power."

"Well, he's probably right there too. But getting access to all of them, getting the partners to cooperate on something like that, well, it's just not going to happen. And then there's the code that would have to be written, debugged and validated. That would take months, if not longer."

"So, let me see if I understand what you're saying." Seth paused and gathered his thoughts into a presentation, his writing experience helping him to organize it in his head. "Sicals is right about filming the avalanche, as you put it. It would just take too much film. And he's right about tracking backwards, but it would require guessing likely vectors to get around periods of blindness. And he's right about the computing power being available, but it would be too hard to get access to it. And he's right about the ability to do it, but it would take too long to set up. I haven't heard you say he's wrong, only that what he's proposing would be hard."

"If something is *too* hard, it might as well be impossible. If we had to go to the moon to catch Screenshot, we could do it. Eventually. But we wouldn't. In the grand scheme of things, it just wouldn't be important enough to squander those resources."

"So we agree that Sicals is probably right? Then what's the harm in going to check him out and see if you're right about the resources? Maybe he has other information that we don't know about. Let's go ask him."

Karen looked at Seth long enough to make him uncomfortable.

Then she nodded once and pressed two buttons on her cell phone.

"Kathy? Karen. Book me two tickets. LAX to OAK. Get me priority on the first flight leaving after …"

She looked back at Seth, the question in her expression. He looked at his watch and said "Ten."

"Nine-thirty," she told Kathy.

Sicals' building might once have housed a successful merchant, probably one serving the shipping industry of the east side of San Francisco Bay. But as transportation and communications improved, these same merchants had moved progressively further out from the bay, and the dominant culture had evolved from maritime commerce to illicit commerce. Lately, an urban renaissance was developing, and many of the neighborhoods had been reclaimed and renovated. It hadn't caught up to Sicals.

It was a brick, three-story row house, unremarkable, an echo of the buildings surrounding it for blocks in each direction. She pressed the button for the building superintendent and got no response. She tried all the other buttons except Sicals' with the same result, guessed it was broken, and banged on the door.

An elderly black man finally answered, standing straight and tall in the image of a veteran at a ceremony, his flannel shirt out of season, and his khaki pants worn and slightly stained, but pressed.

"Good morning," he said without waiting for her to speak. "I apologize for the inconvenience, but I can't seem to fix the problem with that thing, so I am serving as your doorman until I find another solution. How can I help you?"

"You must be Arthur Reynolds."

On the flight up, she had kept her Blackberry running in violation of TSA regulations and received a series of e-mails with additional information on Sicals, including his address and situation, and even his landlord. Additionally, Seth told her everything he remembered about his conversations with Sicals and the results of his research into the guy. She asked a few questions, but mostly listened, planning how to handle him.

"Why yes, I am. Do I know you? I'm sure I would remember you if I did."

Karen laughed for him and said, "No, we've never met, Arthur. May I call you Arthur? My uncle told me your name. I'm Karen Larsen, Dr. Sicals' niece. My husband and I are in town from Pittsburgh and just trying to visit before we go home, but we couldn't get an answer on Uncle Morgan's bell."

"Niece, eh? Well, that's nice. Poor old guy could use some family. He never did mention you, though."

"Unless Uncle Morgan has changed a lot since I saw him last, I guess he hasn't mentioned much of anything about himself. I'll bet you've heard of the Quantum Hall Effect, though."

Now it was Reynolds' turn to chuckle. "Yes, I believe he has mentioned *that* once or twice. Please come in and I'll take you to his apartment."

The stairs down to the basement were narrow and dark. At the bottom, an open door on the left showed a furnace and hot water heater and the other machinery of the building. Reynolds knocked on the closed door on the right and called, "Dr. Sicals. It's Arthur. I have some visitors I'm sure you'll be glad to see."

They heard movement through the drywall partitions that must have been added to the building to squeeze out one more rent check each month. Karen gently edged Reynolds aside to position herself at the door, leading Seth closer by the hand.

A short, somewhat pudgy man opened the door, dressed haphazardly in knee-length shorts and a Hawaiian shirt.

"Yes yes," he said, "what is it?"

Karen broke out a giddy smile and threw her hands wide. "Uncle Morgan! It's me, Karen," and threw her arms around him, forcing him back two steps into the apartment. "You remember Seth, my husband? No, of course you wouldn't. You've never met. Gosh it's been what, nine years now? I know we should have come sooner but ..."

As she continued her non-stop monologue, Karen pulled Seth into the room and smiled at Reynolds, gently closing the door in his face.

"...we don't get out here much and Mom said I must be sure to visit while we were in town." She kept it up until Sicals began to recover from the shock, and object. She put two fingers to her lips and gave him a "shhhh," nodding to the door with her head. She elbowed Seth and he figured it must be his turn.

"Dr. Sicals, it's so good to finally meet you. I've heard so much about you."

Reynolds's footsteps retreated up the stairs while Sicals looked at both of them with calm curiosity, like he was choosing which rat to drop into the maze next. He wore glasses low on his nose, peering over the top of them like he was hiding behind something. His mostly grey hair looked like it had been trimmed by Braille, and combed by saliva-dampened fingers, and there were small, random stubble spots on his face, indicating a haphazard attitude toward grooming. He looked like he should have an odor, but none was evident.

"What is this all about? Who are you people? My sister is dead, and you are most certainly not my niece." His tone reflected his look, curiosity rather than surprise or anger.

"I'm sorry for the subterfuge, Dr. Sicals, but I'm sure you understand the occasional need for absolute secrecy. We're here because we need your help. I'm Karen Larsen, and I believe you've already talked to my friend here, Seth Mathias."

"You're Mr. Mathias, eh? Have you come to apologize? Or are you still looking for free information?"

Seth ignored the sarcasm and followed Larsen's lead, trying for a sincere, enigmatic approach. "No, sir," he said, as his offered handshake was ignored. "I will certainly acknowledge your contributions and opinions in my next article. Our visit is—"

"For other reasons altogether," Karen interrupted. "Mr. Mathias has told me about your theories and I've read your monographs and wanted to discuss them as they apply to identifying the person calling himself Screenshot."

"You've read them? Did you understand them? What are your qualifications to discuss them?"

Karen listed her academic and technical experience, describing her current job without mention of the FBI. After listening and then staring at her for several extra moments, he turned to Seth.

"So you tracked down Phish-Net after all. And then you have the audacity to bring them here." Turning back to Karen, he added, "I'm going to have to ask you both to leave. I will not cooperate with your ersatz investigation."

Before Karen could rebut, he looked at her with some scrutiny and asked, "Exactly what does the FBI know about me? Why are all of you denying me my laurels? How am I a danger to you?"

"I don't know the answers to those questions, Dr. Sicals. That information is not available to me. It's way above my pay grade."

"Yes, well, I don't doubt that. Now I must get back to work. Thank you for your honesty, but I'm afraid I really cannot help."

"Won't, is what you mean, isn't it? Are you going to let past wrongs prevent you from new successes? If your theories turn out to identify Screenshot, wouldn't that validate your claim on the Nobel? People, including my bosses, would have to take you seriously then."

This time Sicals stared in silence even longer, looking directly at Karen, but almost as if she weren't there, like she was a problem someone had scribbled on a chalkboard and he was trying to solve it in his head. Finally, Sicals said, "Let's assume that you are correct. What do you need from me? You have the information. Apply it. If I am right, and I am, my theories will be validated, and any benefits that I might reap will accrue."

"I need you, your knowledge and your vision. You know things never work out as planned in science. You have to make adjustments on the fly, to recognize changes, to evaluate new input. It would take us months or even years to catch up with where you must be already, to write and debug and verify the code, and then more weeks to collect and analyze the data. And we don't have time, Dr. Sicals. Screenshot could kill a dozen more people before we can even begin to analyze data."

When confronted with anything beyond a simple declarative sentence, Sicals seemed to lose track of time. To Seth, he treated the conversation like a chess match, and considered all of the ramifications before moving his piece.

"You are correct, Miss Larsen. There is a higher probability that this Screenshot will die in an automobile accident than be caught by you trying to work my processes without me."

Seth thought he'd actually worked out the probabilities in his head before making the statement.

"However, that changes nothing," Sicals continued. "I do not care about this Screenshot except as a phenomenon to study. As Mr. Mathias knows, I am done with that research."

Now Karen considered in silence while she stared at Sicals. After many seconds, she surprised Seth with her conclusion. "All right, Doctor. If that's your final decision, then that's it. We'll just have to rely on traditional investigative technique. Your ideas probably wouldn't have worked anyway. Goodbye, Doctor. Sorry to have wasted your time."

She led Seth to the door and reached to open it before Sicals spoke again.

"What exactly did you mean by that, Miss Larsen?"

She turned to Sicals and answered with her own question. "Mean by what?"

"That they wouldn't work. Of course they will work."

"They might work, Doctor. You know that no practical theory is proven until it is successfully duplicated. And we won't even try without some assistance. This isn't science to the FBI, Doctor. It's crime-solving."

They reverted to a stare-down. Seth bet on Karen. And won.

"Very well, Miss Larsen. What is it you propose?"

Karen

They spent the afternoon going through Sicals' theories, and Karen became a believer. His abrupt manner somehow complemented his obvious enthusiasm for his ideas, inspiring irrational confidence. This could work, she thought, and it could put her dead center in the Screenshot investigation. One problem remained: Mathias. He was a reporter, whether he called himself that or not, and she couldn't have him meddling and … reporting. At the gate for his 4:54 PM departure for LA, she tried to ease him out of the picture.

"There is one other thing, Mr. Mathias. The Sicals operation will be run out of Phish-Net in Pittsburgh. No local offices or even the Screenshot task force will know about it. If the press or anyone else becomes aware, Screenshot will erase any trail there might be. Then we're dead. So, there will be an embargo on any data about this. I'm going to have to ask you to say or write nothing until it's over. And that includes saying anything to the LA office or any other FBI office."

"An embargo? Like I can't release the State of the Union Address until after the president has delivered it? You can't embargo news. Not in this country. I came by my information on my own, using legal and ethical methods. I can write and publish anything I can sell, FBI embargo or no."

Karen paused before replying. For dramatic effect only, because she'd expected this response.

"Of course, you're right, Mr. Mathias. We can only ask you to cooperate in the interest of solving this series of crimes. We know Screenshot has powerful technical resources, but he believes he's anonymous. If Sicals is right, then Screenshot is wrong. And if you or anyone else brings Sicals to Screenshot's attention, he can cover whatever shadow of a trail there is that we could trace. So it's not really an embargo, it's a request."

"That's a lousy thing to do. Who could turn down a request in a situation like this?"

"You'd be surprised, Mr. Mathias."

"No, I guess I wouldn't be. But you knew that, didn't you? You knew I couldn't. You're manipulating me, Agent Larsen, and that kind of pisses me off."

"I'm not manipulating you, I'm asking for your cooperation. A favor, if you will. I'll owe you one."

"Owed one by the FBI. Is that like a get-out-of-jail-free card?"

"No, it's not a Chance card. It's more Community Chest. Maybe you'll get something good out of it someday."

Mathias was on his way back to LA, and her flight to Pittsburgh wouldn't be boarding for another three hours. It was 8:30 PM back in DC, but if she was going to be up all night on a red eye, she figured her boss could handle a call at home.

"Stanley," she replied to his current objection, using his proper name for emphasis, "I know that. I've met the guy. I've read his history. But you know as well as I that sanity is not a prerequisite for genius. Just the opposite, probably. And there's no denying the guy's genius. All you have to do is meet him and talk for fifteen minutes, and you can *feel* it."

Stan Holcomb, the boss of IC³, and therefore of Karen, was apparently not impressed by her description of Sicals, the software, or her plan.

"Not impossible," she replied to his categorization of it, thinking he just needed a little more persuading to understand the significance of what she'd seen. "Improbable, yes. Difficult? Absolutely. But God, Stan, stop and think about it. Sicals really is right. We're just so used to thinking in conventional terms of load and memory and bits and clock speed that we let ourselves dismiss things as impossible when all they really are is hard."

"Karen," he answered, "this is going to get solved like every other crime, by luck or legwork. It isn't going to get solved by computer forensics unless Screenshot makes a really stupid mistake. There's no reason to think he's going to do that. And if he does, we won't need your crazy doctor to catch it."

Still positive, she played her hole card. "Stan, he's already written the code."

There was a long pause and she thought she had gotten his interest before he replied, "Anyone can knock together some lines of COBOL or C++ or whatever and call it a program. The question is, does it run? And if it does, what does it do?"

"Oh, it runs. Sicals doesn't have a car or a TV or even a cell phone, but he's got a 64-bit RISC workstation that's better than mine. Even with that, he's only able to store and analyze very small data sets, but it runs. We'll have to do verification and validation, but that's it. Then we can find out how it handles huge amounts of data, if it bogs down, or loops, or crashes, or what. I'm betting it works."

"That's not a bet I'm going to permit. Wrap up whatever you're doing out there and get back to Pittsburgh. Bring the programs if you want, and we'll take a look."

"Sicals won't agree to that. He's paranoid, remember? He won't let those programs out of his sight. Actually, there's more. He wants a letter from the attorney general specifically acknowledging his sole ownership of the programs and all of their sub-routines, and any use of them in any current or future application."

"Ha! At least he didn't specify past applications."

"I talked him out of it."

"You're kidding? You want me to authorize Bureau funds and resources to finance a known crackpot, and before that you want me to go to the attorney general of the United States of America and ask him to agree in writing that we won't steal a mad scientist's precious programs?" Stan ran out of breath at the end, trying to get the whole sentence out in one exhale with the necessary emphasis.

"Stan, did you read the second e-mail? I copied you on the report I sent to the LA office regarding their referral of a Mr. Seth Mathias to me for follow up. Mathias is a writer for the *San Jose Mercury News*, and he has been in contact with Screenshot. Verified."

After another pause, this one long enough that Karen thought he might be reading it while she waited, he asked, very slowly and carefully, "Karen, why would the LA office refer this Mathias to you? You're not a field agent. And just how did you verify the contact with Screenshot? And what does this have to do with Sicals?"

"It's all in the e-mail, Stan. Mathias introduced me to Sicals. Screenshot told him who the executioner would be before the fact."

"He told him about our lottery plan? I thought this Screenshot didn't know the identity of the lottery winners."

"He didn't know about that. Screenshot told him the executioner would be a sign. And it was."

"That's it? Someone told Mathias that the shooter in the Helter attempt would be a sign? That's your verification? Karen, leave field work to field agents. Do you have any idea how many lunatics have confessed already? Some religious wacko made a revelation to a reporter, and you're taking it seriously?"

"Read the report, Stan. This was no religious wacko. And he said he will be in contact with Mathias again."

"Okay, turn him over to LA and come on home and we'll get some work done."

"But, Stan—"

"Karen, forget it. Get back to Phish-Net. Do your job. Let others do theirs," is what he said. *Sit down and shut up* is what she heard. *Screw you* is what she thought.

Chapter Fifteen

The FBI

Dave Hendrickson looked up from the latest fallout of the Oklahoma City debacle—a Congressional committee, of all things, investigating the FBI's handling of the event. Dave wished someone *had* found Hoover's phantom files so he could use them now. He understood the irony of Congress investigating anyone else's screw-up, and thought he should remind them that they were in danger of losing Screenshot's vote.

He looked up when Jeff Scoggins, one of his team leaders on the Screenshot investigation, hustled in unannounced, carrying a file.

"We've got an interesting development. Someone over at the Patent & Trademark Office got curious and checked. There really are patents pending on the Drug Rehabinator, the Pediphryer, and the Patriattacker."

That piece of news made the Congressional investigation seem reasonable.

"Patents? On all of them? I don't suppose Screenshot's name is on them, is it?"

"No, but almost as good. Each one was applied for in the victim's name."

"What are the dates for the applications?"

"All filed months ago. Well before any attacks. What we have is a list of targets. I've assigned some admin types to check all the pending patents, but there's a problem. All applications are confidential for eighteen months after filing. The PTO won't give us access."

"What? Screenshot's target list is on some bureaucrat's desk and we can't see it? We need to go to the director on this. We'll get a court order. But keep it quiet. If this gets out, Screenshot might change his targets. I'll talk to the director now. You get your people over to the PTO and find out who knows about this. Isolate them until we get that list and figure out what to do."

The court order came through within three hours, and the PTO commissioner's office grudgingly released their electronic list of over 12,000 pending patents in the categories that might include Screenshot weapons. Fourteen administrative agents pored over the list through the night, identifying likely applications for follow-up. Their search turned up twenty-three new weapons. With three already used, Hendrickson calculated that Screenshot had a six-month extermination program planned.

Then Scoggins gave him the bad news. And Hendrickson dumped it on the director.

"There's an average of forty-seven co-inventors on each application. Of course, only one is the actual target. That makes 1,081 possible targets to find, investigate, and monitor. There is no apparent sequencing to the applications, so we have to do them all."

"Bottom line, Dave. How much?"

"We estimate it will cost about $2,000 each to track them down, then another thousand each per week to monitor their whereabouts, and then approximately five million to cover all of them on D-Day."

"D-Day?"

"Sorry, sir. That's what the agents are calling Tuesdays now.

Death Day."

"So the totals?"

"Our activities to date, including the lottery, total just over $11,000,000. Our estimate to follow up on this and other leads is another $4,500,000, plus $5,700,000 per week until he's caught."

"He's doing a Reagan on us."

"I beg your pardon, sir?"

"He's getting us to spend ourselves to death. It's the Soviet Union in miniature."

The Fourth Victim

When he disembarked from the Air France flight to New York, and before boarding his connecting flight to Houston, Abu Hamir al-Mujahir made his comments to the gathered press brief and moderate.

"I give all praise to Allah for his mercy." His clasped hands and a slight bow testified to his piety. "I will go home now and continue my life as an American citizen. I have nothing more to say."

The crowd of reporters ignored his declaration and, as his security detail cleared a path with the efficiency of a punt-return wedge of blockers, bombarded him with shouted questions.

"Is it true that you met Osama bin-Laden in Afghanistan and trained in al-Qaida camps there?"

"Did your charity really raise over a million dollars for Hezbollah?"

"How do you feel about the French justice system now that you're free?"

Hamir stuck to his vow of silence.

In Houston, the scene repeated itself, except this time Hamir left the airport and got in the waiting black Lincoln Town Car. When the French courts had acquitted him of terrorism and conspiracy charges, he returned to his status as a free American citizen, able to move about and engage in lawful activities without restriction. He chose to return to his Houston home. But first, he had a meeting to attend.

❖   ❖   ❖

Jocelyn brought the *gahwa*, freshly brewed coffee, but without the customary ceremony.

All of Hassan "Sam" Jaffer's law offices and telephones and computers were intermittently swept for any listening devices, but this room was done daily. Four men congregated at one end of the table built for sixteen. Hamir al-Mujahir was one of Sam's most important clients, and a frequent visitor. Sam didn't know the two other men Hamir brought with him.

"Thank you, Jocelyn," Sam said as she turned to leave. "Please lock the door and enable the security system and see that we're not disturbed."

Turning back to his client, he said, "Good to see you home safe. We were all very concerned by the events in France."

"Yes, I know. And I thank you all for your support and assistance. I've called this meeting so you can see first-hand what the efforts of my friends there provided. Sam, you may want to excuse yourself. That is your choice."

Hamir knew that as an officer of the American courts, Hassan had legal obligations that were not protected by lawyer/client privilege and, if violated, would cost him his license. On his part, Sam Hassan knew how to take a hint, and how to take care of himself.

"Yes, of course. Please push the green button on the phone if you have any needs or when you are done. Jocelyn will see that I am notified." They had done this same procedure many times before, but civilized formalities required that they repeat it every time. And it served to categorize the importance of the meeting for the others present.

Hamir started the meeting by handing out copies of a two-page document, written in Arabic. Both men read it while he waited.

When he finished, one of the two said, "This is very disappointing." The other finished and nodded in agreement.

"Yes, it is. It will make our job more difficult. We will have to make up the shortfall, and most of it must come from here. Europe will not be a good source of funds for some time yet."

"The timing does not favor us."

"No, but I have brought with me a tool to aid in our efforts, to demonstrate the seriousness of our mission, to motivate our people. If you please."

He put a memory stick in the USB port of the computer that had been set up with a projector for the conference. After typing several commands, an image came up on the projection screen. It showed four men, one stripped naked and tied to a straight-backed wooden chair, the others in white *thobe* and *ghutra*, traditional robe and headdress. Face masks concealed their identities. Two of them held AK-47s. The third carried a long, curved scimitar.

"Massoud?"

"Yes."

They knew better than to ask the identities of the other three, already knowing that the one with the scimitar was Hamir himself. He walked in a slow circle around the chair, holding the scimitar vertically, his hands clutching the handle and tucked to his chest.

As if a director had said "action," the one with the sword asked Massoud if he had anything to say. The captive looked straight into the camera, as if he knew that the video would be his greatest role, and without flinching, said something. The sound had been deleted, but the others knew enough about his beliefs and likely opinions to lip-read with accuracy. Clearly, the man was ready to die and expected to. And did.

The sword-holder stood behind and to the left of the chair when its occupant began to speak. Before he finished, the sword whirled in a single, spiral motion, lifted vertically and rotated to horizontal, all while swinging counter-clockwise, a right-handed batter swinging for the fences.

Massoud's head fell to the floor, the eyes still open. There was surprisingly little blood, the heart stopping almost instantaneously, and gravity drawing it down, away from the severed arteries. The body barely slumped, secured by the ropes to the tall chair back. The three men didn't move for several seconds. The sword-holder held his follow-through while examining his handiwork, the others waiting for some signal. It came when the executioner brought his legs back together and his sword back to vertical, gave a slight bow to the dead, and walked to his right, out of camera range. A new actor, also concealed beneath his garments, brought a wooden tray and placed the head on it, then followed the same route off camera.

The screen went dark, and Hamir removed the memory stick and handed it to one of the men. "For recruiting. And for discipline."

Hamir pressed the green button and asked Jocelyn to tell Sam the meeting was concluded.

Seth

It was nearing seven when Seth disembarked back at LAX. Two men in business suits stared as they made a direct line to intercept him. He stopped and waited, just to be contrary, forcing them to alter their path and come to him. Apparently, Larsen had phoned ahead, and his ride was here.

"Mr. Mathias," the shorter one said, looking up at Seth. It was not a question. "Please come with us, sir."

"Who is *us*?"

"I'm Agent Wilkinson. This is Agent Sterritt," he said. Both showed their ID. "We're from the Los Angeles office of the FBI, sir. Now, if you'll please follow me, we have a car waiting to take us to our office so you can tell us about Screenshot. Do you have any luggage?"

"What, no Agent Connelly? I would have thought they'd send all my friends from the Bureau to greet me."

"No, sir, no Agent Connelly. Luggage?"

"No, but my truck is in daily parking. Give me an address and I'll meet you there."

"We'll bring you back for your truck when we're done, sir. It will be safe where it is."

"Safe? In an LA parking lot? Fat chance. And who's going to pay the thirty bucks a day?"

"Sir, the sooner we get going, the sooner you'll get back. Think of all the money that will save you."

Agent Sterritt stood quietly to Seth's left rear throughout the conversation, looming in the background, cutting off any escape plans that Seth might have, just as they must have taught him. Both the agents twitched when Seth reached for his pocket.

"Relax, boys. I'm just getting my receipt so I can note the time and know how much to bill the FBI for parking. Okay, let's go."

In the standard-issue black Ford, Seth continued to poke.

"Wow, a limo. And they've got you working overtime. I guess I really must be important, huh?"

Sterritt drove, and Wilkinson paid no attention to Seth, alone in the back seat.

"Wish you had those little chauffeur hats, though. And tinted windows."

When they stopped at the offices on Wilshire Boulevard, Seth got quiet momentarily, impressed by the surroundings. Twenty-three acres of prime Westwood real estate along Sepulveda Boulevard. He followed Wilkinson inside while Sterritt left with the car.

After signing in and passing through security, they went to a conference room upstairs and Wilkinson left Seth alone, telling him he would return. Getting up to see the view through the north-facing windows, Seth was surprised by another expanse of green, dramatically lit as the sun set to his left. He wondered about another wide open space in downtown LA, until the rows of shadows caught his attention and he realized it was the Los Angeles National Cemetery, the Arlington National Cemetery of the West Coast.

Seth was still looking at it when Wilkinson came back with another man.

"Mr. Mathias, I'm Special Agent Embry. Very nice to meet you."

He gave Seth a firm handshake and warm smile.

"Can I offer you coffee, a soda, water? Anything? No? Well, then let's get right to it. I've read your report to Agent Wilkinson."

"My second report," Seth reminded him.

"Yes, of course, the first was somehow misplaced. Would you run through everything for me again and let me see if anything clicks in my head."

Seth told the story again, probably adding new recollections and leaving out others, he thought. He doubted they would cause any clicking.

"In this chat room, are you certain no one else participated?"

"I have no idea what's possible with those rooms. There was a list of active participants, and it showed only the two of us. It was password protected, so if anyone else was there, Screenshot set it up."

"And the e-mail you received with the instructions, do you still have that?"

"Yes, of course."

"Did you send that to us?"

"No one asked for it."

"I'll have Agent Wilkinson go with you to your trailer and take possession of your computer so we can run some tests."

"Wait a minute. No one's 'taking possession' of my computer. I'll be glad to provide a copy of the e-mail, but that's it."

"Mr. Mathias, it's very important that we run these tests to try to locate the source of the e-mail."

Something clicked in Seth's head.

"You think I sent it to myself, don't you? You think I made this whole thing up. What the hell would I do that for?" And after a pause while something else clicked, he continued, "Oh, I see. You think I'm trying for publicity. That I'm going to write about it and make a bunch of money off this."

"Mr. Mathias, it's my job to investigate, not to make judgments or jump to conclusions. It is just good investigatory practice to check all possible avenues, and your computer is the only avenue I have at the moment."

"Some thanks I get for bringing this to your attention. You'd think I'd done something …" Seth stopped mid-sentence and stared at Embry. More clicks.

"You think I did it! You think I'm Screenshot." Seth looked down, thinking about what he'd just said. "No, that's impossible. Even a cursory check of me would show you that I don't have the resources or knowledge. I'd have to have someone backing me, or … Holy shit! You think I'm working *with* Screenshot. That I'm like, his press secretary or something. That's it, isn't it? Well, if I'm the best you've got, Screenshot has nothing to worry about from the FBI. So, no, Agent Embry, you can't have my computer."

"Mr. Mathias, I could get a court order to seize the computer."

"Yes, you could. And I'll be happy to comply once you do. In the meantime, I'd like a ride back to my truck at the airport."

"I think it might be better if you waited here."

Seth's anger overcame his normal acquiescence to authority. At least authority with guns.

"Then arrest me, or I'm walking out of here, calling a cab and going home. And before you even bother to read me my rights, yes, I want a lawyer, and I'm sure the *San Jose Mercury News* would be happy to have one here quite quickly."

Embry again stared at Seth and finally said, "My technician goes with you to the trailer and makes a copy of your drive and any external memory devices. Either that or I'll get the proper seizure orders, then I will seize it. And I will arrest you if I have to.

The FBI has been in the papers before. We'll survive."

"Yeah, I saw you guys in yesterday's paper."

Embry didn't seem to take that well. He turned and walked away, saying, "Take Mr. Mathias to his trailer and copy everything," to no one in particular.

"What about my truck," Seth asked the closing door.

Chapter Sixteen

Karen

As she hurried out the exit of the Airbus A320, dragging her carry-on bag, Karen made sure to give the attendant a sincere thank-you and a smile to validate it. After almost five hours in the air from the plane change in Las Vegas, most of the other passengers, tired from the trip and poorer from the visit, just grumbled something, unaware of the attendant as anything except a flight service module.

She picked up coffee and a croissant at one of the several airport Starbucks and thought about the list she had prepared on the flight and saved in her notebook computer. There were still many gaps, and she needed to be on the office network to fill them before too many people showed up and demanded pieces of her time.

She worked on the premise that Screenshot would stick to his established routine and conduct his lottery over the weekend, announce his latest schedule Monday morning, and someone would die on Tuesday. To find the server that streamed the video of the execution, she needed to convince three of her commercial partners to load a foreign program on their computers, to allocate valuable processor time and network bandwidth to do what would look to them like a hacker's dream, and to collect and store terabytes of data about the process, without them knowing about the two others doing the same thing. And keep it all a secret from her boss and anyone else.

It won't be as easy as it sounds, she chuckled to herself.

❖   ❖   ❖

People were arriving for the start of the work day when she dialed Sicals' phone number. It rang six times before a generic voicemail reply recited his number and asked for the message. Karen left a third one, just in case he didn't understand the urgency of the first two. She guessed he was there, locked into his computer screen, ignoring everything else in the world. She finally gave up and tried a different number. Instead of a greeting, she got a lecture.

"I shouldn't need to remind you that old men like their sleep."

"Arthur, you aren't an old man. And it's only six o'clock there. You should be up and getting ready for another day of breaking hearts."

"Well, I don't know who this is, but even if it's a wrong number, I'll be happy to talk to that voice as long as you want."

"It's Karen Larsen, Arthur. We met yesterday when I came to visit Uncle Morgan. I've tried to call him, but he isn't answering. Would you be a prince and go check on him, and tell him to call me? Wait, better yet, I'll wait five minutes and then call him. Can you answer his phone and make sure he talks to me?"

"Well, I'd be happy to try, but the doc doesn't always answer his door either."

"You must have a pass key. Tell Uncle Morgan I made you do it because it's so important that I talk to him. You need to tell him that Linux just died."

"Oh, dear. I'm sorry to hear that. You have my sincere condolences. I'm sure the doc will want to talk to you. I'll go get him."

When she dialed again, Arthur answered.

"He's kinda mad that I let myself in. Says he doesn't want to talk to anyone. I don't know who Lennox was, but the doc doesn't seem too broke up about it."

"I'm sorry to get him mad at you, Arthur. Don't worry, I'll make it okay. Just put him on."

Sicals got right to the point when Arthur got him to talk.

"That's not possible. What are you using? UBUNTU? Piece of commercial crap. You need to load OpenBSD. It will run fine then."

"I'll try that. And Dr. Sicals, I must insist that you answer your phone when I call. We're on a very tight schedule here, and if we can't get your cooperation, I'll pull the plug on this, and your theories will not get validated or publicized. In fact, I'm going one better. Someone will deliver a cell phone to you today. I will be the only person with the number. Please keep it with you at all times and answer when I call."

Sicals agreed, but Karen guessed he would forget before breakfast. She decided to send Arthur a little gift to make sure he was available for future errands.

Karen returned from picking up her lunch and found her laptop booted and running. Its silence was a relief. Sicals' program had been running since nine-thirty, and her computer was programmed to alarm on any error. No error in three hours meant the program worked, as far as she was concerned. Her immediate task was to finish the phony Verification & Validation documentation, and make the user interface a little more intuitive.

She was halfway through the roasted red pepper and mozzarella sandwich when Roger Parry, her network administrator, charged into her office without warning or invitation, his normal manner.

"What the hell is this program you've been running on my network?"

Karen kicked herself mentally for not anticipating this problem. Roger was a vise: once he got hold of something, especially something he thought he owned, he wouldn't let it go. She would need to slap him down before his grip got too tight. She stared at him for several seconds, trying to make him as uncomfortable as possible before responding.

When he started looking around like he didn't know where he was, she said, "It's the FBI's network, Roger, as you know without my reminding you. At this office, I am in charge of the FBI. You need to keep that in mind. You have obviously noted that I loaded and ran the program. Did it cause any problems on the network? No? Then why are you here?"

"It's a foreign program. No one told me about it. I don't have any documentation or V&V or virus scan. Even you can't go loading programs without following procedures."

"The documentation will be sent to you at the proper time, Roger. You aren't running or maintaining the program, so I'll decide when you need to see that. Here is the V&V," she said as she took it out of her printer tray. "You know the virus scan runs automatically. So, Roger, do you have a valid reason for barging in here and acting like a brat?"

"Well, I didn't have the V&V, and I'm supposed to be notified of new programs being loaded."

"Now you have it. Is that all?"

Roger left behind one more problem for her, what to do with him come Tuesday when she went live with the program. He would go berserk at allowing Sicals access to the network with essentially admin authorities, authorities he felt were his sole domain.

She decided that could wait and get solved over the weekend. Right now she had to ask Bill Gates if she could borrow one of his computers.

Philip

Forget technology or science fiction, Philip thought. If you want to be invisible today, just drive a white cargo van.

His particular model, bought used almost four months earlier from a lot in Baton Rouge, Louisiana, might have been a Ford or a GMC or some other model. It might have been built anytime in the past eight or ten years. It might have been any of the thousands of others cruising Houston on any other hot, sunny weekday. In other words, it might as well have been invisible.

Philip parked next to the railroad tracks that ran directly north between I-610 and the River Oaks Country Club. He drove the familiar route straight to San Felipe Lane, and then the four-tenths of a mile to the end of East Briar Hollow Road. Across the railroad tracks was a cell tower, close enough to the Interstate to provide a link in the telecommunications chain for the very upscale River Oaks neighborhood.

In the back, two crates sat side by side. The large one, about five feet long, contained a large-diameter aluminum tube with several odd protuberances, all protected by custom-cut padding. The other, much smaller, was eleven inches long and about seven inches square, and even better padded to protect its contents. They had been shipped separately and held for pickup at the freight forwarder's facility for three weeks before Philip showed up in his invisible van. On the seat next to him was the electronics case that he had checked as baggage, and a small toolbox, purchased complete from the local Sears that day.

On both sides and the back of the van Philip had stuck magnetic signs identifying it as belonging to a non-existent mobile phone company. Philip saw little risk in this, and figured it would save some business a lot of unnecessary time and effort once the investigation began. He'd designed and printed the signs himself, using standard, letter-sized magnetic sheets that he assembled like floor tiles to look genuine.

Once he arrived at the end of the road, Philip opened the crates and began assembly. The launcher was already mounted in the aluminum tube, designed to look like an antenna, complete with rods and coils mounted asymmetrically around the outside. One of them housed the camera, and the other the radio antenna for controlling the aiming mechanism. Philip loosened the transport lock-down bolts, freeing the launcher to move slightly inside the tube.

The assembled device weighed twenty-nine unwieldy pounds. In well practiced moves, he clipped the tube to a nylon strap and slung it on his right shoulder. Then he climbed the simple single-tube ladder to a cross brace about thirty-six feet off the ground, high enough to get a sight-line above the trees and buildings. The two brackets that he had mounted loosely on the tube matched up to the cross brace, and he quickly connected and hand tightened everything.

The tiny motors and screw-drive rods that adjusted the launcher were mounted inside the tube, and he sighted through it and aligned it dead center at where he guessed the target would be. This left a little room for limited correcting of the aim, and also gave the user the thrill of sighting and pulling the trigger.

Everything mounted and tool-tightened, he climbed down to get the contents of the electronics case. This metal box looked like a circuit breaker housing. It contained the transceiver, wireless network board, and the batteries that would power everything for three hours once brought to life by a radio command. The whole setup blended perfectly with the other odd devices on the tower, and his only concern was that a technician would discover it during maintenance activity.

He saved the small crate for last, a safety precaution. Inside, the TBG-7G rested in special, molded foam, necessitated by the risks of carrying a 105 mm, rocket-propelled, thermo-baric grenade around. Traveling at 1043 feet per second, it would reach the intended target in 3.283 seconds, and he set the timed fuse accordingly. Again going for that extra bit of overkill, the grenade had a lethal blast radius of twenty-six feet. Even outside of that, there would be significant damage and probable death.

After loading it into the launcher, he snapped the two plastic covers over the tube ends, keeping out the weather, curious eyes, and assorted vermin. With the camera on the outside, there was no need for line of sight from inside the launcher, and the only vermin in his plan would be within the twenty-six foot radius. Before climbing back down, he removed the masking tape, uncovering the name: ACME ROCKET-PROPELLED MUSLIMINATOR. Patent Pending.

Chapter Seventeen

Seth

Seth still didn't remember which button to push to silence the alert on his new Blackberry, so he just let it beep, adding another aggravation to his already bad mood. He did look at the display and noted that he had a text message, but decided it would wait. Trying to navigate nearly 24,000 pounds of articulated truck and trailer through the morning LA traffic provided enough challenge. Reading a small LCD display while doing it seemed foolish.

It was late by the time Embry's tech had finished going through all kinds of processes and tests to make sure there weren't any hidden partitions on his hard drive, checking all his file-opening and saving histories for external memory, and installing the recording program that would capture any future Screenshot chats for FBI analysis. When he was done, he answered Seth's request for a ride to the airport to get his truck with a shrug and a statement that no one told him about that, and he wasn't a cab service.

It was even later by the time the cab came to the trailer, for an extra seven dollars because of his remote location, and he recovered the truck and got back. After two hours of sleep, he'd packed up the trailer, secured the loose items, locked the fifth wheel to his truck, and left LA early. Embry wanted him to stay close, Seth wanted to be far away from Embry and his suspicions. He decided the action had moved to the Bay Area, and he would go there and set up camp. Starting Tuesday, Sicals' Oakland apartment would become Screenshot Central, and Seth figured he might as well be there with dear old Uncle Morgan. Screw Embry.

Twenty minutes after the first alert, the Blackberry beeped again, and Seth decided it must be important. The next exit took him onto the Taft Highway going toward Pumpkin Center, a suburb of Bakersfield. As hard as he tried, he couldn't think of an apt joke about the relevance of someplace called Pumpkin Center to his current situation. Except maybe scary jack-o-lanterns, and even flung from the Headless Horseman, they weren't as scary as Screenshot and Embry.

The first text message read, Check your e-mail. The second one got his attention. It simply said, Now. Only one e-mail stood out, the sender identified as shot@censer.com. The subject was Go here. Now. Seth guessed he was about to have his second chat with Screenshot.

Rigging the dish and locating the satellite, even with the GPS auto-locater, took several minutes, and Seth wondered if Screenshot would still be there, and what he would think of Seth's tardiness. At the chat room, he entered *go here* as the password and was denied access. He tried *go here now* with the same result and finally realized that it must be case and punctuation sensitive and typed, Go here. Now. That worked. The occupants' list showed himself and someone called Censer.

The chat window showed a column of brackets along the left edge and, at the bottom, a notation that "Seth has entered the room." No other messages. He waited several seconds without any activity before typing Hello. There was no response, and he thought Screenshot had lost patience and left. Then he remembered the list of occupants still showed someone there. Either he wasn't monitoring the room full-time, or he was teaching Seth a lesson.

Two can play, Seth thought, and went to brew a cup of coffee.

When he came back, there was a message: Censer has left the room. While he considered this development, another message appeared. "The CenserSeth Room has been closed by the Moderator. Goodbye."

I've just been slapped, Seth thought. He broke up with me.

He felt relieved, like getting rid of a clinging girlfriend. He was free of the responsibility of being Screenshot's buddy, and while their relationship had been short, it had been intense. At least for Seth.

He exited the website and started to shut down and stow the dish when his Blackberry beeped again. The text message displayed another link, www.chatnation.com/screenhost. No other instructions, but Seth knew the chat fest was on again.

When he got to the designated room, he realized that there were no instructions to use as the password. He entered "hello_daddy" as his user ID, thinking, I can be cute too, and then hit enter instead of a password. He got instant access. Maybe the games were over.

"Good. You understand obedience *and* humor. We'll get along just fine," the first message read.

Seth considered disconnecting without a response. Obedience? Instead he typed "I obey the law. I laugh at jokes. We're not going to get along."

"Even better," came the reply. "Independence. Maybe we won't get along, but we might find each other useful."

"How? What do you want from me?"

"I don't want anything. I'm giving."

"Giving what?"

"Same as before. Information. Something to think about. I wouldn't want you to get bored."

"Okay. I'll play. What's the information?"

"It's a question. See if your FBI friends have the answer. Why does the next target think he's immune?"

"That's it? What is that supposed to tell me?"

"It tells you the target. At least it should. If your FBI friends are awake and have any intellect at all, it's this week's clue."

"Give me something useful. Why are you doing this?"

"I've already answered that. Someone has to."

"No, they don't. That's just some bullshit rationalization for murder. Did someone have to kill the bystanders? Did the FBI agent deserve to die? "

"There are no bystanders in an AAP audience. And one of their thugs killed Agent Olson, not me."

"Who killed Helter?"

"You start a job, Mr. Mathias, and you finish it. No matter the cost. You should know all about that."

"My guess is that the FBI feels the same way about you."

"Good one! I knew you had a sense of humor. It's the Internet, Mr. Mathias. The great anonymizer. I just made that up. Pretty good, isn't it? Like blog or Google. It's spawning its own language."

"What does that have to do with the FBI?"

"They will never find me because I am one grain of sand on a vast seacoast."

"You were the *only* grain of sand in Helter's room."

"Yes, of course, I'll admit you're right there. But I'm taking precautions to assure that will never happen again."

"What precautions?"

"There will be no need. The jobs will be done right the first time."

"What do you want me to do with this information?"

"Enjoy it. Enjoy being the first to know."

"You want me to write about it?"

"Whatever you like. Just be sure to spell my name right. ;-)"

Even without sound effects, Seth heard the click as clearly as if he'd hung up.

The message was clear, but the underlying import was what Seth thought about. Why was Screenshot talking to him? Why was he giving Seth material? Only one reason: he wanted an outlet, a voice. I do not want to speak for this guy, Seth thought. But he knew he would write it, and that his writing would be influenced by Screenshot, and he *would* have some voice, such as it was.

Theory was fine, but Seth quickly returned to the practical. He had the transcript from the chat, important information that the FBI needed. Calling Embry was out of the question, so Larsen would be the lucky one. He still had her phone number in the outgoing calls log of his cell phone.

The secretary who answered her phone told him Karen was in a meeting and would have to call him back.

"This is important. It's about Screenshot. Please let her know that I'm calling with new contact information. She'll want to hear this, I'm sure."

When Karen came on the line, she didn't seem all that happy to hear from him.

"What is it, Mr. Mathias?"

"I just spoke to Screenshot again. Well, not spoke, but you know what I mean. He gave me another clue to the next victim. It's a question. Why does the next target thinks he's immune?"

"Did he say anything else?"

"He went on about how the Internet protects him, just like you said. He also said that he would make sure things worked right the first time so he wouldn't have to step in again like with Helter."

"That's it? Okay. Thank you for the call, Mr. Mathias, but you need to call the LA office, not me. They will want that information for their own investigation."

"No, I'm not calling them. They tried to take my computer last time I tried to help. They think I'm making this up. Or worse, that I'm working with Screenshot. I saved the transcript. I'll e-mail the file to you. If you want to forward it to Embry, be my guest."

"Fine, do that. Now, I have to get back to my meeting. Thank you for your help. Go ahead and call me if Screenshot contacts you again. I'll keep LA in the loop."

Almost a reason to look forward to a Screenshot chat, Seth thought as she hung up.

Seth turned north onto Hicks Trail, warmed by the easy jog despite the chilly early evening air. Another one and a half miles would get him back to the trailer and the cheese omelet he promised himself after getting hungry while on the Honker Bay Trail. At six foot one, he was well above average height, and since taking up jogging two years before, he had trimmed his weight from, as he liked to phrase it, Duluth to Bayonne, the 218 and 201 area codes, respectively. The eight-hour drive, including several stops to rest, had worn him out, but not in a good way, and he'd decided to jog before dinner.

Another advantage of the mobile life, Seth thought: constantly changing trails. Lake Chabot Regional Park was colder, darker and flatter than the hot and hilly Malibu Canyon he'd left. The lake gave a moist feel to the woods, and was home to waterfowl, which reminded him of eggs, which led to the omelet decision. If he'd seen a wild pig, a possibility, he would have added a side order of bacon.

Since the *Now* e-mail from Screenshot, Seth made it a point to keep the Blackberry handy. It beeped, signaling an incoming message, and it told him it was time for another chat. He figured it would take maybe fifteen minutes to get back to the trailer and decided to reply immediately. Using the Blackberry, he gave Screenshot an estimated time for the contact and waited to see what happened. After several minutes without a reply, he hurried back, not knowing if his message had been received.

In the trailer, he booted up the computer and the coffee maker and launched the session-recording program before entering the chat room, using honey_i'm_home as his ID. He got an immediate reply.

"You're slightly early. Thank you for the message."

"It wasn't a courtesy. It was a reason. What do you want now?"

"All business, eh? Don't want to chat a little? This is a chat room, after all. How are Wes and Rachel doing? Wes graduates next year, right? And the baby must be crawling by now. They grow up quickly, don't they?"

Seth nearly leapt on his keyboard.

"Leave my kids out of this. You want to talk to me, okay, let's chat. But they're off limits, or I'm gone. Now, what the hell do you want?"

"No offense. Just trying to be friendly. No more kids talk. Have you passed on my clue to your FBI friends? Do they have any ideas?"

"Yes. Yes. I don't know."

"Brevity. Good when you're typing. So let's get to the point. Think about this old moral dilemma and we'll talk about it next time. If you could go back in time, with your knowledge of history intact, and you had the opportunity, would you kill Adolph Hitler? Yourself? Up close? Personal?"

Seth inhaled like he would for a doctor with a stethoscope, and let it out slowly. Then he typed, "Yes."

"You had to think about that, didn't you? Most people would jump at that chance. But not you. You know it's not easy to kill another person in reality, even when it's them or you. You did say it was self-defense back there in the woods, didn't you?"

"What's your point?"

"My point? You're special, Seth. You've been there. I'm trying to find out what it takes for you to go back. So, what about old Pol Pot? Or Idi Amin? You're old enough to remember them."

"Yes, I remember them, and yes, I would kill both."

"Now what if Joseph Goebbels was with Hitler and you had two bullets. Would you pop old Joe?"

"This is getting boring."

"Hardly. It's getting interesting. It's going to get revealing. Are you ready for that?"

"All right. Yes, given the chance, I would execute all of them. And before you ask, I would do Osama bin Laden and Stalin and that Somalia warlord guy and Jeffrey Dahmer and Ted Bundy and even Mark Chapman and John Hinckley. Does that save us any time?"

"Yes, quite a bit, actually, although I knew you would. Even knowing what you know, you still would. That's why I chose you. Now, here's the clincher. Would you kill me?"

"That's too easy. Yes."

"When? How about after I killed Redo. Knowing only about that killing, would you kill me."

"No."

"Why not?"

"I'd leave it up to the courts to decide."

"Very good. How about after Glazer? Don't bother. I know the answer. No. Right? So let's get to the bonus round. What about after Helter? Be honest, Seth. With yourself and me."

"Yes."

"So, in my case, it took a dead nine-year-old Jason Hutchins and the Widow Lipscomb and Agent Olson and all the others from the FBI's blunder in Oklahoma City, and possibly the knowledge of my hands-on work with Helter, to get you to the point of murder. Redo and Glazer get categorized with Hitler, and good riddance, no questions asked. Before the so-called innocent bystanders, I was a hero. Right?"

"You were never a hero. Killing history's mass murderers and serial killers before they act isn't murder. It's preemptive justice. I just made *that* up."

"I like it. Maybe I'll use it sometime, if you don't mind. But back to the point. Isn't it true that it took your definition of innocent victims to raise your outrage to the level of retribution?"

"Yes."

"Good. School's out for today."

The next message was the familiar chat room closing.

Seth stared, nothing registering in his mind except the brightness of the screen. Not the words, not the images, not his trailer.

A line from an old movie popped into his head. *Be afraid. Be very afraid.*

Karen

Karen read the transcript a second time before calling Mathias back. After a quick first read at the office, she'd set it aside and hadn't been able to get back to it until she got home.

"What was all that about killing up close and personal and the woods and separating you from the herd?"

"Give me a minute," Seth said. "I'm getting a beer."

She herself was sipping a glass of Pouilly Fuissé, so she couldn't very well criticize.

"I was married for twenty-one years," Seth told her when he got back. "A quiet, comfortable marriage. We were happy with our lives and with our family. Lived in the suburbs, mowed the lawn, did my writing. Pat raised the kids and then worked part-time. Totally unexceptional.

"Then she got sick and died. It took a long time, and it took a lot out of me. The kids were grown, one in college, one married, so I was mostly alone. I guess I got stuck in the depression stage of grief. About a year after she died, I decided to take a weekend camping in the woods, far away from everyone. I told myself I was going to face my past and say goodbye to it, but I discovered I was really trying to escape my present and bring back the past.

"Well, anyway, too much pop psychology. The point is, I ran into some trouble there. I saw some guys murder someone and try to rape and murder a girl, and I got involved and a lot of people died. Some because of me. So I guess Screenshot is interested in me because I've actually killed someone. Maybe he thinks we're simpatico or something."

"You're the West Virginia guy," she said, wondering how she could have missed that, which page she had inadvertently skipped. "I remember. It was in all the Pittsburgh papers. You killed some punks and …" She let the rest go unsaid, realizing that her recollection of the events didn't help him deal with it at that moment.

"I'm sorry, that wasn't very sensitive of me, was it? Listen, from what I remember, you had no choice. You were a hero, nothing like Screenshot. There is no simpatico there."

"No, that's not it. I know I'm no junior Screenshot or something. It's just what you said. I'm the West Virginia guy. That somehow defines me to anyone who finds out. And I'm *not* that guy. Or at least that guy is just a tiny part of me. A part that surprised the hell out of me. So it's not something I announce. I'm out here, living like I live because first, I like it that way, but second, because I can get in my truck and go places where no one knows where West Virginia is, let alone any stories about it.

"I guess it was the surprise of him knowing, of it somehow being the reason I'm in this, afraid for my kids all of a sudden. It keeps following me."

Karen sat in silence for several minutes, sipping her wine. She guessed he was doing more than that with his beer.

"What are you going to do?" she asked.

"I'm getting out. I'm not answering any more of his messages. I'm canceling my Blackberry service. I'm getting in my truck and going somewhere far away until he moves on to someone else and forgets about me."

"Do you think he will? Forget about you? He doesn't seem like a forgetful kind of guy."

"If I ignore him, if he can't message me, there's nothing he can do. He'll have to move on or screw up his plan and schedule."

"Look, Mr. Mathias, as Agent Larsen it's my duty to try to keep you involved because it helps our investigation. As long as I don't put you in danger, I'm bound to enlist your cooperation. So, for a moment I'm not Agent Larsen. I'm not saying this because I have to.

"You have to do what's best for your family, and you need to be real clear on exactly what that is. If he can't text message you, what's to stop him from contacting your kids and forcing *them* to contact you? This isn't some witness protection program thing where they don't know where you are. He knows that. There is no way to hide from him.

"We can put agents on your kids and provide some protection for a little while, but we both know that's not enough. He has time, and he has a million opportunities to choose from. Maybe he'll do nothing. Maybe his path of least resistance is to go to the second name on his list. Maybe he's reasonable, and not obsessed and vindictive. You've chatted with him. You've seen him research you and your history and your family and your life. Do you really believe he'll just drop all that and leave you and your kids alone?

"And what does he want from you? It seems he wants an outlet, someone he thinks will understand his point of view, maybe give him some venue to justify himself, or glorify himself. I don't know. Is that so bad? You're just doing your job, researching a story and reporting on it. There's nothing wrong with that."

Karen knew she made a convincing case, and she wasn't particularly proud of it. Now she was personally invested, something she should never be. Now she was in some way responsible for anything that happened to this man and his family. She wanted to be Agent Larsen again, but it was too late.

Chapter Eighteen

Seth

Arthur Reynolds sat on the front steps, sipping what appeared to be hot coffee, when Seth arrived at Sicals' apartment with his packages.

"Well, well. The nephew-in-law. I thought you were going back east."

"Karen went back. I still have business here. As it turns out, Uncle Morgan might be able to help me with it, so I'm back. I assume he's in?"

"As they say, the doctor is in."

Sicals opened the door after some quiet pleading by Seth.

"What is it now, Mr. Mathias? I'm quite busy getting everything set up with Miss Larsen's network."

"Well, Doc, I thought I'd try to lend a hand, help you and Karen track down Screenshot. I have the communications link to him, so I can be useful keeping you informed and maybe getting any information from him that might help. And just to show you how helpful I am, I brought some supplies. Let's see, I've got a nice, new coffee maker, a little microwave and some food. I'll whip us up some breakfast while you work."

"I do not need your help, Mr. Mathias. I do not need your equipment. I do not want a spy in here reporting back my every move to Miss Larsen. Either she trusts me to do this or not. If I wanted to, I could crash her system while you watched and you'd never know what I was doing. So thank you for the offer, but if you'll excuse me, I have to get back to work."

"First of all, Doc, I'm not Larsen's spy. She thinks I'm in LA being babysat by her associates there. And maybe I can turn that around for you, be your ears to their doings. I'm important to them because Screenshot keeps contacting me, twice yesterday, so I'll be closer than you are to what's going on. Maybe something you want to know about."

Sicals thought about that for a moment and, to Seth's surprise, agreed.

"Okay. Mr. Mathias. You may stay. Make yourself useful, as you said, and please don't interrupt me when I'm working. And under no conditions should you touch my computer. Those are the terms."

Seth set about being useful by unpacking the appliances and making breakfast. He was cleaning up the dirty dishes, with Sicals back at his computer, when the doctor's cell phone rang. Sicals paid no attention, so Seth picked it up and answered.

"Who's this," a familiar voice asked, "and where is Dr. Sicals?"

"Hello, Agent Larsen. It's Seth Mathias. The doc is hard at work on your program, so I'm taking his calls."

"Mr. Mathias? What are you doing there? I thought you were in Los Angeles."

"Being babysat? No, it wasn't very hospitable there, as you no doubt know, so I came to visit Uncle Morgan. I am apparently not his favorite nephew, but he seems taken with you, so he's putting up with me."

"Mr. Mathias, we can't have you involved in this," she said in a polite, firm tone. "I thought I made that clear the other night at the airport."

"That's not what you said yesterday when you promised my

family protection and encouraged me to play Screenshot's game. Got to make up your mind, Agent Larsen." He threw the title in so she knew he wasn't going to be bullied by the FBI.

"I mean we can't have you involved with Dr. Sicals and his programs."

Exasperation was evident behind her voice, and when she asked again to speak to Sicals, Seth eased up on his attitude, and turned to gain some privacy from Sicals, just in case he was even aware Seth was on the phone.

"Listen, Agent Larsen, you know the doc, he's not going to be interrupted while he's doing his stuff. Figure you're lucky I'm here to answer at all. And since I'm here and you're there, maybe I can be of some help. Making sure his phone is answered. Keeping track of his doings. I'll do what I can to get you whatever you want from him."

Larsen hesitated, and then said, "All right, Mr. Mathias. Stay with the doctor. Did the program work?"

A double agent, Seth thought.

"Well, the doc seems satisfied. And lots of little letters and numbers keep rolling up his screen, so I guess it does."

"What is he doing?"

"Just watching the screen, occasionally typing. Printing a few pages here and there. He even smiled once or twice."

"I wonder why he would watch data download and print it. It's just numbers and times in milliseconds."

"Maybe that isn't what he's doing."

There was a pause before she replied.

"Maybe not. I'll take a look at his network access from this end and see what it shows. And you should stay out of his way. I can't have him throwing a fit and quitting. Keep an eye on things and let me know if any trouble is brewing before it happens."

After they disconnected, Seth stood still and watched Sicals work for several minutes, noting his complete focus on the computer, and his apparent satisfaction with what he was seeing. What *was* he seeing?

❖   ❖   ❖

The last of the lunch dishes were cleaned and dried and put away when Seth's Blackberry signaled an incoming message. It was, again, "Go here."

"Doc, I'm real sorry to interrupt, but Screenshot wants another chat. Can you hook my laptop up to your network and I'll do it from here?"

"Must you, Mr. Mathias? I'm quite busy."

"It'll be your chance to see what he's doing, how he's doing it, in real time. Maybe it will give you some more ideas."

After the normal several moments of thought, Sicals said, "Very well. Get your computer and I'll assign an IP address."

After he had played with the computer for a few minutes, Sicals gave it back to Seth and said, "There. It's wireless, so you have access from anywhere in the apartment."

Seth took the hint and moved to the couch, wondering if Sicals had done anything weird to his computer, and what Screenshot wanted this time. More chat buddy stuff, no doubt. More sociological lessons. While he logged onto the chat room, he hoped he was making the right decision. After talking to Larsen, he'd changed his mind and decided to play along. Seth concluded that it all came down to the one simple question she'd pointed out: would Screenshot leave his family alone?

When he'd called Wes and Rachel and discussed it with them,

the FBI agents had already shown up and briefed them. Seth thought they were taking it far too lightly. They didn't understand the evil of this guy. Wes probably thought of him as a vigilante, righting wrongs in a spectacularly entertaining way. Rachel was simply too naïve to worry.

He accessed Sicals' Internet service.

It's go time, he thought as he logged onto the chat room. For his user ID, he chose Eva_Braun.

"Good afternoon, Seth. I trust you enjoyed the trails in Chabot Park. I must get there one of these days."

He knows where I am. Once again, a Screenshot surprise froze Seth.

"Very nice. It's a beautiful day here."

"Good. And your nonchalance about Chabot was very well done. I wonder if you have a poker face too. Now, down to serious matters. Did you think about our lessons yesterday? Do you have any questions or observations?"

"Let me remind you: we're not chat buddies. What do you want today?"

"I'll take that as a 'no' to the questions or observations. If you're impatient to get started, here is my first question of today's lesson. The Hitler/Goebbels scenario. Would you kill Goebbels if he was alone?"

"Probably."

"Please, Seth. Let's not equivocate. Yes or no?"

"Yes."

"But he's not the mass murderer. He's just following orders, like any good soldier."

"He's supporting illegal and immoral orders. He's influencing them. He's enjoying them. He's killing innocent people himself."

"Yes, I suppose that's all true. So it follows that if it was Abu Musab al-Zarqawi alone, with old Osama off at the cave watching a snuff video, you would kill him using the same justification."

"Yes."

"Good. Something to keep in mind as we chat. Let's break for a moment, shall we? How are the kids?"

"Fuck you. Off limits, remember?"

"Okay, break's over. Time to put your money where your mouth is. Time to pay the piper. Time to dance with who ya brung. I could do this all day."

"I couldn't. Get to the point."

"Here it is. On Tuesday someone will die. Someone of the same ilk as the previous criminals. Actually, of a worse ilk, if you can have gradients of ilk. There will be no more lotteries to select the executioner, now or in the future. That phase is done. From now on, I will personally select, recruit, train, and command all executioners. Want to know who the first one will be?"

"No."

"Yes, you do. It's you, Seth. You're lucky number one."

"Forget it. I won't do it."

"And why not? The victim fits the profile we've discussed and agreed upon. He's Goebbels and al-Zarqawi. He's the sidekick. You have a chance to right a wrong *a priori*. Do you mean to say that all of your talk was just that, talk?"

"I don't know who the target is, so I can't judge."

"You'll know before you pull the trigger. And you always have the option to opt out at the critical moment."

"No."

"Consider this: it's a chance for the FBI to mount one of their little operations without the expense of flooding my lottery. Yes, I figured out that's what they did. None too subtle, are they? And it's their only chance because there will be no more lotteries for them to flood. Who knows? Maybe you'll be responsible for catching me. Now that would be a bestseller, don't you think?"

"I can't answer now."

"Oops. Stepped off the moral high ground, did we? And now you're on that slippery slope of rationalization. You'll be riding your preemptive justice toboggan right to the bottom. See you there."

And the screen said, The Moderator has closed the room.

Sicals

Mathias's hurried departure had been a welcome surprise. Right after he shut down his computer, he mumbled "Gotta go, Doc. See you later."

Much later, I hope, Sicals thought.

Now that he was finally gone, Sicals could get to work.

Back at his computer, he checked the progress of the trial download and watched for any glitches. He had selected a corporate web site in China for the first test target, figuring there would be no legal repercussions, and the site might be well-equipped to handle the apparent denial-of-service attack, giving him a better record of effects and reactions. Plus, he enjoyed the irony of an FBI computer assault on a Chinese company.

Data accumulation was proceeding uneventfully at all three servers, and the network attached storage, the terabytes of temporary storage that Miss Larson had obtained, was rapidly filling. He'd based his calculations on four hours of data, the most he thought they would get from any real Screenshot broadcast, and would soon be at that mark. Activity could be shut down at that point, and his software would spend the weekend mining the data to verify it would work come Tuesday.

Satisfied with the results so far, he brought up *his* downloaded data, saved in an encrypted partition on his hard disk. He entered the password from memory—5972 3833 4626 4832 3979 8535 6295 1413—and began the initial analysis. The password was just a little more irony, and a test for anyone trying to access his data. It was easy for him to remember. The eight four-digit numbers were the first thirty-two integers of Pi. Backwards.

It took some time to sift through the data, often going back out into the World Wide Web for more or to verify what he had, but in the end, he found what he needed and began to work in earnest. He stopped often and studied his monitor, sometimes making notes on a pad next to him, sometimes copying large blocks of data to a separate file, always careful to leave the original intact, unedited.

He had thirteen pages of handwritten notes and a sixty-two-page document of segments of data when the cell phone rang. He ignored it. He was on the fourteenth page when it rang again, and he ignored it again. He was still on page fourteen when it rang a third time and, exasperated at the repeated interruptions, he picked it up and clicked the connect button.

"What?"

"Dr. Sicals, it's Karen Larsen. Thanks for picking up, but I must insist that you do it the first time I call in the future. I am the only person with this number, so if it rings, it's because I need to talk to you. And if we are to continue this experiment, then you need to talk to me. Now, how is the data dump going?"

For a moment, Sicals panicked, so immersed in his own work

that he thought she was referring to that and wondered how she knew. Then he remembered the ping triangulation test, and relaxed.

"It went very well. I believe we have sufficient data to run a realistic data-mining test and we should be done sometime very early Monday morning. That gives us plenty of time to set up for Tuesday. It will happen Tuesday, right? I must be sure I am ready."

"Tuesday is the normal schedule, but you know we don't control that, Doctor."

"All right, then. Please keep me informed of any information on the schedule, or any web information like domain names or ISPs that you find. They will help speed up the data mining."

"Is there anything else my people can be doing to help you get ready."

"No, no. It has to be done here. Don't worry, everything will be ready. Just remember to keep Mr. Screenshot broadcasting for as long as possible. We'll need whatever time we can get."

He hung up, and went back to start on page fifteen.

Karen

Karen was comfortable in her long t-shirt and short robe. She watched her *Must Love Dogs* DVD for probably the tenth time, finally unwinding from the day and hoping for a slower-paced weekend. It was after nine when her cell phone rang. She doubted it was good news. The caller ID said Seth Mathias. She thought about ignoring it, but there'd probably been another Screenshot chat, and curiosity trumped weariness.

"Agent Larsen," she answered, deciding not to remind him that she knew when he called.

"Where the hell have you been? I'm waiting four goddam hours. You convince me to get involved in this shit, and then you disappear? Goddammit, this is my *family* we're talking about. This is my *life*. I am not going to do it, and you and your buddies there better figure out a way to make this right."

Karen realized she'd instinctively moved the phone away from her ear, like she could put more distance between herself and the maniac on the other end.

"Whoa, Mr. Mathias. What are you talking about? Waiting four hours for what?"

"Don't give me that. Waiting for a response to the transcript I sent you *four hours ago*. Do you ever check your e-mail? Or is it the weekend, and you have a party planned or something?"

"All right. First thing, you've got to calm down and tell me what you're talking about. I checked my e-mail just an hour ago, and there was no transcript or anything else from you. So please try to tell me what it is you won't do."

"I won't kill anyone, for Christ's sake. He wants me to kill someone, and *I won't do it*."

"Screenshot wants *you* to pull the trigger? When? What did he say? Wait. Let me check my e-mail again and see if it's there."

She turned John Cusack and Diane Lane off just as they were getting together for the third time. Her laptop computer was on her desk, up and running whenever she was.

"Hold on, Mr. Mathias. Here it is, in my Spam folder. I'll read it now and call you back."

"*No.* Forget it. I'll hold. I'm not taking a chance on waiting another four hours."

As she read, her immediate reactions tumbled through her

head. How did he know where Mathias parked his trailer? Was that an implied threat to his kids? Screenshot might be nuts, but he's goddam clever. And not just at building weird weapons. He's got Mathias all twisted around. What the hell can I tell him?

But the thought that overwhelmed the others, the thought that logically followed her last one was, I'm responsible for this. I talked him into going along. What do I do now? She could only think of one thing.

"I'm coming out there. Next flight I can get. I'll send the transcript to the LA office. No, wait, you're in Oakland. I'll get the files to the San Francisco office and to DC. We'll figure out something. I'll be there first thing tomorrow. We will figure something out. Okay?"

"No, it's not okay. I'm not okay. What are you going to do? How about you kill whoever it is? Huh? See how you like it."

"Mr. Mathias. Seth. We'll figure something out." As soon as she said that, she wondered if going there was the smartest move, then decided to hell with smart. "You and your kids will be fine. It's just a matter of time before we get this guy, and we'll take care of all of you until then. I promise."

There was a long pause before he answered, very subdued.

"I sure hope you keep your promises."

And the line went dead.

Chapter Nineteen

Seth

Seth's new sign read San Francisco Welcomes Karen Larsen, with only the last name in a large font so it would all fit on one page. After the call the night before, he'd spent some more time being mad, then a little while feeling sorry for himself, then some time being honest about the real causes for this situation, and she wasn't on his list. He expected to surprise her and hoped the sign and the pick-up service would serve as an apology.

He saw her striding up the concourse, intent, no doubt, on the taxi stand or hotel shuttle she would be using. She wore a navy blue suit, the skirt below her knees and the beige blouse buttoned to her neck, just like any serious FBI agent. Even so, he had trouble reconciling Agent Larsen with the striking woman whose blonde hair contrasted with the suit and complemented the blouse. She looked fresh out of the shower and Seth wondered how she kept doing that, even when she thought the only people she would see were a taxi driver and a hotel desk clerk.

When she got close enough and glanced in his direction, he held the sign up. It caught her eye then her gaze swung back to him, and she smiled in recognition. He wondered how she did *that*, as well, appearing sincerely cheerful after a seven-hour flight.

"Mr. Mathias. What a nice surprise. How are you doing, today?"

"Better. I wanted to apologize for acting so … nasty, so I made a sign, and here I am."

"There's no need to apologize. I should be apologizing for not realizing my laptop would filter that file. My office computer recognizes the format, so it never occurred to me. Anyway, how did you know which flight?"

"There aren't that many flights from Pittsburgh, and I guessed."

"There are plenty of flights, because none of them come directly from Pittsburgh. So how did you crack my security?"

"I picked the earliest connection. And I was prepared to wait and make a day of it, if necessary. Have a picnic. Read my book. Tour the baggage claim area. You can see how full my life is."

She smiled and said, "I guess it's good I got this flight, then."

"It was a safe bet that you would. I can't see you standing around waiting for things to come to you."

"Thank you, I think. To your truck then. Or did you rent a limo to go with the sign?"

"Damn. I wish I'd thought of that."

Oakland Airport parking was no roomier than LA, and they repeated the back-out-of-the-spot-then-get-in procedure for her, and headed downtown.

"Which hotel? Or, the dining room table is still open. It adds new meaning to the term *breakfast in bed*."

"No, thanks. I'm at Marriott Courtyard. They'll bring me breakfast right after I phone them. But I think we should go see Uncle Morgan first and see how the preparations are going."

They drove in silence for several minutes until Karen closed the door on social conversation and brought them back to reality.

"Have you given it more thought? How stupid of me. Of course you have. Do you know what you're going to do?"

"No. I go back and forth. I don't see how I can do it, and I don't see how I can't."

"I've given it some thought too. No one could expect you to do it. I think it's probably my job to prevent you from doing it. We know that Screenshot can pull the trigger himself, so there is always that. What we don't know is what he'll do if you back out. Will he target your family? That's a chance we can't take.

"I e-mailed our attorney, and he's talking to others at Justice. I asked if we could get a court order allowing several people, including FBI agents, to all push the button simultaneously, if it comes to that. Only one signal is needed, so whichever electron gets their first does it. No one can ever know for certain if he was the one. Maybe we can get a judge to sign off on something like that."

"You think so? Because I said that I go back and forth, but in reality, it doesn't matter what I decide beforehand. I know I won't be able to press the button. It's one thing to kill someone because you have no choice. It's quite another to choose to do it. I'd choose not to."

After a few moments of silence, he added, "And then probably live to regret it."

❖   ❖   ❖

As Seth had discovered on his past visit, the intercom at Sicals' building still didn't work, and he took a key out of his pocket and opened the front door. Holding it open for Karen, he signaled her to enter with an elaborate wave.

"Sicals gave you a key?"

"Not exactly gave. I made a copy when I went grocery shopping the other day. I thought it would be best not to disturb him about it while he was working."

"Enterprising. Not legal, but enterprising."

At the bottom of the stairs, they knocked and waited and knocked and waited.

"He might have fallen and can't get up," Seth said, using a second key to unlock the door.

Nothing had changed, including Sicals, still parked in front of his computer, staring at the screen and typing at the keyboard. When he noticed them, he looked like a kid caught with a copy of *Playboy*. He turned back to his screen, typed more commands and clicked his mouse button furiously.

"Hello, Doc. Watcha doin'? Downloading porn?"

"Don't be ridiculous, Mr. Mathias. How did you get in here? Did Arthur let you in again? I'm going to speak to him. This is unacceptable. My home is private, and I will thank you to respect that."

"I'm so sorry, Doctor," Karen interjected. "We needed to see you and no one answered the door. We were concerned for your health." Seth noticed she didn't mention the key, and left Arthur to take the blame.

Sicals looked at her for a moment and relented, probably not buying the health concern, but accepting it from her.

"I'm just here overnight," she said, and the news slightly depressed Seth's better mood. "I wanted to review the results of the ping triangulation tests and make sure we're set up for the real thing on Tuesday."

"Results? I don't have results yet. I told you it would take at least sixty hours of analysis to get final results. I have some preliminary indications, but I won't be done for another twelve hours or so. It looks like the test server is somewhere in southeastern China, possibly Guangzhou, or Hong Kong, or Macau. I can't be more precise than that yet. It's quite a large area, and these are major communications centers."

"And you need twelve more hours? Does that give you enough time to get set up? Do I need to do anything?"

"No, Miss Larsen, you have already given me all I need. Please make sure I am not interrupted again, either by visitors or on my network access."

"You want me to make you some lunch, Doc," Seth asked, making the only contribution he was competent to do.

Before Sicals replied, Seth's Blackberry beeped, and he and Karen jerked their heads and looked at each other. Seth took the device out of his pocket and read the screen. "It's him. He says now."

Karen said nothing and seemed to be thinking about their options. Sicals tired of waiting.

"It's who, if I may ask. And what is now?"

"Sorry, Doctor. It's Screenshot. He wants to set up another chat with me. Can I go ahead and do it here again? He doesn't like to be kept waiting."

"Must you? I have my own work to do."

"Doctor," Karen interjected, "this is important, critical to our program. We have a way to keep Screenshot on-line long enough for you to gather the information that you need, and we must confirm it with him. We can't contact him. We can only respond when he signals that he wants to chat."

"All right, Miss Larsen. You can use my network again. Where is your laptop computer, Mr. Mathias?"

"Uh, it's back in my trailer. I was just picking Agent Larsen up at the airport and I didn't think I'd need it. Can I use yours?"

Sicals seemed uncomfortable with that, although it was hard

for Seth to tell because of his normally cautious conversation.

"Wait one moment while I close down my other work," he finally said. And after some more typing and clicking, careful to conceal his screen from both of them, he said, "There. Go ahead, Mr. Mathias. You can log on now. But I am going to watch you. Please do not do anything except your Internet chat. I don't want you corrupting any of my files."

Seth logged into the chat room and entered his new ID: the_dr_is_in.

"Doctor of what?" was Screenshot's first message.

"What do you want?"

"Your answer, Seth. I need to make plans, to set up systems, to initiate processes. And they all depend on you. So what will it be?"

"You do what you want. I'll let you know when I'm ready."

"No, you'll let me know now. If this chat ends without an unequivocal answer, I will proceed as if you had said no."

"What does that mean?" Seth typed furiously, as if he were challenging Screenshot through the keyboard.

"Just what it says. Now, what is your answer?"

"Who is the target?"

"Don't be ridiculous. You'll see when the time comes. Now, no more delays, please. Yes or no."

"I'll go along, but I won't do it unless the target is clearly what you say he is."

"Oh, he is. I'm quite positive that you will be eager to press the F10 key. That will be the trigger. That will be all you need to do. When the moment comes, press F10."

"How will I know the moment?"

"It will be very clear. I will e-mail you the URL Tuesday morning at six AM Pittsburgh time. Unless I miss my guess, that's where you will be. I'm looking forward to the audience. Don't let them dissuade you from doing what you know is right. They won't dare prosecute you, not when you did it from their facility, using their equipment, with their complicity. They won't want the publicity. Please be ready then."

"I'll be there. Whether I'm ready or not remains to be seen."

"You're ready, Seth. You are so ready."

❖   ❖   ❖

When Seth walked Karen into the restaurant, he regretted the choice. Knowing almost nothing about local dining, he'd asked the hotel concierge for a recommendation. The day had started with her long flight, then the tense Screenshot chat, and they'd been going ever since. Seth suggested dinner, and Karen said she wanted to check into the hotel and get cleaned up first. The concierge must have seen them together and gotten the wrong idea, because someone had designed this restaurant to facilitate what often happened after dinner when couples went out on the town.

"Wow," Karen said. "You sure know how to treat a lady."

"Treat? I thought this was the FBI's treat."

"I'll tell you what, the first $45 are, because that's my food allowance when I travel. After that, you're on your own."

"I don't suppose we could get appetizers here for $45."

The restaurant was quiet and dark, the dark seeming somehow red instead of black. Booths lined the perimeter, tables in the open space, and every surface was covered by dark red carpet or fabric, lit by dim wall sconces and overhead fixtures. The sounds of service and eating were subdued, as if the china and silverware were also fabric covered. The maître d' led them to a booth and told them Albert would be there shortly to take their drink orders.

As promised, Albert came and asked what they wanted to drink and left them with menus, Karen's showing the selections but no prices.

"No prices. Now I know I can't afford it."

"Mine has the prices, and don't worry, a second mortgage will cover it." Seth reflected for just a moment and then continued. "When I was in college, I took a girl to a fancy restaurant like this once to impress her, and they had the same menu thing, only everything was in French. I didn't understand it but wouldn't admit it, so I ordered Steak Tartare to impress her. I figured, what could they do to beef? Well, it turns out they could have cooked it, but didn't, and I had to smile through a raw hamburger with a raw egg on top. I always asked after that."

"Was she suitably impressed?"

"I think so. I told her all about it after we got married."

"I'm sorry. I didn't mean to bring up old memories."

"No need to apologize," he said. "You didn't bring it up, I did. And old memories are not there to be buried and forgotten. They're what we have. I like my memories. They don't make me sad, they make me happy. Without my memories, it was all just a big waste of time, wasn't it? So, what're *your* memories, Agent Larsen? You know all about me, and I know nothing about you."

With her cheerful smile back in place, Karen said, "That's *Special* Agent Larsen, if you please. What would you like to know?"

"First, how did you get to be a Larsen? Married name?"

"No, no marriage. Engaged once, a long time ago. The name is my father's, shortened from Larselaitenen by his father, Matti."

"Still doesn't sound Asian."

"It's not. It's Lapp. My grandfather was born in Lapland and emigrated to America during World War Two with his family when he was fourteen. My father was born here, and he met my mother while serving in Korea."

"Emigrated from Lapland during the war. There's got to be a story there. Tell me if I'm intruding. It's just my writer's nature to want to hear a good story."

"No intrusion, nothing very unusual, unfortunately. My grandfather was born in the village of Petsamo. It's called Pechango now. It is very far north in Lapland, a fishing village on the Barents Sea. They were fishermen, like most of their neighbors. During the war, the Germans wanted the nickel in the nearby mines, and so did the Russians. Anyway, Petsamo got caught in the middle, and when it was over, Petsamo didn't exist, and Pechango was born.

"The fishing fleet was destroyed, and there was no way to make a living and provide for his family, so my great-grandfather loaded them on a Norwegian freighter and they got to western Norway, and then to Iceland and Greenland, which was part of Denmark and controlled by the Nazis at the time. From there they took a fishing trawler to Canada and finally America. It was all very, uh, Bogartish. It's kind of a family legend by now, and no doubt greatly exaggerated."

"Sounds to me like that would be hard to exaggerate. Was your father's Korean tour as interesting?"

"You mean other than meeting my mother? No. But my grandfather went there first, during the Korean War, and he came back with frostbite and a limp and stories he would never tell.

Like many immigrants, my family is very patriotic. When he was old enough, my grandfather enlisted in the army and fought in Korea. My father also enlisted and was stationed there. So that's how Karen Larsen came to look like Kyung-ja Park. Except for the hair, of course."

"What about the hair? Your mother's not blonde?"

Karen started and then caught on, smiling. "No, my mother isn't blonde. Apparently you're not familiar with the Orient."

"Quite the contrary. I've written scads of second-hand information about it. Never been there. And for your information, you aren't the first blonde Korean of my acquaintance. I did a story for *Stars and Stripes* many years ago about the families of GIs stationed overseas who married locals. When I met him, he was their fifteen-year-old son, lived in Jersey, looked absolutely Korean except for the blonde hair. He had it cut so short that he looked bald."

"Maybe I could try that. I've thought about dying mine black, but the thought of blonde roots is just too weird."

"Why? I think your hair is lovely."

"Lovely or not, most people, my superiors especially, can't see past the fact that I am Asian, blonde and female. That kind of description gets you hired, but it doesn't get you promoted."

"You seem to have done well. I mean, Phish-Net. How much more prestigious can you get?"

"Phish-Net is great, but it's so far off the career track at the Bureau that they need Mapquest to find it."

Seth took out the small notebook he always carried and jotted a few key words to jog his memory later when he would write a more detailed description.

"I'm the one who's supposed to take notes while questioning

someone," Karen said.

"Sorry, don't mean to be impolite, but like I said, I'm always interested in new stories. They'll find their way into something I write, someday. And if I don't make notes, I'll forget by the time we leave."

"Fair enough. What else would you like to know?"

Dinner arrived before he could answer, and he waited until coffee before answering.

"How come you're on your own on this? Does the FBI even know what you're doing?"

Seth saw the little inhale and slight twitch backward, as if she wanted to get further away from him but caught herself.

"What makes you say that? Everything I do on any active case is fully sanctioned by the FBI. That's why they give me a badge."

"I keep wondering why you're the only FBI agent here. I mean, they had three agents questioning me, and I'm nobody. Sicals is likely the key to catching Screenshot, and yet no one else has shown up or even called, as far as I can tell. You could take the doc to Pittsburgh where all the big machines are. That would make sense, but I don't think he'd go. I don't know a lot about the FBI, but I do believe if he wouldn't go to Pittsburgh, Pittsburgh would come to him, and we'd see a lot of activity here. I'm guessing that your bosses think he's a crackpot and are giving you no support, or maybe even telling you to drop it. Are you off the reservation on this?"

"Mr. Mathias, this is not an appropriate discussion. We have had a lovely dinner after two very trying days, and we have a lot to do in the next two days to get ready. Or have you forgotten?"

A little of Seth's anxiety leaked out. "That I'm supposed to kill someone come Tuesday? That my family is in danger? No, I haven't forgotten. It's because I remember that I want to know the situation, to understand the rules."

"Obviously the FBI is fully aware of you and of the situation. They have questioned you. You are going to be in our offices on Monday to prepare so that you and your family are safe. Now, we can either finish our nice dinner and enjoy a little respite before I have to get on a plane tomorrow and get ready to wrestle with Screenshot, or, if you insist on pursuing information that is not relevant to you, we can pay the bill and go now."

Seth ignored her protest. "Because if you're on your own, how seriously are they taking the threat to my family? It's already clear that Embry thinks I might be somehow involved. If I get on that plane and trust you and your associates, I'm putting my family at risk."

"We take your family's safety very seriously, Mr. Mathias. We have people working on quasi-legal methods to make sure they are protected. Embry was just doing his job, just being thorough. No one believes that you are in any way involved with Screenshot beyond these contacts."

Again, Seth went on as if she hadn't spoken. "And the other thing is, I don't know a lot about computers, but I do know that the doc's program is just gathering and analyzing huge amounts of information. The computer can do all that by itself. Why does the doc sit in front of his screen day and night, pounding on his keyboard, making page after page of notes? Is he helping the computer analyze? I doubt that. When we showed up today and he scrambled to close the windows before we saw them, I did see one. It was one of those translation sites. You know, where they take foreign text and give you some semblance of an English version. What data is he getting that needs translation, do you suppose?"

"I expect, Mr. Mathias, that he's doing other things that don't concern us or the investigation."

"How do I know that? How do I know he's not off on some crazy adventure of his own that puts my family at risk? So you see, I'm just wondering what those other things are, and why he needs access to your network to do them. And why your FBI isn't living with him."

"That part of the investigation has nothing to do with you, as you very well know. We need to go, now. I have an early flight."

Seth followed her abrupt departure.

Chapter Twenty

Karen

Karen shivered, waiting outside the hotel for the airport shuttle even though the desk clerk invited her to wait in the lobby. The fog made the 51° temperature seem a lot chillier, and the clothes she'd packed for the Oakland daytime weather forecast, warm and dry in July, weren't adequate for the 5:30 AM weather. She chose to stand outside anyway, letting the chill provide a diversion from her new problem. Problems, actually, she thought. Mathias and Sicals. Sicals for what he might be doing. Mathias for noticing what she was doing.

Not noticing Sicals' behavior herself made the problem that much more irritating. She'd let her fascination with his ideas cloud her judgment, and she took him at face value, a brilliant if somewhat deluded man who wanted recognition. She wanted to know what he was doing, and if his access to her network facilitated it. She chuckled to herself, noticing her subconscious attempt to rationalize her mistake. Of course her network would facilitate it, even if it was just playing Sudoku on-line.

The shuttle arrived, and she welcomed the relative warmth inside. The thirty-minute drive to the airport would get her there an hour before her flight. Plenty of time for someone with FBI credentials to get through security.

Instead of opening her computer on the plane, she put on the airline-supplied earphones and listened to the elevator music channel to block out her surroundings while she considered these problems. Sicals first, she decided.

His shutting down open screens for privacy didn't prove anything improper; she would probably do the same thing. Karen went down the list of perfectly harmless computer activities that you wouldn't want others to see, and except for some scientific paper he was writing, or something he wanted to hide from Seth-the-reporter, none of them fit her profile of Sicals. She concluded he knew that his activities abused her trust, whether it was sinister or not. Something that she couldn't just ignore. She didn't have the time to deal with that, but she was exposed. Having let him on the network without proper authorization meant she would be personally, professionally responsible for anything he did.

Using the FBI network security she would be able to get a comprehensive review of his activities: time, bandwidth, CPU load, even the sites he navigated. She hoped it was innocuous, and she could just tell him to knock it off. She didn't want to think about the alternative.

The Mathias problem threatened her work on so many levels she didn't know where to start. He was the FBI's sole contact with Screenshot, and therefore necessary, and privy to information no one outside the Bureau had. And now he knew, or at least suspected, that she was Lone Rangering this one, and that gave him leverage over her. And to top it all off, he was a reporter. It was his job to screw all of them.

The conversation over dinner had brought her back to her senses. She'd begun to like him too much, to feel sympathy for his Screenshot dilemma, and respect for his West Virginia adventure. But dinner reminded her of the risk he posed, and they'd parted the night before with some tension.

She considered this as she dozed off, and it was her first

thought when she woke, almost like she had been beamed forward in time without a break. The pilot announced that they were passing Columbus and everyone should get ready for their final descent into Pittsburgh. She decided she would just have to play Mathias along, minimize his access to information, and encourage his discretion. All good thoughts, but like her original one, none of them had a *how* included.

The drive to her office was easy on a summer Sunday afternoon, at least one when the Pirates weren't playing a home game. Her office overlooked the Monongahela River, and she could see River Front Park just across it with its runners and joggers and walkers and riders. It was a beautiful day for any of those activities, but she had work to do.

On her computer, the network user log showed Sicals had logged on only once, and had stayed constantly connected for a full week. That was unusual, but she could understand that someone like Sicals would not want to be bothered by the housekeeping of log-on and log-off, and just stayed connected.

She next opened a record of his transactions, and found that he'd visited and accessed the three servers doing the ping triangulation test, and the Phish-Net server running the data mining. All kosher so far. The only unknown was a site in Moldova that he had logged onto at 1:27 AM last Friday, and where he was apparently still active. When she checked out the site, she discovered an anonymizer, a portal that allowed Sicals to enter as himself and exit into the Internet world as any identity he chose, his movements from there untraceable.

That caused her concern. If Sicals needed an anonymous identity, and was willing to put up with the inconvenience and delay of this additional layer of access, then he was doing something he wanted kept secret.

She could thwart him by restricting his access to only the three servers doing the data gathering and analysis, but his access was her access, and she couldn't restrict that. And Sicals wouldn't react well to any restrictions.

Her other options were illegal, and therefore out of bounds for the FBI. She had to decide if they were out of bounds for Karen Larsen. The easiest would be to install a keylogger, a program to record all of Sicals' keystrokes and upload a transcript to her. While she had any number of these, taken from some of the more talented hackers they'd caught over the years, it would only tell her what he typed, not show her what he read or downloaded. She would have to retrace every step, and in the Internet world, many of the commands that got you one thing yesterday, got something different today.

She stared at the screen for a while, not really seeing it as she tried to come up with another solution, or a justification for leaving it alone. In the end, it boiled down to two choices: slap a tap on Sicals, or shut down the whole tracker effort.

"Shit," she said as she started reviewing her menu of confiscated bugs and spyware to find one with a chance of working without tripping Sicals' anti-virus protection, which she had to assume was formidable.

Sicals

Mathias's article on Digital Gold had been thorough and accurate. And now that he'd confirmed it with his own research, the last piece of the puzzle was in place.

As he did with anything new, Sicals analyzed Digital Gold in his head, considering the phenomenon from its root causes to its projected effects. The cause was simple enough: the Internet provided anonymity, while at the same time making access public. You could pretty much say or do anything, and everyone would know it. They just wouldn't know who said or did it. Anonymous money wasn't only the logical result, it was an imperative, probably second only to pornography as a concept in search of a vehicle.

Its use was simple: put money into an untraceable, numbered account, transfer it anywhere, anytime, and do it without any control, reporting, or oversight. Digital cash. The effects? He thought these would be revolutionary. People worried about the cashless society, where everything would be paid for by card, access would be instant, no bounced checks or deposit delays. Where everything had a source, a path and a destination, and it was all instantly recorded. With digital gold, they were right about everything except the instantly recorded part. And that, to traditional society, was the important part.

The account open, he clicked Next on the web page, and got a blank screen with the message that the page could not be accessed. He tried again, and got the same result. Using the command screen, he pinged the university web site and got no reply. He'd lost his Internet access.

The computer clock read 2:23 AM. Could the FBI have shut down for network maintenance? That seemed unlikely. They would have backup for such an occurrence. Had they shut him down for some reason? They couldn't know about his other work, his tracks were hidden. Maybe they'd detected his subterfuge and shut him down until they got an explanation. That would be very bad.

There was nothing he could do from his computer, so he went to bed, telling himself to sleep three hours and thirty-seven minutes.

At six, he awoke. He didn't need to look at the clock in the icon tray of his computer, the only one in his apartment. He'd decided to wake at six, and his internal clock had done just that. It's all in your head, he knew. If only other people realized that, it would be a world more to his liking.

At six, it would be nine in Pittsburgh, and if he still didn't have Internet access, then something was wrong. At his still-running computer, he pinged the university again, and got replies in an average of seventeen milliseconds. Acceptable performance, his access re-established.

He got up and put a fresh pod in the new coffee maker, taking out the used pod that he always forgot about, and throwing it away. His undersized freezer was fully stocked with things he could heat in the new microwave oven, and he decided a breakfast burrito and orange juice would get his day started right. While it heated, he got himself ready.

Clean, fed and rejuvenated, he sat back down at his computer and played with all that server power at his disposal.

The FBI

Dave Hendrickson looked again at the doodles on his desk pad. Names of bizarre weapons and little drawings of what they might look like. The patent descriptions gave him some clues to their design, but not to their reason. Some of the names helped. The Defrocker clearly targeted some church official, probably a pedophile priest or something. But the Defibrillator? Was he targeting a cardiologist?.

His phone rang and Scoggins told him they had the evaluation of the patent titles and the correlation with the contacts between Mathias and Screenshot. Hendrickson told him to get everyone together and he would meet him in the main conference room to review them and decide on a course of action.

At the meeting, Scoggins projected a two-column list on the screen. The first column included the names of the historical villains mentioned by Screenshot in the chats, and the other column listed many of the names from the patent applications, with a web of connecting lines between the two. Hendrickson looked at it like he might an abstract piece of art, not fully sure which side went up.

"Jesus, Jeff. Could you have made this any more complicated? What the hell is the purpose of this? And what the hell is a Lesso-lator?"

"Several times in all of the communications with Mathias, Screenshot has given and hinted at clues," Scoggins answered. "We've tried to correlate the people's name or category of names with the weapon names, and based on the frequency of their use, project which weapon will be used next. Then we can narrow the targets to those on the patent and have a chance at covering all of them, or at least the most likely ones. And *lesso* is Italian boiled beef. The Lesso-lator is essentially a very big capacitor."

Back in her office, Karen could see the computer projection on her own screen and, over the speakerphone in the conference room, said, "It's the Terroroaster or the Musliminator. Screenshot focused on bin Laden. He's going after a domestic terrorist, probably a radical cleric."

Scoggins, possibly smarting from the comments about his

slide, said, "You can't really be sure. He started the whole polemic with Hitler and Goebbels, and came back to them the most often. It could be some Skinhead or Neo-Nazi."

"Yeah, it could be. But he wants Mathias to pull the trigger, and Nazis and Skinheads don't present much of a threat to our way of life. I doubt he's confident he can get Mathias to kill one of them. My guess is that he's going to present an unequivocal bad guy, someone history will record as one of the preeminent bad guys of our time. That means a Muslim terrorist, and since bin Laden is clearly out of his reach, we need to focus on his US-based lieutenants. Check out both weapons and I'll bet two or three names jump out as the clear favorites. They might even be on both patents."

"I agree," Hendrickson said, ending the debate. "Next question, do we tell the targets? If we do, they're likely to refuse to cooperate. They may even leave the country, and we'll be right back where we started."

"It's going to be hard to explain it if someone dies and we knew beforehand and didn't protect them."

"I know, Karen, but what choice do we have? Anyway, if we start watching these guys too closely, they'll see us and get spooked. These are not citizens. They're killers, and they expect to be killed themselves at some point, so they're paranoid. Jeff?"

"We put loose surveillance on them, prep the teams based on our best estimates of where they'll be on Tuesday, and count on Mathias and Karen to delay long enough for us to hit in force and get them out. It would be a coup to have a televised rescue after Oklahoma City."

"I agree with Jeff," Karen added, "except for the swarming and scooping them out. Like you said, these guys are paranoid.

And well armed. We might end up with another televised fire-fight instead."

One of the field agents spoke up. "Target the weapon. As soon as the video goes live, we'll have the weapon's perspective on the target. We should be able to backtrack and spot it and disable it before Screenshot fires."

"Good idea," Hendrickson said. "Examine the patent designs and figure out exactly what this thing will look like, and have the necessary means to take it out. Jeff, you and your guys get on that. Karen, you and Mathias are doing good. See what more information you can get from Screenshot, and maybe we can confirm his plans. What else?"

Karen asked, "What are we doing to cover Mathias's kids?" One of the other agents answered.

"We've got twenty-four-hour escort, three shifts. We're watching both areas for any unusual activity, vehicles, etc. We've notified the local police and the campus security, and we're working with them for further coverage."

Unusual activity on a college campus, Karen thought. Wasn't that the usual activity? The coverage was window-dressing anyway. If Screenshot wanted either of his kids, FBI presence would only mean law enforcement fatalities along with whichever kid he targeted. No, their best shot at protecting the Mathias kids, apart from pulling them out and storing them somewhere until this was over, was to get to Screenshot before he had a reason to target them. Or anyone else's kids, for that matter.

Chapter Twenty-one

Seth

As he struggled upstream against the current of departing passengers, Seth scanned the crowd, looking for the familiar blonde hair and smile. Instead, he saw an earnest-looking young man in a blue suit, scanning the passengers and looking down at his hand. When he got to Seth, he checked his hand and then called to him. Seth figured his hand had a picture, and he wondered from where.

"Good afternoon, Mr. Mathias. I trust you had a good flight. I'm Agent Barrows, and I've been assigned to assist you. Do you have any baggage? The others are waiting at the Phish-Net offices, and we'll go directly there if that's okay with you."

"Yeah, fine," Seth said, trying not to seem disappointed. "I just have my carry-on, so we can go."

As they drove, Barrows told Seth what he knew of the plans.

"We're set up for tomorrow. We'll do a quick run-through for you, and then I'll take you to your hotel and get you checked in. I'll pick you up at five AM tomorrow so we're here in plenty of time for the Screenshot e-mail. We'll have breakfast set up."

"What about the judge? Did he sign the order?"

"I don't know anything about that. I just know that the network has been set up for you and a bunch of HQ people. Special Agent Hendrickson from DC will be here. He's running the show. He can answer that question for you."

"And Agent Larsen?"

"She's at Phish-Net now, getting ready. She'll be in charge of the technology."

At the offices, they signed in and were greeted by Hendrickson at the guard desk, then followed him to the conference room where the rest of the team was waiting to review the plans.

While they walked there, Seth asked his only question. "Did the judge sign the order?"

"Here we are," Hendrickson said, opening a door. "Let's discuss that with the others."

Seth took that as a *no*, and stopped short of entering, Barrows almost walking up his back.

"He didn't sign it, did he?" Seth turned and walked across the hallway and stood facing the blank wall for a moment, looking down, his head swiveling back and forth. "Goddamit," he whispered and slammed the wall with the heel of his fist.

Then Larsen was behind him, her hand on his shoulder. "We'll take care of it, I promise you."

He turned his head to look at her and asked, "*Do* you keep your promises?"

"Yes, Mr. ... Seth. I do."

He stared at her for several more seconds and she didn't flinch.

"Let's get this done." He followed her into the conference room.

Meetings done, preparations made, Seth got up to get his third cup of coffee and decided to switch to decaf. He started to cross the gymnasium-sized room to get to the pot, and Karen stopped him.

"Stay here in case he calls. I'll get it."

"Thanks. Decaf. A little milk, a little sugar."

"I know. I've probably seen your coffee ritual about seventeen times now."

They sipped the fresh coffee together and Seth looked at the big digital clock on the wall: 7:22. They had been watching blank monitors since six, as instructed by Screenshot, and nothing had happened. Yet. He hoped the target had done something unusual and was out of range. Maybe he would get a reprieve.

Seth thought the room, with its rows of desks and computer monitors, its perimeter of glass-walled offices, and the conference rooms with their huge flat-panel displays, felt like the Johnson Space Flight Center when *Discovery* launched after the *Challenger* catastrophe. Anxiety seemed to be the predominant feeling, with anticipation and optimism trailing behind. Frustration and impatience were both closing on the outside.

The monitor on the desk in front of him showed a blank blue image, not even a screensaver. He rolled that word over in his head for a moment. Maybe today he could be the Screensaver.

Larsen's desk faced his, butted up against each other. She had a computer and monitor of her own that he couldn't see, mirrored to his to provide backup, and a headset for Internet communications, which he didn't have. There was a murmur of activity in the background, the white noise of twenty-seven agents and technicians moving about and speaking quietly into microphones or to each other. Seth knew that about thirty field agents were covering the likely targets. Local offices were on alert with lists and locations for the other possible targets.

At 7:46, Seth's Blackberry beeped, and just like the *Discovery* launch, the final countdown started.

He typed the web address from the cell phone and entered the familiar chat room environment, this time using the I'm_from_ Missouri user ID, a carefully thought-out name intended to start the conversation on his show-me terms. It would probably be his only chance to dictate terms, and he wanted at least that.

"Good morning, Seth. Are they treating you well there? Coffee. Donuts. Guns. Help yourself to seconds, it's taxpayer money, after all. Yours and mine."

He never misses a chance to let me know who's in control, Seth thought, not in the mood for their electronic sparring. "Get to the point."

"We've got a few moments. Let's chat. But first, let's go over the instructions so there'll be no mistakes. You'll get the video when it's time. Then you'll press the F10 button when I tell you to. Not before. Not after. When. This is a very short window of opportunity, and you have to act quickly. Clear?"

"I'm not making any promises."

"I don't need them. You'll do fine."

Seth didn't answer, determined to avoid any gratuitous conversation and deal strictly with the task at hand. In the pause, he heard Hendrickson whisper to his field teams that there would be little time to react, and to be ready.

"No response, eh? You must be all excited. The chance of a lifetime. The first. We're having some fun, now."

Again, Seth ignored the taunts and waited for the real action to begin. It began.

A new web address appeared with instructions to keep the current chat window open. Seth opened another browser window and typed the address. In the window, an image of part of a building appeared. It was the right end of a three-story brick structure, covered with ivy, minimally landscaped, serene, with no people in view.

"We have video, all teams to ready," Hendrickson said.

"Oh, Christ," Seth blurted.

"What's wrong," Karen asked.

Before Seth replied, the chat window displayed a new message.

"Recognize it?"

"Yes. It's Cascadilla Hall."

"Been there, have you?"

"Yes."

"Which room is his?"

Larsen figured out what was happening and spoke urgently into her headset. "It's his son's dorm at Cornell."

Hendrickson's face came to life, like someone had turned it on. "Call Wes Mathias's agent. Tell him they're targeted. Get them out of there. Now. Use a back or left side entrance. Evacuate the dorm the same way. Get Cornell security alerted. Also the local PD. Where's Cornell?"

"Ithaca, New York," someone responded.

"Get Ithaca PD and NYSP moving. Where's our nearest office?"

"Syracuse."

"Alert them."

On Seth's screen, Screenshot asked again, "Which room is his?"

"Second floor, second from the right." If his typing could have shown inflection, it would have been monotone.

"Center of my screen. Where do you suppose he is right now?"

"Somewhere safe."

"Yes, I suppose that's true. After all, his own father text messaged him earlier where to be during this execution. To stand by because he wanted to talk to him. What could be safer than a father's directions? Oh, wait. Maybe that was me. Do you think they'll get out in time? And which door were they told to use? Not the back one, I hope. Or the side. Maybe the front? That would be good."

Hendrickson read over Seth's shoulder and stepped back to issue more commands. Seth didn't hear them. He heard nothing except the noises generated in his own head, in his heart as he tried to process all of this. The noises coalesced into blind anger.

"You fucking bastard. There's no reason to hurt him. He doesn't fit your profile."

"You're absolutely right. And there won't be any reason to hurt him, will there? My new device is called The Remediator. It's there to remind you of lessons learned."

Before Seth could reply, another web address appeared, and Seth opened a third browser window. The new address showed a video of the front of a luxurious suburban house. The view came from slightly above and to the left. A black Cadillac Escalade was pulling into the driveway, next to a pole with a basketball backstop and net. Three men dressed in dark business suits and ties got out and two went to the front door of the house. The third lit a cigarette and waited at the vehicle, scanning the surroundings.

After several moments, three men emerged from the house, walking in single file. "It's Hamir," someone called.

"Are we sure? You can't see his face clearly at this distance," Hendrickson said.

"That's his house. That's his car. I'll check the surveillance team."

"No time," Hendrickson said out loud, and then spoke rapidly into his headset.

The chat screen displayed a new message.

"Push F10 when he gets in the back seat. Not before. Not after. When."

Seth froze, like he couldn't even read the words. The man was getting in when Karen called, "Seth," and he glanced up at her, then looked back at his screen and pressed the F10 button.

Nothing happened. Seth pressed it again, and again, hammering it with his index finger, yelling, "Why won't this fucking thing work?"

FBI

"East-northeast," Sandovar spoke distinctly into his headset, giving the direction of the weapon to his team. "Have you got it, Castillo?"

"Not yet," the response came over the ear phones. The video image came from Castillo's quadrant.

Agent Sandy Sandovar commanded the six-man sharpshooter squad, and four of his men were positioned to cover Hamir's house with .50 caliber Barrett sniper rifles. Hamir was one of seven high-risk targets taken from the patents, and Sandovar's team became the most important FBI agents in the country at that moment.

"Air one, what do you have from that vector?" Two helicopters with spotters and his remaining snipers held station a mile north and south of the residence.

"Nothing. Wait, there's a cell tower about 3,000 meters west-southwest. No one on it."

"Get in close. Come from the east. Castillo, can you see the tower?"

"I see it, but it's too far. I can't tell what's on it except antennas and shit. Nothing with a barrel or a scope that I can see."

"Air two, break off and come at it from the west."

"Command, air one. I've got a tube mounted just above the second horizontal cross-member, on the northwest vertical. Could be it. Looks like the drawing, and it's pointed toward the house. I don't have a shot yet."

"Air two, do you have it?"

"We're coming in range now. We have to get closer and hover before I can get a steady shot. Four seconds."

"Castillo, can you take the shot?"

"Negative. Too far, bad angle."

"Somebody take the goddam shot!"

Karen

Karen watched him hammering at the button, yelling at it. She'd watched a guard walk around the front of the car, the driver get in, and Hamir step into the car with his right leg, then his left, almost ready for the other guard to close the door, and for the SUV to leave. And she understood what had happened, understood that they had disabled Mathias's F10 key, making sure the FBI was not involved in any assassination no matter what Seth decided. She looked at Hendrickson and saw she was right, his face set, but set in a look of shock, like he was watching a disaster unfold.

"Dave," she said quietly, and he looked at her. With an exaggerated motion, she raised her right arm, index finger extended, and brought it down hard on her own F10 key.

The screen image shook, and a burst of smoke blocked the view. Almost immediately, a huge flash of red and orange shone through the smoke, followed by the sound of an explosion, muted by the low volume settings on all the computers, but permeating every direction.

"Holy shit," someone said, and the whole room burst into activity, everyone moving and speaking at once.

As the target scene cleared, the damage became evident. The big SUV lay on its left side, engulfed in flame. One body lay huddled against the splintered garage door, having apparently been the guard coming around the front of the truck when the explosion occurred. The other three bodies were nowhere in sight, and were likely in or under the wreckage.

"Pull our team back. Way back," Hendrickson ordered into his mic. "Let the locals handle it. Screenshot is to see no hint of us. Everybody clear on that?" They were, and he continued, "Let the local office know to handle this as a normal call-out."

"Seth, are you okay?" Karen asked.

"Huh? Yeah, yeah. I'm fine. He would have killed Wes. Is he okay? Is Rachel?"

"Both of them are fine," Hendrickson said. "Our agents report nothing unusual. In fact, Wes was in class, not his room."

Seth's screen blinked a new message.

"Nice shot, Seth. I knew you could do it. You just needed that little reminder of your place in history. Do you know who that was?"

Seth started to type, "Fuck you. Wes wasn't …" but Larsen came around to his side and stopped him.

"Don't let him know what we're doing, or what we know. Make him tell us information. Don't offer any."

It took him a moment, and then he erased the text and typed, "No."

"You're gonna love this. That was the late Abu Hamir al-Mujahir, member of the Saudi Royal Family, friend to oil barons, and terror mastermind. Oh, and head of the diplomatic mission in Houston, making him immune from prosecution under our laws. You remember immunity, Seth?

"The French recently released him after a sham trial, and believe it or not, he is a US citizen, having been born here while his father was a senior diplomat in their embassy in Washington. He's never been implicated in any activities here, but is believed—no, make that known—to be the financial brains behind most of the money raised by several of your better-known Islami-fascist organizations in recent years. You just rid the world of one of the most important radical Muslims. Now, don't you feel good?"

"No, I don't. I'm going now. Don't ever contact me again."

Before he could press "enter" and send the message, Karen stopped him again. "Keep him talking. We need the live video as long as possible."

Seth erased another message, giving her an angry look, and typed "No," once more.

"No? You should feel great. Oh, I get it, you're pissed about Wes. Relax, he was never in danger. There was no weapon, just a camera. If you hadn't pushed the button, the worst that would have happened is a few minutes of uncertainty after I shut it down and your screen went blank. They will never be targeted, Seth, you have my word on that."

Seth's hands sprang to the keyboard, but Larsen put a hand on his shoulder and squeezed, leaving his opinion of Screenshot's integrity untyped, and offering no reply.

"Nothing to say? No 'thank you'? No appreciation?" Seth's hands trembled, but held firm.

"Don't be petulant. Mr. al-Mujahir might not be Joe Goebbels, but a major coup just the same."

"Seth," Karen said softly, "you've got to say something. Keep this going. The doc is getting his data as long as you do."

He typed, "Congratulations. You've successfully coerced me into murder. No, I don't feel good."

"Oh, look, the Houston Police have arrived. Can justice be far behind? Too late. Justice has already been served."

They all watched as the police screeched to a halt then slowed their approach on foot, not certain of what they were dealing with. It finally occurred to one of them that this was not an accident, and they all became more cautious, scanning for any threat, taking care with each step as they approached the burning wreck.

Screenshot continued his color commentary, like an announcer at a sporting event.

"And now we have the fire fighters. At least they'll be useful. And what happened to your FBI this time, Seth? No helicopters landing dramatically and rescuing everyone? Maybe I should have given better clues, but I really thought the whole bin Laden and al-Zarqawi stuff was enough. Never underestimate the ignorance of government employees."

"So you can get me to do your killing by threatening my family. Is that how you're going to get all your assassins? That doesn't make you very smart or righteous. The just makes you a murdering blackmailer, regardless of your victims."

"You are so naïve. This is all part of my marketing strategy. I will have people lining up for the opportunity once they know they can do it safely, once they know that there is no evidence, nothing that prosecutors could use or juries believe beyond a reasonable doubt. It all goes away as soon as they press the off switch.

"Let me spell it out for you and your FBI friends. Redo was proof of concept, a simple demonstration to show the process works. Glazer and Helter were market research, establishing the availability of buyers and sellers, and the value of the product. Today was go-to-market day. The free trial offer.

"Do you think that William Buchanan would want the opportunity you just had? Don't know who he is? Ask Glazer. Oops, can't do that. Glazer's dead, and Bill is no doubt happy to see his twin daughters avenged. You don't think that Adele Cresteen's family and friends wouldn't have done Redo? He burned her and her family alive in their own home when they tried to interfere with his drug business. Look at the lottery applicants. Thousands of them. I even made a profit on my market research. My problem won't be finding applicants, it will be picking them."

"How are you going to make money off any of them? They can't afford your fee. I wouldn't have paid it."

"No more fees, Seth. Everyone gets a free shot."

"You must be very rich."

"I don't need to be. We're going commercial with this now. That's right, pay-per-view. Fifty dollars for the opportunity to watch it live. That's about the price for one of those silly wrestling extravaganzas."

Seth looked at Karen and then Hendrickson. Everyone had the same astonished look. Pay-per-view? This was a promo to sell tickets?

"You're doing this to get fifty bucks from some pervert? You're killing people as entertainment?"

"Not just *some* pervert. Thousands of perverts. Tens of

thousands of perverts. A hundred thousand perverts. And not killing just any people. Killing people the audience can root to die. Five million dollars per week. Production costs maybe one tenth of that. A real cash cow."

"He can't do it," Scoggins said. "How can he collect fifty dollars from each one without us finding him?"

Seth thought that was a very good point. "Do you accept VISA?"

"Why? You want a ticket? You get a free lifetime pass. And I didn't need VISA or any other traditional financial tools to get my fees, did I?"

Seth thought about that for a moment. "Digital gold?"

"Offshore banking for the masses. Don't you love the Internet?"

"Not for this. Not for some demented asshole murderer to use."

"Gee, Seth, with these four, and counting West Virginia, that makes eight dead bodies that you are responsible for. What does that make you?"

"Let's take it to a judge and jury and see what they say. I had no choice. Either time."

"Really? So those four dead men on your screen are less important to their parents than your son is to you? Why don't you go and apologize to the parents and families of those men, and then tell me how much better than me you are. Tell them it was their son or yours. Except, it wasn't. Sleep on that, Saint Seth."

"He's right," Seth said to no one in particular.

No one moved; no one spoke. They looked at their monitors, or at the floor, or at Hendrickson. Some looked at Seth, waiting for some clue, some guidance on how these next few moments would play out.

"I killed four strangers because I thought my son was in danger. I traded their lives for his. And the thing is, I'd do it again. What does that make me?" He looked up at Karen.

His face slowly collapsed, growing old, like time-lapse photography, and Karen thought he might actually break down and cry. She started to speak to him, but Hendrickson stopped her with a hand gesture.

"You didn't kill anyone, Mr. Mathias."

At first, Seth didn't seem to understand his words, and then came to the wrong conclusion. "Thanks, but you don't need to cover for me. I faced this once before. I can do it again."

"No one is trying to cover for you. You really didn't kill anyone. Your F10 key was disabled. That's why it didn't work when you tried."

"Disabled? Then what happened?"

"We had a backup keyboard on-line as a precaution," he said. "Agent Larsen assessed the situation and made the decision to fire the weapon when it seemed a dorm full of college students was in imminent danger. She took the lesser of two evils, and we'll pay the price for that, whatever it is."

Seth looked at Karen, astonished. "You did it?"

Karen nodded once, going along with Hendrickson's little white lie about precaution.

Chapter Twenty-two

Karen

"Goddammit, Larsen. You had no authority to act. Do you have any idea the position you've put the bureau in? An agent murders four foreign nationals, all live on the Internet, recorded by thousands of viewers, and in a bureau facility using bureau equipment. Jesus Christ, I've never heard of anything so outrageous in my career. You should be prosecuted."

The assistant director glared at her. Karen had expected some problems, but nothing of this magnitude. Did they remember a dorm full of college students?

Dave Hendrickson tried to come to her rescue. "Sir, Agent Larsen really had no choice. The circumstances—"

"And you, Hendrickson. You're supposed to be in charge of this, and you give her a live keyboard? She's not even a field agent. What were you thinking?"

Karen maintained a calm exterior. Inside, she thought about pulling her weapon and pistol whipping this once-an-agent-now-a-bureaucrat jerk who hadn't been there, hadn't been responsible for lives, hadn't had to make judgments with only seconds to act. It was a good thing they made everyone check their guns on arrival.

"Sir, I acted when it was clear that I had to. We were presented with an untenable choice. I took control of the situation."

"Who was controlling you, Agent Larsen? Apparently not Hendrickson, there."

"Sir, I did not and do not require control in my own facility. As I have done my entire career, I followed procedure and took action based on the circumstances and on our sworn duty. You have not mentioned a college dormitory full of students at possible risk. A decision had to be made. Doing nothing was a decision, a decision that as far as we knew would cost many innocent lives."

"Yes, well, that career is somewhat tenuous, wouldn't you say? And what risk? There was no weapon, only a camera."

"We had no way of knowing that. If there had been one, and I hadn't acted, we would be having a very different meeting today. Every indication from Screenshot, including the immediate communications and the thirteen bodies he'd amassed, suggested very strongly that he was going to blow up that dorm if Mathias didn't act. Since we had precluded Mathias from acting, I did."

"I don't mean to sound callous, but if Screenshot had done that, it would be on his head, not ours. That is the difference. 'Screenshot kills students' versus 'FBI kills Saudi Royal Family Member and Diplomat.' Which headline do you think works better for the bureau."

She couldn't get any more screwed, so what the hell. She stood up, gathered her papers and mentally waved goodbye to her career. They couldn't fire her over this, not unless they wanted even more damning headlines. But they could, and would, dead-end her in Pittsburgh, probably re-organizing some day to put her in charge of network administration with Roger as her boss.

"Where the hell do you think you're going?"

"Back to Pittsburgh, and back to work. Yes, I am aware that there are four dead foreign nationals. I was there. Live. But those foreign nationals were four thugs. So would I trade their lives for one innocent American college student? In a minute.

"And here's the headline you should consider. 'FBI enables Screenshot to murder college students.' Or maybe 'FBI fires agent who saved college students lives.' How do those work for the Bureau?"

And she left.

Philip

"Philip, you've been to Miami what, four times in the last six months to meet with these guys. The due diligence is done. The lead investor wants you in, but they're closing Monday, with you or without you. You've got to get your head around this and decide."

He'd decided long ago, after the first trip, in fact. He liked the people, he liked the idea, but most of all, he liked the location. The other trips provided intelligence for planning, and a paper trail should anyone ever question his itinerary. This meeting to discuss his investment in the start-up would get him on record as still considering, being cautious, justifying his previous meetings. But he knew the money was going in. It was only $4 million. He'd turn a profit even if the venture failed.

"Yes, all right Greg, I say we go for it. Tell them we're in, and get me the papers to sign. Do they want me in Miami for the closing? I'm busy Tuesday, but I can do it Monday."

The waiter cleared their lunch dishes and asked if anyone wanted coffee. Philip looked to his left to answer, and saw the TV in the lounge. Someone in Arab robes was speaking to reporters. More coverage of yesterday, he guessed.

"What's going on?" Philip asked the waiter, pointing toward the screen with the paper in his left hand.

"It's about that Hamir guy that was supposed to be blown up by Screenshot. That's him talking. Turns out the FBI knew about it and warned him. He put a look-alike stooge out and got him blown away instead. That's a hell of a job. Hope it came with a life insurance policy."

Philip tensed, and if anyone had been paying him any attention, they would have seen his jaw muscles flutter as he ground his teeth in an effort to control himself.

"No coffee for me," he said after he suppressed the growl that grew in his throat and got his voice under control. "I've got to wrap this up and get to another appointment. You guys can go ahead and finish up the details. Let my secretary know if I need to be there Monday." He hesitated for a moment and then continued. "Although on second thought, I'd rather not go. There are things I need to take care of here."

Used to his comings and goings, his frenzied lifestyle, the lawyer and accountant thought nothing of it and prepared to drink coffee and discuss the deal at a leisurely pace, billing Philip.

Philip didn't walk the eight blocks to his condo, he stomped them, releasing some of the pressure that he felt building from his gut outward. He would be laughed at, he would be made a fool, outwitted by the FBI and a raghead. Four dead men as a joke. A joke on him. Someone would pay for this.

He knew his list of weapons by heart, and he reviewed them in his head, starting with the two primed and ready for Tuesday. The Lesso-lator and the Well-Don. It wouldn't matter which weapon he used, either way an organized-crime boss would occupy a morgue table come Tuesday night, and either the Miami or the Detroit medical examiner would be putting in overtime. Both weapons were positioned and enabled. Re-targeting either would be impossible.

The other nineteen, while not in place, were in storage or concealed in controlled locations waiting final prep. Getting any of them to Hamir would be a monumental task, especially in the time available, and with the security he would no doubt add. Hamir would take time, and probably a new weapon as well. Philip would wait. Right now, someone had to pay, and the list of possibilities was very short.

Sicals

It had taken forty-three hours, but it was less time than he'd expected. The raw power at his hands impressed Sicals. He had never before had the luxury of such a resource, not even at the height of his QHE research. Knowing the theory of modern computers didn't adequately prepare him for the reality when it came to completing his project. He watched his screen and saw what the woman saw, or what she would see on her computer screen when she woke up and went to work in about seven hours. He needed the last piece of the puzzle, and she would provide it, and then the fun could begin.

She was the assistant comptroller, and it took many hours of intense research to find her name and e-mail address before he could even start his forty-three-hour campaign. Before that, it had taken sixteen hours of programming and testing to create the signal that he could correlate to get access to her server, and then waiting for her to get to work to implement it.

His tracking program would find her, he had known, but signal correlation required two things: a signal, and something to correlate it to. In her case, he had no video patterns to track, no way of knowing what she typed into her keyboard or scanned on the Internet. His solution was as simple as it was elegant: get her to send a signal at a precise moment, then send another hundred thousand or so correlated signals, and he would be in her computer, ready to install his keyboard trap and monitor her keystrokes.

Getting a microsecond accurate signal required that her computer send it. His new program, R^3, as he called it, stood for Return Receipt Requested. He had sent her an e-mail with a virus he'd developed and embedded in the standard return receipt request. When she opened the e-mail, she would get the pop-up box that asked if she wanted to send a return receipt, as requested by the sender. His program sent the receipt whether she accepted or not, and her computer continued to re-send the return receipt at very specific times that he could decode from his end. Forty-three hours later, he was in.

Tomorrow when she came to work, she would go on-line and go about her daily business. She would have no clue that someone was recording every keystroke, and that soon enough, her password would open that business to an old enemy.

Chapter
Twenty-three

Seth

Back at Oakland airport Friday afternoon, Seth waited for Karen's flight, but without a sign this time. Her voice on the phone when they'd spoken the night before told him it wasn't appropriate, and he wondered what had happened since he'd returned to California after the disastrous events in Pittsburgh. She'd claimed she was fine, even tried to sound upbeat, when she told him she was flying in to meet with Sicals and review progress.

He almost missed her, subconsciously looking for the blonde hair and scanning right past the Asian woman in a tan beret. His gaze was four people to the right of her when the familiar face registered in his mind and he looked back. She smiled and waved when she saw him, still looking fresh and cheerful, but with some melancholy tint, like she was tired and concealing it.

"No sign?"

"Not this time," Seth answered. "Now that I'm a not-so-special agent, I'm keeping a low profile. What's with the hat?"

"Me, too. I carry it with me so I can disappear a little if I want to. I guess that makes us a team."

Seth wasn't sure how to take that, but he knew she wasn't celebrating.

"Anything wrong?"

"No, just tired from the flight. From all of this. The repercussions from the Hamir stuff have kept everyone on edge, then he turns up alive and it all has to be rehashed again. The bureaucrats take credit for saving him, reminding everyone that it's us lowly agents who screwed up. Just another week of Washington law enforcement. I hope Uncle Morgan has made some progress because I'm ready for this to be over."

They reached his truck where he'd managed a parking spot with an empty space next to the passenger side. He put her bag in the crew cab behind the front seats and helped her up, getting a smile and a thank-you in return.

"We'll get you checked in and then I'll buy you dinner. I know they didn't feed you on the plane."

"That's okay. I think I'll just go to bed. We'll meet for breakfast and then visit Dr. Sicals."

"Breakfast it is. I'll be there at seven."

He arrived at 6:30. Twenty minutes later, she came into the hotel restaurant and smiled when she saw him there. Today her hair flashed against a black jacket, like a light in the dark.

"Good morning," she said, and seemed to mean it.

Seth stood and held her chair for her. "Eggs Benedict on the way. Coffee and juice right here. Better than room service."

"I've been stereotyped. Will I have to eat Eggs Benedict every morning?"

"Only if we eat out. I can't do Hollandaise, so it's omelets for our breakfasts at my place."

"Then Eggs Benedict it will be, won't it?" She smiled, looking to Seth like a teacher encouraging a particularly slow student.

The waitress brought the meals, and Seth concentrated on eating his food instead of his foot until it was time to go.

The key still worked, and so did Sicals, sitting at his computer. He barely acknowledged Seth's arrival. Then he saw Karen and perked up a bit.

"Miss Larsen, I didn't know you would be here. I'm getting used to your partner, and you are a welcome change."

There was an insult in there somewhere, but Seth kept silent.

"Dr. Sicals," Karen replied, striding towards him with a smile and an extended hand. "It is good to see you again. Seth tells me you've made some progress."

"Progress? Yes, of course we have made progress. Your computers are wonderful, and we shall have results soon."

"Soon enough?"

"Yes. Right now I can tell you that your Screenshot is using a server in Bhutan, and his video is streamed through E-nunC8 servers exclusively. Neither of those matters to my programs, only the pipes in and out. I should have those identified later this morning. We will start packet analysis by Sunday at the latest. Again, we'll run the program for testing and for baseline data, and be ready to go live on Tuesday."

"That's good news. What can I do to help?"

"Now? Nothing, really. I have everything I need to get done. On Tuesday, you will need to keep the event going as long as possible so I will have sufficient data to analyze."

"What are you working on now?"

"Just monitoring the data-mining and doing some of my own puttering around. Nothing really interesting to anyone except me."

"Can you show me what's going on? And some more about how the programs work?"

"Certainly, Miss Larsen, I would be happy to. Why don't you just make yourself a cup of coffee in that fine machine that Mr. Mathias was kind enough to bring me. I'll go ahead and close out the other things I'm working on. They would be of no interest to you, just the obsessions of a scientific mind."

Seth spent the rest of the day watching them play, Dr. Sicals entranced by Karen, and Karen enjoying the lesson and the attention, flirting just enough to keep Sicals under her spell. By the end of it, Karen said the jet lag had caught up with her and declined Seth's dinner invitation. They arranged to meet the next day and take a break from work to do some sightseeing before Karen had to fly back.

❖   ❖   ❖

Seth picked her up early on Saturday morning, and they arrived at The Duck Club in the Bodega Bay Lodge in time to get one of the only three tables by the window overlooking Doran Beach. This time the concierge at Karen's hotel got it right, both the recommendation for lunch, and the advice to get there early for the view. From their seats, Seth could look left and see the Pacific about a Tiger Woods drive and three-wood away. The analogy was apropos because a little farther left the Bodega Harbor Golf Links ran along the ocean, just a duck hook away from a penalty stroke. Seth didn't play golf, but he'd written enough golf vacation fluff pieces to know the language.

Karen's view angled more northwest, toward Bodega Bay and the upscale shops and marina that you would associate with waterfront in Sonoma County. They'd followed the shore coming up, driving through the spectacular redwoods of Mount Tamalpais and Muir Woods, and then the Shoreline Highway 1 along the beach and through the woods to get to Bodega Bay. The wine country would come on the trip back, when they planned to head inland and then south through Santa Rosa and Sonoma, stopping at a vineyard or two along the way.

Their lunch conversation was quiet, mostly about the remarkable scenery of the drive and the plans for the rest of the day. Seth thought Karen looked somewhat recovered, less worn. He hated to interrupt their interlude, but he had things to discuss, and she would be a captive audience for a few more hours.

"So, Agent Larsen, just how bad did they beat you up back in DC?"

Karen's face scrunched a little, her head moved back just the smallest bit while she adjusted to this abrupt jerk back to reality.

"Beat me up? What do you mean?'

"Come on. On the phone the other night, you sounded like a boxer after losing on points. And when I picked you up, you moved like you had a flat tire. What's going on? It's about Hamir, isn't it?"

"If I am out of sorts, it's just that this whole case has got me tired. And worried. Screenshot demonstrated a willingness to do things that we hadn't considered. This whole thing has escalated, if that's possible. If Sicals doesn't come through, we're screwed. So, yeah, maybe I'm not as perky as usual. I'll get over it."

"That all may be true, but that's not what's got you down. I think about this stuff, as you know. And I think you pulled the trigger on Hamir without authorization. I think the whole blackmail-the-assassin thing caught everyone by surprise, and no one knew what to do. There was no plan or procedure, and everyone there froze. Except you. You made a decision and you acted. And I think that when it turned out that there was no threat, someone had to take the fall, and they elected you."

Karen didn't say anything. She stirred her coffee and took a sip.

"Hendrickson said you assessed the situation and made the decision to fire the weapon. He said your keyboard was enabled and ready. My question is, why did the FBI, emphasis on bureau as in bureaucratic, leave the decision to a, pardon the expression, computer geek? Why didn't Hendrickson make the decision? Why didn't he have the keyboard? He's the senior guy. This is his case."

Karen still said nothing, looking out over the Pacific, her face blank. Seth let the silence sit for a few moments and then tried to help her wrap it up.

"You got blamed, didn't you? Nobody cares that there was a weapon pointed at my son and his friends, do they? There wasn't a weapon, and they think on Wednesday that you should have known that on Tuesday. They weren't there, and they're hindsighting you. An FBI computer sent the signal to kill some foreign nationals going about their lawful business, and there is no justification for that in their minds. So why are you still a special agent?"

She looked away from the ocean and directly at Seth, as close to tears as Seth had ever seen her.

"Because the alternative is worse, in their opinion. There's going to be a headline no matter what, and they would rather it focus on Screenshot, leaving the impression that he did it, than fire me and have the truth come out. So I've still got a job, but it's clear that my FBI career ends in Pittsburgh, whether it's tomorrow or ten years from now."

"Are you going to stay? Put in those ten years, knowing that's all there is?"

"If that's all there is, then no, I won't. But I'm betting that Uncle Morgan can change all that. His success will more than offset the Hamir thing, especially since Hamir didn't die. I'll be back."

Seth took his turn looking out at the ocean while he thought about that, adding this information to his inventory and considering the ramifications.

"So you really are off the reservation with Sicals. Otherwise, his success would be the FBI's success, not yours. You would still be buried."

Karen slumped slightly and mouthed the words "aw shit" clearly enough that Seth could lip-read.

"They don't know about Sicals, do they?"

"Yeah, they know about him. They know about his history, and they want nothing to do with him. I snuck him onto the system through some of our commercial sites and turned him loose. Sooner or later someone's going to figure it out, and he better have some results before then or being fired will be the least of my problems. So now you know. Will I see this in the *Mercury News* tomorrow?"

Seth flinched at that. "No, of course not. Why would you think I would do that?"

"You're a reporter. That's what reporters do."

"Listen, Karen, I'm a writer. I happen to work for the *Mercury News* right now, but that doesn't make me a reporter."

"All reporters are writers."

"Not true. I'm not reporting a story, I'm writing one, and it will get written the way I see it when I'm ready. And I see you as one of the heroes of this story. Maybe the only hero."

She went back to looking out at the ocean, her expression just a little sad.

"You've got to remember," he added, "I have some experience trying to do the right thing and causing unintended consequences."

She looked back at Seth and said, "Thanks. I did forget that. Now I think we better get to that vineyard tour and slam down some Cabernet before this gets maudlin."

Karen

With two hours until Seth would be back to pick her up for dinner, Karen took her time and enjoyed the anticipation, the uncertainty, treating herself to a little pampering before their night out. She slipped out of her shoes and slacks and had the bath running, and a mouthful of toothpaste when her cell phone rang.

"Ffit," she muttered and spit into the bathroom sink, leaving an unrinsed toothpaste tingle in her mouth.

"I know what Sicals is up to," Seth said. "Turn on your TV to Headline News. I'll be back in a couple of minutes. What room are you in?"

"610. Give me a minute to get dressed."

It took several minutes, and by the time Seth knocked, she was fully dressed and up to speed on the news.

"They haven't read the story yet. Just the news ticker along the bottom," she told Seth when she let him in.

They watched the ticker in silence, waiting for it to come around again. Before it did, the news reader picked up the story.

"In Stockholm today, the Nobel Prize Committee acknowledged that they have been the target of a computer hacker, and that funds have been diverted from their accounts into several of the anonymous and untraceable so-called digital gold accounts. While officials refused further comment, authoritative sources in the Cyber Crimes Division at Interpol put the amount of the theft at seventeen million dollars. These same officials commented on the digital gold process, whereby money can be stored, transferred, and spent with no oversight or regulation. Once into these accounts, they say, the money is unrecoverable."

Looking like she'd caught her husband cheating, Karen said, "I guess we better go see Uncle Morgan."

They drove in silence, and when they got to Sicals', found a dark and empty apartment. Karen saw any chance of catching Screenshot disappear, along with the remainder of her career.

"Where do you suppose he went?" Seth asked.

"With seventeen million in untraceable cash? Any goddamn where he wants to. Look around and see if he left *anything* useful behind."

Sicals' computer was still there, still on. Karen saw that it still monitored Screenshot data, and she untensed ever so slightly. Maybe the Screenshot search could go on. She had the software, and everything worked so far. Could she finish without him?

Seth finished his tour and found her sitting at the computer, staring at rows of numbers scrolling from bottom to top, like she actually could read and understand them, like she found some solace in their very existence.

"I can't see anything missing. Not even clothes. But with that kind of money, he's probably planning a new wardrobe. Are you okay?"

"No, I'm *not* okay." She flung her arms up and let them drop, her hands flopping on Sicals' desk. She looked up at Seth, wanting to cry. "Do you *remember* our lunch conversation? Sicals was supposed to resurrect my career. Now I'll be lucky if I don't end up in prison."

Seth ignored her anger and continued gently. "Let's check the computer for any travel reservation or anything else he might have done on-line. Maybe that will give us a clue where he went."

"*No*. Let it run. It's working on baseline data analysis, and it might get through the process and give us results. I don't want to take a chance on crashing the program and leaving us with nothing. Maybe this was his going away present."

"What, then? You have any ideas?"

"I've got several, but they all involve close combat with a crazy old man."

"Any useful ideas?"

"No. The guy's a hermit. His only contacts were computer geeks with names like buzzsaw and sparkle333 or something. I don't know where to find them, and it's not real likely any of them want to cooperate with the FBI if I did. He's estranged from any family. We can check cab companies and see if anyone picked him up, but that's just going to get us the time and the station he went to—bus, train, or plane. He's probably using cash. God knows he has enough of it now, so tracking him will be impossible without huge manpower commitment."

She thought for a moment and added, "Let's go see if Arthur knows anything."

On the trudge up the stairs, her next thought was, I am totally screwed.

❖   ❖   ❖

Arthur answered the door, smiling and happy to see them.

"Ah, the children are here. The doc said you would probably be coming around. Come in, come in. You're just in time for coffee and cookies."

"You saw him? Where did he say he was going?"

"Going? Why, nowhere."

As he stepped away from the door and signaled for them to enter with an arm flourish, Karen jumped and her hand went to her mouth, covering the little "Oh!" that escaped like she'd been pinched on the butt.

"I guess you heard the news," Sicals said, a mug in one hand and a cookie in the other.

Before she could comment, Arthur interjected. "What news? You didn't tell me there was news, Doc."

"It's nothing, really, Arthur. It's just that I've come into a bit of money. And I expect my, um, niece and her husband have come to try to help me manage it. Isn't that right, dear?"

"Uncle Morgan, it's just that your withdrawal was a little premature, and the accountants think you should put it back for the time being. Where it will be safe."

"Nonsense. It's perfectly safe where it is. When your accountants have paid me my due, I might refund a balance. But let's not talk about that right now, shall we? Arthur was just telling me about his recent experience with the rent control commission. Fascinating stuff. Come. Sit. We can discuss all of that later."

Karen's willingness to play this game was short-lived, and she glared hard at Sicals, without any movement in response to his invitation. After a few moments of that, with Arthur looking back and forth between the two like it was a shouting match instead of a staring contest, Sicals broke and said, "Yes, well, maybe it's time to go. I've a lot to do, and these two are bound to be a nuisance until they've said their piece. Wonderful dinner, Arthur. We must do this again sometime. But next time, we'll go to a fancy restaurant. I'm buying. I can afford it now."

Sicals led the way down to his apartment, stepping on one stair and then bringing the other foot to the same one, doubling the time it took to negotiate their way to the bottom, and increasing Karen's impatience and anger proportionally.

"I ought to arrest you right now!" she said when they got into the apartment.

"Yes, Miss Larsen, I expect you should. But you see, that wouldn't do anyone any good. It certainly won't get the money back. There is only one thing that will do that, and it's not your concern."

"Not my concern? Everything you do is my concern until we've got Screenshot. And anything you did using access that I provided is more than my concern. It's my responsibility. I can't believe you abused the opportunity I gave you like this."

"Opportunity? To use some simple code to muscle information from machines? That hardly ranks with my years of research and my discoveries, Miss Larsen. No one is going to even notice my involvement in this, let alone give me back my reputation. You may think me eccentric, but that doesn't make me stupid. The opportunity was always yours. The opportunity to do what no one else will be able to: identify Screenshot. It is your reputation that would soar, Miss Larsen. You would be the one getting the prizes, whatever the FBI gives out to its minions. I would be forgotten in a week."

Karen said nothing, knowing he was right, only surprised that he'd figured it out. And more than a little ashamed of herself. But it was too late to worry about any of that, now.

"None of that excuses the theft of seventeen million dollars. You are now a criminal, Dr. Sicals, and it is my job to call you to account. I have no choice but to arrest you and take my chances with my role in this."

"Yes, that would be a law enforcement coup, choose to capture the crazy old man and let Screenshot go. And make no mistake about it, if I am not personally monitoring my programs, Screenshot will get away."

"I'll have to take my chances there, as well. The program is running, and I have the source code. We should be able to complete the process."

"You misunderstand my participation. Every four hours, the program asks for my password. Without it, the program will terminate itself and erase any data that it can access. That gave me a bit of concern when you crashed the system to place your little keyboard tracer, but fortunately it came up again before the deadline. So you do have a choice, don't you? There are always choices, Miss Larsen, and now you must make yours. Screenshot, or myself."

Chapter
Twenty-four

Karen

Somewhere over Nevada, or maybe Idaho, Karen finally acknowledged the situation: everything was officially out of control. She'd never controlled Screenshot, so that part of it was no surprise. It was actually the one bright spot, the one aspect of her life trending towards control.

Sicals was fully out of control, and now she knew he'd been that way all along, happy to accommodate her agenda, unwilling to relinquish his own. She had two concerns. First, could his crimes be traced back to her? She knew the answer: if they looked hard enough. And eventually they would. So it wasn't a matter of if she would be screwed, but when.

Which led to her second concern: how to get the money put back. Sicals made that clear, and all but $900,608.87 would be returned immediately upon granting one small request: give him his Nobel Prize. He would share it with von Klitzing. The $900,000 plus was half of the prize money, compounded annually since 1985, and he figured they owed him that.

He did concede to delay any ultimatums to the Nobel Committee until after the next Screenshot assassination. Otherwise, it wouldn't take long for her bosses to connect his name with her previous requests and reports, and from there to learn the truth and shut down the program. She needed the Screenshot success before the Nobel Prize hit the fan.

The hardest control issue to accept was herself. She was trending out of control in a totally unexpected and undesirable way: Mathias.

Their afternoon together, the air between them cleared by the lunch conversation, had been, well, glorious. The best she'd had in recent memory. There'd been laughter and stories and sharing and wine. Plenty of wine at the two vineyard tours they had taken. Enough wine that Seth had taken her hand while walking through the grape arbor, providing support and signaling a developing intimacy. It was the wine, she thought, knowing it wasn't true.

The drive back after that tour had been tinted with anticipation. Where was this going? How serious would it get? And when? Would dinner that evening be the prelude to something more that night? At the time, these thoughts were pleasant, fun to express with harmless flirting, the expected answers all welcome. And then Sicals blew everything up, and who knew if the mood would ever strike again. When Seth had dropped her at the airport, there was little emotion between them, just a fog of sadness.

The plane finally landed in Pittsburgh, after the stop in Chicago, and put her back in control of that little part of her life.

Seth

Dag Vellvort understood the value of publicity, and had been accused more than once of courting it. As Seth read the article in the Sunday *San Jose Mercury News*, he guessed that old Dag wasn't happy about this particular story. Among other endeavors, Dag chaired the Nobel Prize Financial Oversight Committee. The criticisms were totally unfair, Seth knew. Fort Knox would probably yield to a determined assault by Uncle Morgan.

Seth sipped the last of his coffee while he considered what the newspaper postulated, and how far off it was. Sicals had told them that once he had found his way into the Nobel system, and found a likely identity to co-opt, the rest was easy. He'd simply set up thirty-three accounts at The Gold Standard, one of the digital gold providers, and started making transfers of random amounts. Over the fifty-one hours that he'd maintained access, his automated program made 386 transfers, about one every ten minutes, and would have kept running until the money ran out if someone at one of the affected banks hadn't noticed transfers at some very odd hours and investigated.

Seth knew The Gold Standard from his digital gold research. One of the newer players, TGS had enjoyed respectable initial growth, and then leveled off, well below the publicly stated goals of the venture capital company that financed its launch. Their strategy had been to bring digital gold to the masses, to make opening accounts and transferring funds as painless as using a credit card, becoming the VISA of the digital age.

Sicals didn't fit the profile of the TGS target market, small account holders using it like a debit card, only without the bank trail. He used TGS because of Screenshot, telling Karen, "If they can't find him, they won't find me."

The theft story had made the front page, with Dag's picture prominent, but below the fold. When Seth turned to the continuation on page seven, he found his own article on digital gold reprinted as a sidebar. It had been, what, ten days since he wrote that? It seemed a lot longer, like time was moving slower. In reality, he knew it was events moving faster. Two sides of the same coin.

According to the story, TGS refused comment, refused access, and refused cooperation. Seth wondered at this unwanted publicity. Did they view it like the famous public relations mantra—any press is good press—or were they hoping it would go away so they could get on with justifying their poor results to the stockholders? The influx of tens of thousands of new accounts must be just what the venture capitalists ordered. No wonder they weren't cooperating. Screenshot had just laid the golden egg for them.

This might be a story, he realized. How does a respectable business deal with perfectly legal, but morally reprehensible, revenue?

The phone rang after his chicken salad dinner, left over from his chicken salad lunch. He didn't recognize the caller ID and when he clicked the Send button, he was pleasantly surprised to find Karen on the other end.

"Hi. I just got home and wanted to let you know I made it back okay."

"I'm glad. Just got home? Was the flight delayed?"

"No, I just had some things to do at the office."

Seth thought about that in the context of the Sicals revelations. "Making sure the Sicals tracks are covered?" he said, trying to make a joke of it.

"Whatever," she answered, and he realized his response hadn't been as clever as he'd intended. "Anyway," she continued, "I'm back, and thanks for your help."

"You're doing the right thing, whether your bosses realize it or not. See it through. I'll help any way I can."

"Thanks. I'm sorry for the way I acted last night. The whole Sicals thing really caught me off guard, and I guess I wasn't very pleasant to be around."

"Is Sicals' program still running?" he asked.

"Yes," she answered. "There's no reason for anyone to make the connection between Sicals and the Nobel theft, and they probably never will unless he goes public."

"Well, we should be a lot closer after Tuesday, and then it won't matter."

"Trust me, unless Sicals puts the money back, it will matter. At best, getting Screenshot will cancel out my letting Sicals use our resources to do his hacking, and I'll only get fired. Without Screenshot results, I could face some serious charges. Even jail for aiding in an Internet fraud."

Seth thought a change of subject might keep the conversation going longer.

"You want to know about my day? It had to be better than yours."

He filled her in on the article in the morning paper and his decision to examine the story from the business angle.

"Rather than approach them directly like every reporter out there, I'll use my history of writing about digital gold and go through the venture capital firm that's the lead on their financing. It's called Obsidian Capital. One of their previous start-ups was E-nunC8, the firm Sicals says owns the streaming video servers that Screenshot uses. Maybe I'll probe a little there as well. They're down in Menlo Park, a forty-five minute drive from here. I'll call tomorrow and see if I can get in to see anyone."

"Good luck with it. Will you be around Tuesday for the next one?"

"I was going to skip it. Maybe see the film at eleven, or whatever. Why? Do you want me to baby-sit Uncle Morgan?"

"There's that. But I wanted to know in case I want to get in touch with you after."

Seth paused to consider that, and decided to schedule his day around her. "Listen, I'll bring Sicals some breakfast and spend the day with him. That way I'll be available to help if you need me, and we can talk after."

"Thanks. I have a feeling that I'm going to need it."

Chapter
Twenty-five

Philip

Philip was working at his desk in his home office when the phone rang, and the caller ID displayed Obsidian, his venture capital firm.

"Hello, Mr. Hurst. It's Sylvia. I have a Mr. Seth Mathias calling …"

Philip's comprehension of her statement ended with Mathias's name, and he asked her to repeat what she'd said. He wanted a meeting?

"Did he say what it's about?"

"He said it was about The Gold Standard. I think he's a reporter. Do you want me to transfer him to Sandy at the PR firm?"

Philip tried to fight an unfamiliar feeling: fear. It caused an unusual reaction for him: indecision. How had Mathias found him? What did he know? And just as importantly, what did he want?

"No, I'll meet with him. Is the executive conference room available today?"

"Mr. Wesley has a lunch meeting scheduled, but he'll be out and everything cleaned by two."

"Fine. Go ahead and set it up for then. I'll be in at one. Have Sandy send over a complete media kit. And have someone work up some figures and talking points so I'm briefed beforehand."

Philip hung up and waited, not moving. He waited while the

fear and indecision leached out of him, as he forced himself to think, to consider, to understand. Mathias wanted to talk about TGS. That made some sense—Philip had read his article on digital gold, so he knew Mathias covered that. But why did he call Philip about it? Why not call TGS directly? He would be the obvious choice for a reporter. They had the facts and figures at hand. They would have the company responses prepared.

Maybe that was it. Maybe Mathias realized that, and didn't want canned responses. But why choose me? There are six partners here, and we don't advertise which partner handles which investments. How had he known TGS was mine?

There were too many questions, too many hows, and too many ifs, and too many whys. But they all had the same answer, and he would discover it sometime after two PM.

Philip tried to concentrate on the FAQs and figures in front of him. Tried to get ready and appear to be the fully informed and confident money man, ready to explain to the world why digital money was the greatest idea since paper money. His concentration kept slipping, and the answers on the page got displaced by questions in his mind, questions that no talking points could prep him for.

Sylvia came in to clear the remnants of the roast beef sandwich she'd ordered for him, and to get the room set for a visitor. It was a quarter to two, she reminded him. "Yes, thanks," he said, and went to the men's room to clean up.

What did Mathias know? How did he find out? What did he want? The questions followed him down the hall and kept him company while he washed his hands and rinsed his face and put his tie straight. Show time, he said to himself, a reminder that this was an act, and he was an actor. *Break a leg.*

Sylvia knocked lightly and opened the conference room door without waiting for a reply.

"Mr. Mathias is here, Mr. Hurst," she said as she stepped aside so Seth could enter the room.

Philip stood, his hand out to shake, a sincere smile on his face, and all remnants of anxiety gone. In its place stood a confident and wealthy entrepreneur, Hugo Boss-suited, Bruno Magli-shoed, and Jerry Garcia-tied, the last for that hint of Silicon Valley rebellion.

"Seth Mathias. It is a pleasure to meet you. I read all of your work in the *Mercury News,* and I was impressed by the digital gold piece. Good, solid research, no judgments or politics, just a fair presentation of the facts. And reprinted yesterday. Your bosses must have liked it as well."

"Thank you. I'm flattered. Especially coming from someone like you."

"Like me? What about me?" he asked.

"An expert on the subject. Someone who knows enough to bet his money on the business model."

Philip grimaced inside and wondered how he would make it through the interview if he was going to interpret every question as an accusation.

"And *not* know enough so we lose that money more times than win," Philip chuckled to cover what he thought must be obvious distress. "What would you like to know, Mr. Mathias? And why come to me? I am just the slightly informed money man. Why not go to the source? To TGS directly?"

"Call me Seth, please. And I came to you because I think you're the man with the answers. After all, you're The Wizard."

Another jolt, like someone stomped on his toe and he could follow the pain as it shot up through the nerves from his foot to his brain, he could trace its progress with the physical sensations. He does know, Philip thought. Only a few insiders ever called him that name. Who had he talked to? Why is he here?

"That was then, Seth, and this is now. I'm just a glorified banker, trying to make money from money."

"And that's why I'm here. To talk about making that money, and the impact the Screenshot-based business will bring, is bringing, to TGS. How do you and your partners feel about that? Aren't you concerned it will taint your reputation to be even peripherally involved with Screenshot."

Philip relaxed a degree or two. A very plausible reason for being there, for talking to him. Yes, Mathias had always taken a different tack in his reports. That was why Philip chose him in the first place. That, and West Virginia.

"Yes, of course we are. But no reasonable person would hold us in any way responsible for Screenshot."

"Really?" Seth asked. "Then why not cooperate with the authorities and let them examine your records for leads to Screenshot? Or freeze his accounts? Or block the PPV transfers?"

"First, we have no control over that. The company and its board decide policy on customer privacy. And secondly, even if they decided to allow such access, the political ramifications are significant. TGS is not a US corporation, and we have to abide by the laws and regulations of our nation of registry. So you see, I am not the man with the answers."

"Let's look at your reasons. Obsidian controls the board, don't they? You and another partner sit on it."

"That's two votes out of five. Hardly control."

"Yes, but that third vote is an outside member selected by Obsidian. Does that constitute independence? And as far as your corporate registration goes, São Tomé and Príncipe has a population of 150,000. Their only industry is issuing Elvis and Marilyn Monroe stamps for gullible collectors. You could buy any law or regulation that you wanted there."

"Whether we could or not is immaterial. We don't. And we won't. Our registry there is for taxation and privacy issues, not political. Our customers would not trust a company that made privacy guarantees conditional."

"That raises another point. Aren't you concerned that TGS and other digital gold providers are suspect as venues for money laundering, pyramid schemes and Internet scams? Doesn't this reinforce the taint that your best customers are those with something to hide?"

"First, our customer base is small merchants and consumers. Most accounts are less than $5,000. Hardly organized crime numbers. And no, we are no more a vehicle for illegal money management than any offshore financial entity. No more than a VISA card issued by a Cayman Islands bank. We are not in the law enforcement business. We're in the money business. We don't ask law-makers and law-enforcers for any special treatment, and we don't offer any in return."

Philip relaxed with the give and take, a forum where he was comfortable. He didn't need talking points or FAQs to discuss these points. They had been raised many times before, by questioners much more hostile and persistent than Mathias. As the interview began to wind down, as Mathias's questions became repetitions of the same issues under a different guise, he became more and more certain that it was all a coincidence, and that he had let his imagination get away.

And then Mathias stomped on his other foot.

"And you know, of course, that TGS isn't the only one of Obsidian's investments to be tied to Screenshot. E-nunC8 is the provider of the streaming video servers that Screenshot uses to broadcast his events. The exclusive provider, I might add. You're on their board as well, aren't you?"

That was not possible. How could Mathias possibly know? The servers should be buried in the Internet landscape, just one small link in a constantly changing chain, one leaf in an autumn wind.

"No, I wasn't aware of that. In fact, I'm not convinced that it's true. Who told you this?"

"It doesn't matter who told me. I checked the information myself, and it's accurate."

"You had better check again. Screenshot himself would be the only person to know that. Did you get the information from him?"

"No, but from someplace just as good. And I'll ask him about it. The next time I talk to him."

Later, Philip couldn't remember if Mathias emphasized *next*, and if that inflection was a hint that Mathias knew he was already speaking to Screenshot.

Seth

"Special Agent Larsen," she answered the phone.

"Well, hello, *Special* Agent. How's the crime-busting business today?"

"And hello to you, Ordinary Civilian. The criminals are winning.

How's the investigative reporting going?"

"Nothing much to report. The guy was a bust. He has to be the only venture capitalist in San Mateo County with a Hugo Boss suit. And the attitude to go with it."

"Nothing interesting? Not even an investment tip?"

"No, the guy was straight up about it, I guess. They're ambivalent, one foot on the platform, the other foot on the train. The PR clearly helps TGS, though he wouldn't even acknowledge that. But they're only one of many Obsidian investments, and an under-achieving one, at that. I think it's an embarrassment to them, but one that could make them a few bucks. They don't seem to know what to do, so they're doing nothing."

"No story?"

"No, there's a story there, he just didn't have it. The one thing that I did get was his reaction when I dropped the E-nunC8 information. He seemed genuinely surprised, either that they were involved, or that I knew about it. How could he not know? Wouldn't E-nunC8 know?"

"Not necessarily. The streaming video uses UDP packets instead of the TCP ones that data uses. It makes it easier for Sicals to do a high-level filter, but the packets would still look the same to E-nunC8 unless they did some analysis. And I don't see why they would without something suspicious."

"So what you're telling me is that they could know, and probably should know. Maybe they haven't told the board members like Hurst, but I'll bet someone knows Screenshot is using their servers. How is everything really going there?"

"Quiet. Nervous. Everyone is hoping Screenshot died in a car accident with a signed confession in his pocket. That's our best investigative avenue right now. Official one, anyway."

"Hopefully we'll get the information we need tomorrow."

"We'd better. I'm almost out of time here. My network administrator is an aggressively curious, anal geek, not a guy who's going to stand quietly in the corner no matter what I say. He is bugging me daily about the processor time and the bandwidth that Sicals is chewing up."

"Tomorrow's the day. Look's like I'll be lunching with the doc. I'll get there early and call you."

"Good. And Seth? Thanks."

"You're welcome. I'm glad to be able to help."

Chapter Twenty-six

The Fifth Victim

In Blauvelt, New York, Barbara Adkins, along with slightly more than 100,000 paying customers, guests and various law enforcement agents, watched the action unfold on their computer screens. Barbara enjoyed the show as an invited guest, although she would have paid for the opportunity.

Dominic D'Amico did a leisurely flip turn at the end of the pole section of his flagpole-shaped swimming pool. With each stroke, he took a breath and caught a glimpse of the palm trees bordering his Bermuda-grassed and stockade-fenced back yard, the hot, South Florida sun on his back. The pole part was his exercise area, and he swam sixteen Olympic-length laps at lunchtime every day, taking forty-five minutes to do it. Respectable half-mile times, especially for a sixty-five-year-old man.

On the fifteenth lap, Alycya, with two *y*s, came to join him, wearing a short, silk robe. She stood at the edge of the flag part of the pool, the entertainment section, and waited for him to finish, so he would be fully focused on her before she took off her robe to join him in the pool. He stayed focused because she was naked.

Dom's wife spent most of the spring and summer traveling, getting away from the brutal Miami heat, going to Europe or New York or California, once even to South America to try skiing.

Dom stayed at home and spent most of his spring and summer getting acquainted with various Alycyas. The arrangement suited everybody.

Dominic 'Dropkick' D'Amico had retired the previous New Year's Day, symbolically turning over the organized crime reins of power in Atlanta. A well-deserved retirement, he thought, after years of hard and loyal service. A very successful career, and the earnings paid for the Key Biscayne home, and the Maybach that chauffeured his wife around, and for the Porsche that Dom drove himself. His legitimate retirement investments threw off enough income to validate his lifestyle, but the real money came from his pension. His own off-the-books 401K. A percentage, a gratuity really, from the on-going operations that Dom had built back in Atlanta, and the current management inherited. Financially, Dom was very well established.

His 'Dropkick' appellation resulted from a repetitive sequence of actions that defined his early life, and had nothing to do with football. It came from the habit of punctuating his work, dropping someone with a fist or blunt object, with a final, brutal kick. Sort of a signature. For more than a few of the droppees, it signed their death certificate.

His laps finished, he stood and watched Alycya tiptoe down the stairs into the pool, where she swam with the grace of a six-year-old doing the doggie paddle. It didn't matter to Dom.

She paddled and thrashed over to him, her wake rocking the pool skimmer floating at rest in the corner, turned off for their swim. She could stand with her head and shoulders and the top of her substantial breasts just above the water at the deep end of the pool, and she cooed to Dom, "Swim another lap, baby. I love to watch you *slice* through the water." It didn't matter to Dom if she lied or not, he chose to believe it every time she said it, and do the extra fifty meters.

He had swum just a few strokes when he felt an odd, tingling sensation over his whole body. He stopped as Alycya said, "Ohhh. What was that? That felt good, Dom. Do it again."

Dom looked at his two bodyguards, standing a respectable distance away at each end of the pool, and said, "There's something wrong with the pool. I just got—"

His body arched rigid, his face tightened in a grimace. Then just as suddenly, he loosened and sank. Surfacing, he yelled at the guards, "Get us the fuck outta here," while he frantically tried to swing his leg over the side of the pool, grasping at the pebbled edge without the strength to lever himself up. Alycya was slower to recover, and barely managed to stay afloat, her legs incapable of fully supporting her even in the water.

The nearest guard ran to Dom and grabbed his right hand to pull him out. The second guard frantically waved at the stunned Alycya to come closer so he could do the same for her. As he did, Dom went rigid again, his face contorted in a scream, but no sound came out. The guard who held his hand looked straight ahead, crouched over, and vibrated in place. Alycya stood straight up, her back arched, her arms flung out, looking like she was on stage trying to sing the "land of the free" passage of "The Star-Spangled Banner." She'd used the same pose for soft-core porn auditions.

Again, their bodies loosened after a few seconds. The guard let go of Dom and collapsed. Dom and Alycya sank. Dom came up again, but Alycya's face stayed in the water, and she floated better than she ever did while alive. Dom tried to grab the edge of the pool and, with the small part of his considerable strength that was left, struggled to pull himself out, his expression not dissimilar to that of many of his victims just before the kick. But he couldn't get his center of gravity over the edge to roll away from the hammer blows in the water, and he was still trying when they hit again. The other guard, the only person left moving under his own power, watched in shock, having no idea what was happening, or what to do.

This time, Dom didn't come up either.

The images on Barbara Adkins screen were static, with no camera movement or sound. Three cameras provided the split-screen images, and she could see everything clearly from multiple angles. The slider at the bottom of her screen was positioned all the way to the right, at the mark labeled 100 percent, to where she had moved it, stopping at several lesser numbers along the way to experiment with the results of the F10 keystroke.

Screenshot told her that the capacitor was good for one three-second burst at a time, and would need several seconds to recharge after each. When the Ready icon came on, she pressed the F10 key again, and even though Dom was floating face-down, gave him one last shock just to be sure. Her own signature. Her repayment for the kick that had burst her father's spleen when she was just six, all those years ago.

In the pool, the green light on the skimmer turned to red while it recharged. The guard didn't notice it, or the label, but the police eventually would.

ACME LESSO-LATOR. Patent Pending.

Karen

In the grainy, wide-angled shot on her computer screen, Karen watched the police arrive and the survivor gesture wildly. He waved his hands, turned constantly and pointed, and, if she could have heard him, no doubt shouted as well. The picture quality seemed poorer than usual and the lack of audio made it seem like one of the hundreds of copycat events that were all over the Internet, mostly harmless, but a few fatal. Paramedics attended the other guard, and the man and woman were laid out on the patio next to the pool, covered in large towels. Her phone rang, and she lurched, startled, and banged her knee on the slide-out keyboard tray, sending a moment's numbness through her leg.

"We're screwed this week," Seth told her. "He took the feed from the home security system and there aren't enough packets to analyze. Sicals just gave me the bad news."

Karen sat silently and stared at the calendar on the file cabinet next to her station. They might be screwed this week, but every delay increased the likelihood that her scheme would backfire and she would be screwed every week.

"It's a security camera feed," she told no one in particular, but all nine people in the room heard her.

"No shit, Sherlock," Roger Parry called back, his social skills not honed for anything except the Internet chat he did until late into every night. "The question is, whose? I guess we'll know soon enough."

And then all the screens went black, matching Karen's mood. One more week, she thought over and over. Maybe she could weather one more week, if it just didn't rain.

Chapter
Twenty-seven

Karen

The storm clouds came rolling down the hall toward her office early the next morning. Thunder and lightning wouldn't be far behind, no doubt coming west out of Washington. Roger Parry plopped himself uninvited into one of the two chairs in her office. Abnormal rudeness, even for him.

"You shut down early this week. What happened?"

"Roger, what do you want? And what are you talking about?"

"Your mystery program. You shut it yesterday at 4:14. You usually run for several days after peak activity during the Screenshot events. Problems?"

So far, it was just a squall, Tropical Storm Roger. The question was, how bad would it get?

"Problems, no problems. Turn it on, turn it off. It is, all of it, none of your business. I thought I made that clear during our last conversation about this."

"Oh, you did. And I'm not interfering or anything. The network clocks significant activity, and I guess it thinks yours is significant. I watch the network, and if it thinks something is significant, I usually do too."

Maybe this one would blow itself out quickly if she clamped down hard, and the fair weather would hold for the week.

"Well, it's not. Not in computer network terms, anyway. Is it causing you any problems? Are you having any slowdowns, or interruptions? Program crashes? Anyone complaining?"

"No, not yet."

"Good. Then once again, we're done here, are we not?"

"Okay," he said as he got up to leave, then paused dramatically at her door. "I'll let you know if I hear anything back from Holcomb," referring to her boss in Washington.

She thought she heard distant thunder. "What about Stan?"

"It's monthly report time. Well, a little early, but you know me, I like to keep on top of things. He probably won't even notice, though. I don't think he actually reads them."

"Stop being childish, Roger. Notice what?"

"The description of unusual occurrences that is always included in the report. This is certainly an unusual occurrence, isn't it?"

"Thanks for reminding me. I need to get my monthly ready, and now I'll remember to include that."

Now Roger clouded over, and she could see that he hadn't thought about giving her a heads-up so she could cover herself. He was hoping for an ambush, but he had pulled the trigger too soon. He left, slightly deflated.

Karen's head felt like a claxon was sounding a tornado warning inside it. Of course Stan read the reports, every word of every one. Roger knew that. Everyone did. Stan put the anal in analysis. And it wouldn't matter what her report said. Stan would want to know the details.

In her head, the wind rose with a fury, and the storm broke. Abandon ship.

Philip

Before starting the tricky part, Philip decided to take a break and brew a cappuccino so he could review the procedure one more time before actually risking fragmentation. It wouldn't be good to accidentally turn himself into Screenshit.

The glare in the machine shop was so uniform that it wasn't apparent, its impact softened by its pervasiveness. Light bathed everything, and with no shadows to hide texture, every screw and lever and motor and table looked ready for the glamour photo, clean and bright. The ambiance looked more clean room manufacturing than machine shop functional.

The hot water sounded hollow as it pressured its way through the espresso grounds, followed by the hiss of steam from the wand and the growl of rapidly heating milk as he foamed it. Industrial sounds, fitting their environment. Philip decided that if he were a comic book hero, ACME would be his Fortress of Solitude, his safe haven, surrounded by his toys and his tools. This was where he would come to consider problems like Mathias, and decide how to respond.

He sipped the sweet, strong coffee and thought about inserting the PETN—Pentaerythrite Tetranitrate—into the four-inch metal tube that he had tack-welded vertically in the center of an empty propane bottle. In the empty plenum between this core for the explosives and the wall of the bottle, he dumped every nut, bolt, screw and scrap that would fit. He knew that was overkill, more shrapnel than necessary to do the job, but overkill was the design basis for all of his weapons.

The espresso finished, he went back to work. He had cut the top off the new, empty tank, at the circumference of the housing for the fitting and valve at the top. He replaced this with an identical-looking mount that he could screw in place after loading the explosives, the joint between the mount and the tank hidden by the new housing. Underneath this screw cap he mounted a cellular phone connected to a simple electrical switch. On the third ring, the electrical connection would be made, and everything within a thirty-foot radius shredded instantly.

Weapon design and fabrication relaxed Philip, gave him the opportunity to focus on one complex problem and come up with one elegant solution. The crude design of the new weapon bothered him, but he'd had to improvise on this one, and rush the fabrication. And now he would need to observe his target and wait to detonate the device at the appropriate moment, rather than do the normal careful research and planning.

All done, he prepared the straw-filled crate—no Styrofoam peanuts to become electrostatically charged. He placed the four tiny cameras in separate boxes, ready for batteries and placement. It had taken some research to design suitable housings for them, something ubiquitous enough to be in rooms that he had never actually seen. He'd settled on an air vent for the main camera. The others were more creative: a window blind mount, a wall-mounted thermostat and a bathroom light fixture. His replicas might not be exact, but they would likely go unnoticed until it was too late.

Only making and mounting the nameplate remained. He really wanted to work barbeque into the name somehow, the propane tank being designed for an outdoor grill, but he couldn't make it fit. Maybe he would find a target named Barbara. That brought an audible chuckle, and he thought he should find targets to match the clever names he liked, rather than the other way around.

Not coming up with anything suitable, he decided to shelve that issue and consider the more important one: how did Mathias know about E-nunC8? He had to be wired into the investigation somehow. Philip decided to drop by E-nunC8 and talk to the techies. He would discretely see if there was a legitimate way for Mathias to have discovered this.

Maggie, the pretty receptionist who always flirted with him, answered the phone, and he asked for Phil "Magnet" Hyslop, the Chief Technical Officer, so named because once he got onto something, he wouldn't let go.

"He's in a meeting with that writer. Do you want me to interrupt him?"

"What writer?"

"The one you talked to and sent over. Mathias."

Philip swallowed his shock and tried to maintain a calm voice.

"No, don't interrupt. Just tell him I'll be over later, and he should be ready to brief me fully on his discussion."

After he hung up, it popped into his head, and he machined his nameplate.

ACME DISETHEGRATOR. Patent Pending.

On Thursday he would pay a visit to Chabot Park.

Chapter
Twenty-eight

Karen

It seemed like a three-week day. Karen went about her normal Phish-Net activities, tried to stay focused, tried not to picture Stan levitating behind his desk as he read the monthly reports. He must be curious why theirs were early this month, when he normally had to send out at least one e-mail reminder to get them submitted anywhere near on time.

Her report mentioned a data-mining trial she'd been running to try to correlate Screenshot activity to any unusual Internet incidents, and she glossed over it as if it was just an administrative chore that hadn't yielded any useful data. There was a chance he might buy it, and each minute that passed increased the possibility that he had, that he'd read the reports and was satisfied.

Her back to the office door, she typed on the computer keyboard at the workstation behind her desk. Someone knocked on her open door, and she turned to see Stan and a man she didn't know. The first thought that ran through her mind was, I'm under arrest.

They came in and closed the door while she tried to organize and speak normal greetings. She wasn't sure exactly what she said, but doubted that it sounded casual.

"Karen, this is Al Siebel from legal affairs. I asked him to come along to let you know exactly what your options are, and to help us resolve this quickly and harmlessly."

"Resolve what?" she asked as they sat down.

Stan didn't answer immediately, as if he were choosing an answer from a long menu of possible selections. He apparently decided on something bland.

"The data-mining operation that you've been running. We've looked into it at our end, and we simply cannot figure out what you're doing, or how, or why. All we know is that you've installed some rogue software on our network without authorization, and you seem to be collecting huge quantities of Internet traffic, storing it and then sifting through it. Looking for what?"

Legal affairs? Karen decided that staying close to the truth without actually getting there was her best option.

"I'm not sure, Stan. I think it's like pornography. I'll know it when I see it. It just seemed to me that the Internet traffic surrounding Screenshot events might yield clues, and we should grab it in real time and look. There's no harm here, just some disk space and CPU time."

"Karen, that's like saying the space shuttle is just a three-hour plane ride. Do you know how much disk space and CPU time? Of course you do, so don't try to make it sound trivial. But that's not even the issue. The folks in Al's office say that this could constitute an illegal wiretap of immense proportions, and could get all of us fired. And some of us put in jail. Do you get the drift of what I'm saying?"

Jail? She had told herself that was a possibility, but it was like saying, if I smoke I might get cancer. No one really believes it until the MRI comes back and they pump you full of poison.

"That's ridiculous, Stan. Internet traffic isn't private, protected communications. There's no law or precedent that I know of that would make this illegal, or even unethical."

"See, that's where you're wrong. You might be able to make

that case in a courtroom if you were just collecting data packets, but that's not what you're doing, is it? You're trying to decode the contents, and that's invasion of privacy. In the legal sense, I might add."

"So I'll shut it down. What's the big deal? You didn't come all the way here, unannounced, with a lawyer for God's sakes, to tell me to do that."

"No, I came here to find out what you're doing, and I brought Al to tell me what our exposure is, and how to minimize it. How to isolate it."

Very nice threat, she thought. Subtle, but effective. Isolate it meant blame it all on her. Which of course was a perfectly reasonable thing to do from their perspective, and easily done with her attempt at secrecy. She'd provided deniability for them.

"Fine. I'll shut it down now. You can come with me. Then I'll explain what we're doing, and you can see for yourself what we have for data. Public domain data. Then you can send your lawyer home, and I'll pretend that you trusted me."

She was pushing the envelope, but she had known Stan for a long time, and she hoped to put a little guilt on him, turn his caution against him. She was likely screwed anyway, so a little righteous anger couldn't make it any worse.

"Fine. Roger can come along and help you explain it all to me."

With that command, he'd parried her thrust, trumped her play, and sealed her fate.

Seth

His shoulders ached and his butt hurt and the trailer seemed smaller, no longer big enough to contain his restiveness. Seth picked up his Dos Equis and went outside into the cool afternoon. The rain had kept him inside, learning more than he cared to know about Internet streaming video, trying to figure just what the E-nunC8 boys might be up to.

He sipped the beer and thought about the research, but it couldn't hold his concéntration. It wasn't the technology that had him impatient, it was the time. It was seven PM back in Pittsburgh, and he wanted to know how her day had gone. He climbed the two stairs back into the living area and recovered his cell phone. Two speed-dial clicks and her cell phone rang. She answered on the second ring.

"Hi," he said, "how did it go today?"

"It's still going. I'm at the office. My boss showed up today with an FBI lawyer, and right now that twerp of a network administrator is explaining all the techniques of data mining so they can crucify me and protect themselves."

"Protect themselves from what?"

"I can't talk now, but it's all politics and cover-your-ass. This whole Screenshot thing has everyone heading for the fallout shelter, and there's not enough room inside. I'll call you when I get home."

He drank the next Dos Equis pacing in the trailer, angry and frustrated, wanting to be there, helping her, defending her, even, although he knew that was ridiculous. She didn't need it, she could defend herself. It was just a natural reaction, he thought. Rescue fantasy. A way to act on his feelings.

When confronted with a challenge, Seth paced, bleeding off the excess energy so no explosion would follow. Outdoors, the pacing would be relaxing. Confined to the trailer by the rain, it became an aggressive act, getting up speed before hitting the opposite wall, then turning at the last possible moment to do it again. He was a big cat in his cage, and the onlookers were glad for the bars.

He kept this up through his second Dos Equis, drinking slowly so as not to fuel the fire he felt inside, and he was only released when the phone finally rang.

"I don't believe he brought a goddamned lawyer with him," she said after the brief pleasantries. "They're treating this like I'm a criminal, like they think I'm embezzling money or something. And that little shit, Roger …"

He could picture her head shaking, almost in grief, mourning their loss of trust in her, realizing it had never fully been there.

"Do they know about Sicals?"

"Not yet, but they will. Tomorrow, Monday at the latest, they'll pull it together. All they need is Hendrickson to hear about it. He's the only one who knows about my tie with Sicals. If they find out about him and the Nobel stuff, I'm finished. Then *I'll* need the lawyer."

"What can I do?"

"I don't know. Put the pillow and blanket on the table. I may need a hideout. Anyway, let's talk about something else. Anything going on there?"

Seth filled her in on his day, but it didn't hold their interest for long, and they got more personal. Seth took the leap.

"I miss you. Will you be coming out this weekend?"

Karen didn't answer for what seemed to Seth like a very long time.

"Thanks for saying that. I, well, I miss you too. I'll see what happens tomorrow and then decide. I might not be able to come if I think they're monitoring me. No sense putting them onto Sicals any sooner than they will be on their own."

"Do you want me to come there?"

"Let's wait until tomorrow and see. I'll call you when I can."

After the conversation, Seth opened his last Dos Equis, and resumed pacing.

Chapter
Twenty-nine

Seth

Seth let himself into Sicals' apartment early, while the doctor slept, and made breakfast of scrambled eggs with red peppers and chorizo sausage, toast, juice and coffee. The activity and the aromas woke Sicals, grumbling.

"Shall I put you on the lease, Mr. Mathias? You could share the rent."

"Morning, Doc. I thought you should have some nourishment because we've got some work to do today."

"I do work every day. My own work. What work did you have in mind?"

"We're going to figure out how to cover Karen, Agent Larsen. She's in a lot of trouble because she took a risk on your programs, and you used that to play your Nobel games. Now we've got to figure out—*you've* got to figure out—how to make your Screenshot programs seem benign, and how to bury your extracurricular activities so deep that it will take tectonic plates rubbing together to uncover them. Cream and sugar, right?"

After eating, and after Sicals showered and dressed, they sat down to discuss the problem.

"My activities vis-à-vis the Nobel committee are immune from any kind of investigation, I assure you. The trail stops cold at poor Miss Bergfors and her unfortunate security lapse. They will know nothing until I want them to. And my programs are benign. Any network administrator will understand that. So it seems we don't have any work to do after all. But thank you for the breakfast. It was very good."

"If we don't need to do that, then we can spend the day figuring out how to speed up the Screenshot investigation. We need results fast or Karen will be fired, maybe even arrested. So, Doc, your challenge for today is to get your packet analysis or signal correlation working or whatever and point me to Screenshot."

"As you know perfectly well, I need two more video sessions to run the programs. Until then, I won't have any signals to—"

"What? What did you just think of?"

"Hush, Mr. Mathias. Let me consider this."

Sicals sat in his chair, his head drooping and moving slowly back and forth. His lips moved without sound, and his stubby fingers bounced like he was playing air keyboard. After several prolonged minutes of this, his hands dropped to the arms of the chair and he looked up at Seth.

"Yes, that would work. Good, good."

"Come on, Doc. What would work?"

"I needed to use signal correlation to track down Miss Bergfors, but I didn't have the luxury of a prolonged video stream, so I used a variation of the return receipt to do it. If we can open an e-mail communication with your Mr. Screenshot, then we could try it on him."

"What is the return receipt variation?"

"Return receipt requested is just a way for senders of e-mail to request an acknowledgement that their communications have reached, and been opened by, the intended recipient. It's just like a postal return receipt, only it records the delivery electronically rather than by a signature. Because it requires an active process on the computer, the recipient is queried as to whether he wants to send the receipt or not, and then the appropriate action follows.

"The program I wrote simply overrides the refusal of the option and sends the receipt anyway. It then continues to send receipts at exact, predetermined intervals as long as the computer has power and an Internet connection. With the known interval, the message duration and the fixed content of those signals, I am able to run my signal correlation."

"Why are we screwing around with these other programs? It sounds like this is much simpler and quicker."

"It is both. The problem is that the program is inside the target computer, and therefore subject to detection. Screenshot would then know we are tracking him."

"How long would it take to locate him using this?"

"Quite a bit longer, now."

"Why?"

"Oh, Agent Larsen didn't tell you? They cut off my access at 10:44 last night. I am back to my own resources, and those are woefully inadequate to do this with any alacrity."

"Then we need to get started quickly. Can we add whatever resources you need?"

"Of course. Resources are always available, they're just very expensive. But the real problem is initiating the e-mail communication with Mr. Screenshot. We would need his current, active e-mail address, and he would have to open our communication and accept or decline the return receipt query."

"He'll open an e-mail from me."

"Yes, probably. Do you have his current e-mail address? We can't just address this to Screenshot, North Pole, like a letter to Santa Claus."

"I have the e-mails he sent me. I don't know if that account is active or not. But we can try to reply to them."

"What will you say to him? He can't be suspicious that the e-mail is infected or he will find the program and delete it."

Seth went to his laptop computer and pulled up the return address for his last Screenshot e-mail, *scores@then.com*.

"All right, here's what I'll do. I'll ask him who pushed the F10 key on D'Amico. He laughed that he will have willing triggermen standing in line. Maybe he'll want to gloat. Let's see, for a subject line, I'll use … 'Who dropped the Dom?' "

Karen

Karen had two hours and thirteen minutes to kill, and nothing to do it with. No time-zapping machine to jump ahead, not even a book to read to fill the 133 minutes. O'Hare was crowded, as always, and she felt diminished by the abstract nature of an airport, people hustling to be somewhere else, seemingly forbidden to take note of the here and now, focused ahead on the there and then. So she called Seth. It was either that or sit in a corner and cry.

His first question was, "Where have you been? I've been trying to call you all morning. They said you weren't in and wouldn't tell me anything else. I must have left a dozen messages." His second and third questions followed before she had a chance to deal with the first. "Are you all right? Where are you?"

"I'm at O'Hare, changing planes. No, I'm not all right. I've been put on leave, which is the last step before being fired," she said, answering his questions in the opposite order. "I'll land at SFO in five hours. Can you meet me?"

"Of course." He hesitated before asking, "Are you crying?"

"Not yet. Well, maybe a little."

"I'm so sorry, Karen. I'll be waiting for you when you land, and we'll figure something out. Why SFO? Why not Oakland?"

"Bad enough that they find out I'm in the Bay area. No sense leading anyone to Uncle Morgan's door."

There was a silence, and Karen figured Seth was processing the need for subterfuge.

"Is it that bad?"

"Yeah, that bad. They found the network access that Roger was tracking, but it doesn't show up as foreign because Sicals was coming in using my ID and password. When they start mapping access, and they will, they'll know someone unauthorized was using mine. I can't be in two places at once."

"Tell me what happened," he said. She still had 127 minutes to kill, so she told him.

❖   ❖   ❖

Just going back to her office that morning had put her in a bad mood. Of all the scenarios she'd imagined, of all the punishments that they could mete out, of all the bad faith they could show, a lawyer was the worst. A lawyer was worse than saying you screwed up. A lawyer said that you couldn't be trusted. It said they thought they might need to throw your ass in jail without appeal. All the years of work and success, the achievements and relationships, all wiped out in a second when your boss says, "This is our attorney."

She had no idea what they had done after telling her to go home, but her pass card still worked when she came back in the morning, so unless they were going to ambush her, she knew nothing had been finalized yet. She found no one waiting in her office with a warrant, so she settled down to work, waiting for the lawyer to use the handle on the metaphorical toilet and flush her career away. It happened at precisely nine.

Stan, lawyer in tow, marched into her office without ceremony and took one of the chairs. The lawyer took the other. After an uncomfortable few seconds of silence, Karen determined not to start with pleasantries, Stan did.

"Karen, you're on leave until further notice. It's paid leave for the moment. You will spend the remainder of the morning briefing Mr. Siebel and myself on everything pertinent to the unauthorized use of FBI computer resources, and everything that you know about the Screenshot investigation. Then you will turn in your badge and weapon and any other Bureau resources or equipment that you have. You are to call me personally each morning to get an update on our internal investigation, and you are to make yourself available to Mr. Siebel or myself or anyone else we designate, to answer any questions we have. You are to be forthright with your answers, and they are to be accurate and complete. At our request, you will submit to a polygraph test. Is all of that clear?"

Karen remembered a phrase she'd heard somewhere: hard to get happy after that.

"Yes. Perfectly clear. Let's get this done," she said, and then spent the next four hours doing it.

❖ ❖ ❖

"When I left," she told Seth after describing the interrogation, "I was so upset I didn't even go home. I drove right to the airport and got the first flight to San Francisco. I don't even have a toothbrush."

Relating the story made her mad all over again, wiping away any vestige of tears.

"I'll take care of all that," Seth told her. "You just get yourself here in one piece. Maybe this will help." He told her about Sicals' R-Cubed program and the possibility that they could still find Screenshot during the next event, even without the FBI network.

"I don't know. If Screenshot finds that program, we're screwed. He'll know we're tracking him."

"Even if he does, so what? If he shuts it down, we still have the other tracking. It's not like it puts us in any danger."

"What about Uncle Morgan's other quest?"

"That's on hold, and he assures me it will remain undiscovered until he says otherwise."

"It had better, or he's going to have to use some of those millions to pay for my lawyer."

Seth

Standing in the crowd, even a little above the crowd with his height, Seth saw her almost running down the pier, carrying only her handbag. He didn't have a sign to hold up, but his face had concern written all over it. Her face read relief once she saw him.

Her momentum launched her into his hug. They stood there for several moments, her face turned sideways, lying against his chest, arms around each other, blocking the other passengers whose grumbles they didn't notice. The hug didn't end so much as evolve, opening like a clamshell, one side swinging out, the other still connected, holding each other by one arm each. They walked toward the exit, still connected, her head leaning against him.

Neither spoke during the walk to short-term parking, or during the now familiar routine of backing the truck out and then getting in, or during the wait in line to pay for parking. They said nothing until they were heading south on Bayshore towards the San Mateo Bridge and Lake Chabot Regional Park. Neither of them even considered the possibility of another destination, such as a hotel for her.

"What's this," she asked, pointing to the several Nordstrom and Rite-Aid bags on the back seat of the crew cab.

"I did some shopping. I figured you'd need a change of clothes and toiletries and stuff."

"Stuff?"

"Yeah. Stuff."

"All right, let's see some stuff." She searched the bags.

"Jeans, that's good. Size is close enough, although they might be a little tight. Either good planning or bad memory on your part. Knit pullover. Hard to go wrong with that. Nikes. And exactly the right size. Do you have a foot fetish? What's this at the bottom? A thong! You got me a thong? And this isn't a bra, it's tissue paper."

Seth grinned, and Karen had her first laugh of the day. "Good thing that single-wide of yours has a washing machine, because these are going back. And you're taking them. I just wish I could have watched you pawing the ladies' lingerie and picking these out. I don't see pajamas or a nightgown."

Seth was still grinning.

They rode in silence, and gradually the goofy grin relaxed as the moment passed. It disappeared completely when Karen brought them back to reality.

"Did you see the Screenshot e-mail today? What's the news?"

"I don't know, I didn't have time to check my e-mail after your call. I had to learn about lingerie."

The joke went unnoticed, and her mood stayed somber.

"They took my computer and PDA, so I don't have e-mail at the moment. I wonder what he's got planned for this Tuesday." After a pause, she added, "And if it will help us get to him."

"Hopefully Sicals will have made progress and we won't even have to wait for Tuesday."

"He'd better. I don't think I have much time left."

"We'll take some breakfast to him tomorrow and catch up."

"You mean lunch. It'll take a bomb to get me out of bed before then," she said.

"Lunch, then, 'cause I'm all out of bombs."

He parked next to the trailer and made her wait in the truck. His key wouldn't work right, the bolt sticking, and he made a mental note to check it out in the daylight.

He went inside with the packages, and without turning on the lights, lit the nine candles he'd bought and distributed around the room, casting a soft, flickering glow. The trailer looked different in the candlelight, a little eerie.

"Wow," she said softly when he escorted her in. "What's all this?"

"This is for you. That," he said, pointing to the bed set up from the dinette table and benches, "is your very own massage table. You are going to relax and sip a lovely Montrachet whose vintage you might remember, and I am going to start on your feet. And before I'm done, you will have forgotten this day."

"Not all of it, I hope."

"No, not all. I expect there will be memorable moments. In the bedroom you will find boxer shorts, a robe and a very soft towel, all brand new. I will pour the wine while you prepare."

She hesitated at the bedroom door, peering inside. "You're not one of those weirdos with hidden spy cams, are you? I'd hate to end up as voyeur bait on the Internet."

"No, and even if I did, I'd keep it for private viewing. "

Karen came back wearing the robe and carrying the towel. She took off the robe, and in the boxer shorts and bra, she lay propped in the bed, the towel draped over her.

"Are you good at this?"

"I will be. Practice makes perfect."

Seth gave her a glass of wine and sat at the foot of the bed, taking her left foot in both hands, rubbing the insole with his thumbs, and the top with his fingers. Her eyes closed, Karen made soft noises that Seth wasn't sure she even heard. He moved to her right foot. And then her left ankle.

When he finished her calves, he took the wine glass and had her roll over. He started at her neck and moved down, shoulders to shoulder blades to lower back, unhooking her bra along the way. She said nothing, communicating with sighs and groans, and he understood every message.

When he got to the boxers, he slipped his fingers under the elastic and slid them down her legs. She lay naked while he massaged her with his eyes. In the candlelight, colors faded and he could see only shades. She looked shaped and polished from some gemstone, but he didn't know which one might match her tone. Her upper back rose and fell slowly, and he thought she might be asleep.

"How do I look to you?"

"Perfect. If I could have made you from my dreams, this would be the result."

"Mmmm. You are a silver-tongued devil, aren't you?" Her eyes still closed, her breathing her only movement, she said, "I think it's time." She didn't need to say for what.

She rolled to her side and Seth took her hand as she stood, inhaling sharply at the full view of her. She still seemed made of gemstone, but now it was liquid, like some sort of topaz lava, slow and fluid and smooth and hot. Still holding hands, with her leading the way, they went up the two stairs to the bedroom at the front of the trailer.

Seth lay in the dark, listening to her soft breathing, and tried to remember when he'd last felt quite so fulfilled. He knew it was a long time ago, but the immediate memories allowed no room for reminiscing. I can die a happy man, he thought.

Chapter Thirty

Seth

The alert on his PDA, recharging on the counter on the small built-in desk, woke Seth, and he took only a second to orient himself, to remember the events of the night before, leading up to Karen's being in bed next to him. And the events that happened after she got there. He ignored the alert, and it stopped after a few moments.

The curtains muted the bright, morning sunshine, making the light soft, almost tangible, as if they floated in it. Karen lay to his right, curled in a loose fetal position, her back to him, uncovered to her waist. He admired her back for the three minutes it took for the PDA's automatic snooze to chime again.

"Umm," she murmured. "Let it ring."

That was the reminder he didn't need. The PDA was using the default ring tone. He'd programmed custom ring tones for everyone who called him, and there were only four of them. He left the default ring tone for the rare other caller, including Screenshot.

"I'd better check," he reluctantly decided.

He sat up and slipped on the boxer shorts on the floor next to the bed, then went to retrieve the PDA. As he feared, it was another URL, and the instructions, Go here.

He booted up his laptop, letting Karen sleep, and waited. He typed in the URL, and instead of the expected chat room, he got an immediate streaming video picture. It took a moment for him to realize he was looking at himself, the picture from above and to his right, toward the front of the trailer.

"Oh shit," he said.

"Yes. Oh shit is right," his computer said, the voice tinny through the small speakers, and Seth jerked back like he'd touched a live wire. "We have sound to go with the video this time. Isn't technology great? You can talk to me too, right through your computer's built-in microphone."

"Who're you talking to?" Karen asked from the bed.

The image on his screen changed, and he saw her climb out of bed, naked, and slip on her robe. Seth almost knocked over his chair as he jumped up and ran to the bedroom to locate the camera.

"What's wrong?" Karen asked.

Seth whispered to her, "Don't say anything about Screenshot. He's planted cameras and microphones in here, and he's watching us right now."

The picture had come from the foot of the bed and up high. Seth looked closer and saw that one of the curtain brackets was different. He grabbed his shirt and hung it over the bracket.

"Ah ah ah," said the voice over the computer speakers. Seth and Karen walked to it while Screenshot continued. "Here are the ground rules. You don't interfere with the cameras. You don't turn off the microphone. You don't try to leave. You don't try to contact anybody. Pretty simple stuff, really."

"And if we do?"

"I'll know. I can see everything inside the trailer. And I can see everything outside. And I know about the emergency window exits. It's not that hard to contain you, Seth. You live in a fiberglass box. You might as well be a mime for all the chance you have of getting out. If you try, you will *very* briefly understand the meaning of my new word: DISETHEGRATOR. Catchy, don't you think?"

Karen gasped loud enough for the microphone to pick up, and Seth understood that this wasn't just spying, that he was the next Screenshot event. Why? Why the sudden reversal from chat buddy to target?

"Yeah," Screenshot continued. "You picked the wrong guy this time, didn't you? Well, sorry, Miss, but you've seen the previous episodes. No one gets out alive."

"Change the rules this time," Seth said. "She'll be great advertising for you. She'll be on every talk show, drumming up interest. Sex and violence. You can't beat the combination. You'll have created a star."

"A good point. I'll mull it over while we talk. Her life is my bargaining chip, a good reason to abide by the rules and give the fans a show."

Seth felt a desperation building and made a conscious effort to suppress it. The other victims flashed through his mind and he understood their emotions for the first time. Some, like the pedophile, not understanding anything except he was being murdered. Others, like Redo, never knowing what hit them. He wondered how he would look, how people would remember his death.

"Look, the police or someone's going to come for us soon enough. We're live on the Internet. What's happening isn't a secret, for Christ's sake. What then?"

"There are a couple of things wrong with your reasoning, Seth. First, who knows where you are? Besides me, of course. I'll bet no one. You like your privacy, don't you? And second, a new rule: no trying to give clues or solicit rescue. First, rescue is impossible. You remember the F10 key, don't you? It doesn't take long to press. And second, if the police or anyone else tries to get in, then they will have DISETHEGRATOR defined for themselves. And here's the definition, in case anyone is interested. It's not Webster's, but it's accurate.

"DISETHEGRATOR. Noun. A device that, when activated, shreds any soft tissue within thirty feet, damages that tissue within sixty feet, and adversely affects that tissue to a distance of eighty feet."

"So we're trapped and you can kill us anytime. Why shouldn't we just get it over with?"

"Because of human nature, Seth. You'll take every second I'm willing to give you. Anything can happen, can't it? I could have a heart attack and die. Or your FBI could come crashing through my door and save you. I think you'd better hope for the heart attack."

"Why are you doing this? I don't fit your profile. I thought we were finished."

"Let's just say it's a little personal preemptive justice. See, I got to use your term after all."

Not knowing what else to do, and watching himself in his shorts, Seth said to Karen, "Let's get dressed, at least."

"Take the computer, Seth," Screenshot directed. "I want to continue our chat. This is my first talkie."

They went to the bedroom and Seth set the laptop on the bed.

"Use the bathroom," he told her, and she took her clothes in and closed the door.

Seth watched himself for several seconds and then the picture changed, giving a clear if awkward view of Karen putting on her panties. He opened the door, startling her, and quickly covered her with the robe, pointing up to the light fixture. His arm around her shoulders, he led her out and closed the door; the picture immediately switched to the bracket view. Letting go of her, Seth walked to the device and stood directly in front of it, the screen showing only his raised hand.

Karen quickly slipped into her bra before Screenshot spoke again.

"Another new rule, Seth. I'm the director and you two are the actors. I get to tell you where to stand and what to do. You're welcome to ad lib your lines, but I'm in charge of everything else. So step out of the way and let the audience enjoy the show. Keep thinking F10."

Without moving, Seth turned his head toward Karen. She shrugged, as if to say *what more harm could it do*. She'd already been shown naked, so Seth figured the worst was past and stepped aside.

"Much better. Continue dressing, miss. I can always show a rerun later."

Seth slipped on his jeans and a shirt and his sneakers and took the computer back to the desk. He sat in one of the lounge chairs in the main living area at the very back of the trailer. A large rear window behind him took up nearly the whole back wall. Karen followed him, stuffing her hair into her beret, and sat in the other chair.

"Are you going to let her go?" Seth asked.

"Let's examine that possibility, shall we? First, who is she? Don't lie. You know I can find out quickly for myself."

Seth took a chance. "Her name is Karen Ryan. She's from LA. She's a producer at Universal. I met her when I did celebrity interviews there for a series of magazine articles six weeks ago.

We're just dating. There's no reason to kill another innocent bystander. Especially one who can help you. She works at a studio. She has access to all that television time. She could be your best advertisement."

"Let's hear from the lady. Tell me about your work. What do you produce? And what's with the hair?"

Karen picked up without hesitation. "AM/LA on KTTV," she said. "It's the local Fox affiliate. Cynd Simpson and Jules Avery are the hosts. We do local interest pieces and audience participation. You might have seen it. Starts at nine every weekday morning." She ignored the hair question.

Seth did his best to conceal his admiration. She never missed a beat. Even he believed her.

"I would have to be in LA to see it, wouldn't I? And since we don't know where I am, whether I've seen it or not will be my secret. So, what do you think of your Mr. Mathias now? Less appealing when he might cost you your life?"

Seth hoped Karen would be smart with her answer and stay in character.

"Honestly? Right now I wish we'd never met. But ten minutes ago I was quite happy with him."

"Funny how things can change so quickly. For instance, did he tell you about our relationship."

"He didn't have to. I knew about it from the news. Remember, I produce a news and talk show. I would have booked him if he wanted. And it doesn't change anything. Didn't change anything, until now."

"Did he ever tell you about West Virginia?"

Seth looked up sharply. She knew all about his adventure, but he didn't want the world to hear about it. Just as quickly, he caught himself. Who cares now? I'll be dead in a few minutes.

"No. What about West Virginia?"

"It seems about fourteen months ago, your boyfriend killed four men in one exciting weekend. As I recall, he clubbed two of them to death, broke another's neck, and strangled the fourth."

Karen turned to Seth, performing brilliantly. "Is this true?"

He looked at her for several seconds, trying to play his part. "Yes. But it was self-defense. This gang murdered an innocent couple just for sport, and I stumbled into it. I had to defend myself."

While he talked and negotiated for time, Seth tried to think of a way out. There was none. No secret trap doors, no windows out of view of the cameras, no hope for rescue. He was going to die. He had nothing to offer in exchange for his life. No appeals to reason or mercy were going to work. *I'm going to die.* There was a time when that wouldn't have been so undesirable. No longer.

Karen continued to stare at him while Screenshot said, "That's certainly one interpretation. But I'll bet there are some mothers in old Bascomb, West Virginia who believe otherwise. Right, Seth?"

"All right. You've had your fun with her. Now let her go."

"I don't know. My viewers might like to see more of her. Even more than they've already seen, if that's possible. We'll leave it up to them. Give me a minute and we'll set up an Internet poll to let the audience decide. Kind of like American Idol, only more … definitive."

The picture stayed on them, but the narrative by Screenshot stopped. Seth took the opportunity to try to look his feelings to her, and he hoped she understood his care and concern. Suddenly, a pop-up appeared in the corner of the screen with two words: Live and Die. Under each was a counter and there were already several votes.

"We'll let this run for, say, fifteen minutes and see what they think. Looks like the early returns are in," Screenshot continued, "and they're running in favor of Miss … What did you say your name was again?"

"Ryan. Karen Ryan."

"Yes, that's right. I forgot there for a moment. We wouldn't want to be wrong about her identity, would we, Seth? We wouldn't want any other mothers to grieve, especially the wrong ones."

Screenshot was suspicious of Karen's story, and had tried to trip her up, and even though she got it right, Seth wasn't sure if Screenshot believed them. He lost his patience, and his temper went as well.

"Goddammit, what are you trying to do? Let her go. Press F10. Whatever. Get this done. I'll put on a show for you after she's gone. What do you want? Begging? I can do that. We could do some hostage thing and I'll confess to anything you want. I'll confess to being you. Then this will be suicide and you'll go free. How's that sound?"

"I am free, Seth, and I will remain that way." Screenshot's voice hardened, the glib gave way to authoritative instruction. "You can't confess to being me. You don't have the brains or the talent to be me. Do not make light of this. And do not patronize me. This is how you will be remembered. This is your legacy. Take advantage of it. Show us the Mathias backbone that was so evident in the woods of West Virginia."

"At least those thugs gave me a chance. At least I was able to fight back."

"And look what it got them. All dead. Enough of this. Let's go to the tote board, shall we? Why it looks like the public wants to see more of Miss Ryan. We have 897 votes to live against 461 to die. Almost a 2:1 margin. A landslide in politics. What do you have to say to your public, Miss Ryan?"

"Just let me out."

"Not so fast. We have one more vote to count. Mine. But before we do, would you like to say anything to Julianne Foster?"

"Who?"

"Why, your replacement at AM/LA. According to their web site, she's the show's producer. They must have acted very quickly when they realized you wouldn't be showing up for work on Monday."

Seth's heart sank. She would die with him.

And then his phone rang.

"Don't answer," Screenshot commanded.

"Fuck you," Seth said. "You're gonna kill us anyway. Do it or don't. I'm answering."

"Actually, that's a better idea. Maybe it's Wes or Rachel. They should have gotten the e-mails I sent. I expect they're watching. Maybe they're calling to say goodbye. It will be a nice moment to capture live."

The phone continued to ring as Seth almost vibrated, like his tire had thrown a weight at sixty mph, and the whole trailer was shaking. "You bastard," was all he said, and looked down at the PDA screen. He didn't recognize the caller ID.

"Mr. Mathias. I'm glad you answered. This is Dr. Morgan Sicals calling."

Seth glanced at Karen.

"Uh, listen, Uncle Morgan. I can't talk right now. I'm a little busy at the moment."

"Yes, yes, of course you are. I've been watching you and Miss

Larsen on the Internet. I didn't realize that you two were, uh, intimate."

"Is there a point to this?"

"Yes, there is a point to this. What do you take me for? A voyeur? You're in a travel trailer, if I'm not mistaken. Is that right?"

"Who is it?" Screenshot called in a lilting voice. Seth ignored him.

"Yes, that's right," he told Sicals. "So?"

"Do you have a power supply? Answer quietly, please, so the microphone doesn't pick it up."

"Yes. I'm connected to external power, and I have a generator."

"Can you control it from where you are?"

"Yes. There are cut-off switches on the panel."

"Good. Here's what I want you to do. Switch the power inputs off. Go to your circuit breaker panel and cut the main power there. Then find the hot lead to the main breaker. It will be the big one. Disconnect this and secure it to a metal frame piece of the trailer. Next, turn the external power and the generator on, at the same time, if possible. This might create sufficient current to charge the entire trailer frame and body and set up electrical interference. If Mr. Screenshot is controlling his weapon by radio or cell phone, this might block his commands momentarily."

"Are you sure this will work?"

"No. Would you like me to do some research and get back to you later today?"

"No, no. Thanks, Doc. We'll give it a try."

"Three other things. First, do not touch anything metal once you have turned the power on. And make your escape quickly because the circuit will eventually fail, probably quite quickly, and he will have his link back."

"What was the third thing?"

"Well, there is a measurable possibility that the electrical field that you create will itself detonate the weapon."

"How measurable?"

"Again, I don't know. I can still do the research, if you like. That would take me until tomorrow."

"Don't bother. We'll go right to the real thing and hope for the best." And he hung up.

Screenshot's impatience came through clearly, even over the computer speaker. "Who was it? And what did you tell them?"

"It wasn't Wes or Rachel, so you won't get any sick enjoyment over that. It was a relative, my Uncle. He just gave me his prayers." It would take a prayer for this to work, Seth knew. Karen stiffened at the mention of an uncle, and he flashed her what he hoped was an encouraging look.

Seth went to the breaker panel in the small storage closet next to the kitchen counter. Karen joined him, and Screenshot asked, "What are you doing?"

"I'm activating the escape pod so we can get out of here," Seth taunted, hoping Screenshot would give them some latitude if he thought it would demonstrate their vulnerability and his superiority. "Just give me a couple of minutes."

To Karen, he whispered, "In the switch panel behind that cover is an External Power switch and a Generator switch. Turn them both off. Be ready to turn them back on when I tell you. As soon as you do, take this hammer and smash the rear window. Do not touch anything metal, the whole trailer will be one big live wire. Use a chair cushion as insulation and vault out the window. Then run like hell for the woods."

"Where will you be?"

"Right behind you. If it works, we'll only have a few seconds, so don't hesitate, don't look back. Just go."

With the hammer claw Seth loosened the paneling next to the box. The hot lead cable was easy to spot, just like Sicals had said.

"Cut the power," he whispered.

He disconnected the cable and taped it to the trailer frame. There was no perceptible change in the trailer, the bright sunshine maintaining the light, and the laptop operating on its battery. He went to work on the lug holding the cable and listened to Karen answer Screenshot's increasingly urgent demands. He finished quickly and stepped out of the closet, trying to look innocent.

"Problems with your pod, Seth?"

"Yeah. Damn thing's stuck. I'm gonna complain to the pod people."

"I'll do it for you," Screenshot said. "You'll be indisposed."

"Thanks. It's a little dark in here. Would you turn on the lights, Karen?"

Philip

Philip's screen went blank. Using his keyboard, he toggled between all four cameras. Nothing.

"Mathias, I'm giving you three seconds to re-connect my cameras, and then it's F10. Do you hear me?"

Mathias didn't answer. Philip heard only static. From his seat at his computer, he could see the trailer through the windshield, an angled view from its front and along the door side, with the back and far side hidden. That view showed the truck still there, and the trailer door still closed. No one had come out.

"All right, then. Three. Two. One. Goodbye." He pressed the F10 key and waited for the third ring. Instead, he got the familiar recorded voice telling him the cell phone he dialed was out of service, and he should try again later.

Out of service? Before he could act on that thought, the static on the computer disappeared. Whatever had interfered with his call was over. He hit the F10 key again, watching the trailer as the phone connected.

This time the third ring brought results, instant results. The trailer seemed to evaporate, with no transition from trailer to dust. The sound hit the motor home at the same moment, the light not having much time to outrun it. Without the support of the leveling legs, retracted in case he had to make a hurried getaway, the shockwave rocked it on its suspension. When the initial smoke and dust cleared, the scene looked like the debris field from a small plane crashing into a pickup truck.

Many of the other trailers and motor homes were damaged, and campers came out to investigate. Some of them were clearly hurt, others in shock, some panicked and screaming. The calmer ones cautiously approached the destruction, unsure what had happened, and not entirely certain it wouldn't happen again. Philip left his motor home and moved slowly toward the wreck, not wanting to attract attention in his impatience to confirm the deaths of Mathias and the girl. If there was anything identifiable left of them.

Seth

When she'd hit the switches, there was a loud crackling sound, and the air around them seemed to animate, crawling all over their bodies like a million invisible insects. Karen swung the hammer and the window dissolved into a glass mist. She grabbed the cushion and was gone. Seth glanced at the laptop as he followed her, and saw only black and grey fuzz swimming on the screen. The field was working.

He grabbed a chair pillow and raced to the window. His foot slipped on the broken glass, and he pitched forward, arms outstretched. He hit the window frame hard, cushion first, but the impact broke the grip of his left hand and his palm hit the metal frame. It felt like an infinite number of Mike Tysons all decided to hit him at the same time from every possible angle, and he was knocked backwards onto the floor.

Somewhere in his head, commands were issued without his initiative, and he stumbled to his feet. Using the cushion, he slid forward and fell through the window, landing on the ground hard, sending spikes of pain through his shoulder and back. Stunned, he looked up at the clear blue sky and thought how pretty the day was.

Karen grabbed his arm and shirt and dragged him to his side, frantically trying to get him standing. She yelled at him to move. He did, but he didn't know why she was so angry. He stumbled along, dragged and urged by her, gathering his wits and coordination as he went.

They were nearly to the woods, about fifty feet from the trailer, when the world erupted and knocked them flat.

Something stung his legs and back, like he'd been attacked by huge hornets. He landed on top of Karen and struggled to get off her so they could keep going. When he tried to stand, he found that someone had disconnected his legs. He tumbled over, landing first on his knees, then on all fours.

Karen stood. "You're bleeding. It doesn't look too bad, I think. Can you walk?"

"Give me a hand."

She helped him to his feet and, with his arm over her shoulder, they moved as quickly as they could, looking like the losers in a three-legged race.

"Head for the office. There'll be people there. Maybe we can get out."

As they limped down the trail, two men in Lake Chabot work shirts, running toward the explosion, stopped and asked if they needed help. Seth said yes, and one of them took his other arm and helped Karen take him to the park office. The other one headed for the campsite.

Seth answered the ranger's *what happened* question before Karen could. "I don't know. We were just walking to our camper when the explosion happened. Maybe someone's propane tank or something."

"We'll get you to the office and see how bad those cuts are."

Karen said. "If you have a first-aid kit, I can dress the wounds while you go help your friend."

"Good idea," he agreed as they helped Seth up onto the porch. "It's in the cabinet behind the desk. I'll be right back."

He took off running toward the black smoke they could see above the trees.

"Karen, there's a park van right over there. See if you can find the keys. We've got to get out of here before the police arrive. If they figure out it was us on the Internet, we'll never get back to Sicals."

She ran inside and came out a few moments later holding the

first-aid kit and a set of keys on an oversized Smokey the Bear keychain.

"Grab some gauze and disinfectant and leave the rest in case anyone else is hurt," he said. She also thought to bring a wet towel.

Seth climbed into the rear seat and lay face down. Karen tore the holes in his shirt and jeans and cleaned the cuts with the towel. The worst one was in his left thigh. A piece of bent metal was lodged in his leg.

"This is gonna hurt," she told him, and when she pulled it out, it did.

She used the disinfectant and left the gauze lying loosely on each cut and told him not to move too much.

"Go to Sicals' place. Can you reach in my pocket and hand me the phone?"

While she drove, he dialed Sicals.

"Mr. Mathias! How grand to hear from you. I'm gratified my idea worked. I couldn't tell from here, of course, I just lost the signal when you turned the power on. Are you and Miss Larsen all right?"

"I've got a couple of cuts, but we'll be fine. We're coming to you now. Can you meet us and let us in?"

"Yes. But come to the back entrance. There is an alley next to the building and a courtyard back there. I'll tell Mr. Reynolds it's your truck so he won't have it towed."

"My truck got blown up with the trailer. We borrowed a van from the park ranger. We should be there in twenty minutes."

Before Sicals could answer, Seth's call-waiting tone sounded and he said goodbye. He looked at the Caller ID. It was Wes.

"Dad?"

"Yeah, it's me. I'm fine. Call Rachel and tell her, and I'll call you back soon."

"What about your friend?"

"She's fine too. Thanks for asking. Now call Rach and we'll talk later."

When Seth hung up, Karen asked, "He asked about me? He doesn't even know me."

"I guess he figured that any naked woman in the trailer with me is part of the family."

That brought a smile to her face.

Chapter Thirty-one

Philip

He skirted the thickest of the smoke and dust, moving toward what used to be the back of the trailer. When he got far enough to see past the haze, he caught a glimpse of three people disappearing down the trail. One, apparently Mathias, limped noticeably, wounded but mobile. A ranger and the girl helped him along. Philip cursed and hurried after them.

The trail from the vehicle campgrounds to the park office ran through sparse woods and emerged across a gravel road from the log cabin that served as ranger headquarters. A ranger ran past him in the other direction, toward the wreckage, pausing only long enough to ask if he was hurt, then hurrying on.

Arriving at the trail's end, Philip stepped onto the road, and when he didn't spot them, he figured they must be inside the ranger station. As he stepped back into the woods to wait, a park van pulled out and headed for the exit. He caught a glimpse of the girl driving, and cursed again.

Philip looked around for another vehicle. There were others, including a pickup truck that belonged to the park, but as quickly as the impulse came, it went. Stealing and chasing were high-risk ventures, and he didn't want to attract attention to himself. With one last curse, he turned back to the camping area.

A siren oscillated in the distance. Soon there would be organized chaos and managed confusion. He had expected that, prepared for that, even counted on that. He originally planned to video the explosion and resulting police and fire activity for his own enjoyment, possibly even editing for broadcast if it could be done without leading back to him.

The camera! Bugger!

He'd mounted it on the dash of the motor home with a suction cup device, aimed at what was left of the trailer, hooked up to his computer to initiate recording when he hit the F10 key. The computer would provide enough memory to hold several hours of video. That would look suspicious, the whole event captured perfectly. He ran to put it away.

A police car, its siren off, looped around to the campsite, following the circular road while he crossed through the woods. They got to the scene at the same time. There was only one officer. The destruction and confusion should keep him busy, Philip thought, while he got inside and moved the camera. He kept walking as the cop got out and talked into a shoulder-mounted radio while he scanned the area. When he finished, he frustrated Philip's plan.

"Everyone," he shouted, even though everyone was looking at him already, "I want you all to come over here and stand by my car. No disturbing the scene, no leaving the scene."

"Officer, can I wait in my motor home right there?" Philip asked.

"No, sir, I'm sorry. Everyone is to stay right here until more officers arrive to control the scene and take your statements."

Philip persisted. "I'm not going anywhere. I just want to get inside, away from this … mess."

"I can't allow that, for you or anybody. We can't be too careful these days. For all I know, someone has an empty RPG launcher and a full AK47 inside. I need everyone to stand where I can watch them."

They stood, milling slightly but mostly just standing, stunned, a few of them asking questions nobody could answer. Nobody except Philip.

"Shouldn't we check the damaged campers for any injured?" someone asked.

"The paramedics will be here in two minutes. Just be patient until I get back-up."

The sirens sounded in the distance.

Police, firemen and paramedics converged on the site amidst much sound and activity, in one huge emergency caravan. Soon the area swarmed with professionals in uniforms and gear. The overall effect was chaotic, just as Philip had foreseen, and it was all being captured on an incriminating video.

The emergency personnel fanned out to their respective duties, and the temporary control that the officer had asserted broke down as people moved out of the way or angled for a better view. Philip tried to ease unnoticed to the motor home and covered about two thirds of the distance when one of the newly arrived officers selected him as his interviewee and asked which vehicle was his. Philip pointed to the one with the camera visible through the windshield, and the officer motioned for Philip to accompany him to it. Standing outside the door, the policeman took all of Philip's contact information, checked his driver's license for confirmation, and asked if anyone else was inside.

"No. I travel alone, doing my videography. Nature videos are sort of my hobby."

His attempt at planting a legitimate reason for the video set-up sounded phony even to him. Who would believe it if they investigated further? No one had ever accused Philip of hugging trees.

"Tell me what you saw and heard," the officer said.

Philip did, answering the follow-up questions about any strangers (they're all strangers to me) or unusual comings and goings (how can you tell what's usual and unusual?) without any apparent reaction. He hoped for a cursory examination of the motor home to confirm no other occupants or any obvious links to the explosion. Better yet, no examination at all. The officer shattered that hope.

"Let's take a look inside. You first, please."

Philip went in, resisting the urge to grab the offending camera on his way by. The officer had him sit in a chair, too far from the camera to grab it, while he checked the bedroom and bath.

"Okay, everything looks fine," he said, and Philip had a moment of optimism. "Is that a video camera on the dash?"

"Yes. I keep it mounted there when I drive through woods and such in case anything interesting jumps out in front of me. I can either turn it on using my computer or grab it and shoot by hand."

He tried to sound convincing, but it didn't divert the policeman from his examination.

"Was it running at any time before or during the explosion?"

"No. I was just cleaning up when it happened. There's nothing interesting to tape in a campground."

"Well, if you wouldn't mind, I'd like to see for myself. Start it at the beginning and let me scan what's there."

Philip didn't have to do it. He could refuse. But then he would have to wait while they got a warrant, increasing their focus on him and making the contents even more suspicious. He would have to play the video and try to think of a valid reason for the recording. Maybe he could say that he hit the computer by accident while cleaning up. Even if they believed him, he would become a part of the Screenshot investigation, his name and story in the file, just waiting for some other little piece of evidence to be connected and for someone to notice.

The heat would be on, and while there was little chance that they could link him to Screenshot, future events would have to be deferred, and he might have to stop altogether. It was fun while it lasted, he thought.

The camera recorded to a small disc, so he just had to press play. He considered erasing it, but that would take several seconds and arouse the officer's suspicions. Even if he succeeded, the data could still be recovered with sophisticated forensic software. He had trapped himself.

Philip picked up the camera and nonchalantly disconnected the Firewire connection to the computer, hoping the officer would look at the internal memory and not realize everything was on the computer. He pressed the play key, and handed it to the officer, who watched the blank screen in silence for several seconds.

"How do I fast forward?"

Philip showed him the button, and he watched a blank screen at high speed for several more seconds.

"Okay. Nothing there." Philip almost sighed in relief but stiffened when the officer asked, "What's the cable for?"

He briefly considered lying, but if the officer knew computers, he would recognize it.

"It's for memory overflow. In case the camera memory fills up, the computer will continue the recording." Close enough to the truth to sound plausible. "But since there's nothing on the camera, the computer wouldn't have started recording."

"May I," he asked, pointing to the computer. Philip shrugged his acquiescence.

"Is this the video program," he asked, pointing at the miniature camera icon on the computer screen. "What's the file extension?"

So, the cop knew computers. Philip watched, sweating now, inventing explanations in his head and testing them against his own analysis, trying to remember if he'd erased any other incriminating videos after transferring them to his network server at home. The cop did a file search for all files with the *vdo* extension. Sixteen popped up, the most recent one just minutes earlier. It took all of Philip's self-control to maintain his poise.

The cop opened the newest file and played it. It showed a view of the park from the windshield, centered on Mathias's trailer, and Philip struggled to maintain a calm expression. Then it stopped, after maybe eight seconds of the static campground view. Again, Philip's composure almost slipped, this time in surprised elation.

The policeman watched the blank screen for several more seconds and then asked, "Is there any more to this?"

"No, that was just a camera check I ran earlier."

"Okay, Mr. Hurst. Thanks for your cooperation. If there's anything else we need, we'll be in touch. And if you remember anything at all, please call us right away. No telling what can be important in a case like this."

"You're welcome, Officer. Am I free to go then?"

Philip was out the door, disconnecting the water and electricity hookups as soon as the cop said, "Yes."

On the highway, he played the events over in his head, trying to understand what had happened to the video. The trailer cameras went dead. He gave Mathias a warning. No response. He hit the F10 key. It didn't work. He hit it again. *Again*. That was it! He had hit the F10 key twice, toggling the camera off.

Whatever Mathias did helped me escape too, Philip thought, smiling for the first time in hours.

Karen

She found the alley and wondered why she hadn't noticed it on her previous visit. Finding it and negotiating it were two very different things, the narrow space made more so by protrusions on the walls of the buildings. Litter obstructed the way, including a large plastic garbage can that she pushed down the alley with the truck's bumper.

What Sicals had called a "courtyard" included the backyards of the buildings on either side of the alley, if old concrete, rock-hard dirt, and discarded appliances could be termed a yard. A tall brick wall, overgrown with vines, and apparently held in place by gravity, surrounded the area. A partially collapsed, prefab storage shed in one corner provided a convenient ramp to the top of the wall, compromising what security the wall might have provided. Beyond, she expected she would find similar courtyards, walls and junk.

Karen took the extra time to turn the van around, requiring several forward-turn-back-turn maneuvers. She wanted it hidden from the alley entrance so it wouldn't draw attention, and aimed out because they might need to leave in a hurry. The arrangement positioned the sliding door on the passenger side of the van closer to the building entrance, making the transfer easier for Seth.

He lay on his side, taking the pressure off the wounded left thigh, bent slightly at the waist and knees to fit in the seat. Karen helped ease him to an all-fours position, one foot and hand on the floor, one knee and elbow on the seat, and backed him out like a horse from its trailer. Her arm hit the deepest of the wounds, causing him to flinch.

"Sorry," she said.

"That's all right," he answered. "It was more reflex than pain. I just need to get this bandaged and I'll be fine. What are the odds Sicals has first-aid gear?"

"For himself, or for the computers?"

She helped him stand and once upright he seemed better. She steadied him as they walked. The back door to Sicals' building was below grade, five steps into a concrete pit parallel to the rear wall. She went down first, backwards, holding one hand while Seth steadied himself against the wall with the other. A book propped the door open about two inches, and Karen glanced at the title when she picked it up. *Feynman Lectures on Physics, Definitive Edition -Volume 2*. A *New York Times* bestseller, no doubt. It had a note attached, asking that she bring it in with her.

The door opened into a tidy basement storage and furnace room. Another door on the opposite wall led to the hall outside Sicals' apartment. A book held it open, too. *Volume 1*, she guessed correctly. It also had a note requesting its return.

Someone kept the path to that door clear, no doubt Arthur's doing. She walked backwards in the narrow aisle, holding both of Seth's hands. Sicals answered her knock without his usual delays.

"Welcome, Miss Larsen. Let's get you inside and we'll tend to Mr. Mathias's wound."

Karen led Seth to the couch against the front wall of the basement apartment, the small, curb-height windows above it. While she helped him off with his pants, Sicals brought back a clean sheet and spread it on the cushions, whether to protect the worn fabric from Seth's blood, or Seth's wound from whatever might be living there, she wasn't sure. Mentally she scolded herself for being snobbish.

Sicals brought a prepackaged first-aid kit, the plastic wrapper still intact despite its apparent age, and nudged Karen gently aside, saying, "Let's take a look at that." After a quick examination of the four wounds, he said, "This one will need stitches. The others we can bandage. I'm certain that you'll be good as new in no time."

"We can't do stitches, Doc," Seth said. "I'm not going to the hospital, or anywhere, for that matter. The whole world saw us this morning. I'm not taking a chance that someone will recognize me. Right now, this is the safest place for us. No one knows about you, so they won't be looking. Use a butterfly or something."

"Nonsense. I'll get my sewing kit and do it myself."

Karen almost burst out laughing. "Doctor, you're a Ph.D., not a physician. Wouldn't it be better to use the bandage?"

"Miss Larsen, you are correct, I am not a physician, never having done my internship. I did, however, spend three years attending the Weill Medical College of Cornell University, a very prestigious school, I might add, where I specialized in medical physics and graduated with honors. I thought at the time that I might go into research in nuclear medicine, but I found it too limiting. I *am* qualified to suture Mr. Mathias."

Karen found herself once more astounded by this man. Seth chuckled. He stopped when Sicals brought back his sewing kit, a clear plastic envelope with the Holiday Inn logo printed on it, and Karen got a chance to chuckle.

After threading the needle, Sicals dipped it and the thread in alcohol, giving Karen some confidence that he knew what he was doing: she wouldn't have thought to cleanse the thread. He put four quick stitches in, tying each off with minimal fumbling, and Seth never grimaced or indicated pain.

She put a fresh bandage on his leg then set about examining the kitchen cabinets and found them well stocked from Seth's grocery trips. She made eggs and bacon and toast for everyone while Sicals questioned Seth on the implementation and results of his plan, as if preparing to write the experiment up for a scientific journal.

"Yes, well, that is very good," he said when Seth finished. "I was a little worried that the field would be sufficient to detonate the device, but I expect he had some safety mechanism or delay so nothing could set it off accidentally. All's well that ends well, I suppose. So, what will you do now?"

"We're going to spend the night here, Doctor, and then tomorrow we'll all have to pack up and find somewhere safe to go," Karen answered.

"Stay? Go? Whatever for? You would be far more comfortable in a hotel, or with your FBI guarding you. And I am perfectly content here."

The dangers they faced, and their isolation from any help, had not registered with Sicals, so she explained them to him.

"First, Seth, Mr. Mathias, has to rest that leg, so we can't move him today. And what he said about the hospital is true for hotels or any other place. There's too great a risk we'll be recognized and found, and it will be in the media, and Screenshot will be after us again. And somehow I don't think he's the type to miss twice."

"Then you must go to your FBI. They can certainly protect you."

"They are no doubt frantic, although they should know by now that we're not dead. They'll be looking for us, but it will be for questioning, not guarding. By Monday, Tuesday at the latest, they will be looking to arrest me, and you, and probably Seth as well, just to be thorough."

"Arrest? Why? Why me? They have no reason to want me."

"Doctor, you stole seventeen million dollars from the Nobel Commission. Do you think that will go unnoticed? It won't take long for someone to connect the dots between your Nobel history, access to FBI computer resources, and the missing money."

"She's right, Doc," Seth added. "And with Screenshot after me, we're all in trouble. We need a place to hide while we finish running your R-cubed and identify Screenshot."

"How is that going?" Karen asked.

"It's going very slowly without more processing power and network storage. We will need at least several more days of uninterrupted signal to complete. Forty-three hours is my actual estimate, plus or minus twenty minutes."

"Almost two days," Seth pointed out. "We can get him before Tuesday. Think we can ditch your friends for that long?"

"That's not the problem," Karen said. "It's ditching them that long while maintaining computer access that's the problem. And that's presuming Screenshot doesn't shut down at night. Has he, Doctor?"

"Not so far."

"Good. We'll lose the data while we move, but hopefully that won't take long. Any ideas, Seth?"

Before he could answer, Sicals interrupted. "Moving is out of the question. This is all very sensitive equipment that I have here. It can't just be thrown in the trunk of your car and rushed off to some hideout. And we will need very high-speed Internet access.

Cable modem at the least, and a fractional T-1 would be better. I don't expect you could get a dedicated T-1, could you?"

"T-1?" said Seth.

"The highest speed individual Internet access line available. Usually a T-1 serves hundreds of computers, an entire building or company. And no, Doctor, I don't expect I could get a dedicated T-1."

"What about your commercial contacts through Phish-Net? Would any of them help?" Seth asked.

"Not once they realize I'm persona non grata. I don't have any ideas. It's not like we can just advertise in the paper for a T-1 equipped hideout."

Seth looked up sharply and said, "Maybe we can. Get me my phone from my pants pocket."

Karen fetched it and waited while he scrolled through his contacts and then pressed the Call button.

"Sid. Seth Mathias … You saw? No, we got out. I'll explain it all to you, but I need to meet with you in person. Privately. No one can know. Can you do it now? … Good. Do you remember the woman with me? She'll pick you up in an hour, out in front of your house. She's not stopping, she's not waiting, and she's not getting out. Will you recognize her? … Yes, dressed. Just go with her and don't ask questions until you get to me. Got it?"

Karen and Sicals looked at Seth, waiting for the explanation.

"Forget freedom of the press, we'll try to maintain freedom *with* the press."

Chapter Thirty-two

Philip

The trip home gave Philip the opportunity to examine the day's events, and their implications for his plan. He came to one conclusion: everything was screwed up. Mathias and a mystery woman were on the run with information about him, and he didn't know how much or where it came from. And then there was the phone call just before Mathias's escape. The events had to be connected, meaning Mathias had other resources, technical resources. After thinking about it, the screwed-up conclusion seemed optimistic.

Once inside his condo, Philip poured himself a shot of the Evan Williams single-barrel bourbon that he preferred over scotch when he didn't need to show off his collection of expensive single-malts. He took the drink into his office and opened the curtains with the push of a button. He sipped his drink, looking out over the city. With a conscious effort, he focused himself, put the emotion out of his mind, relaxed the tension from his body and thought about his next move.

Philip wondered most about Mathias's information and its source. It couldn't be complete or the FBI would have been there by now. Then he worried about surveillance. Were they watching him now? He would put more effort into observation until he was certain. And he would call the security company to re-check his office and home for bugs.

The Obsidian visit, by itself, could have been coincidental.

The E-nunC8 visit held the key, making the other too much of a coincidence. E-nunC8 should have been lost in the background noise, indecipherable from all the other traffic. Did someone at the company stumble onto it and contact Mathias? That seemed the only likely way for him to know, and Philip decided to reconsider the streaming video system for the next Screenshot event. In fact, he would have to reconsider the entire process before the next event, double- and triple-checking for loose ends that could lead back to him.

The woman in the trailer and the phone call—how did they connect? She could be an innocent bystander, someone unfortunate enough to spend the wrong night with Mathias. Then why did they try to disguise her identity? That made sense only if her true identity risked her life. Then again, she could be anybody who didn't want her identity broadcast over the Internet. Maybe she needed to hide from a husband or a boyfriend.

On the note pad, he scratched the simple message *how?* to remind him to consider the phone call and the escape. How had he interfered with the cell phone signal? How did he even know there was a cell phone involved? And why hadn't they used the door?

He remembered the image of Seth after the call, half-inside the cabinet, talking about escape pods. He went to the trailer manufacturer's web page and discovered the cabinet housed the electrical circuits. Mathias had used some kind of electrical field, he realized, and someone called him with the idea and instructions. The door would have been charged, and therefore unusable.

Who called? What did they know? And most important, what to do about it?

Karen

Karen found the address without difficulty with her Mapquest directions. She drove slowly, not concerned about attracting attention by low speed in the quiet residential neighborhood, although the big Lake Chabot Regional Park sign might make her memorable. She wore her beret, another effort to keep a low profile. The man standing at the end of the driveway matched Seth's description: 50s, tall, African American, receding hair, big guy. "Could have been a power forward," in Seth's words, whatever that meant. He wore slacks and a short-sleeved pullover with the familiar crocodile patch. He seemed very comfortable in his surroundings.

She stopped next to him and he climbed in. He told her his name, probably expected hers in return, but did not get it. She drove far enough away to be out of sight of the house and then stopped.

"Here are the ground rules," she said. "No one is to know about us or this meeting, or who we are or where we are or what we're doing or how we're doing it. No one means no one, not your wife, not your boss, not your priest. If you agree, then you'll get the story, fully and exclusively. If not, then this all stays a secret."

"What story? Screenshot? Do you know who he is? Is that why he tried to kill Seth?"

"That would be covered under the next ground rule that prohibits questions at this point. Do you agree with these rules?"

Sid Beecher, publisher of the *San Jose Mercury News* and Seth's temporary boss, nodded, and Karen asked him to speak out loud so he'd think he was being recorded and stick to the rules.

"I agree," he said. "How far are we going? Oh, right, no

questions. Well, at least it's not more than an hour each way since you got here that fast. Wake me when we get there." But he didn't go to sleep, he watched her and the route.

Karen drove the alley with the confidence gained from practice, and executed the turnaround procedure better than the first time. The books in the door provided access, and Sicals answered with the first knock.

Seth sat upright, his left leg on a pillow to ease the pressure, but he looked uncomfortable.

"Jesus, Seth. Are you hurt?"

"Took one in the butt. I'll be fine. Sit. Before I introduce everyone, you went over the rules and agreed?"

"Yes, of course. I saw what happened, like everyone else. You don't need to worry about me. Now tell me what's going on."

"First, the legalities. Doc?"

Sicals brought two printed pages that Karen knew were identical copies of the simple rules; another motivation for Beecher to keep his word. He asked, "What's this?" and got an explanation before reading both copies and signing them, keeping one for himself. Seth then told him the story to date, leaving out any mention of the Nobel Prize money theft.

"She's a rogue FBI agent on the run? He's a hacker using the FBI computers to do things they think are illegal? You're the next Screenshot target? And you want me to hide you all in my office? Get you resources so you can continue this crime spree? Jeopardize everything I've worked for on the off-chance that you might identify Screenshot? Does that pretty much summarize it?"

Karen felt disappointment and saw that Seth seemed to as well. Neither of them spoke, but Sicals did.

"Off-chance? Is that your estimate of the probability of my programs working? You are clearly an ignorant person. My programs have worked exactly as they were designed. Within," Sicals walked over and looked at his computer screen, "forty hours and forty minutes, I will have identified the originating computer of Screenshot. And I am a scientist, not a hacker. In my work, I use the scientific method and proper grammar."

He stared at Beecher, waiting for a response.

"You need private space where you can work and live for the next four or five days. With a high-speed Internet connection and a top-end workstation," Beecher said, without the sarcasm this time.

"Preferably a rack of thirty-eight Sun servers, a fiber hook-up with ten megabits per second, and two FAS3070 network-attached storage racks, about 500 terabytes should do it," Sicals added.

"And you need it when?"

"Tomorrow," Seth said. "We're staying here tonight and pulling out first thing."

"In a stolen van?" Beecher kept focusing on the broken laws, and Karen worried about the length of that list.

"We have no options," Seth said.

Beecher sat back and looked up, saying nothing for several minutes.

"I'll be here at eleven to pick you up. Leave the van for the FBI to return. Are you bringing all this equipment?"

Karen interrupted Sicals before he could start on his delicate equipment speech. "No. Just the software and memory. We'll pull the hard disks and bring them." Sicals looked disgruntled.

"Where are we going?" Seth asked.

"I've got one office with a connected conference room and

private entrance, and the Internet connection. I'll move the current occupant for the time being and you can work there."

"Won't he be upset? Or suspicious?"

"No. No one will complain. It's my office. This had better work, Seth. We're talking about my business. My career. I'm not too keen on turning it over to your … um … team, here, so show me some results. Soon."

Chapter
Thirty-three

Philip

Philip woke when Laura climbed back into bed.

"Ohh, what's this?" she asked, looking under the covers. "Let me take care of that for you."

She straddled Philip and with a little maneuvering, put his morning erection to its intended use. "Oh, Jesus," Philip said, and he repeated it over and over. His entreaty grew increasingly urgent, and ended with a final "Oh, Christ," completing his prayer of passion.

"Amen to that," Laura said, collapsing next to him.

Since her overnight stay the night of the Redo kill, Laura had spent one or two or more nights a week at Philip's, and their relationship continued at the same fevered pitch as that first time. The previous evening's fundraiser ended after midnight, and their lovemaking continued well into the single-digit hours. Philip looked forward to a relaxed Sunday morning, especially after the events of the day before, and the climactic start to this one.

He waited in bed while Laura used the bathroom again. Wearing the robe she kept there, part of her moving-in beachhead, she then went to make coffee. Philip cleaned up and put on his own robe before going into the office to check his e-mail. As he expected, there was nothing new and he shut down the program. Instead of closing immediately, a dialog box said, Cleaning messages from the server. It did this little bit of housekeeping automatically after every e-mail check, but today it took longer than normal, and, always wary of security, he made a mental note to find out why later.

Breakfast turned into a leisurely review of the Sunday papers until Laura left, and it was one o'clock before Philip got back to the computer. Checking his e-mail from his local Outlook program showed nothing new, and again there was a noticeable pause while his computer was cleansed of all messages sent to Philip's local machine. Since he hadn't sent or received any, he guessed that it had to be cleaning filtered spam. Philip methodically checked all of the folders and found nothing unusual. He closed Outlook and decided to go right to the Internet Service Provider's computer and see what was there.

Bypassing Outlook meant he could see the messages directly on the ISP's server. What he found startled him: 137 e-mails, sent in the slightly more than seven minutes since he'd deleted all the previous sent mail. His first thought was malware, a program that hackers secretly attached to a computer and used it to send spam or run phishing schemes, providing extra processing power for the hackers and making the e-mails look genuine. His firewall and security system should have caught something like that, but the fixes were sometimes hours or days behind the schemes.

He checked the header, the information listing the path of the e-mail, including its origin and destination, and found it was sent to seth.mathias@gmail.com. Philip jerked his hands back from the keyboard, like it was suddenly contaminated with something repulsive.

Impossible, he thought, and instantly went to full alert. All the other ones went to Mathias as well.

"Bugger," he said, and he knew that somehow Mathias had

tracked him to this computer. The e-mails must be providing a trail. Philip didn't know how this could be done, but that didn't matter. First he had to stop it. Then he could study it.

Looking through several of them, he discovered that they were identical Return Receipt Requested responses. Mathias's last e-mail had asked for one, but Philip had declined and thought nothing more of it. Apparently it had planted code to keep sending the message. The problem should be easily solved; he only needed to delete the offending e-mail from the ISP's server and from his own, and then re-boot. If that didn't work, he could use any of a number of commercial sweeper programs to clean it off his computer.

It took only a few minutes to accomplish that, and he found no further sent return receipts. Now that he had stopped the process, he would do the study.

Several hours brought him no closer to the "how did he do it?" answer, but it did give him an idea, one that would help him find Mathias now that he'd gone to ground. Philip went back on-line and did a Google search, finding what he wanted in Palo Alto. He then deleted the e-mail account Mathias had used, packed up his video equipment and laptop computer, grabbed his keys and headed for the garage.

The FBI

The meeting had been called in haste after the previous day's events, after an FBI agent had, live on the Internet, evolved from voyeur cam subject to phony TV news producer to near murder victim. Then she evolved to something else altogether.

"She's what?" Hendrickson half rose from his chair, his eyes wide and his mouth gaping.

"A fugitive, sir. Technically, anyway. She was suspended Friday, pending an investigation into her role in allowing unauthorized access to FBI computer resources. She was warned to stay available for further questioning. I can't reach her at home or on her cell phone. When she didn't conference in for the meeting, she became a fugitive. She may be hurt and unable to contact us, but we canvassed all the hospitals and clinics and found nothing. And, of course, the ranger at the park said she seemed fine when she stole his truck. I contacted Stan Holcomb and he's on his way in. He's her boss and has the information about her."

"I know who he is, Leonard. Did he tell you anything else?"

The other four agents in the conference room looked back to Leonard Lyons, who wouldn't answer to the name Leo, for his response.

"Only that she had some software doing data mining that was possibly illegal, and that she'd given her ID and password to someone else to use to run the software. He said to pull the file on a Dr. Morgan Sicals and he would brief us when he got here."

Hendrickson picked up the conference phone and requested the file. It arrived at the same time as Holcomb, who then briefed the group.

"Karen, Agent Larsen, has this crackpot scientist with some theory about tracking Screenshot through his Internet connection. Some crazy theory about following hoof prints in a stampede backwards through time.

"You can see from the size of this Sicals character's file that we've kept tabs on him and some of his more notorious activities, mostly involving his feud with the Nobel people. This guy's ball is not fully inflated, and I told her no way we were going to involve him, but she must have gotten over-zealous. We aren't certain of our legal exposure, so she was put on leave while Justice sorts things out."

Hendrickson picked up the narrative, updating Holcomb on the meeting.

"We tried to contact Agent Larsen after yesterday's Screenshot event, but we haven't heard back from her. According to the local police, there is no sign of anyone dead or wounded in the trailer, but a couple answering their description apparently stole a park van and left the scene. We want to question them, especially about Screenshot's reference to something Mathias was doing, and about the phone call he got just before the explosion. Do you know anything more? Have you been in contact with her?"

"No to both," Holcomb answered. "My people are sifting through the logs, trying to understand what was done and what she might have learned. We've got nothing, so far."

"Uh, sir," one of the agents reading the Sicals file said, "it says here that Sicals has a grudge against the Nobel committee, and has been trying toget recognized for some work he did that was credited to someone else."

"That's right. The guy's been writing everyone for … Oh, shit. You don't suppose?"

"It does seem like kind of a coincidence."

Everyone sat in silence while Hendrickson's expression went through severalvolutions, from eyes-wide surprise to furrowed-brow thoughtful to squintingconcern before settling somewhere near face-collapsed resignation.

"If it's true, we are really fucked. The press will have a field day with this, and we'll have Congress so far up our ass they'll be tasting our dinner. Well, let's see if we can't make something good out of it. Leonard, find out who has the case at Interpol and set up a conference call today.

Pearson, get Sicals' address and have a team bring him in. Tell them to be on the lookout for Larsen and Mathias. What am I missing?"

"The locals?"

"Right. Pearson, make sure the local authorities are notified and invited in. See if they have anything from the explosion yet, or if our information helps them. What else?"

"Mathias's cell phone records," one of them suggested. "Let's find out who called him."

"Good. Take care of that. Stan, do you have anything that will help?"

"No. If she's with Mathias, and she certainly seems to be, then our contact information, family and such, is probably useless. I'll check on it. And I'd better confirm that her network access is terminated."

"Sir?" Leonard offered tentatively. "What if she and Sicals are working together? What if the whole Screenshot tracking thing was just a cover? What if she's sitting on $17 million?"

Hendrickson didn't answer for many seconds. Then he told Leonard, "Get warrants for their arrest. All three of them."

Chapter
Thirty-four

Karen

The crash awoke Karen with a start, a hostile sound that increased her disorientation as she sat up and looked around the unfamiliar room. Before she had the chance to react, a familiar voice said, "I beg your pardon, I seem to have dropped the pitcher," through the closed bedroom door. Sicals, she thought. His bed, his apartment, his clumsiness. Then she remembered the sleeping arrangements and wondered where Seth was.

Half asleep, she looked at her watch and saw the big hand on the nine, but no small hand. She realized it was under the big one and it was 8:45. Much later than she normally slept. She dressed and went to the bathroom to splash water on her face. Her hair scared her, and she ran her damp hands through it until it fell easily into its naturally straight form.

She found Sicals cleaning up the spilled water and refilling the plastic pitcher to make coffee. Seth sat on the couch, looking like the graveyard shift had just ended and he wanted his replacement to show up.

"Good morning, Doctor," she said as she walked past him to check on Seth. She put her hand on his shoulder and kissed him on top of his head, suddenly realizing the intimacy of the act and feeling more nervous about that than their night together. But Seth reached up and stroked her back, and she felt relieved and happy. "How are you feeling?" she asked him.

"Stiff. Sore. I'll be fine once I get moving."

"Yeah, we better get moving. Doctor, may I check my e-mail from your computer? I haven't looked at it since Friday night."

"Certainly. Let me enter my password." He typed what seemed an entire sentence.

She tried to access her FBI e-mail, but the network didn't recognize her ID and password. She checked her personal account and found one from Hendrickson. She read it and jumped up.

"We've got to get out of here right now."

"What's wrong?" Seth asked.

"Hendrickson set up a Sunday meeting that I was supposed to conference into over an hour ago, East Coast time. They'll be onto the Doctor by now. Doctor, get all your hard drives, memory sticks, back-ups, cds, everything."

"But—"

"Doctor," she interrupted, "do it now or the FBI will be reading them in an hour." That convinced him, and he started pulling the hot-swappable drives from his computer.

"Seth, can you travel?"

"Yeah, I'll be fine. Here, just help me stand up and I'll walk it loose."

She did, and then told him, "Find anything that we brought with us and throw it in a bag to take. Leave nothing they will know was ours. And the sheet, too. It's got your blood on it. I'm going to warn Arthur and see if he'll keep quiet about you and me and maybe stall them when they get here."

Karen bounded up the stairs and hammered on Arthur's door. His look of anger evaporated as soon as he saw it was her, and he smiled. "Why, Miss Larsen. Visiting your Uncle again?"

"Look, Arthur, you know, right? I'm not his niece."

"Yes, I kinda figured that. Especially after seeing you on the news."

"The police or the FBI are going to show up looking for the doc. We're leaving with him. Could you not mention we were ever here? And maybe stall them a bit?"

"Is the doc in trouble?"

"We all are. Can you help?"

"For you, I'd be happy to. Po-lice and I ain't too friendly to begin with. But you'd better hurry out the back, 'cause here they come."

She turned to the window and saw three cars coming down the street, identical Ford Crown Vics.

"I'll just go out on the stoop and sit for a spell, and chat with them."

"Thanks, Arthur," she said and gave him a quick kiss on the cheek before jumping three stairs at a time down to Sicals' door.

"Now! We've got to go now," she shouted. "They're here. Seth, grab our blankets and bring them." She tucked her hair into her beret while they gathered them.

Karen peeked up the stairs. The front door was still closed. She pushed Sicals and Seth in front of her through the door to the storage area. "Doctor," she said, "open the back door carefully. Make sure there's no one out there." As soon as he did that, she closed her door and followed them up the stairs to the back courtyard.

"Wait here a second," she told them, and ran to the corner of the house. She peeked to see if anyone was coming. The alley was empty, but one of the FBI cars was parked at the end, mostly blocking the exit.

"Come on, over the wall," she said, pointing to the collapsed shed.

Sicals balked. "Over the wall? But why not just take your van?"

"Doctor, there are FBI agents out front with cars and guns. We wouldn't get very far in a car chase. Now hurry."

She helped both men up and over, but remained on the wall herself.

"Doctor, where are we? What's down there?" she asked, pointing directly away from the apartment.

"More houses and a church."

"Church? Perfect. Sunday morning. There'll be people. Wrap those blankets over your heads and try to look homeless. Head for the church, but not too fast. Find someplace to wait, under a tree or on a bench. Keep wrapped up and don't talk to anyone. Seth, call Beecher and get him here fast, then turn your phone off so it can't be traced. If I'm not back by the time he gets here, go without me. I'll find my way to the newspaper and meet you there."

"Back? Where are you going?" Seth asked

"I'm taking the van and leading them the other way. You'll have a chance to get away. I'll dump it fast and meet you at the church."

"But that's—"

"No time to argue. I'm exposed up here. Now go!"

And she slid back down the shed and ran for the van.

Seth

She disappeared. He started to call her back, but caught himself. Attracting attention wouldn't help. And there was no way he could climb back over to catch her. He balled his fists and jerked them down like he was slamming the top of a counter, demanding attention from an inattentive clerk.

"Mr. Mathias? Someone is watching us," Sicals said, pointing to a window in the house belonging to the wall they had just crossed. "Perhaps we should leave."

Seth looked up. An elderly black woman in an apron, visible from the waist up, held what he hoped was a kitchen utensil, and not a weapon. Or a phone.

"You're right, Doc. Let's go."

As they walked down the alley to the street, Seth kept glancing over his shoulder, hoping Karen would appear. Sicals waved to the woman in the window, raising his right hand like he was taking an oath, and bowing his head. She scowled in return.

On the street, Sicals led the way toward the church, his blanket around his shoulders, walking upright, determined, a gowned professor on his way to teach a class. So much for subtlety, Seth thought. With his limp, Seth thought he looked the part. When they reached the church, Sicals plopped himself down conspicuously on a bench facing the street. He sat upright, like he was waiting for a bus.

"Doctor," Seth said, "why don't you wait in the shade under that tree, and I'll call from here."

Sicals looked behind and said, "That's quite all right, Mr. Mathias, I'm fine here. You go right ahead and call."

"We can't be seen together. We'll be easier to spot. And I need to be where I can signal Beecher when he comes."

Sicals seemed to analyze Seth's reasoning, maybe looking for flaws, or maybe just unwilling to sit on the grass. Either way, he said, "Very well," and walked to the tree. He spread his blanket out like he was preparing a picnic and sat, leaning against the tree, hands folded on his lap, eyes closed. Seth couldn't tell if he was sleeping, or perfecting Einstein's Unified Field Theory.

Seth sat on the bench and dialed Beecher, concealing the cell phone under his blanket. He wondered how Sid would react to being the getaway driver.

"Sid? Seth. We've got some problems here. Can you come and get us right now?"

"What problems?"

"I'll explain when you get here. We're at the Holy Trinity Church—"

"Are you crazy? What are you doing out in public? You'd better explain these problems before I come to get you."

Seth tried to downplay their situation, but as soon as he mentioned FBI agents at Sicals' apartment, Sid went sour on him.

"You're running from the FBI, and I'm supposed to save you? Seth, I'm a businessman. I don't do that kind of thing. You'd better find another place to go."

"There is no other place. If you want the story of the year, hell, the decade, you've got to help us. Now."

"I can't. I can't aid and abet fugitives. I want the story, but I need my job so I can publish it. Sounds to me like I can't have both."

Seth played his hole card and hoped it trumped the objections.

"They're looking for Karen, not me or Sicals. At least not yet. She took the agents with her," he said. "It's just me and Sicals, and we're up against the clock. If we don't get on-line pretty quick, we'll lose Screenshot. You'll lose the story."

After a long pause, Beecher said, "Tell me where you are. But you're on thin ice, Mathias. I want results fast or you're going to need a new hideout."

Karen

She climbed into the van and struggled to get the key, on its bear-shaped wooden key chain, into the ignition.

She hesitated and took a deep breath to stop her hand from trembling. Just let Sicals find Screenshot, she thought. Then everything will work out.

She started the van and drove slowly down the alley. She approached the parked Bureau car until the front bumpers touched. She pressed the accelerator tentatively. The engine strained. Karen gave it more gas. The van moved slightly forward, pushing the FBI sedan. The car's alarm sounded, the horn honking and the lights flashing.

Now or never, she thought, and pressed the accelerator to the floor.

The tires spun, smoke filled her rearview mirror. The van bucked once, twice and again. The sedan moved backwards each time. Just as she cleared the building, an agent ran out and shouted. Karen backed clear of the sedan, turned hard left, and drove up the sidewalk, over the curb and down the street in the opposite direction that the FBI cars faced.

At the first intersection, she turned left and found herself speeding directly into on-coming one-way traffic. After the initial shock, she realized this might help her get away, and drove straight up the center of the two lanes. The sparse Sunday morning traffic swerved left or right as she played chicken with each of them and won. She glanced briefly in the rearview mirror for signs of pursuit.

After two blocks, she saw an opening and yanked the wheel to the left, now going with the traffic on a two-way street. Two blocks later she took a right. She stuck to the pattern, figuring if she stayed more than two blocks ahead, they couldn't see her and wouldn't know her direction. Two blocks and turn left, two more and turn right, repeat.

She lost count but guessed she was ten blocks east and ten blocks north of Sicals' apartment. Or maybe west and south. She made the next turn and glanced in the mirror. Flashing red and blue lights on the familiar bar across the top of yet another Crown Vic.

If the locals are in the chase already, I'm screwed.

She pulled over to the right curb and decided to stall. The young officer approached the van, reading the Lake Chabot Regional Park graphic on the side. He hesitated, his right hand on his holstered pistol. When he reached her window, he stood a little back.

"Morning, Miss. May I see your license and registration, please?"

That was an odd request if the FBI has alerted them, she thought. She handed him her license then searched the glove compartment.

"Miss, step out of the van, please. Slowly."

He had taken two steps backwards and put his hand back on his pistol. She dropped the contents back into the glove compartment and exhaled slowly.

"Please take off your hat," he said, again surprising her with an odd request.

Her blonde hair tumbled out.

"It *is* you," he said, glancing from her license picture to her and back. "From the Internet. They told us yesterday that you were an FBI agent and you were in some danger and we were to be on the lookout for you."

Before she could answer, his expression changed and his hand went back to his pistol.

"Is there anyone else in the van?"

"No one else. I'm alone. And if you know about the Screenshot stuff, then you'll know I'm in a hurry. Can I have my license and get going?" She stepped closer to him as she asked, her hand extended.

"I've got to call this in. I'll need your Bureau ID for my supervisor."

"I don't have it. I'm undercover, remember? And I can't wait for your supervisor to call his supervisor and so on. Call it in. And have your supervisor call the Bureau if he's upset. I expect he knows the number." She wheeled around, holding her breath and walked back to the van.

"Wait," he ordered, and she stopped. "You forgot your license."

Karen drove off. Three turns later she pulled in next to a convenience store with a dumpster on one side. She parked around the far side of it to conceal the van from the street. As soon as the officer called it in, the police net, guided by radio and maybe helicopter, would quickly close on the moving van. She left it there and walked away.

She considered her situation. No money, no friends, no phone, no car, police and the Bureau in pursuit. It was going to be a long walk to San Jose. A thirty-mile walk.

Chapter
Thirty-five

Seth

The knock on the conference room door startled Seth, and he opened it to a security guard.

"She says she's with you," he said, pointing to a smiling Karen.

Seth took two quick steps around the guard and wrapped her in his arms.

"Guess she is," the guard muttered as he walked away.

"You've got to pay the cab driver out front, then I'll tell you what happened. Are we set up?"

"Sicals is in the office," he said, pointing to the open door between the two rooms, "and he should be set up by now. This is the living quarters. As you can see, we have all the amenities. Coffee pot, microwave, mini-fridge, mattresses on the floor. Make yourself at home and I'll settle the bill."

When Seth got back, he found Karen had brewed them each a cup of coffee, and she told him of her escape. After ditching the van, she had walked until she found a hotel and then had taken the shuttle to the airport. Hoping to get lost in the maze of cabs, she took one to the newspaper building. Seth didn't much care how she got there, just that she did. She had just finished when Sicals surprised both of them.

"Drat," he said.

Seth looked at Karen, his head tilted.

"What's wrong, Doc?" he called to the next room.

"We've lost the return e-mails. I thought maybe he shut down his computer, but I sent an anonymous e-mail and it bounced back as undeliverable. His e-mail account seems to be invalid."

"What does that mean?"

"He closed the account. We're at a dead end."

Seth and Karen jumped up and hurried to the office.

Seth asked the logical but useless question, "How can that be?" He got a look of disdain from Sicals.

"It can be that he closed the account, as I just said. Possibly he discovered the R-Cubed program, or it's a coincidence. He might transit through e-mail accounts for security reasons."

"It's not a coincidence," Karen said.

"I'm inclined to agree with you, Miss Larsen. That makes our position untenable until the next Screenshot event. We are back where we started five days ago."

"Can't we just send another e-mail? Maybe to one of his other addresses?"

"We can try, Mr. Mathias, but even with a valid address, if he is aware of the program then he will stop it before it gets a chance to do anything."

"So, what have we got to lose? If he knows, he knows. If he doesn't, we're back in."

Three hours later, they were no closer to success.

"Doctor, you said you sent an anonymous e-mail to check the account status and it was returned as undeliverable," Karen said. "Is it possible that his spam filter kicked it back to you?"

Sicals thought a moment and then said, "You might be right, Miss Larsen. The filter would have to be on the ISP server if his computer was off, but that is not unusual. We should try a new e-mail from Mr. Mathias and see if that goes through."

"What will you say, Seth?"

He thought a moment, and then said, "I'll just ask him why."

Philip

In the second-floor office directly across the street, Philip could see a woman working at a desk. The telephoto lens on his video camera pointed at the doors below her window, and he watched the frequent comings and goings of the patrons, looking for a familiar face.

The café had opened at six, and Philip watched from his hotel room when it did. He didn't know how long it would take, or even if it would work, but the plan to lure Mathias to him required patience. So he set up shop, did some work, made some calls, ordered in room service, and watched the doors. After four hours, everyone began to look like Mathias in disguise, and he found his mind wandering to how each person could be him, rather than looking specifically for him.

The day before, Philip had gone to The One World Café, an Internet café in Palo Alto, and re-opened the e-mail account that Mathias had used to send the return receipt program. He hoped Seth would try again, and he intended to let him succeed. If they tracked him down, it would be to here, and Philip would be waiting.

After opening the account, he had a latte and surfed military and technology sites looking for inspiration for new weapons. He didn't find any, but the search filled the time until the e-mail arrived. It simply said, "Why?" Following the same process that had got the worm installed on his computer the first time, he opened the e-mail, closed it, and declined the return receipt request. He didn't bother to answer. The *why* question was unimportant. He thought about when and where.

After getting the e-mail and making what he hoped was the link that would lead Mathias to him, Philip had crossed the street and checked into the Tremont Hotel, tipping well to get the room he wanted and the privacy he needed. There would be no housekeeping during his stay. At seven that evening, the café doors closed for the night, and Philip went home. He planned to repeat the six AM to seven PM surveillance Tuesday, the next day, through Friday, hoping Mathias or the girl would show up to investigate.

With plenty of time to think about it, Philip considered the other possibilities. He still only half-believed that he could be tracked, and expected nothing would happen. Or, someone could come in Mathias's stead, and Philip would not recognize them. Or, once they saw the café from a distance, they could realize Philip had set a trap, and then they would run without his spotting them. So he put the five-day limit on his plan, gave it a 5 percent chance for success, and used the time to consider the options if it didn't work.

But it did.

Chapter Thirty-six

Karen

"Doctor, how did you get this?" Karen asked when Sicals woke her with a note.

"What is it?" Seth asked.

"It's the name and address for One World Associates LLC in Palo Alto, who I presume is the owner/operator of the Screenshot computer we're looking for."

"You found it? Great work, Doc. Let's go check it out."

"Wait a minute. Doctor, your programs were intended to get us the DNS for the Screenshot computer. The only way to tie that Internet address to a physical address is through the Internet Service Provider, and ISPs don't give out that information. Not without a court order. Or at least the imminent threat of one. So how did you get this?"

"The latter."

"You threatened them with a court order? Doctor, I don't think even you could hack out a court order."

"I didn't. This morning, the ISP received an authentic request from a reputable law enforcement agency for the information, with the implied threat of expensive legal action to get it. They decided discretion was the better part of valor and gave up the information, sending it by reply e-mail to me."

"What law enforcement agency? And why to you?"

"The FBI. And mine was the address they were directed to send it to."

Karen stared at him for a long moment, unsure she wanted to know but asked anyway.

"What the hell have you done now, Doctor?"

"Miss Larsen, you clearly understood from the beginning that my programs would only get us Internet information, nothing more. You fully intended for the FBI to use that information to secure the physical location from the ISP, and then proceed with whatever plan you had to capture Screenshot. So we are proceeding as planned."

"You didn't answer my question, Doctor. How did the FBI inquire to the ISP for this information?"

"Through your offices at Phish-Net. I simply re-activated your access and profile and sent the request."

"Simply? You can't 'simply' re-activate profiles and access. You have to be on the FBI network, and you have to be authorized way up the food chain from me."

"Yes, and I was." Sicals stopped and watched Karen, who said nothing, waiting him out. "All right, then. While I had your access previously, I created a profile for myself and activated it as a precaution against the very thing that happened. I am currently on the FBI payroll as a GS-15 special technical advisor. I happened across the order changing your status and de-activating your access, and I just reversed them. We GS-15s are allowed to do that. I also printed out and laminated a facsimile of your FBI identification. It's not authentic, of course, but they have very good equipment here, and I doubt anyone will notice."

Karen examined the card he handed her. "You are a very dangerous man, Doctor."

"Nonsense. I am just an old scientist who wants what is due to him, and who wouldn't harm a fly."

"Are we done now?" Seth asked. "We've got what we want. Illegal access to the FBI computers isn't going to significantly increase our rap sheet when they prosecute us. Let's just get this over with."

Karen forced herself to stop thinking about it, to stop constructing a list of charges in her head, to forget legality for a moment, and the bureaucracy and complexity that it created, and to think about simple justice. She decided that law enforcement had had their chance; it was her turn now.

"Okay then, let's go. Seth, you'll drive me and wait in the car while I go check it out. Doctor, you wait here and stay out of trouble."

"I'm going in with you," Seth said.

"No, you're not. First of all, someone has to drive and be ready to get away quickly if anything goes wrong, and this little adventure has proven that things always go wrong. Second, Screenshot knows you and if he sees you, he'll run and we'll never find him. He couldn't have gotten a very good look at me and is less likely to recognize me in passing. Third, I have the FBI credentials, you don't. And finally, when it comes time to flee, you're working with about one and two-thirds legs. I've got both of mine."

Seth drove the *Mercury News* sedan, a plain tan-colored Ford Taurus with 48,649 miles on the odometer, and Karen guessed most of those were accumulated between stoplights, accounting for the shabby condition of what should have been a reasonable used car.

The short drive to Palo Alto took over forty minutes in the morning traffic. They exited the Bayshore Freeway at University Avenue and drove south into Palo Alto, following the Mapquest directions as Karen navigated. They found Cowper Street, and drove slowly, reading the visible numbers until they got to 706. The sign, all stainless steel cursive letters on a ceramic tile background, read One World Café, and they knew they were at the right place.

Seth pulled into a loading zone across the street and they sat in silence for a few moments, Karen trying to decipher this development.

"It's a cyber café," he said. "Do you suppose that's how he maintains anonymity? Using public computers?"

"I'll go check it out. Wait here. If someone wants you to move, drive around the block and come back."

She walked around the front of the car then darted through a break in the traffic. On the other side, she stopped at the café door and turned to look back at Seth. It was possible that Screenshot was on the other side somewhere, maybe a patron, maybe an employee, maybe the owner. She wasn't sure how she would know, or even what she would do, but it was their best lead, and they had to know if it led anywhere. Most likely, she knew, this was a dead-end, designed by Screenshot for the express purpose of building another layer of isolation between himself and the real world. The thought didn't help.

Inside was what looked like a big Starbucks with computers. They were mounted at angles on a saw-tooth pattern counter along the far walls of the café, in front of her and to the left. An island service counter had a huge, four-station espresso machine, looking to her like a chromed control panel on an old-fashioned steam locomotive, complete with hissing noises from the steam wands. Two baristas manned the machine, echoing the called-out orders from the two cashiers, and placing the completed drinks on the counter under the smaller version of the outside sign, this one reading Pickup. A fifth person filled pastry orders from a tempting array in a glass display case.

Karen went to the pastry server as the least busy of the workers and said, "Manager?" The girl pointed to a thirty-something California male, big, blonde, healthy, working the cash register. Karen went to the head of the line with her fake ID and held it where he could see it. "I need to talk to you."

He wanted it to wait until the rush was over. She didn't. "Hey, Elvis," he called to a younger version of himself who was bussing tables, "take the register for a few."

They sat down at a small, round table that Elvis hadn't gotten to yet, and the manager dropped the empties in the trash, leaving the spills for later.

"Let's do this quick. This is when I make my money."

First she got his name and driver's license and copied the information in a notebook she had lifted off Beecher's desk.

"Is the owner here?" she asked.

"Geez, I doubt it," he said. "Place is owned by some corporation in Atlanta. They've got fourteen of these scattered around the country."

"Explain the system to me. How do you get access to use the computers? Do you have records of users? Any controls on access? That sort of thing."

He looked at the lengthy line at the registers before he answered. "Customers come in. They show a driver's license. We hold onto it while they surf. They're done. They pay. They get their ID back. End of transaction."

"Do you keep records of the users' IDs?"

"No. Our customers want anonymity, we give it to them."

"What about controls?"

"No porn, nothing illegal. No spamming, no hacking. We see it, we throw you out."

"So if I wanted to take a streaming video download and redirect it, I could?"

"No. Our servers would see that as an attempt to spam, you know, someone trying to zombie the computers to dump ads for bigger dicks and lower interest rates. No, it comes in through the firewall, it can be viewed, but stays here until it gets deleted."

"How about e-mail?"

"You can access your own, we don't have it for customers. They want it, we send them to Yahoo or Gmail or Hotmail."

"What's your computer usage like?"

"Overall, about 70 percent. Peak hours, there's a line. Weekends are slow and steady."

"What about during special events?"

"Like what? The Victoria's Secret fashion show or WWF Smackdown or something?"

"Like Screenshot."

Without a pause or a blink, he answered, "No change. I don't allow that shit in here. Worse than porn."

"Is that corporate policy?"

"Don't know. Didn't ask. Doesn't matter. We about done?"

Karen didn't know what else to ask. This seemed like a dead end, but she didn't know how to confirm that. Maybe Sicals would have an idea. She thanked the manager for his time and left.

On the sidewalk, she looked across the street for Seth, and got her picture taken.

Philip

Philip brewed his second cup of lousy hotel coffee, half-watching through the window as customers entered and exited the café. He wondered how he would make it through the day, let alone tomorrow and the next. Maybe the whole thing was a dumb idea.

He had suppressed the video camera's motion sensor and alarm because the high volume of morning customer flow kept it sounding incessantly. The video recorded when it detected any motion in its field of view, in case he missed anything that he might want to review later.

The last sip of coffee was no better than the first, the opposite in fact, and he set it down on the desk, thinking that maybe he should go across to the café and get a proper cup. When he looked up, he caught a glimpse of someone entering the café, but not the face.

He looked at the computer clock and saw it was getting close to nine. The crowds would thin and he could relax his diligence a little, let the video camera do some of the work. This set off a little train of thought that asked the unanswerable question of when the most likely time for Mathias to show up would be. The answer was, *as soon as he could,* and that didn't help establish Philip's timetable.

The café door opened from the inside and, to his amazement, there she stood, looking around and then across the street in his general direction. The girl with two names. It took a moment to process what he saw, then he grabbed his room keycard and bolted out the door.

He'd parked the Lexus in a two-hour metered zone on the cross street, aimed at the café to give him the best view and a chance to follow his quarry. The timer on his computer reminded him to feed the meter, and make sure there would be no parking tickets to draw attention to himself. He couldn't avoid the credit card charge for the hotel, but he could stay off the radar of anyone looking at his traffic history. Without a good reason, no one would be checking the hotel anyway. He just had to make sure no one had a reason.

He pressed the unlock and remote start buttons on his key fob as he dodged traffic to cross the street, and the car started with a soft whirl. He'd glimpsed her getting in a light-colored sedan. Philip scanned the streets from his driver's seat and saw it going up the street directly away from him. The red light at the intersection stalled him, but he saw the car take a left. Philip forced his car to the left lane, drawing the ire of the driver he cut off, and took the turn, closing the distance. He decided to stick close as long as they were in traffic and make sure he didn't get caught by another light.

At University Avenue, Mathias turned right. At least Philip hoped the driver was Mathias. He followed onto the southbound ramp of the 101 to San Jose and onto 880 North, exiting at E. Brokaw Street. Philip had only the vaguest idea where they were, and no idea at all where they were heading. The area was industrial, and he didn't expect to find any hotels or homes where they could be hiding.

When they pulled into a building entrance, it all became clear to him. Mathias had gone home. The newspaper. He would be working from there and then going to wherever they were hiding, probably a hotel nearby, at the end of the day. All Philip had to do was make himself comfortable and wait. Figuring they wouldn't be leaving anytime soon, he went on a quick search for a Starbucks and a newspaper, and a sandwich for lunch later.

Hours after he ate that sandwich, Philip lost patience and seriously considered going inside and shooting everyone until he got to Mathias. He had the gun, but only sixteen rounds, and that might not be enough. Besides, going postal would lower Screenshot's very high standards for creative killing. So he waited, getting hotter and stiffer and madder by the minute.

Sometime after six, she came out through the same door she had gone in earlier, an entrance off to one side, not the main one. Her hair was hidden under a soft hat, and if she had used the front door, he might have missed her in a crowd, her most noticeable feature hidden. She left the parking lot in the same car they'd arrived in and Philip followed at a discreet distance. At the intersection with the city street, she turned right into a steady flow of traffic. That made it easier to hide himself, but harder to follow her, and Philip concentrated hard until he remembered that she would have to come back this way to get Mathias, so he could always pick her up again.

Just as he started to relax, she turned left into a restaurant, Carlos Goldstein's. Maybe she was after kosher enchiladas. He parked several places further into the lot and followed her inside.

She spoke to the hostess and then walked to the bar where she spoke to the girl serving drinks, who nodded and said something in return, and Miss Two-names sat at a stool to wait. The bar was u-shaped, with her at the center of the base, the food-to-go pickup spot. Philip sat at the side to her left, about twelve feet away, and ordered a beer. The restaurant name and phone number were printed on the cocktail napkin, and he dialed the number on his cell phone, holding it out of sight under the bar. Watching, he saw the hostess pick up the phone at her station and answer. He turned away and spoke into the phone, asking for the bar.

The bartender picked up the phone and Philip said, "Sorry to bother you, but my friend is picking up our order and I wanted to add something. Would you see if Karen Ryan is there yet?"

The girl held her hand over the phone, and looking toward the stools at the pick-up point, asked "Is there a Karen Ryan here?" No one acknowledged the name.

"Oh, she may be waiting in the car while my other friend picks up dinner. Try Julianne Foster."

When she called that name, his quarry's head jerked up, and she looked frantically around the room. Philip had lowered his phone and his eyes, looking disinterested while she tried to locate the source of the page. Just as the bartender started to raise the phone to speak, the woman said, "I'm Julianne Foster," and reached out her hand. She answered with a very tentative "Hello," still glancing around.

"Well hello, Miss Foster-Ryan, or is it Ryan-Foster?"

"Who is this," she asked.

"Silly question. Who do you suppose it is?"

"I suppose it's some sicko who saw me on the Internet and enjoys sadism."

"Good point. I hadn't considered that. I didn't see you on the Internet. I put you on the Internet. How about this? An escape in a stolen park van with Mathias taking some shrapnel in the butt."

"You were there?"

"Wouldn't have missed it for the world. But enough small talk. I see your order is here. Go ahead and get it and go outside normally. And Miss Ryan-Foster, if you try anything, I will shoot you. In the face. And then the nicely dressed gentleman to your right. And then the man next to me who might remember my face. And then the perky blonde bartender. And then I'll escape in the stampede, and no one will ever be the wiser. Do you understand?"

"Yes."

"Will you do as I say?"

"Yes."

"Good. See you outside."

Philip closed the phone and watched while she paid and took her bag. He put a five on the bar and followed her closely. Outside, he said, "Walk toward your car, but keep going past it. I'll tell you when to stop."

At his car, he said, "Here. Set the food on the trunk and go to the passenger door." She did as he told her and then followed his instructions to get in the car and fasten her seat belt. He cuffed her hands with plastic cable ties from the glove compartment, anchoring her in the loop of the shoulder and lap belt.

He went around to the driver's side, picking up the bag of food on the way and setting it on her lap after getting in. They looked at each other, and he asked, "What's for dinner?"

Chapter
Thirty-seven

Seth

Seth paced, stopping on each round-trip to the other end of the conference room to pull the blinds aside and look for her car.

"She should have been back twenty minutes ago. Something's wrong."

"Perhaps she got lost. Or there is a long line."

"The car has a GPS. I'm calling the restaurant."

The hostess transferred him to the bar where the bartender remembered the pretty Asian lady, wearing a hat that didn't quite hide her blonde hair.

"Yeah, she picked it up a half-hour ago. You the guy who called her?"

"What guy? Who called her?"

"I dunno. She got a call. Some guy wanted to change the order. She didn't, though. Just picked it up and left."

Seth thought for a moment.

"Who did they ask for?"

"Oh, man, I don't remember. I called her name and she answered."

"Was it Karen Larsen?"

"Yeah, maybe. That could be it. Wait, there were two women on that order. She have a friend with her?"

"No, we must be talking about someone else. But the order for the *Mercury News* was picked up?"

"Just like I said. Half hour ago. And I really think there were two of them."

Seth put the phone down and thought about it for a while. There can't be two blonde Asian women picking up dinner at the same time at the same restaurant. Either the bartender was mistaken about her appearance, or something was wrong.

"We've got to go look for her. I'm calling Beecher to see if he can get us another car."

Beecher said to stay put until he got there. When he did, about thirty minutes later, he found Seth pacing at almost a jog, muttering occasionally and swinging his fist down like he was using it to pound a nail.

"No word?"

"None. You have a car for us?"

"Before we do that, what do you think happened? Where is she?"

"I don't know. Maybe an accident. Maybe broken down. Let's just go look, okay?"

"Do you think someone recognized her and called the police?"

Seth had been suppressing that possibility, but it continued to surface, the cause for the muttering and fist pumping and agitation. When Beecher said it out loud, he stopped and looked at him for a long moment before answering.

"That's the most likely answer, isn't it? Can you check with your police contacts and find out?"

"Yeah, I can, but there will be questions asked. Questions you don't want me to answer. I can put them off with 'confidential sources,' but they won't like it and will probably send someone out here. Just to piss me off, if nothing else. Someone here asking questions might get some answers from the others. You guys aren't exactly invisible. If they have her, who would she call?"

"Probably not here, for the same reasons you just said. She wouldn't want to give away our location. Arthur! She would call Arthur. Doc, do you have his number?"

"No, Mr. Mathias, I do not carry my landlord's contact information. However, it is not a secret. Why don't you try the telephone book."

The phone rang seventeen times at Arthur's before Seth hung up. Not even an answering machine or voicemail. He tried the number again and this time waited for eleven rings, and then called information to get the number verified.

"Sid, can we get that car? We'll go to Arthur's and see what's up."

Sicals answered before Beecher could. "If he doesn't answer the phone, then he is not at home. He has a daughter up north somewhere, Sacramento, I think. He goes to visit her sometimes. Even if Miss Larsen called him, she wouldn't have gotten through."

"Couldn't he be somewhere else? Getting groceries or something?"

"That is unlikely. He shops during the day, one day per week. He makes a project out of it."

"Maybe he went to the police station after she called him," Beecher offered.

"Maybe, but she probably would have told him to stay put for my call. Shit, we're right back where we started. What the hell are we going to do?"

"Sorry, Seth, but this changes things. You can stay another night, but tomorrow I'm taking the both of you wherever you want to go and dropping you off. If they have her, it's only a matter of time before they find you. And it can't be here."

"All right. I understand. You've gone above and beyond already. Before you go home, how about we take one ride to the restaurant and drive by, see if there's anything."

He agreed, and they got into his Audi, leaving Sicals to monitor the phone. Seth kept telling Beecher to drive slower while he tried to see every feature in the growing dusk. When they got to the restaurant, Seth stared off into the distance, lost in thought about what to do next.

"There's our car," Beecher said, startling Seth.

"Go, go. I'll look inside it."

He found nothing—no food, no signs of anything unusual, no messages.

"Face it, Seth, the cops got her. Shit, they might be watching the car right now. Let's go."

Seth reluctantly got back in Beecher's car, moving like something held him attached to the empty Taurus, something elastic that pulled harder the more he stretched the distance. It snapped when he closed the door, and they drove off.

Karen

So this is where they'll find my body, Karen thought. If they find my body.

Screenshot drove the Lexus slowly through what looked like, in the myopia of the headlights probing into shadow, a graveyard for dilapidated buildings. There was nothing to indicate that life currently visited this place. No lights over doors, no windows with a faint glow, no signs on the buildings where the headlights swept by, not even street signs.

The road was potholed and he drove slowly. Even so, the car jounced left and right without warning. Her restricted hands prevented her from compensating and she hit her head on the doorframe and window several times. They had been traveling for nearly an hour according to the clock on the dash. Karen had no idea where they were, except that they had traveled north on 101 toward San Francisco, exited on Cesar Chavez and then ranged through city streets to get to this desolate tract of decay.

Screenshot drove directly to a one-story warehouse-like building, indistinguishable from its neighbors. He stopped in front of a rusty roll-up door that appeared to be sealed closed, and pressed a button on a garage door remote. The door rose and he drove in before it completed the process. He pressed the button again inside, and the door closed behind them.

He turned off the headlights and the car, enveloping them in total darkness and said, "Welcome to the Acme Machine Tool Company. Exclusive suppliers to Screenshot."

He got out of the car and left the door open, the interior light providing a dim, dusky glow that faded quickly into dark and made the building seem never-ending.

To her right, Screenshot unlocked a door to another room, propped it open with something he slid in place with his foot, and disappeared into the room. A light went on in what seemed to be a vacant office, two of its walls solid to waist height with glass above. He played with something on the wall and then propped open another door on the far wall of the room, but she couldn't see into the dark beyond it.

Her mind raced. Acme Machine Tool Company? The Screenshot weapons? But the place was just a dingy old warehouse, with an electric door opener that worked. Before she could make sense of the incongruity, Screenshot opened her door.

"I'm going to take you out now, but there are a few things you need to understand. First, if you make any trouble, I will kill you without hesitation. Or maybe just wound you painfully. I'll decide at the time. Second, trying to escape is futile. As you saw, there is no one anywhere near to hear you or help you. There is no place to hide that I won't find you. Third, if you cooperate, you will see your Mr. Mathias again, soon. If you don't, he can identify your body."

Without waiting for any acknowledgement, he sliced the plastic ties with a very sharp folding knife then stepped back, putting the knife in his pocket and pointing his gun at her.

"Undo your seat belt and step out," he said, waving her into the office. He closed the door behind them and pointed to the open door, indicating with another wave of his gun that she should go through it into the room beyond. She hesitated, somehow more afraid of that room, and its ominous dark. Screenshot nudged her in the back with his gun, and she moved in small, tentative steps, tip-toeing to sneak up on her fear.

Enough light filtered in that she could see a clear path on what looked like a Lego floor, with row after row of thin buttons, spaced very close together and painted grey. It was, she realized, industrial, non-skid flooring. Another incongruity is this dilapidated building.

Screenshot followed her and flipped a switch that made a sturdy click. The room came alive with light from every angle, like she'd stepped inside a light bulb. When her pupils contracted enough to see anything but white, she found herself surrounded by two rows of gleaming machines, as if on display, ready for a buyer.

Shelves and cabinets and bins lined the walls, holding metal and plastic pieces of various size and shape, components that looked like electric motors and hydraulic cylinders, fasteners, more tools, and other things she couldn't identify. She realized she was in do-it-yourself heaven, and that Screenshot, if he operated alone, was a very talented designer and fabricator. No wonder they could never get a line on his weapons. They were just raw materials and individual components until they left here.

"What do you think? Pretty cool, huh? You're the first person ever to see this. Once the room was renovated, everything came in one piece at a time, delivered to a warehouse far from here. Picked it all up myself and brought it here. The forklift you see got everything in through the movable wall there."

He pointed to the wall dividing the machine shop from the empty warehouse. Massive hinges were placed along the top and electric motors and cables strung from the ceiling.

"The whole wall lifts up, tilts open like a garage door. From the other side, you can't tell it's anything but a block wall.

"Come. We'll get you settled for the night," he said, granting her several more hours of life. Hours in which lots of things could happen, she told herself. Good things. "Please cross your hands behind your back. This will only be temporary while I prepare something more comfortable."

She did as instructed and he used another plastic tie to secure them. He led her halfway down the length of the room and told her to sit on the floor next to a pedestal holding the biggest electric drill she had ever seen.

"Now just scooch on over to my pillar drilling machine and wrap your legs around the base." The way he said it sounded like he needed more room to sit on the couch at a cocktail party. Once she had done it, he secured her crossed ankles and she was anchored to the machine.

The position was terribly uncomfortable, adding to the stress and fright she already felt. Sitting up required holding herself with her stomach muscles because the pedestal and table of the machine made it impossible to lean forward enough for gravity to do it. Lying down on her bound hands would be just as bad, but after a few moments of holding the ab crunch, she gave it up and lay back on the floor.

He took a length of steel cable from a reel and cut it off with a large scissor device. He wrapped one end around her left ankle and secured it with a metal clamp and bolts. Then he cut the plastic tie and freed her legs from the pedestal and dragged her across the bumpy floor away from the machine. About eighteen inches from her ankle, he made a loop in the cable, loosely clamped it, and slipped it over her right ankle. When he tightened this, she was hobbled by a fifteen-foot steel tether.

Leaving her there, he walked to the near wall and folded down a bed, latching it to something recessed in the floor. Finally, he took the free end of the cable and fed it through a steel ring that flipped out from the wall. He used another clamp and bolts to secure the loop to the ring.

He stood still and admired his work, then seemed to remember something he had forgotten. He went to a rack of hand tools across the room and selected what looked like a large electric toothbrush, and Karen's imagination showed her all kinds of horrors that could be inflicted with such a device, even though she didn't know what it was.

Once he'd plugged it in and turned it on, she understood it was a grinding tool, and she wondered what part of her needed to be ground. None, as it turned out. He smoothed the heads of all the securing bolts so they could no longer be undone as designed. They would have to be destroyed to open.

"Do you think I can undo those with my teeth?" she asked, trying to show some defiance in her untenable situation.

"No, but you and Mr. Mathias are resourceful people. And I gather from the news that you are an actual FBI agent. Imagine my surprise. That explains your reluctance to identify yourself back in Mathias's trailer, and I'm more than a little curious about how you came to wake up in his bed, but that can wait. Right now, I'm trying to make this as comfortable for you as possible, but anything I do for your comfort increases your range and options. Why, you could tear the bed sheet into little strips and make a lasso and get a wrench from the wall over there, and undo yourself. So you see, I must take care to cover all the possibilities. Try not to move around too much. That cable will chafe your ankles, even through the socks."

He put the tool back in its place and told her, "This is where I sometimes sleep when I'm trying to get one of my toys done. The bed is quite comfortable, and you will find food and drinks in the fridge. You should have just enough length to reach it. I'm sorry about the lack of toilet facilities. I have them, of course, but you won't be able to reach them. If you need to, there's a basin near the bed. Do you have any questions before I go?"

"Yes. Why are you doing this? I mean, why Seth and me?"

"He knows too much. I don't know how or what, but I intend to find out. I'm going to leave the lights on for you. It gets very, very dark without them. And I want you to be able to see all my machines. Study them, figure out what they can do." Here he paused and looked at her for a moment.

"Pick the one you like best," he said, and left her alone.

Chapter
Thirty-eight

Karen

She had a favorite. She'd tried to ignore them, to cover her head with her pillow to block the light and the scene, the landscape of machines and tools stretching over her entire visible world.

The light and the tension teamed up to chase sleep away, and she could clamp her eyes closed for only so long while lying awake. She opened them to get a drink and a fruit yogurt from the refrigerator, and there was no direction she could look that didn't say *the little machine shop of horrors*. Even the wall next to her, covered when the bed was folded up, had engineering drawings hanging on it, whether for reference or decoration, she didn't know. She recognized the Pediphryer, but two others were unfamiliar.

So despite herself, she liked the cream-colored one best. It was about five feet high with a curved, smoked-plastic door that concealed the inner works. A flat-panel video display, now dark, was mounted next to the door on a stalk so it could be adjusted to different viewing angles. She didn't know what it did, and wasn't sure she wanted to. Whatever it was, her body was unlikely to present much of a problem for it.

She'd tried to sleep, to forget the situation, to concentrate on other things, but couldn't. She'd tried not to be afraid, but when the door opened, she was. She'd tried not to think of rescue, knowing she'd only be disappointed, and she groaned when she heard him.

"Good morning, Agent Larsen. Did you sleep well? How did you like the bed? It's that Swedish foam rubber stuff that molds to your body. Pretty comfortable, isn't it? Looks like you don't want to get off. But you must. I need you to stand so I can look at you and see if you have improvised anything during the night. So, please do. Don't make me use force."

Karen peered out from under the pillow and saw him standing out of her reach, relaxed, his hands in the pockets of his khaki pants, wearing a navy-blue short-sleeved pullover and brown leather deck shoes, looking posed for an advertisement. She did as he directed.

"Turn around please. Good. Now let me see your hands. Good. I expect you have to use the facilities, so I'll cut you loose for the moment. As you can see," he reached in his pocket, "I still have my gun. Please don't try anything stupid because I will shoot you."

With that, he tucked the gun back into his back pocket and fetched another one of the clamping devices, a wrench, and the cable-cutter he had used the night before. He cut the cable about five feet from the end at the wall, and pointed to a small room in the corner.

"You will find washcloths and towels in there, but I doubt the efficacy of a shower as you won't be able to undress with the cable around your legs. A sponge bath is the best I can offer. I brought breakfast, so don't loiter or it will get cold."

She decided to maintain silence as long as possible, to withhold any satisfaction he might get from her questions or comments, and to try to hide her fear, even as she hobbled to the toilet.

The facilities, as he called it, were complete, in an industrial way. Stainless steel toilet, sink and shower cabinet. Towels and washcloths and fresh soap were on the shelf above the toilet. Before she opened the medicine cabinet, hoping to find a forgotten Uzi or even something to throw in his face to blind him, he called, "You'll find a new toothbrush in the cabinet above the sink." He seemed pretty up to date on the contents, and she found only the toothbrush, toothpaste, a razor and shaving cream, and Excedrin.

She looked for the morning Karen in the mirror, the disheveled but alert Karen, eager to get on with the day. She couldn't find her. Instead it was a Karen she recognized from bouts of the flu, or a rare hangover. A wan and drawn Karen, eyelids drooping even as the eyes tried to focus, shoulders slumped, breathing through an open mouth, each exhale more of a sigh than a necessary reflex.

She thought about staying in there, but knew that would only get her harsh treatment and make the ordeal even more difficult. She tried to put herself together as best she could, washing her face and hands and brushing her teeth, running her damp hands through her hair to get it in place. Remembering the camera in Seth's trailer, she wrapped a towel to cover herself on the toilet.

"Feel better?" Screenshot asked when she came out. "I brought us some breakfast. There's pancakes and scrambled eggs and Egg McMuffins. Take your pick. Orange juice and coffee, cream and sugar there in the bag. But first, let's get you secured."

He overlapped the two cable ends and used another clamp to link them, and her world became six inches smaller.

"These stupid Egg McMuffins are my weakness. I sneak off to McDonald's on weekends and have one for breakfast. Their coffee is actually quite good, don't you think? I prefer fresh orange juice, but this is okay."

Questions rebounded in Karen's head like the silver ball in a pinball machine. Sneak from where? Why sneak at all? What is the place? But the biggest one, the one she knew had already sealed her fate was, who are you? She ate the scrambled eggs and sausage in silence, looking around like she was at a sidewalk café, refusing to give in.

Screenshot continued his chatter, giving her a synopsis of the news and weather, news that did not include any mention of her disappearance. "Makes you wonder," he said.

When they were finished, he packed up the remains and threw them in a large industrial trash can.

Trash pickup, she thought. This place has to be inhabited sometimes, and trucks had to come around to haul away the refuse. So escape wasn't quite as impossible as he said. Something as simple as a fire and smoke could bring the fire department. A metal trash can would be perfect for that, but there wasn't one. She did see a couple of large metal boxes on wheels, and containers that looked like they might hold kerosene or something else flammable. Her mood improved: there were possibilities.

"Feeling better? Let's make a quick phone call and then I'll get to work."

He took out a cheap-looking cell phone, probably one of those prepaid ones that couldn't be tracked to a user's account, and dialed a number. When he asked for Seth she wanted to grab the phone and hear his voice. She didn't have to. He said, "Please hold for Special Agent Karen Larsen," and handed it to her.

"Seth?" she said. "I found Screenshot."

Seth

The line went dead before Seth could even comprehend what Karen had said.

"Hello? Hello? Can you hear me?"

"If you would like to place a call, please hang up and dial again," the recorded voice told him.

"Goddammit," he shouted, slamming down the phone and startling Sicals, busy at the computer as usual.

"Is something wrong, Mr. Mathias?"

To Seth, the query that would take the Blue Ribbon in the ridiculous-question-of-the-day category.

"Yes, something's wrong. Screenshot has Karen. Shit. How the hell did he do that?"

"Clearly he—"

"It was a rhetorical question, Doctor. Do you have an actual idea to contribute, or just some God damn … drivel?"

"I'll wait. You're obviously not rational at the moment."

Seth almost laughed at that. What did it take to fluster this guy? Besides the Nobel Committee.

"You're right. Sorry, Doc. What were you about to say?"

"It's quite simple, really. The cyber café discovery was planned. Mr. Screenshot must have found the R-Cubed worm and set up the e-mail account there to see if we could track him down. When we did, he somehow knew about it and followed you from there. There is no other explanation."

"You're right. Shit. Pack your stuff, Doc. We're getting out of here. If he followed us, he can notify the FBI or come after us anytime he likes."

"It's already packed. Mr. Beecher made it clear last night that we would be leaving. I'll just pull this hard drive when he gets here and I'm ready."

Seth gathered the few belongings he had. "Is there anything on the computer that anyone can use to prove we were here?"

"No, I've done everything from removable memory, and I'll take that with me. Where are we going, by the way? Somewhere with computer access, I trust."

If the earlier question had been ridiculous, this one was astute, and Seth didn't have an answer. He hoped Beecher did.

Beecher, he remembered and grabbed the phone, searching his pockets for the card with his cell phone number on it.

"It's Seth. We've got big problems. Screenshot has Karen. He must have grabbed her last night at the restaurant." He explained the call and Sicals' analysis.

"I'm on the Nimitz Freeway. I'll be there in fifteen minutes. Tell me when I get there."

Beecher used the private entrance into his office where Seth and Sicals waited, their few belongings wrapped in the blankets they carried. After Seth filled him in, he said, "I've arranged a safe house for you until we get this resolved. I've got someone to take you there."

"Sid, I can't go. I've got to call the FBI and tell them everything. It's the only way to get Karen back before Screenshot kills her." Saying it out loud was like taking a blow. The words took his breath away, and he paused to recover before going on. "You take the doctor and go. It's better I don't know where he is."

"I thought the same thing," Beecher answered. "While you're going to the house, I'll call my attorney and set up a meeting on the condition that you are free to go at any time, without interference or surveillance."

"You think they'll agree?"

"I don't see why not. There's no reason for them to arrest you alone. They only want to question you about Karen and the doctor. We'll give them the Karen information and say nothing about Dr.

Sicals. There's a computer and printer at the house. Why don't you write up the chronology and facts of what went on so far. Include everything except any mention of Doctor Sicals. As far as you know, Karen bought the software at Office Depot."

"Excuse me," Sicals interrupted. "I have an interest in this as well. I think I should be consulted about the arrangements. I, too, am worried about Miss Larsen. I might be able to provide some information or offer some opinion that will help find her, and I want to be included in any meeting with that purpose. You do not need to protect me from your FBI. I am not afraid of them. They have been after me for years, and there is nothing they can do to me. I am thoroughly protected."

"Doctor, I appreciate your offer," Seth said, "but if you're there, the meeting will inevitably include other ... issues, and it's better we focus on Karen and let them deal with the other stuff later. You can help me write up the report, and if we need anything further, we can call you from the meeting."

After some harrumphing, Sicals agreed, and Beecher left to check on the arrangements.

He came back a few minutes later and told them to follow him. They walked through the office corridors, attracting some attention with their unique luggage, and entered the printing facility. They followed Beecher as he wound past the printing presses, quiet for the moment. Men worked with huge rolls of paper and drums of ink, getting ready for when they weren't. A *Mercury News* delivery truck was backed into the loading dock, its doors open and its cargo bay empty.

"Brian will take you to a safe house in this. No one will know you're in there. Go with him and wait until I get there. You'll find what you need, including food. Get me that report so my lawyer can review it before the meeting. I'll call you at the house as soon as everything is set."

Karen

Before she could hear Seth's reply or say anything more, Screenshot snatched the phone and disconnected. He rocked his head back and gave the *touchdown* signal. "That was perfect. I couldn't have scripted it better myself. You just earned yourself a treat. Think about your favorite lunch and I'll get it for us. But right now, I have a lot of work to do. Please make yourself as comfortable as possible. It may get noisy at times, but I'll try to keep it down."

He acts so normal, she thought. How can that be? No one would ever suspect this guy murdered people for sport. She blurted, "Who are you?"

"So, you *can* talk. You don't waste words, do you? The answer must seem very important to you right now. But it's really not, is it? What you should be asking is 'what are you doing?' That is much more germane to your situation than who is doing it."

"All right, what are you doing?"

"I thought about it a lot last night, and I decided to modify the ACME Suffer-cator and use that. It's quite an interesting device. I originally designed it for two men, one of them is the CEO of a chemical company that is solely responsible for 40 percent of the air pollutants in southeastern Louisiana. The other one is the politician who makes sure he's allowed to, in return for very large campaign contributions from the employees in his company.

"The way it works is there are two sealed chambers connected side-by-side with a clear plastic divider so you can see between them. They're large enough for a person to sit comfortably. Each chamber has a pair of numbered buttons. Simple, huh? Now here's the fun part: there's only one air inlet. When I say *go*, it gets closed. To open it, both occupants have to agree which chamber will get the air and which won't, and press the appropriate buttons simultaneously. Until they do, it stays closed. They've got about two hours to decide, then one or both suffocate. Apropos, don't you think? They ruin our air, I take away theirs."

"Modify how? And what does that have to do with me?" She asked the last question knowing the answer in the back of her mind.

"I'm making it mobile. I've got a cargo van in the other bay, and I'm installing the Suffer-cator in it. Then I plan to populate it with you and Mr. Mathias and park it out of the way in the lot of the *San Jose Mercury News*. Let them get the jump on all the other papers. What do you think?"

Karen said nothing, her fears confirmed, and tried to control her rising panic. Locked in the glass box and watching Seth suffocate while she did the same. Under other circumstances, she might have been able to imagine something worse, but at that moment, the Suffer-cator topped the list.

She had time, though. Time to do something. He would have to build his device and capture Seth. How would he do that, she wondered. At least Seth would be alive when he got here.

"You said he knows too much. What do you think he knows?"

"He knows who I am, or at least he is getting dangerously close to knowing."

"He doesn't know."

"Yes, he does. He may not realize it yet, but he knows."

"How does he know?"

"We've met. And we've discussed the Screenshot events. And he is putting things together, and soon all the threads will intersect at me. I need to cut them before they do. Now, I need to get some work done, so we'll have to wait and have this conversation at lunch. Remember, you have a treat coming. And please honor my request for silence. I don't want to have to gag you."

Screenshot went to work, and Karen tried to concentrate on escape. She studied the machine shop for weaknesses, but there was only one door and no windows. No, she remembered, there were two doors, including the one Screenshot had said opened for moving large items in and out. Would that be of any use? Where were the controls? And even if she got it open, there was still the matter of her leash.

Screenshot answered her first question.

"Karen, you don't mind if I call you Karen, do you? Would you move to your right just a couple of steps?" When she obeyed, he said, "That's fine right there."

He took a remote from his pocket and aimed it at a large motor and metal box mounted on the ceiling. The motor whined, and with a thump, the wall next to her bed swung outward. A white van was parked in the empty warehouse on the other side. When the door was fully open, he went to the van, started it up, and backed it into the open space in the shop.

Karen watched the door close with particular care. Would the door and frame be sufficient to act as a huge slicer and shear the cable? If she could get the door open, the cable would reach to the other side and she could try. She looked for another switch.

He went back to work, measuring inside the van, then measuring pieces of clear plastic and heavy sheet metal. He cut these with various tools and machines, drilling holes, experimenting with fit, trimming, and repeating the process.

As she watched and thought, she kept coming back to Screenshot and his Suffer-cator. A gruesome way to die, she thought. Trying to convince someone else to die instead. In the case of the businessman and the politician, someone who cares about you as little as you care about him. She guessed both would die, neither able to sacrifice for the other.

In her and Seth's case, who would die? She couldn't imagine consigning Seth to death, and knew she would choose to die. Was that love? She hadn't thought about love and Seth previously, consciously avoiding the topic. There was attraction, that much she knew. Going both ways. But there was also the situation, and how much of that attraction was driven by their need for each other to get through this? So she had shelved the love question to be reviewed at some future date.

Today was the future date. It had to be because there probably was very little, if any, future left. Did she love him? Did he love her? With the pillow over her head, she closed her eyes and fell asleep with those thoughts.

Seth

It took many more hours to get organized than Seth wanted and, report done and lunch over, he was back to pacing, waiting for the call from Beecher. Instead of a call, Sid walked in with a man Seth didn't recognize and interrupted his trip between the living room and dining room of the small, two-bedroom ranch house.

"We're set. This is Ed Higgins, the paper's attorney. Let's go. The meeting will be at the newspaper. We'll discuss the rules with Ed on the way."

When they arrived, everyone briefed and ready, Beecher again took them through his private entrance to the conference room that had been home to Seth for the past three days, and restored since their departure. Three men waited there, and Seth was introduced to Agent Canaan and his boss, Rich Avrakotos, the Special Agent-In-Charge in the Bay area. The third person was their lawyer, Andrew Kraus.

Higgins started the meeting with a reiteration of the ground rules.

"For the record, we," and he named everyone in the room, "are meeting to discuss the whereabouts of Special Agent Karen Larsen, and how her disappearance is related to the FBI's Screenshot investigation. Mr. Mathias is here voluntarily, and is under no threat of arrest or detainment of any kind. There will be no interference with his departure at any time, nor will he be the subject of any surveillance for the next twenty-four hours. The discussion will include only those topics germane to Agent Larsen, and we will be the sole arbitrator of that. Finally, I will do all the talking for Mr. Mathias. Are we agreed?"

The FBI lawyer responded. "What about Mr. Beecher? Why is his presence required, and what will he report in his newspaper?"

"Mr. Beecher plans to excuse himself from the meeting once we have agreed on the rules. As far as reporting goes, he is not restricted in any way from reporting anything and everything he knows or finds out legally and ethically within the performance of his duties as a newspaper editor. If there is anything said during the meeting that you do not want available to the press, then specify that at the time and we will discuss it and agree on its confidentiality as appropriate."

Everyone scanned and signed the one-page agreement that

Higgins had prepared, and Beecher took it with him to get copies made for everyone. As soon as the door closed, Kraus spoke up.

"Right off, Mathias's report is public information now, and I can't stop Beecher from publishing it verbatim, if he wants. But from this moment on, everything we say is confidential and, while you may speak to Beecher about it or not, it is embargoed for forty-eight hours, or until we recover Agent Larsen or her body. And I would urge you to restrain Beecher from publishing anything at all until either of those conditions has been met. Are we agreed on that?"

Seth stiffened at the mention of Karen's body, but he knew it was intended to shock him and establish the FBI's importance to the investigation. Without them, he knew that was the only thing they would recover. He leaned to Higgins and whispered, "Sid's not gonna like that."

"Actually," the lawyer answered, also whispering, "he anticipated something like this and left it to me to decide. I'm fine with those restrictions."

That agreed, Agent Canaan took the lead and started at the beginning, asking about the first time Seth heard about Screenshot and his decision to write about him. After twenty minutes of questions, Seth and Higgins consulting, and Higgins responding, the FBI lawyer interrupted.

"Look, this will go much faster if we drop the lawyer/client conferences. How about we all stipulate that anything said from that side of the conference table is said by Mr. Higgins there, and in no way is attributable to Mr. Mathias directly. Are you comfortable with that?"

Everyone agreed. The direct questioning began and continued smoothly until they got to Seth's first meeting with Sicals a month earlier. Seth simply said, "I interviewed Dr. Sicals for my third article on Screenshot, and from that point on he had nothing to do with my work."

Canaan tried to press the point, but Seth insisted that he had nothing to add to the report concerning Dr. Sicals, and they would be welcome to ask Karen about his involvement, once they got off their conference chair asses and found her. Kraus responded to that emphatic statement.

"Look, Mr. Mathias, we understand that you have a strong interest in finding Agent Larsen quickly and in good health. We have the same interest, for many of the same reasons. She is one of ours, and we take this very seriously. The search is already under way with, how many agents and police, Bruce?"

"Thirty agents and nearly one hundred local and state police."

"That's an extraordinary level of effort, Mr. Mathias, and the phone call that Agent Larsen made to you has provided us with the best lead to Screenshot so far. The fact that he kidnapped her locally means that in all likelihood, he is local and has her held somewhere local. We are tracking the phone call as we speak, and any further help you can give us could be crucial to finding her. So, we'll leave the Sicals issue for future consideration and proceed. Bruce?"

They left an hour later, and the value of any additional information gained was lost on Seth. The value of the hour wasted wasn't. They seemed motivated more by their process, their procedures, than by Karen's well-being, and Seth decided that would have to change.

Chapter
Thirty-nine

Seth

The thing about doing nothing is that it takes so damn long, Seth thought. He looked at his watch and did the same calculation again: thirty-seven hours and fourteen minutes since she'd left for the restaurant. Twenty-three hours and fifty-one minutes since the phone call. One-hundred and sixty-six dog hours and fifty-seven dog minutes.

He lay on the couch in the safe house, staring at the ceiling, counting the seconds in his head. The phone rang, and he did a credible imitation of a slapstick comedian falling off the couch while groping for the cell phone on the coffee table.

"Hello, may I speak to Seth Mathias, please?"

"That's me. Who is this?"

"You may not remember me, but I'm Philip Hurst. You interviewed me for one of your articles on Screenshot."

"Yes, of course I remember you, Mr. Hurst. Obsidian, right? Venture capital."

"Yes, that's correct. And please, call me Philip."

"Okay, Philip, what can I do for you?" Those were the magic words for Seth—do something—and he hoped Hurst might have something constructive for him to do.

"When we talked, you surprised me with some information about E-nunC8. I investigated further and found things that might be relevant. The problem is, I have fiduciary responsibilities and this needs to be discreet. And I need time before it becomes public to cover our exposure. Could we meet somewhere quiet and talk about it?"

"Relevant how?" Seth asked,

"Well, there seems to be some connection … no, that's too absolute. There *may be* some connection between E-nunC8 and Screenshot. I'm not in a position to pursue it further, and I'd prefer not to be involved with the authorities, so I called you."

"Of course. Where and when?"

"How about back at the campground you were at on the Internet? I saw that, and it was a very close call. Congratulations, by the way, on getting away."

"All right. I'll meet you there in an hour. How about at the ranger station at the entrance."

"Good. We'll find someplace quiet to talk. I'll be driving a plain, white cargo van."

Seth jumped up and nearly ran to the bathroom to get cleaned and ready. A quick face wash, toothbrush, no shave, and a change of clothes would suffice, he decided. That done, he found Sicals in the den, working at the computer.

"I've got an errand to run and I'll be gone for several hours. If anything happens, call my cell phone."

"What errand?"

"Some guy I interviewed before might have Screenshot information, and I'm going to meet him."

"Why doesn't he go to the FBI with it?"

"Maybe for the same reason that you wouldn't: he doesn't trust them. He has a financial interest in a company that might be connected somehow to Screenshot, and he wants to keep the information quiet while he gets out."

"Is it Philip Hurst?"

The question shocked Seth. *How does this guy keep coming up with these things?*

"Yes. How did you know?"

"You mentioned his name when you were discussing this with Miss Larsen, and I ran across him while doing my Digital Gold research. Coincidence intrigues me. I don't believe it happens, so I make note of it and investigate. His company has interests in several high-tech start-ups. Which one is it?"

"E-nunC8."

"Ah, yes. Streaming video. I should have realized the connection. Well, good luck, then."

But Seth was already out the door.

The FBI

"Bruce, we caught a break." The agent bounded into Canaan's office like he had been propelled. "Some kid, well, some twenty-something manager in one of those discount store-front electronics joints downtown remembered one purchase that has the right timing. Guy bought four phones, $160 each with a bunch of minutes. Paid cash. Kid says four phones is unusual, and so is that much cash. But here's the kicker. The kid recognized the guy."

"Who is it?"

"Well, the kid, like every Internet geek his age, has a business plan for the next big thing. He recognized this guy because he's a big-shot venture capital type from up on Sand Hill Road. Anyway, the guy was on the cover of a local business magazine, and the kid told him about his business plan and the guy said, sure, send it along, and gives him his card."

Canaan took the offered card and read: Philip Hurst, Obsidian Capital, Partner.

"That's it? That's our big break? Some rich guy buys cell phones for his girlfriends? Tell me there's more."

"There's more. We ran an MVA records check, and the guy has two vehicles and a clean driving record. One of the vehicles is a new Lexus, what else? The other is a motor home. That rang a bell, so I checked the incident reports. That motor home was parked 200 feet from Mathias's truck and trailer when they blew up."

"So we've got a rich guy with cell phones and a fancy motor home. Not much of a case."

"The local cop who interviewed Hurst wrote that he had a video camera mounted on his dashboard that had about a fifteen-second clip of Mathias' trailer before the explosion. Nothing else. Why would a rich guy be videotaping Mathias' trailer? And why did he stop? *Did* he stop, or did he erase evidence?

"Does this guy show up anywhere else in the file?"

"No, just the motor home."

"All right, it's the best lead we've gotten so far. Let's get this organized and do it right. Get four men tracking down his current, specific whereabouts. More, if you need them. Make certain we know where he is and don't let him disappear. Call Mathias. See if he knows this guy. Play it down, just a routine lead. Tell Jenkins to get his squad prepped. Full equipment, body armor, the whole nine yards. No telling what this guy has stashed. As soon as we have a confirmed location, we liaise with the local PD and set up the grab. Keep me fully informed. I'm going to tell Avrakotos."

As the agent left, Canaan called, "Wait. I'll handle Mathias." He called the number in the file and asked for Seth.

"Who is calling, please," the man who answered asked.

"This is Special Agent Bruce Canaan from the Federal Bureau of Investigation. Now, may I please speak to Mr. Mathias."

"How did you get this number?"

"What? We're the FBI. We get any number we want. Put Mr. Mathias on."

"I cannot."

Loose Bruce tightened. "And why not?"

"He's not here at present."

"Do you know where I can reach him?"

"Yes."

"Where?"

"I cannot tell you that."

Canaan could almost hear that theme music from the old TV show about supernatural events.

"Why not?" he asked, resisting the urge to shout.

"He asked me not to."

"Who is this?" He did shout this time.

"This is Doctor Morgan Sicals, and if you want to locate Mr. Mathias, you'll have to find some other way to do it. After all, you're the FBI."

The line went dead and Canaan just stared at the phone, like he had caught an alien being and didn't know what to do next. He made a mental note to find and torture Dr. Morgan Sicals when this was all over.

Going back to the file, he found Mathias's cell phone and dialed the number. It rang and rang, not even a voicemail system.

Philip

When Philip turned onto the park access road, Mathias was standing next to a plain sedan, and waved at the white van. Philip slowed and waved for him to follow, then watched as he jogged the few feet to a plain Ford Taurus, just like the one Larsen had been driving. Fleet cars, he realized. The *Mercury News* cars.

He drove to the remote overlook he had reconnoitered and found it empty, just as he had expected. Mathias virtually leaped from the car and walked quickly around to the back where he waited for Philip.

"Thank you for coming way out here on such short notice. I appreciate your concern for my privacy."

"No problem, Mr. Hurst, I mean Philip. Can you tell me what this is all about? I am in a hurry."

"Of course. I'm cutting into your workday. Deadlines and all that."

"It's not that. It's just very important that I find any clue to Screenshot quickly. I know you said you wanted discretion and some time to protect your business, and I will do whatever I can to cooperate, but Screenshot has kidnapped my friend, the one from the Internet, and he is going to kill her if I can't find her soon."

"You're sure of that? That he would kill her? Maybe this is just some game he's playing with you. You seem to attract his attention."

"I'll be happy to sit down with you and explain everything as soon as I find her, but right now, if you could just tell me what you've found out, I'll follow up on it."

"I think what I have *will* help you find her. Wait, let me get it out of the van."

Philip opened the back door and picked up a stack of men's clothes: jeans, shirt, underwear, socks and sneakers. On top, right next to the sneakers, was his gun. When he turned, he held the clothes in his left hand and the gun in his right, his arm extended straight from his shoulder, almost parallel to the ground, pointing at Mathias' forehead, not four feet away.

"Please say nothing, for your own safety as well as others'. Take off all your clothes and pile them at your feet. Once you are naked, spread your arms out wide and turn slowly around for me. All the way around. Once I am satisfied, you may put these on." He dropped the clothes on the ground, near Mathias.

Mathias stepped back. Philip wiggled the gun and shook his head. Philip almost laughed at Mathias's expression, his face gone slack but his eyes open wide, like they were the only muscles that worked. The shock didn't last long, and as his eyes narrowed, his face seemed to pull together, everything drawn to the center until he was focused on Philip like there was nothing else in the world.

Mathias started to speak and Philip put his index finger to his lips and said "Sshhh," while signaling toward the clothes with his gun.

Once Mathias was dressed, Philip told him to lock his clothes in the Taurus. He followed close behind while he did this, and then directed him back to the van.

"Okay, no microphones or bugs or locators, you may speak now."

"You? You're Screenshot?"

"See, I told Agent Larsen that you would inevitably arrive at that conclusion, although I have to admit this is a pretty big clue."

"Where is she? Is she all right?"

"Of course she is. You know I don't do things in private. If anything happens to her, everyone will see it live, on the Internet. Now please get in the van and I will secure the door. Then I will drive you to your happy reunion with Karen. The ride will be bumpy, at least until we get to the highway, so you might want to sit on those cushions. And there is a microphone and speaker in the box so we can chat on the way. No need to mime your questions to me. I expect you have several, so let's get started, shall we?"

Waving the gun, Philip directed him into the back of the van and closed the door, the airtight seal giving a solid thump. Leaving the car like it belonged to hikers who planned on returning later to fetch it, Philip left the overlook and started back to the park exit. He flipped a switch on the small control panel mounted between the seats.

"Can you hear me all right, Seth?"

After a moment's delay, he heard Seth through the small speaker next to the control switches. "Yes, I can hear you. Where are you taking me?"

"Back to my lair. What a great word 'lair' is, don't you think? All sorts of ominous connotations. Very primal, very … wild animal. Now, my turn. How did you find me?"

"We didn't."

"True, but you would have, wouldn't you?"

"My turn for the question, then I'll answer yours. Is Karen okay? And by that I mean no physical or psychological damage."

"She is just as she was when you last saw her. Probably a bit more tired, and certainly scared, but that's all. Now, how did you almost find me? And by that I mean a description of the technology and techniques you used. I can be precise in my questioning, too."

"We ran a program called Signal Correlation comparing each return receipt from your computer to track back to your DNS. Then we got the One World Café name from the ISP. What are you going to do with Karen and me?"

"This is fun, don't you think?"

"No. Now I have two questions coming."

"Very good, Seth. You're right into the swing of this game. The answer is, I'm going to kill you. One or both, it will be your choice." Philip described the Suffer-cator design and process. "It will be my first prime time event. Do you think it will be a hit?"

"Yes. What can I do to get Karen freed unharmed?"

"Wait, it's my turn to ask."

"No, you had yours, and I answered. I think it will be a hit. Now, about Karen."

"You already know the answer to that: convince her to push her button."

"She won't do that. I want you to rig the game so no matter what happens, she gets the air and goes free. What can I do to get you to do that?"

"We're going out of turn here, but to answer anyway, I can't think of a thing. The device is built, the event arranged, it's simply too late to make changes. Now, my turn, who wrote these programs? The FBI? Karen?"

"Screw you. I'm not playing anymore. If you have nothing to offer, I'm not giving you shit."

"I do have one thing to offer. I can promise I won't hurt her before she dies. How's that?"

"I don't believe your promises, and we're going to die anyway. I'm not helping you because right now someone else is using those programs and others we have to track you down. You won't last the week. And grant me this one last request: resist arrest when they come to get you."

"I'm curious about this tracking software. Properly marketed, it would be a big hit. But if you want to know the truth, I don't believe you. I don't believe you can backtrack a return request signal, so you used some other means, something your e-mails planted in my computer somehow to identify me, like an Internet Lojack. But we're here, so we'll talk some more about this later. We have all day to get ready. Showtime's at eight."

Chapter Forty

Seth

When Seth arrived, he took in the room only in the most abstract sense, noting color and position and shape, but unaware of any detail. His mind, and therefore his eyes, had only one focus, and when he saw her just twenty feet to his left, and when he heard her call his name, he relaxed and tensed at the same time, releasing imagined horrors and feeling an urgency to get closer.

Seth ran to her, seeing her hobbled by the cable. "You're all right," she said, not quite a question, and he replied, "You are too." For a moment, everything was all right in the little piece of the world just big enough for the two of them. But when he opened his eyes, Seth saw that their little world was surrounded on all sides by Philip's world.

After Philip had hobbled Seth in the same manner, and after their initial questions and examinations to satisfy each other that they both really were all right, they spent the last hour whispering, bringing each other up to date on the events they had endured, and discussing the impossible rescue scenarios. Karen told Seth her back-up plan, for what it was worth.

"Here's the only thing I could think of. He said he was going to park us in a remote part of the *Mercury News* parking lot, and that we have about two hours of air. That's two hours to maybe catch someone's attention by making some noise, especially if they're looking for us because of the Internet broadcast. The cameras might show the inside of the van and people will be aware of what to look for. The problem is that the effort to do that will cut the air supply, probably in half. So, as soon as he parks and leaves, we'll open the air vent on your side so you can yell and pound as long as possible without running out of air. I'll lie down and use my yoga to slow my heart and respiration, maybe getting another thirty or even sixty minutes."

"That's not bad. But let's flip roles. You pound, I'll rest."

"Seth, do you know yoga? Do you think you could really slow your heart rate? And do you think I could pound as long or yell as loud as you? No, it makes more sense to do it my way."

And before he could protest, Philip interrupted.

"I have to go out and run some errands and make sure everything is set for tonight's show. I should be back by about four. Lunch is in the fridge. I want you two to play nice while I'm gone."

And with that, Seth and Karen were alone, surrounded by enough tools, equipment and supplies to make the steel cable that anchored them, let alone cut it. And they couldn't reach anything.

Karen's hours of observation provided the content for their planning. She told Seth of the fire and automatic door ideas, and of Philip's jest about lassoing something. Seth thought about these and offered his opinion.

"The problem with the fire is that we could be dead from smoke and suffocation before the fire department gets here. The problem with the door is if it doesn't work, we're out there with no options. And the problem with both is reaching something to start the fire or activate the door switch. It would be best to find some way to cut the cable for sure."

"I thought of that and looked and looked. If we use his lasso idea, we might be able to get the metal box thing on wheels and see what's in there. And we could use it to start the fire and try to keep in contained."

"Can't hurt to try. It's better than sitting here watching the clock. Let's make a rope."

They tore the two sheets into narrow seven-foot strips then braided them together before tying the ends together, creating a long, thin rope.

"Shit! This isn't going to work," Seth said after about the tenth unsuccessful attempt to lasso the box. "We need a hook, not a loop."

To their right about ten feet out of reach stood a large industrial shelving unit, eight feet long and the same height, made of angled steel corner posts, with steel-framed wooden shelves. Seth stared at it for a few moments, taking an inventory of the items stored there. He then looked around their little space to see what was within reach, and focused on the refrigerator.

Opening it, he took all the contents off the small, wire rack inside and took it out. He tied each end of their rope to a corner of the rack, making a single loop linked by the rack like a giant necklace. He handed one end to Karen and told her not to let go. Then he picked up the rack and flung it like a Frisbee toward the top shelf. After three muttered curses, one for each miss, the rack finally caught on the top of one of the posts. He pulled until the shelf tilted slightly, and then pulled some more. The shelf creaked and groaned as its joints were bent out of shape, but it continued to tilt. Then one of the knots came untied, and Seth stumbled backward onto the floor, and this time the curse wasn't muttered.

"Help me check and tighten all the knots," he told Karen, his urgency giving an edge to his request.

He caught the post again, and this time the knots held. The shelf tilted until it reached the point where the gravity of down was more compelling than the resistance of up, and the shelf toppled toward them, hitting the floor with a crash and spilling its contents everywhere.

Seth reeled in the rope and grabbed a small electric motor, about the size of a football, from among the debris. He untied the rack and cast it aside, then tied their rope to the base of the motor, creating an anchor. He got as close to the metal box as his tether would allow and threw the motor underhand. It landed in the box on the first try.

"Ha!" He pumped his fist once. "Let's see if the wheels work."

They did, and the box rolled easily to them. It turned out to be a parts bin and inside they found dozens of plastic cubes and balls, some hollow, some solid, of varying sizes. Seth had no idea of their use, but he discarded them along with the idea of using them as fuel, fearing toxic gases.

Karen pointed out the plastic garbage can, and Seth used the same technique to hook it and pull it to them. There was flammable material in it, but not enough to make a significant fire. Another garbage can, hooked and landed, contained used shop rags, and the big clear plastic bag next to it contained clean ones, bundled tightly by plastic ribbons and dense enough to burn for some time. Seth hooked that and reeled it in as well.

Next he grabbed the shelf post closest to him and removed the shelves, giving himself a pole to reach another eight feet beyond his range.

"Here's my idea. See if you think it will work," he said to Karen. "We'll start a fire using the trash, then feed it some loose rags to get it going good, then throw in the bundled rags. Then we'll trip the door switch with this pole and get into the other bay and close the door. That will get us out of the smoke, and hopefully cut our cables. If it doesn't, we'll use the motor like a hammer and eventually the cable will give."

"It sounds good, except for two things. Let's open the door before we start the fire, and how are you going to start it?"

"I was hoping there might be something on the shelves. Look for any torch-type equipment, something that sparks. Or maybe a gas grill or something for making food."

"There's a little electric space heater in the bathroom," Karen said, pointing at the closed door. "Maybe that would work."

"Is the door latched?"

"I don't know. He was the last one to use it. But it opens out. We'll have to pull it open."

Seth recovered another post from the toppled rack and they overlapped the two ends about eighteen inches and used half their rope to bind them together. It sagged in the middle when he lifted it, but held together. Seth took the rest of the rope, made a small loop at one end, and dangled it over the end, running the rest in the V of the pole.

Getting to his knees, he slid the pole to the bathroom door. "Help me lift it slowly. I'll stand behind and take the weight. You stand in front and try to hook the knob."

The process was surprisingly easy, and they got it on the first try.

Seth pulled the rope, applying slow steady pressure to the door, and after some resistance, it popped open.

The space heater sat on the floor, facing slightly to their left. It was about eighteen inches high and twelve wide, with a large handle on top.

"We'll have to hook the handle with something. It's plugged in and we won't be able to pull it easily. Let's see if there's something we can use in that stuff," Seth said, pointing at the shelf contents spread all over the floor.

"How about this?" Karen asked, holding up a large "C" clamp.

"Very good," he said, and he tied the clamp to the rope like a hook, and used the pole like a fishing rod.

Hooking the handle proved difficult, and Seth's arms soon tired, making the pole wobble even more.

"Give me a minute, then we'll try it together. I'll take the weight again and you see if you can hook the handle."

That worked, and the heater fell over when Seth pulled it. With several soft tugs, the plug pulled out and he dragged the heater to them.

He plugged it into the receptacle with the refrigerator. "While it's heating, let's get ready."

They set their fuel next to the steel box, ready to feed once they started their fire, and placed metal debris in the bottom to serve as a grate so air could circulate. Seth placed the electric motor and rope near the door to take with them, and then used the pole to press the Open button on the wall, about six feet from the end of his leash. The door swung up, revealing the dark, empty bay on the other side.

"We'll need a bundle of rags for a small fire in the other bay," Karen said. "It will be dark in there, and we won't be able to reach the light switch if the cable doesn't break."

They moved their stuff into the bay, except for the pole Seth would use to close the door. He used his motor/hammer to break up one of the wooden shelves attached to its metal frame to use as more fuel, and as a torch for the other room. He twisted a discarded sandwich wrapper tight, leaving one end loose, and held it against the bright, red heater coil.

"I just realized," Seth said, "I don't see a sprinkler system. There's probably no alarm, either. We'll have to hope that someone sees the smoke."

The edge of the wrapper caught, but only as an ember. Seth tried again.

"Come on, come on," he urged, softly blowing and willing a flame, and finally getting one.

Walking slowly, his left hand cupped around the torch, he went to the box and lit the trash in the bottom. The trash burned quickly and they fed some rags and then added the bundles, like logs on kindling, and the scrap wood on top. Karen held the wooden torch in the flame and got it burning.

"Okay," Seth said. "That's it. Take the torch, go on in, and I'll close the door and be right behind you."

"Wait. The last time you said that you fell on your ass and nearly got yourself killed. I've seen the door come down and it is nice and slow. Please don't rush."

"Thanks for the vote of confidence," Seth answered, and gave her a kiss on the forehead before pushing her toward the door.

With everything ready, Seth got as close to the wall-mounted switch as he could and fumbled with the pole until it connected and the door began to lower. Taking a quick last look, Seth could see the fire burning nicely, and he left, bringing his pole with him. He doubted the tolerances between the moving door and the fixed frame would be close enough to cut the cable, and they would need the edge of the steel angle to use as a chisel.

The shadows stretched as the closing door blocked more and

more of the light, until it went dark, except for Karen's torch. The door didn't protest the cable in its path, and there was no sound of anything ripping or breaking. Seth gave a pull on his cable and it snapped taut. Karen did the same, and said, "I hope Plan B works better."

"Twist one of those rags around each hand and hold the pole like this." He set the edge of the pole on the cable like a guillotine blade. "I'm going to hammer it with the motor. The vibration will hurt, so make sure you keep the rags between your hands and the pole."

When she was ready, Seth knelt next to the pole and raised the motor about three feet above it. "I'll go easy for the first few just to make sure nothing happens. Here goes."

He slammed the motor, base first, into the pseudo blade. Karen yelped and let go, shaking her hands. "I need more rags."

Seth repeated the procedure, halting occasionally so they could twist another rag tight and light it to keep their torch burning. After a dozen hits, Seth checked the cable. Several strands were broken and others mashed but intact, and he went back to hammering. After forty minutes, and when Seth's arms felt as heavy as the motor, the last of the strands gave and he was free.

"I'll turn on the light and check the doors. If I can get back in, I'll find the cable cutters. I don't know if I have the strength to do that again."

"What about the fire?"

"It will have burned out by now, and the ventilation system should have cleared most of the smoke."

Karen pointed out where the light switch was, and they were basked in the soft fluorescence of the single fixture. Seth found the door unlocked and called to Karen that he would be right back with the cutters. Inside, there was not a trace of smoke, but Seth immediately started gasping and stumbled back out into their bay.

"There's some kind of gas in there. I can't breathe. I'll have to hold my breath and try again."

He found the cable cutters right where he had seen Philip put them after making his tether. He closed the door behind him, cut the loops from his ankles, and hurried to Karen to cut her loose.

They ran to the roll-up door and hit the Open switch. The door slowly rose, but in their impatience to get away, they ducked under before it had risen fully and then stood up on the other side.

Philip leaned against the white van, his gun dangling from his right hand, and took a long look at his watch.

"One hour and fifty-three minutes. Not bad. But that ends the pre-game show. Shall we all go back in and suit up? It's almost show time."

Chapter Forty-one

Sicals

In the office of the *Mercury News* safe house, Sicals thought about the irony of his illicit FBI network access. Everything he was doing, all that he had done already that day, they could have duplicated, using the exact same computer network. They could have discovered the exact same information, searched the California tax files and business registrations, checked the SEC filings for the publicly held companies and their officers and directors, followed the same trail to the Acme Machine Tool Company, 7220 Shoreline Ct, Brisbane, CA, 94005.

And they could have gotten to the other site he'd hacked into, and done what he did, officially, with far less fuss. He looked at his watch, thought about it for a moment, and typed in some final keystrokes before turning the computer off. He checked the side and back pockets of his baggy trousers to make sure he had everything he needed, picked up the printout from the computer, and went outside to wait for his cab. He had to follow a strict schedule now, and he wanted to be sure and meet it.

Sicals gave the driver the address and told him he needed to be there by 4:45.

"Brisbane? Geez, that's fifty miles. That'll cost you ninety bucks."

"If you follow this route, $93.45 to be precise." Sicals handed him the Mapquest driving directions he had printed. "Plus gratuity, of course."

The driver turned in his seat to look directly at him. "Nice to see you come prepared."

"Yes, isn't it?"

The drive took almost an hour, and Sicals sat in silence the entire trip. The driver gave up on conversation when it became clear he would be doing all the talking. They arrived at the turn onto Shoreline Ct. two minutes early, and Sicals had the driver park and wait. At 4:45, the driver asked, "Can we go now?" Sicals told him to continue to wait.

At three minutes before five, Sicals handed the driver a $100 bill for the fare, and then another for the gratuity he'd promised. With $17 million in the bank, he felt he could afford to be generous.

"This is for you, so please follow my exact instructions. Take me to the specified address, it's just up ahead, stop just long enough for me to exit, then drive away, out of sight. Then stop and call your dispatcher and tell him that Dr. Morgan Sicals said to send the police to this same address. Tell them that Screenshot is inside with, and you had better write this down, Mr. Seth Mathias and Special Agent Karen Larsen of the FBI. They are hostages, and he intends to kill them at eight o'clock tonight. Tell them to hurry. The likelihood of my being killed increases exponentially with each moment. Do you have that?"

"You're kidding, right? You got a hidden camera somewhere and I'm gonna be on one of those make-the-guy-look-like-a-jerk shows, right?"

"No. That would be in very poor taste. The facts that I gave you are accurate, and if you fail to carry out the instructions, there is a 97 percent probability that the three of us will be killed. I repeat, do you have the instructions straight?"

"Yeah," he said, glancing at his notes. "Screenshot, Mathias,

Larsen, hostages, killed at eight, hurry. That pretty much cover it?"

"Yes. Now you can proceed."

"One question first. Why are you going in there? Why not wait for the police?"

"The likelihood of Mr. Mathias or Miss Larsen or both of them dying is 94 percent if I leave it to the police. If I go in and prepare the scene, and you follow those instructions, the probabilities fall to 68 percent. So, my presence is required to gain them the 26 percent advantage."

"What are you? Some kind of human computer?"

"No, I am a fully computerized human."

In his hurry to get away, the cab driver spun the wheels on the dirt and gravel covering the old macadam street. Sicals walked up to the personnel door and pounded. Then he stepped back and looked up into the camera he knew had to be hidden in the light fixture. When there was no response, he pounded again and spoke in the direction of the camera.

"I am prepared to keep this up until you answer, or until you have to leave for your eight o'clock appointment."

After some delay, the door opened and a man, whom Sicals recognized as Philip Hurst from the pictures he had seen, stuck his head out and said, "Who are you? What do you want?"

"I am Dr. Morgan Sicals, and I am here to arrange the release of Mr. Mathias and Miss Larsen. Now, if you will be so kind as to let me enter, we can discuss the terms of that release."

Hurst swung the door open and pointed a pistol at Sicals face and said, "Come in."

Once inside, Sicals saw an empty warehouse with an equally empty office with glass windows, and a white van parked about halfway down.

"Ah, the Suffer-cator, I presume. It has been well advertised on the Internet today."

"I have one question for you, Dr. whoever. Why don't I just kill you now?"

"Because then you will only learn the downside harm of your choice, and never know the upside benefits of the wiser course of action."

"Good answer. Next question, how did you find me? Wait, I know the answer. You're Mathias's technical resource, aren't you? You're the guy who called him with the idea to electrify the trailer. You must be the author of the software he told me about."

"You are correct on both counts. Now, may I please see Mr. Mathias and Miss Larsen to verify their well-being before talking terms?"

"Terms? You are, as they say, a piece of work, Doctor. Before we get to that, I have to know who else knows you're here. Who else even knows about this location?"

"At present, the cab driver who brought me here."

"At present. What does that mean?"

"The present would be the upside of your choices. The downside is the near future. Shall we proceed?" And Sicals walked away, toward the van, his back to Hurst, ignoring the gun as it swung to follow his progress.

When he got to the van, with Hurst following, he checked the door and saw that it appeared normal and would likely open using the handle.

"Please open this and let them out so I may be certain they have not been harmed. Then I will answer your questions, and you can make your decisions based on a full and complete understanding of all of the parameters."

Sicals knew the flaw in that offer: Philip could simply shoot all of them and disappear. The unknown, the answers to the questions that were certainly racing through Hurst's mind, was all that was keeping them alive. Hurst needed to know how compromised he was. And he needed to know who else was waiting outside.

"I've got a better idea. How about you answer my questions now, and I won't shoot random holes in the van. Kind of like that battleship game where you take shots in the dark and hope for the best. Or worst."

Hurst had found the flaw, just as Sicals had expected, and a novel way to counter it, as he also expected. He reached into his pocket for his equalizer.

"Wait, Doctor, what's that? Please take it out very slowly."

Sicals brought out a flashlight.

"What the hell is that for?"

Sicals looked down at his watch and smiled as the seconds ticked off. Then he looked up at Hurst and said, "Why, to see in the dark, of course."

And the lights went out.

The FBI

Loose Bruce Canaan had the same information that Sicals had. More, even. He had the same computer resources. More, even. And he had the same goal: find Hurst before he killed Mathias and Larsen in prime time, as advertised on the Internet that morning. He just had a different approach to such problems. He threw agents at it instead of thought. When the two agents looking at Hurst's condo didn't find him, it became four looking at his motor home and then eight looking at his office and then sixteen looking everywhere. By mid-afternoon, he had all thirty looking, and with the help of the local police they turned up his first good lead.

It took nearly two hours to pull everyone in, to get the building plans, to determine the best approach so they wouldn't be spotted, to brief everyone, to get the weapons and equipment ready, and to do everything this near-military campaign needed. They were all in position, and his man on the electricity waiting the command.

"Last check," he said quietly into the microphone clipped to the shoulder of his body armor, and listened as each station acknowledged they were ready. When he heard "Station nine, ready," so was he.

"Cut it now," he said, and the lights went out.

"Go," he said, and the lead agent pounded on the door and yelled, "FBI. Open Up."

"Hit it," he said, not waiting for a reply, and the two agents with the battering ram took the door right off its hinges, leaving a gaping hole that the others rushed through, pointing weapons and flashlights, shouting commands, demanding compliance.

Canaan heard his men calling "Clear" as they searched, then he heard a woman scream, and then a man shout in pain. No shots fired. That was good. Then it turned bad.

"Bruce, you better take a look at this," an agent said and pointed out a man and a woman sitting on the bed, both naked, hands secured behind their backs.

"Who are they?" he asked the agent, who handed him a man's wallet and a woman's purse. He didn't need to look because the woman introduced herself.

"I'm Laura Fascio, and I'm a lawyer with Welsh, Carson, Edgerton & Stowe, and I'm going to personally crucify you."

"Who's he?"

"He is William Edgerton, Managing Partner of the firm. I don't know why you're here or what you're looking for, but what you found is a big load of legal problems. Now cut us loose and leave this room."

"Where's Philip Hurst?"

"Philip? I don't know."

Edgerton looked curiously at Fascio, and Canaan said, "We have a report that he entered the building with you about four hours ago. Was he here?"

"William entered with me, and as you can plainly see, Philip is not here. Now get these things off my hands and get out while I dress."

"Weapons?" he asked the agent and got a negative. "All right, everyone out to the other room." He turned to the woman and said, "I'll be waiting for you both there." Finally, he told the agent, "Keep someone on the window."

"The window doesn't open," the woman shouted, "and we're eleven stories up. Who do you think I am? Spiderman? *Get out*!"

The couple still hadn't come out when Canaan's cell phone rang.

"Special Agent Canaan," he answered. "Where? … Brisbane? … A cab driver? … How sure are they? … Okay. Have the locals seal the area. Absolutely no one in or out until we get there. See if someone can get us a plan of that building." He looked at his watch. "Yeah. Thirty minutes."

He hung up and did a scan of the room, checking who was there. "Pierce, you and Holt stay here and try to smooth things over. Call the office and get help, if you need it. Everyone else, saddle up. We'll do this again. Right, this time."

Chapter Forty-two

Seth

Before the lights went out, Seth had no idea how long they'd been in The Suffer-cator. He thought of it by Hurst's appellation now, with the air close and hot and humid from his own perspiration. They were still parked in the empty bay, backed up to the roll-up door to the machine shop, halfway between the exit door and the dark end of the building. Only vague light from the dim overhead fixture penetrated their plastic cages, creating crude, defective shadows, and then even that disappeared.

They'd talked very little, saving their breath and their strength. Karen had practiced her yoga to see how well it worked. Even knowing they were only testing the process, that at any moment the doors would sweep open and fresh air rush in, Seth had felt defeated, lacking the emotional energy to feel even panic. That wouldn't be the case when the real thing happened, sometime soon.

Back then, he'd liked Karen's plan more and more, and felt disappointed in himself for it, not knowing if it made sense to him, or if he feared the finality of opening her air, and closing his own. He wondered if she felt the same, and he watched her back rise and fall very slowly, almost not at all. She was curled, fetal, looking away, he knew, so she could concentrate on her body, and not watch and worry about him.

He also knew that Hurst watched them, maybe guessed their plan, and probably enjoyed the hopelessness of it. Seth knew that Hurst would never park them where they might be found in time, and he guessed that Karen knew it as well. Her plan had the same chance of success as going to Mexico for almond extract injections to cure cancer. It gave the patient something to do, some hope that could be fantasized into a percentage, a veneer to spread over the grisly image of impending death.

Seth heard a noise and started, disturbing Karen from her trance. "What?" she asked.

"I heard banging. He must be coming to get us. I wonder how long it's been. Are you all right?"

She turned to look at him, and he was surprised to see just how composed and calm she looked, like the yoga really did work.

The doors didn't open, but Seth heard voices. "Do you think he's on the phone?"

"No," Karen said. "It sounds like two of them. Should we try banging?"

"Why not? If it's someone with him, then at least we'll know if we can be heard. I'll try kicking the side."

As he unbent his stiff muscles and joints and positioned himself, curled on his back for kicking in the cramped quarters, the lights went out.

"Seth," Karen whispered, "what happened?"

He knew the question was rhetorical, he had no more answer than she did. It was just a way to be reassured that he was still there in the absolute dark that entombed them.

"Maybe it's time. Maybe he's moving us," he said to her, guessing it was nothing good.

After a few seconds, the rear door opened and fresh air gusted into his box. A flashlight shone in his face momentarily, blinding him, then swung to Karen behind her Plexiglas wall.

"Mr. Mathias. Miss Larsen. Once again, I am gratified to find you in good health, and pleased that this plan also worked. Very good."

Seth had a moment of pure intellectual anarchy, his mind trying to gain traction so it could move from resignation and despair, speed through confusion, and arrive at comprehension.

"Doc? How did you find us? Where's Hurst?"

Sicals started around the side of the van to open the other door and let Karen out. "I found you through organized, rational research. And I tasered Mr. Hurst. He's over there, on the floor," he said, pointing past the van toward the office. "It will be seven minutes before he is able to function, so we should get him secured and call the authorities."

"You have a Taser? What for?"

Sicals opened Karen's door and looked back at Seth. "That's a foolish question, don't you think? You've seen where I live," he said.

Karen stepped out and gave Sicals a hug and said, "You're amazing, Doctor. This should get you a Nobel Prize."

"We should probably discuss that when we get out of here," Seth said. "What happened to the lights?"

"I accessed the Pacific Gas & Electric maintenance site and left a very specific electricity turn-off time. They should be coming back on in twenty minutes."

Karen gave him another hug.

"That means the roll-up door won't work, either," Seth said. "Karen, would you open the personnel door and let some light in. I'll turn the van around and aim the lights at Hurst. We'll get his gun and tie him up with something. Doc, would you close the back door, there?"

Seth got in the driver's seat and found the keys still in the ignition. He looked in the rearview mirror and saw Sicals, his flashlight still on, come to the back and reach for the door. He heard an odd, pressurized sound, like someone rapidly filling a helium balloon at the fair, and Sicals grunted, spun halfway around to his left, and fell face-first on the floor, dropping the flashlight.

Before Seth could react, before he even realized what had happened, a bullet shattered the window next to his head, showering him with safety glass shards, and two more ripped through the door itself as he dove to the passenger side and out that door.

"Karen! Look out. Hurst is up and shooting."

Another bullet followed his voice and clanged against the steel wheel that he hid behind. The wheel vibrated, and he hoped no shots would make it through. That's five shots, he thought, as if that would do him any good. He had no idea how many bullets were in Hurst's gun.

His next thought was the flashlight, lying close to Sicals, illuminating his left arm, flung out to the side, and a dark pool under him. The flashlight nullified Sicals' plan, removed the weapon of invisibility. If Hurst got it, they were dead.

Without thought or plan, hoping only for surprise and luck, Seth leapt up and dove for the flashlight, picking it up with his right hand and fumbling the switch off as he continued his forward momentum to the side wall. He heard two of the balloon sounds, followed instantly by the crack of bullets hitting the back wall, only after one passed so close by his head that Seth thought he felt the shock wave as it whistled by.

Against the big swing-up wall that opened into the machine

shop next door, he slid slowly and silently toward the back of the building, watching the direction that the shots had come from, seeing nothing, but knowing he wouldn't until it was too late. When he had moved about eight feet, he put his foot against the wall and set up like a sprinter in the starting blocks.

"Karen. Get out and get the police," he shouted, using his voice as the starting gun and launching into a full sprint into the dark toward the opposite wall.

One shot, this time, not even close, eight total. Seth wondered if Hurst had to conserve bullets, or if he had spare ammunition. When he'd run eight strides, he stopped dead in the open space and crouched low.

"I wouldn't do that, Karen," Hurst said, somewhere near where the shots had first come from. "You will present a lovely silhouette at the door, an almost perfect target." Seth heard a slight quiver in his voice, a slurring of his words, like maybe he hadn't fully recovered from the Taser, and maybe he hadn't moved from where he fell. Seth knew tasers, and had even fired one into a police cadet as part of an article on the new police officer. It was a painful and disorienting experience. Something must have interfered with the full discharge of this one, but Seth had no idea how it could happen. Clearly Sicals hadn't expected it, thinking them safe for several more minutes.

Put the van between Hurst and the door so Karen can get out. Do it quickly before he's up and moving.

A good plan, except for one flaw. Where was the van? Seth thought he was about two-thirds of the way across the room, facing the front, so it would be ahead and to his left. The problem was the word *thought* substituting for the word *knew*.

He lay down on the floor, his head facing where he thought

the van was, and reached up above himself and to his left with the flashlight as far as he could. If Hurst thought he was standing and holding it in his right hand, he would aim left, even further from where he lay. He counted to himself and on three, turned it on, swept it right to left, and turned it off. Shot nine passed over him.

He'd spotted the van and scrambled to it without waiting or trying to creep silently, again counting on speed, surprise, and the dark to protect him. The passenger door was still open and the keys in the ignition. He jumped head-first into the van, staying on its floor. He reached up and twisted the ignition, pulled the gear lever as far as it would go, fumbled for the headlight switch and pulled it out, grabbed the steering wheel with his left hand, and pressed the gas with his right.

As it started moving, he risked rising to see where he was. The bay was now flooded in light and he saw that he wasn't turning sharp enough, so he pulled harder, turning the van more left. As it did, the headlights briefly illuminated Karen, huddled against the big, roll-up door, before passing over her and leaving her in the shadow. Seth guessed he was positioned correctly, shielding her and the exit door, and let go of the steering wheel to press on the brake with both hands. As he did, a bullet smashed into the dash in front of his face. Plastic exploded into him. He fell and pressed the accelerator all the way to the floor.

The van jumped forward, the tires squealing on the concrete floor, and crashed into the front of the building, smashing both headlights and stalling the motor.

Seth slid out onto the floor, groggy from whatever hit his head when he was flung into the dash, and Karen was there at his side. The van motor made noises, hissing and crackling, as it came to equilibrium with its new circumstances, and Seth whispered to her, "Let's go quick while he can't see us."

"We can't," she whispered back. "You crashed into the door and it's blocked. We're trapped."

Rapid footsteps, Philip's hard leather soles against the concrete, came up to the other side of the van. Seth pushed Karen ahead of him and they scuttled to the far wall.

"Well, looks like you screwed up that time, Seth. There is no other exit. I'll just wait here until the lights come back on and we'll get on with this. What did your Dr. Sicals say? Twenty minutes? We've probably used five or six of those already. Enjoy your last few minutes of freedom."

Embraced in the corner with Karen, Seth tried to envision any circumstances that would save them, a series of events that didn't lead back to a new and improved Suffer-cator. He could only hope that Sicals had called the police, but his arrival here by himself didn't bode well for that. Sicals was not a police kind of guy.

A flashlight against a gun was not a fight he thought he could win. On the other hand, he remembered, a gun was useless as long as the lights were out. That was why Hurst was biding his time, waiting for the lights to come on, waiting for the moment that he had the absolute advantage. The real battle was between light and dark, and dark was scheduled to lose very soon. Seth needed to act, to finish, before that happened.

Taking advantage of the distance and the hissing van, Seth whispered his new plan to Karen, hoping it would work better than the old one.

"Take the flashlight and wait a few seconds until I move away. Then, I want you to hold it away from yourself as far as you can and shine it at the spot where you think Hurst is. Swing it until you see him, or until you're risking exposure. Shut it off, move to a new position fast. Wait a few moments and do it again. Don't move in the same direction each time, and try to move left or right from him, not forward or back. He has already taken ten shots, so I don't think he'll waste any shooting at you in the dark. He'll be trying to find you, to get close to you so he can shoot you. Figure he'll be moving to where you were, or where he thinks you'll be next."

"Where will you be?"

"I'll be trying to find him."

Seth made a mental map of the empty warehouse. He and Karen were in the far front corner of the building, the office was in the opposite front corner. The roll-up door was about midway between them and the office, and the personnel door, now blocked by the van, just past it. The fake wall that opened in to the machine shop was along the far wall, about halfway down it, with Sicals lying nearby, dying unless they hurried. Or maybe dead already.

Hurst was between the van and the office wall when he spoke, a pretty good location, the equivalent of the high ground in the open bay. He was protected on three sides by the front wall, the office wall, and the van. He would likely stay there until moved by something, hopefully by Karen's light. Seth thought about crawling under the van and trying to trip Hurst, but if he failed, or if Hurst looked under, he would have no way to escape, no chance to run. The best chance was to bring him out in the open, where he would have to watch 360°, so he moved quietly away from Karen, into the dark.

Seth settled into a crouch and waited for Karen's light, and in a flash of mental brilliance understood the flaw in his plan:

the closer he got to Hurst, the more likely the light would reveal him. The light came on, and Seth really wished he'd thought this through better.

She had aimed the light at the van, and as expected, he saw Hurst's shoes light up as the light tunneled low, underneath the van. He oriented himself as being maybe two-thirds of the way across the bay, heading toward the swing-up door on the wall and Sicals on the floor. As soon as the light went out, he angled left and forward, aiming for the corner where the office wall met the bay wall. He took four quick steps and then stood up straight, in profile to where he expected Hurst to be.

He decided this would be his method: four steps, stop, stand. It allowed him time to get set for each light, and he could move instantly at Hurst if he was close enough, or away if Hurst spotted him.

He guessed that Hurst would do nothing after the first light except become wary. When Karen turned it on the second time, he saw Hurst lying on the floor, sighting under the van in Karen's direction. Hurst squeezed off one shot, and all of Seth's planning and intent were blown away by the sound, and by the possibility of Karen lying in her own pool of blood. Eleven, he thought, and moved.

He expected Hurst would do the same, moving toward the rear of the van to get a better view of the building. Seth moved toward the false wall. He had to get behind Hurst as he emerged, if he emerged.

Karen's light came on, and Seth exhaled, not even realizing he'd been holding his breath. This time it came from the middle of the room, further from the van than before. The beam swept the area around the van briefly and then went out. Seth hadn't seen

Hurst. He wondered what Hurst had seen, and why there was no shot this time.

Hurst must have circled around to the far side of the van to get a clearer shot when the light came back on. Seth moved four steps up the wall and bumped up against the office. He crouched.

When the light came on again, Karen had moved back toward the east wall but kept her distance from the van. The instant the light came on, Hurst snapped off two quick shots. The flashlight dropped to the floor with a clatter and went out.

"Looks like your game of light tag is over, Seth. Now we'll just wait for the lights to go on and see how bad Karen is hurt. And, yes, I did figure out what you are up to, and it had to be Karen with the light so you could sneak up on me and beat me senseless. That was the plan, wasn't it?"

Seth said nothing. He did nothing. It was easy to do nothing because he didn't know what *to* do. And that made him angry. Angry because he'd failed Sicals, who lay dying on the floor even as Seth wrestled with indecision. Angry for letting Karen use the flashlight, for not having a better plan, for probably killing her. The only thing he could think of was anger, and the only action he could take was attack.

He shifted his body weight somewhat to the rear, getting ready to launch a do or die charge at the taunting voice. His brain sent the message and his right leg muscles flexed, ready to push off. But before he could, the flashlight came on from behind Hurst, silhouetting him perfectly. Hurst jumped, unprepared for this. He spun and fired two shots. The flashlight went out.

"Well, Karen, you pussycat. You have more lives, do you? Are you hurt? Did I just wound you? Or were you playing possum? No matter, we are back at our standoff, and I win as soon as the lights come back on."

And they did.

Hurst stood at the rear corner of the van, almost directly between Seth and Karen. She was fifteen or twenty feet away from him, near the roll-up door. Seth smiled at seeing her alive. Hurst raised his pistol and aimed it at Seth's face, some ten feet from the business end of the barrel.

"What do you think, Seth? Nice gun, huh? It's a Ruger 380, hollow point bullets, fifteen shot clip. They'll make a hole in the back of your head the size of an orange."

"Fifteen shots?"

"Yes. Fourteen more than I need at this range."

"More importantly to me, fifteen more than you have in the clip."

A brief flicker ticked across Hurst's face, and then he smiled.

"You counted? How certain are you? It doesn't matter, really. Fifteen in the clip, Seth. One in the chamber. I think I'll just shoot you in the leg and go back in the shop for more bullets. Then we're going to do the Suffer-cator right here, where it sits."

"Are you sure of your count, Seth," Karen called.

"Yes."

She started to walk toward Hurst. "He's bluffing."

Seth wasn't sure who was bluffing, Hurst or Karen. She cleared up his indecision. "To set the gun with sixteen rounds, he has to insert the clip, chamber a round, remove the clip, replace the round, and put the clip back in. Nobody bothers. They just carry extra clips."

"Are you willing to bet your leg on that, Seth? Are you willing to bet Karen's face when I pistol whip her with my empty, sixteen-round gun?"

"And our choice is to just do as you say, to get into your box unharmed? Maybe the viewing public should see what you are, not some high-tech vigilante, but a psychopath who likes killing and rationalizes it as social policy."

"Seth," Karen said, kicking off her shoes and, watching Hurst, slipping off her socks. "On three. One."

"So, Special Agent Larsen. You're going to kung fu me, or something?"

"Two."

"The FBI teaches martial arts to computer geeks? And you practice it? No, I don't think so."

"Nothing to do with the Bureau, asshole. I'm Korean. We invented *tae kwon do*. Three." And she charged him.

Philip swung his arm 180° and shot her. It happened so fast that Seth never even moved. Karen lay on the floor, blood on her shirt, not moving. Philip flipped the gun in the air and caught it by the barrel, holding it like a hammer, and turned back to Seth.

"Look *around* you, for Christ's sake," he shouted. "*Think* for a moment. What do you *see*? What have I ever done that would make you believe I wouldn't take the time to put the extra bullet in?"

Chapter
Forty-three

The FBI

"Talk to me," Canaan said into his phone. The police officer at the other end, the first to arrive where the cab driver waited, did.

"The driver says he brought some weird old guy here from San Jose. Guy talked percentages and numbers and crazy stuff about FBI agents and Screenshot. Made him write down the Mathias and Larsen names. He says that's all he knows."

"What was the guy's name?" Canaan listened while the policeman asked the cab driver.

"He doesn't know. Says the guy told him to write the names of the others after he'd said his own, and he didn't write it down."

"Ask him if the name Sicals rings a bell. Dr. Morgan Sicals."

"Yeah. He says that's it. How soon you gonna be here? It's just my partner and myself at the moment, but more cars are on their way."

"Shit," Canaan muttered and then said, "Call them off. I'm sending two agents to check it out. You wait there with the driver and he can show you where to look when my guys get there. They'll get back to me."

"Call them off? It's Screenshot, for Christ's sake. Four of us ain't gonna be enough."

"Listen, Officer. I appreciate your good work, but Screenshot isn't there. I guarantee it. Sicals stole $17 million and he's apparently working with Mathias and Larsen. This is all some trick to throw us off their trail while they get away. I doubt he'd call the cops and say, *here I am, boys. Come and get me.* We got burned once today. Not gonna happen twice."

Philip

"Now what are you going to do? You want to kill me, and right now you might be angry enough to try. Before you do something stupid, you should know she's not dead. Yet. She could use medical assistance, no doubt. Probably too late for your doctor friend, but someone ought to stop her bleeding before she goes into shock. Killing me will take time, if you can even do it, which I doubt. I don't think she has that much time."

"I think I'll take my chances with you first," Seth muttered through clenched teeth, his fists compressed so hard they looked almost white.

"Well, let's consider the probabilities," Philip said, reaching into his pants pocket and coming up with a folding knife. He opened the blade in his right hand, the gun a hammer in his left, and said, "What are the chances, now?"

Seth did nothing, and Philip decided to motivate him.

"Maybe your doctor did call the police. Or maybe his cab driver did. Maybe they're on their way now. What do you think? Will they get here in time to save Karen? Should you help her? Or should you make some futile, macho gesture while she bleeds to death?"

Seth circled to his right, maintaining his distance from Philip, who turned with him. But Seth kept moving until he was near Karen, and bent to help her.

"Good choice," Philip said, lowering the gun, his path to the shop no longer obstructed. "Now I won't have to hurt you too. Why don't you see if you can move the van while I'm gone? Open the door for your police. You'll need it because the roll-up won't be working. The circuit panel is just inside the shop door, and I'll be cutting its power."

He eased himself backwards toward the shop, watching Seth. While he moved, he said, "Oh, and by the way, your little let's-start-a-fire-and-see-who-comes plan didn't work. The shop has a halon fire suppression system, and both the doors are sealed. As soon as the system detected your fire, high-pressure tanks released halon gas and fans pulled the air out, taking all of the oxygen from the room in a matter of seconds. No oxygen, no fire. No fire, no rescue."

"We don't need the fire," Seth answered. "Sicals found you. The police won't be far behind."

"Let's examine that thought." Philip was at the office door, now. "Do you really think your friend called them? It's been over twenty-five minutes since he came in. Are they on a break? Did they stop for donuts? How long do you think they'd take to get to me if they knew where I was?

"Here's what I think," he continued. "I think your high-tech sidekick there planted some locator device on you or in you. Maybe you swallowed it, or maybe it's under some fake-skin patch, or up your butt, and he followed you here. Maybe he was your back-up after my call. Maybe you were already suspicious of me. Lots of maybes.

"But here's a fact. Karen is an FBI agent. Why is she running around with you, and not in a pack of white-shirted civil servants? And why are you two hiding in the newspaper offices? There's something going on I don't yet understand, but I will. We'll discuss it while you're relaxing in the Suffer-cator."

He turned and walked through the warehouse office and into the machine shop.

Philip knew that Seth was resourceful and lucky, and hoped he would be too concerned with Karen to act while he was gone. There were four dead guys in West Virginia who had underestimated Seth.

In any event, Philip would be fully armed and very careful when he came back out.

Chapter Forty-four

Seth

Seth prepared himself to rush Hurst, the impulse coming unbidden from somewhere in his brain that he had only visited once before, back in the West Virginia woods, and he hadn't liked it there. Then the knife appeared in Hurst's hand and everything changed. He'd handled the punks in those woods, but it was one at a time, and they were young and stupid and too sure of themselves to fight smart. Hurst was an experienced killer, well-armed. He went to Karen instead.

She lay on her back, slightly on her left, the side where the bullet had entered her shoulder just below the collar bone. Both arms were sprawled wide, ready for a hug. Her legs were together, bent at the knees. Seth felt her carotid artery, another skill acquired writing magazine articles, and found a pulse. Hurst hadn't lied, there was a pretty strong pulse. He lifted her left shoulder to see the damage made by the exit wound. He tore her shirt and used it to dab some of the blood away. The wound didn't look too bad, but he needed to stop the bleeding before she went into shock. He grabbed her socks from the floor where she'd dropped them, turned them inside out and pressed them against the entry and exit wounds. He took off his belt and wrapped it around the makeshift bandages to hold them tightly in place.

As soon as Hurst moved out of sight into the shop, Seth ran to Sicals. He didn't have time to check and tend to his friend, and that was how he thought of him, a friend. He could only see if

Sicals remained true to his nature the same way Hurst had, taking care to load the extra bullet.

The Taser was in Sicals' pocket, the spent cartridge discarded on the floor a few feet away. Its two leads stretched to where Hurst must have gone down. In his other pocket, Seth found what he counted on him to have, a spare Taser cartridge. He snapped it into the weapon and hoped that surprise would let him get close enough to use it.

Seth scuttled through the office and at the door to the shop, he stopped and peeked around the corner. Past the shelves lining the left wall, he saw Hurst at the desk, near the debris of their escape attempt. He seemed intent on whatever he was doing, and Seth knew it had to be fitting fifteen bullets into a clip. And one into the chamber.

The first machine, a five-foot wide lathe on a metal base, was mounted about seven feet from the door. A perfect spot for an ambush when Hurst returned to the warehouse. Seth dodged across the open space and ducked behind the lathe. Then he heard Hurst slam the clip into the gun, jack the slide once to seat a bullet in the chamber, and replace the bullet in the clip, slamming it into the gun a second time.

Seth tensed, waiting to hear the leather-soled shoes on the plastic flooring. He began to worry after a few moments of silence, and glanced around, but no one was there. He ventured another peek over the machine. Hurst was still looking down at the desk. He wondered why he seemed so intent on it, and not in a hurry to get back.

"The thing you didn't think about, Seth," Hurst said, never looking up, "was the cameras. I can stand here at my desk and watch you on my monitor while I reload sixteen bullets into my gun. Be sure you count them again, Seth, although I wouldn't bet you'll get past three. I took the silencer off so you won't miss any."

There comes a point, Seth knew, when there is no fight left, and no flight possible. A point where you just give up and say, *get it over with*. He could almost reach out and touch that point. He felt no panic, no fear, just overwhelming regret that he couldn't help Karen and Sicals, and that Hurst was going to get away with it. He slumped, the tension released like air from a balloon.

"You know I know weapons, Seth," Hurst continued, "and I'm figuring that your dead friend out there had a spare cartridge for his Taser, and that's what I saw you doing, reloading. That Taser is good for fifteen feet. It surprised me once. It won't again. Your challenge is to get within fifteen feet of me with as few bullet holes in you as possible."

Just get it over with.

"Think you're up to it? Think you can handle me like you handled old Hutch and his little gang of thugs back there in the woods? Back in ol' West Virginny? There's only one of me."

Would you just shut up and get it over with?

"I'll give you this much, you're very good at improvisation. Against a bunch of other improvisers, it's clear why you came out on top. But I'm a planner, Seth. Improv rarely works against planning. The only time it does is when the plan is bad. And my plans are never bad."

Why don't you shut the fuck up?

"Let's recap, shall we? You've got a Taser, one cartridge, and a fifteen foot range. I've got a Ruger, sixteen bullets, and let's say conservatively, fifty feet of absolute accuracy. That pretty much means I can shoot you from anywhere in the room anytime I want to, as long as I stay sixteen feet away. Is that how you see it?"

Fuck you.

Seth sat, leaning his back against the lathe, listening to Hurst blather on, staring at the workbench that stretched along the entire width of the front wall, just six feet away. Staring at the array of hand tools hung neatly from pegboard, each outlined in black ink so you always knew what wasn't there. Staring at the set of hammers, starting with the little jeweler's hammer on the left, and incrementally increasing in size until you reached the two-pound hand sledge on the right.

"Here's what I think you'll do. I think you'll toss out your little battery-operated device so you can get back to tending to Karen. That's really what you want to do, isn't it? Stay alive. Buy time. The cops could still show up. We've got hours until the regularly scheduled broadcast of the Suffer-cator. The alternative is to wait here while she oozes blood until there's none left."

Fuck you, asshole.

The circuit panel was right where Hurst had said it was, next to the door, seven feet to Seth's right. Six feet to the hammer. Seven feet to the panel.

Put the Taser in your pocket. Improvise.

And fuck you twice, asshole.

Without thinking about it, without setting himself up for it, without giving Hurst's cameras any warning, Seth jumped to his feet and vaulted across to the hammer. He grabbed it with his right hand and pushed off the bench with his left. He dove to his right, and with one step, flung his body at the wall, swinging the hammer with every bit of strength he had left.

The first bullet hit just below and to the right of the black outline of the hand sledge. The second hit the wall next to the circuit panel. The third went right through the spot Seth would have been if he hadn't knocked himself silly when he hit the wall.

The sound was like the world's biggest moth flew into the world's biggest bug zapper. And all the lights went out. Again.

The FBI

The cab driver rode with the agents, repeating his story as he directed them to Acme. They drove by the building, looking for anything suspicious, and saw only trash and weeds.

"You sure this is the building?"

When the driver confirmed it, they all got out.

"Did you see Sicals go inside? Or open the door, or even knock or anything?"

"No. He told me to leave and call you and just stood there until I was out of sight."

"Well, let's try the door."

Everyone drew their weapon, except the cab driver, who hid behind the FBI sedan. The police took up positions behind their car, and the agents bracketed the door. One reached over and tried the knob. Nothing moved. They both examined the steel door in the steel frame and could see that even though it bulged out slightly, they wouldn't be able to kick it in.

"Did you guys search the back," the lead agent asked the police.

"Yeah. Nothing. No doors. No windows. Not even a vent. Maybe there's another way in from the roof."

"Or out. One of you watch the roof. I'm gonna announce."

Before he had a chance, they heard three quick shots from

inside, and dove for cover.

"Shots fired. Call it," he yelled to the police at the car. At the same time he took out his cell and speed-dialed Canaan.

"We're under fire here," he nearly shouted. "Three shots from inside the building."

"Anyone hit?"

"No. We don't even know where they were aimed. Or if they were meant for us. We haven't announced yet, and there's no windows and the doors are closed. Could be shooting at each other inside."

"Stay there. We're on our way."

"Bring something heavy. The doors are steel, and the roll-up looks welded shut."

Seth

Seth didn't move, lying on his left side, propped with his left arm, the Taser out of his pocket and back in his right hand. A small flame in the electrical panel dripped molten plastic on the floor eight inches from his right foot. Otherwise, he heard no sound, saw no movement, and as the flame flickered out, he went blind.

So much for planning over improvisation, asshole. Where's your sixteen feet now?

Seth got his answer when a flashlight beam came on, a powerful one, like one of those big lantern lights. It swung slowly toward Seth and he scrambled back behind the lathe.

"You're full of surprises, aren't you? More improv. You know the trouble with improv? It's trial and error. You never know what will work and what won't until you try it. Planning would have asked the question, *what will he do when the lights go out?* And one of the answers that would be considered is, *he'll pick up his handy flashlight, and then we'll be right back where we started.*"

Not right back, Seth thought. It's just a flashlight. You haven't got me yet.

"Let's count. Was that two shots, or three? Do you think it will matter in the end?"

The flashlight beam swung slowly back and forth. It wasn't a search for Seth, just a leisurely illumination of his end of the room. The industrial shapes, and the changing orientation of the light, created strange and fluid shadows that leapt away from it, like they wanted to escape. But they were anchored. Seth knew how they felt.

"My beam is a lot longer than fifteen feet. Did you notice that? Let me help you out by showing you some of the hiding places you might try. See those shadows? Your best bet is to stay in those, because that means there's something between you and my light, and as long as my light is in my hands, that means something's between you and my gun. The thing that you don't want to happen is to get stuck in one of those shadows after I put the light down, because then you won't know where I am, but I'll know where you are."

The source of the beam moved for the first time, not coming directly toward Seth, but towards the far side of the room, away from the door, still moving closer. Seth thought about the door and wondered if Hurst was trying to lure him into going for it. As if to punctuate the situation, to remind Seth of his vulnerability, the light paused briefly on the lathe with each sweep. *I know where you are*, Hurst was saying.

The beam swept from right to left, following the top of the workbench, lighting the tools hanging there and creating miniature shadows that almost danced against the white pegboard. At the far end of the bench, twenty feet away, were shelves with rows and stacks of cans and bottles. Glass bottles and plastic bottles. Aerosol cans, screw-top cans, paint cans, even a red, five-gallon can on the bench.

A flammable liquids can.

"The base of the lathe makes a good hiding place. The problem for you is, it's actually a metal frame covered in sheet metal. Sure looks solid, though, doesn't it?"

The shot was almost physical, not just a sound, but a huge presence, especially next to his right shoulder where a jagged hole appeared in the metal.

"Did that hit you, I wonder? I didn't hear you make any noise, so I'm guessing you got lucky. Let's try a different angle."

Now the beam moved back toward the door that led to the warehouse. It was still too far away for the Taser, but created new shadows angled toward the can. Seth waited for the shadows to be where he wanted, and as quietly as he could, scrambled away from the door, further into the shop to the next machine in the row, this one closer to the red can. The next bullet clanged through the sheet metal of the lathe, right about where Seth had just been, and he heard it ricochet off the floor and into the cabinets below the bench.

"Now that one had to hurt. Are you dead? I sure hope not. Won't be much of a show with two bodies in the Suffer-cator. We'll have to pre-empt it. Maybe replay one of the other ones."

The beam was steady now, aimed at the lathe. It cast enough peripheral light that Seth could see the outline of the can, about twelve feet away. He crouched, setting himself to move fast, aimed, and fired.

He dropped the Taser and dove face down to his right, toward the door out. He was still above the floor and sinking fast when the room erupted. Hot things rained down on him, some hard pieces, some liquid fire. The darkness of seconds before was replaced for an instant by a brilliant flash, and then more, smaller flashes as other flammable cans exploded. Seth hit the floor and without pause managed to get part-way up. He scrambled on all fours toward the open door.

Two more explosions followed Seth out the door and into the warehouse office. He thought they were bullets, but decided not to include them in his count just to be safe. He grabbed the door handle as he went by and it jerked him to a stop. With the reverse momentum, he slammed the door closed, and leaned against it, waiting for Hurst to try and shoot his way through.

Thirteen bullets. Eleven if I'm lucky.

He shoved the old metal desk hard against the door and leaned against the other end, getting himself five more feet from the muzzle once Hurst started shooting.

The fire must be going by now. Hold on for just a few more minutes.

The length of the desk got him within three feet of the opposite wall of the warehouse office. Seth sat on the floor, his back to the desk and his feet braced against that wall, giving him the leverage to hold the door closed.

The doorknob rattled hard, followed by hammering on the door, violent shaking and more hammering. The halon must have started by now, Seth thought. The door is sealed, he'd said. Seconds to no oxygen, he'd said. Then the bullets began.

Seth got to three in his count, just as Hurst predicted, before one of the random shots made it through the door and the sheet-metal desk and found its target. His last thought before the pain exploded in his back was, How long did you plan to hold your breath, Phil?

The Best Defense, Inc.

Seth looked up from his computer as the Avianca agent announced boarding. He started the shutdown process, his mood turning darker with the reminder that the many weeks of recuperation had put him further behind on the nuclear fuel terrorist article for the *Mercury News*.

He'd been lucky, he knew. The bullet that hit him was a low-energy fragment of its original self after getting beat up by the metal door and desk. Hurst's other bullets had no such obstruction, and they had been able to vent their full force on Karen and Sicals. The thought of Hurst suffocating in the sealed machine shop, his lair, as he called it, was ironic. And gratifying. He couldn't have come up with a more fitting end if he'd planned it.

Bogotá was the only destination left for him to see first-hand the spent fuel recovery process that was at the center of his delayed assignment. Fuel that could be turned into weapons in the wrong hands. Fuel that had been handed out by the US before anyone knew what a terrorist was. And fuel that was now in unruly places like Colombia and Indonesia and the Congo. The National Nuclear Security Agency folks promised to meet him at Bogotá airport, but he knew they weren't happy to have him working on the story, and he didn't entirely believe they would be there.

He decided to make sure the contingencies were in place, and dialed the private line from his cell phone.

"Hey, it's Seth. I'm about to board. Is everything set for me?"

"Of course it is, Mr. Mathias. When have I ever let you down?"

"Never. Yet."

"Be careful. I won't be there to back you up."

"If everything's set up right, I won't need back-up."

"Nothing is ever set up right. And you always need back-up. I'm sorry to be brusque, but my crisis phone is ringing, and I have to answer it."

Seth closed the computer and slipped in into his briefcase. After the DISETHEGRATOR and the SUFFER-CATOR, he thought, how bad could Colombia be?

"Dr. Morgan Sicals," he said into the unnecessarily red phone.

"We're under attack, Doc. Thought you'd want to know."

"How bad?"

"Not massive, but not insignificant, either."

"Who is the target?"

"Looks like DoE. We can't be sure until they get through the first firewall and then focus."

"What is the source?"

"We're backtracking now. We should know within ninety minutes or so."

"I'll come down."

Sicals hung up and pulled the right-hand lever. The wheelchair backed away from the desk. A tap to the right, and a push forward and he was on his way to the war room, the command post for all TBD Software installations, the very successful IT security start-up he had endowed, financially and intellectually. From there, they could monitor and coordinate all their resources worldwide, and operate v3.0 of *The Best Defense* cyber-security suite at efficiencies that surprised even him.

He accelerated the customized wheelchair to dangerous speeds down the corridor towards the elevator. It was such an efficient and pleasant way to travel, he wondered why he hadn't thought of it years ago, when it would still have been an option. Hurst's bullet had hit him low in his left side, and tracked across his back, taking a small chunk of his spine with it, leaving his legs useless. Well, I never had much use for them before, in any event, he thought.

Sicals swung the wheelchair to the right, into the executive offices, and barely slowed down to wave to the administrative assistant outside the private office. The door was open, as required unless circumstances dictated privacy, and he brought the wheelchair to an abrupt stop in front of the CEO's desk.

"What's up, Doc?"

"I wish you would stop saying that. We are under a somewhat concerted attack, with a government target. I thought you'd like to know. I'm on my way down now."

"How serious?"

"Enough. We'll have it identified in ninety minutes, and we can start the countermeasures. There will be some very dead computers in two hours."

"Perfect timing. The investment bankers will be here in an hour, and they can see our technology eat some viruses in real-time."

"Must you? I still don't know why we need outsiders. We've already had one venture capitalist involved, and he tried to kill us. The Nobel Prize money they belatedly awarded me, and the $300,000 software fees that I got from your FBI should be plenty."

"As you know perfectly well, we burned through that and much more getting the commercial versions of the software developed and to market. If you want to see the consumer version on the shelves by Christmas, we need the cash."

"And I wish you wouldn't call it a consumer version. It is a very powerful network, hive-computing if you must use the jargon, combining resources of all the users to thwart hackers and other miscreants. Just because it functions better with large numbers of users to share information and processing power doesn't make it consumer. That sounds like a game."

"We've covered this once or twice, Doctor. It's your company, but you hired me to run it, so I've got to do what's best. You better get down there and get ready to tap dance for the money guys."

The wheelchair swiveled and rolled away as Sicals called, "You're the boss, Miss Larsen."

"Doctor," she called after him.

"Oh yes, of course. How forgetful of me. Mrs. Mathias."

About John Darrin

John Darrin is a consultant on preparing for and
responding to attacks or emergencies involving nuclear
weapons and radioactive materials. His work has taken
him all over the world, from China to Finland, from Central
America to Canada, and includes dismantling obsolete
nuclear reactors, the safe treatment and disposal of
nuclear weapons waste, and the recovery from the Three
Mile Island accident. *Screenshot* is his first novel.

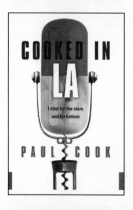

Cooked in LA ■ Paul Cook

How does a successful young man from a "good" home hit bottom and risk losing it all? *Cooked In La* shows how a popular, middle-class young man with a bright future in radio and television is nearly destroyed by a voracious appetite for drugs and alcohol.

Non Fiction/Self-Help & Recovery I US$ 24.95
Pages 304 I Cloth 5.5" x 8.5"
ISBN 978-1-60164-193-9

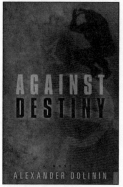

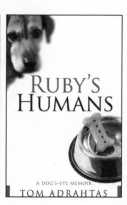

Against Destiny
■ Alexander Dolinin

A story of courage and determination in the face of the impossible. The dilemma of the unjustly condemned: Die in slavery or die fighting for your freedom.

Fiction I US$ 24.95
Pages 448 I Cloth 5.5" x 8.5"
ISBN 978-1-60164-173-1

Let the Shadows Fall Behind You
■ Kathy-Diane Leveille

The disappearance of her lover turns a young woman's world upside down and leads to shocking revelations of her past. This enigmatic novel is about connections and relationships, memory and reality.

Fiction I US$ 22.95
Pages 288 I Cloth 5.5" x 8.5"
ISBN 978-1-60164-167-0

Ruby's Humans
■ Tom Adrahtas

No other book tells a story of abuse, neglect, escape, recovery and love with such humor and poignancy, in the uniquely perceptive words of a dog. Anyone who's ever loved a dog will love Ruby's sassy take on human foibles and manners.

Non Fiction I US$ 19.95
Pages 192 I Cloth 5.5" x 8.5"
ISBN 978-1-60164-188-5

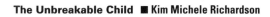

The Unbreakable Child ■ Kim Michele Richardson

Starved, beaten and abused for nearly a decade, orphan Kimmi learned that evil can wear a nun's habit. A story not just of a survivor but of a rare spirit who simply would not be broken.

Non Fiction/True Crime | US$ 24.95
Pages 256 | Cloth 5.5" x 8.5"
ISBN 978-1-60164-163-2

Save the Whales Please
■ Konrad Karl Gatien & Sreescanda

Japanese threats and backroom deals cause the slaughter of more whales than ever. The first lady risks everything—her life, her position, her marriage—to save the whales.

Fiction | US$ 24.95
Pages 432 | Cloth 5.5" x 8.5"
ISBN 978-1-60164-165-6

Screenshot
■ John Darrin

Could you resist the lure of evil that lurks in the anonymous power of the Internet? Every week, a mad entrepreneur presents an execution, the live, real-time murder of someone who probably deserves it. *Screenshot*: a techno-thriller with a provocative premise.

Fiction | US$ 24.95
Pages 416 | Cloth 5.5" x 8.5"
ISBN 978-1-60164-168-7

KÜNATI

Touchstone Tarot ■ Kat Black

Internationally renowned tarot designer Kat Black, whose *Golden Tarot* remains one of the most popular and critically acclaimed tarot decks on the market, has created this unique new deck. In *Touchstone Tarot*, Kat Black uses Baroque masterpieces as the basis for her sumptuous and sensual collaged portraits. Intuitive and easy to read, this deck is for readers at every level of experience. This deluxe set, with gold gilt edges and sturdy hinged box includes a straightforward companion book with card explanations and sample readings.

Non Fiction/New Age I US$ 32.95 I Tarot box set with 200-page booklet I Cards and booklet 3.5" x 5" ISBN 978-1-60164-190-8

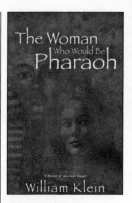

Sleepers Awake
■ Patrick McNulty

Monstrous creatures invade our world in this dark fantasy in which death is but a door to another room of one's life.

**Fiction I US$ 22.95
Pages 320 I Cloth 5.5" x 8.5"
ISBN 978-1-60164-166-3**

The Nation's Highest Honor
■ James Gaitis

Like Kosinski's classic *Being There, The Nation's Highest Honor* demonstrates the dangerous truth that incompetence is no obstacle to making a profound difference in the world.

**Fiction I US$ 22.95
Pages 256 I Cloth 5.5" x 8.5"
ISBN 978-1-60164-172-4**

The Woman Who Would Be Pharaoh
■ William Klein

Shadowy figures from Egypt's fabulous past glow with color and authenticity. Tragic love story weaves a rich tapestry of history, mystery, regicide and incest.

**Fiction/Historic I US$ 24.95
Pages 304 I Cloth 5.5" x 8.5"
ISBN 978-1-60164-189-2**

The Short Course in Beer
■ Lynn Hoffman

A book for the legions of people who are discovering that beer is a delicious, highly affordable drink that's available in an almost infinite variety. Hoffman presents a portrait of beer as fascinating as it is broad, from ancient times to the present.

Non Fiction/Food/Beverages | US$ 24.95
Pages 224 | Cloth 5.5" x 8.5"
ISBN 978-1-60164-191-5

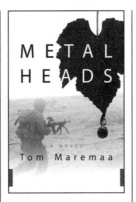

Under Paris Skies
■ Enrique von Kiguel

A unique portrait of the glamorous life of well-to-do Parisians and aristocratic expatriates in the fifties. Behind the elegant facades and gracious manners lie dark, deadly secrets

Fiction | US$ 24.95
Pages 320 | Cloth 5.5" x 8.5"
ISBN 978-1-60164-171-7

Metal Heads
■ Tom Maremaa

A controversial novel about wounded Iraq war vets and their "*Clockwork Orange*" experiences in a California hospital.

Fiction | US$ 22.95
Pages 256 | Cloth 5.5" x 8.5"
ISBN 978-1-60164-170-0

Lead Babies
■ Joanna Cerazy & Sandra Cottingham

Lead-related Autism, ADHD, lowered IQ and behavior disorders are epidemic. *Lead Babies* gives detailed information to help readers leadproof their homes and protect their children from the beginning of pregnancy through rearing.

Non Fiction/ Health/Fitness & Beauty | US$ 24.95
Pages 208 | Cloth 5.5" x 8.5"
ISBN 978-1-60164-192-2